REVENGE

By Martina Cole and available from Headline

Dangerous Lady
The Ladykiller
Goodnight Lady
The Jump
The Runaway
Two Women
Broken
Faceless
Maura's Game
The Know
The Graft
The Take
Close
Faces
The Business
Hard Girls
The Family
The Faithless
The Life
Revenge

MARTINA COLE

REVENGE

headline

First published in 2013 by HEADLINE PUBLISHING GROUP

3

Cataloguing in Publication Data is available from the British Library

Hardback ISBN 978 0 7553 7561 5
Trade paperback ISBN 978 0 7553 7562 2

Typeset in ITC Galliard by Avon DataSet Ltd,
Bidford-on-Avon, Warwickshire

Printed and bound in Great Britain by Clays Ltd, St Ives plc

Headline's policy is to use papers that are natural, renewable and recyclable products and made from wood grown in sustainable forests. The logging and manufacturing processes are expected to conform to the environmental regulations of the country of origin.

HEADLINE PUBLISHING GROUP
An Hachette UK Company
338 Euston Road
London NW1 3BH

www.headline.co.uk
www.hachette.co.uk

For Darley and Adele,
with all my love

Prologue

The Lord shall smite thee with madness

Deuteronomy 28:28

2012

'Hello! Are you not listening to me? My little girl has been missing for three *fucking* days. I think that might be worth your attention, don't you?'

Michael Flynn was so angry he was almost spitting his words down the phone. Over six feet tall and with a heavy build he was a big man and, as everyone in the room knew, he was more than capable of great violence. He was paying them for their expertise, which they currently seemed to be lacking in. In fact, they were irritating the arse off him with their stupidity.

'Her mother is giving me serious grief, and that alone is a fucking bugbear. I need to know where she is, people! So I think you lot had better get me the information I need before I start to think you're all mugging me off. I know she isn't exactly what you might call a wilting fucking violet and, believe me, when I locate her I will personally launch her into outer space for this. But I want her found. You are the *Filth* – this is what you fucking do! You locate errant fuckers. So you had better start doing it quickly. I am not a man who is known for his patience, and I have a very low threshold for idiocy.' He slammed down the telephone.

Jamie Gore listened to his boss rant at the policemen in his employ. Everyone knew that Jessie Flynn, Michael Flynn's daughter, was about as dependable as a Nigerian marriage broker; therefore, she held no importance whatsoever to anyone, especially to the police. She could get away with anything – from possession of any substance, including a bomb, should she ever purchase one, and that was all thanks to her father's influence. He'd paid the Old Bill handsomely to *ignore* her over the years; now suddenly he wanted them to make her a priority? Bit of a turnaround there. He spoke up. 'Look, Michael, with all due respect, you know your daughter as well as we do, she could be fucking anywhere. She goes on the missing list regularly . . .'

Michael Flynn was dark-haired and dark-skinned, he had the Irish gypsy in him there was no doubt about that. He was a handsome fuck, and his good looks were part and parcel of his persona. Both men and women were attracted to him, and he had always used that to his advantage. His startling blue eyes were now trained on Jamie Gore, and the man felt the first prickle of uneasiness at the intensity of his gaze.

'You having a fucking laugh, Jamie? You think I brought you lot here for nothing? My old woman is like a fucking lunatic! My little Jessie is on the missing list! No one, and I mean *no one*, has seen her for *three fucking days*! I know she is a lazy mare, I know she lives on her own fucking time-zone, and I know she is the biggest pain in the rectum since records began. But she is still my baby girl. So my advice would be to fucking well find her! Track her down, let me know where she is so I can deliver her back to her mother and then we can go home.'

Michael looked around the room, and he knew that every bloke in there was thinking the same thing: Jessie Flynn was probably tucked up in bed with another lowlife, another fucking no-mark she had picked up on her travels. She was a trollop of the first water, having been sleeping with the enemy since she was fourteen years old. He wondered how many of his workforce had serviced her at one time or another. She was a beautiful-looking girl, with the morals of a fucking alley cat. It didn't matter – he still wanted to know where she was. More to the point, her mother *needed* to know. Josephine was deeply concerned for her daughter's whereabouts.

Jessie was not a girl you could lose sleep worrying about all the time – she stumbled from one disaster to the next (usually the disaster was a man), but she always seemed to come out on top. He made sure of that. She came home at some point and then her mum would be so pleased to see her there would be no retribution of any kind. That was the trouble. Michael personally believed that his daughter needed a fucking good slap, but his wife would never agree. If Jessie murdered the neighbours with an axe and it was caught on CCTV, his wife would say, 'Well, they must have upset her.' Jessie could do no wrong in her eyes.

He too had indulged her once, when she had been small and still lovable, but that had changed the moment she discovered the power of her sexuality and the harm it could bring to the father she had once adored. He had given up trying to force any kind of fatherly rules or regulations on her. Jessie wouldn't listen to him anyway – she was a girl after his own heart in many respects. She did exactly what she wanted, and she did that with the maximum amount of energy she could muster. But she was a whore, and that fact broke his heart. Not that he could ever let that be known – in his game that would be seen as a weakness.

He sighed heavily. The men in this room were some of the hardest men in the south east; they *all* worked for him and were pleased to do so. He was a hard man, everyone knew that, but he prided himself on being a fair man, a decent man in some respects. These were men who were at the top of their particular games, and he used their nous and their instincts for his own ends – and made sure that they earned a good fucking wedge at the end of the day. Michael Flynn was a one-off; in his world he was a man who was not only feared, but who had also earned the respect of his peers, and who had managed to rise to the top without treading on too many people's toes. He had embraced his partners in crime, and made sure that they earned enough to prevent them coveting what he had. Now he had the partnership and the major earn from every Face in the country – well, in Europe, if truth be told. And the men he dealt with owed him, respected him for his achievements, and did not begrudge him his percentage because, without him, most of them would never have got as far as they had. He had worked his way up the ladder, realising early on that to keep on top you had to have a loyal and willing workforce, and that if you wanted to earn a place of importance in the criminal world, you also needed a very lucrative and honestly run legitimate business, as well as the wherewithal to not only invest heavily in other people's businesses, but to also be able to offer them a modicum of protection should Lily Law decide to investigate them at any time.

Well, Michael basically owned Lily Law, and it was not fucking cheap. He paid out a serious fucking wedge to the Old Bill, and they, for their part, did fuck-all the majority of the time to earn their crusts. It was one of the things that really irritated him, but they were what his old partner Patrick Costello used to call a 'necessary evil'. He had worked hard to get them in his pocket, and many of them had *him* to thank for their additional wages, nice cars, and kids' educations. Because of that, he held all the major cards: he could negotiate a prison sentence, he could make certain charges disappear, he could fit up anyone who he felt was getting a bit too big for their boots. It was a win-win situation. No one had ever had that much power over the law before. He had orchestrated that by himself, and now he was a man who was settled at the top. No one in his game would ever feel the urge, or indeed the need, to try and take his place and run his businesses. He was too shrewd for all that old fanny. His legit businesses were huge earners as well – he could explain away everything he owned. In short, Michael Flynn was virtually untouchable.

But now he was looking out at the men he knew as friends, not just as business associates, and he felt the prickle of shame wash over him. His daughter going AWOL was not something they saw as in their remit to sort but, as they were on his payroll, they had no option but to listen to him and offer their help in any way they could.

His Jessie's reputation had preceded her as always. They all assumed she was drugged and/or drunk out of her head somewhere, because that was what she was famous for. Twenty-two years old, and she was already a legend in her own lunchtime. She had been excluded from every school he sent her to, and instead she had embraced the underworld from an early age – from the drug dealers, to the scumbags who hung around the council estates, the burglars, gas-meter bandits with homemade tattoos – she spent her time in filthy squats until he brought her back home to her mother time and again. After cracking open a few heads, of course.

Michael had given up on her completely by the time she was sixteen. Once he had found her naked on a filthy mattress in a condemned house in Hackney with a junkie three times her age, who had given her not only a black eye but a dose of gonorrhoea as well. He had known then that he had no choice but to step away from her emotionally. He loved her, but he could not get through to her. Nevertheless, he had gone back and almost kicked the man to death for doing that to his baby. He had vented his anger, looking around at how she had been living. She was available to any man who tipped her the wink and who she thought would anger her father, and bring him shame.

He didn't understand it. She had had a home that was not only full of love for her, but was beautiful. She had everything she could have desired: the chance to go to a good school, and a good life ahead of her. But, from fourteen years of age, she had made it her business to find the lowest of the low, and make a home there for herself with them, and she had broken her mother's heart in the process. Unlike her father, her mother still felt her daughter could turn her life around, redeem herself. But Michael refused to get involved any more; she was his Achilles heel, his only real weakness. Her antics were common knowledge in his world, and it was only his status that stopped people from gossiping openly about her.

He had tried everything, and she had fought him every step of the way. She was his daughter, and he would protect her as much as he could but, in his darkest moments, when he heard about her latest escapades, or the police informed him she had been arrested once more, he had wished her dead, and he hated himself for that.

Seeing the suffering she caused his wife made him resent Jessie all the more. Jessie had broken her mother early on. She still cared what happened to her daughter; she hoped that she would come home one day, and it would be forgotten, and they would live a normal life together, like everyone else. Michael knew better. He just provided Jessie with the means to live her life, but at least her need of money allowed him to police her in some ways.

Jessie had given birth to a child at sixteen, but the child was no more to her than a doll she dressed up on special occasions. She left him to be brought up by her own mother. Michael loved the bones of his handsome little grandson, who had more of the Flynn family in him than whoever had been the fucking piece-of-dirt culprit. Not that Jessie had any fucking idea of her son's parentage of course; the poor child had been no more than a whodunnit and, with Jessie, that meant it could have been literally *anyone*. Oh, he'd accepted the reality of his Jessie a long time ago. He loved her, but he didn't *like* her one bit.

Now her mother was worried about her and, if he was really honest with himself, so was he. He understood her much more than she had ever realised; she was a ponce of Olympian standards, but she had never missed an opportunity to pick up her allowance. She should have been at his offices the night before to pick up the money, but she had been a no-show. That was not like his daughter at all – she craved money like a junkie craved a fix. She spent like a woman with no fucking arms – on clothes, shoes and, unfortunately, men. His Jessie never missed her cash payment; she had her credit cards as well, but he could monitor them, so she knew the value of a pound. Jessie was a druggie, a drunk and a waste of space, but she was never late for her allowance. He made sure that it was far too lucrative for her to turn down.

So where the fuck was she?

Jessie Flynn opened her eyes, and fear enveloped her.

It was pitch dark, and she was aware that she was bound, both her hands and her feet tied. For all her exploits, she had never found herself in a predicament like this. She was racking her brains to work out not only who the fuck she had upset recently, but who would have the guts to do this to her knowing who her father was. She knew, on one level, she was in serious trouble, but she was still having a problem accepting that.

She was Jessie *Flynn*, for fuck's sake! Her dad was the biggest Face in town. That had always meant she was immune to aggravation of any kind – even when she caused outrageous problems for herself, those problems were automatically negated by her father's timely intervention.

She strained her eyes to see where she was being held captive, but the darkness was total. There was nothing to see at all – just a pure blackness. She was actually truly frightened, and that shocked her. She had never felt real fear before – it was an alien concept – and she swallowed down the scream that she could feel building inside her throat. She would never let anyone know that she was scared or worried about anything. All her life she had lived behind a mask of defiance, and she was not going to let this situation freak her out.

She took a few deep breaths to calm herself; her heart was hammering in her ears, and she could hear it so loudly it was like a drum beating in the room. It bothered her more than she liked to admit. It was too quiet, that was the problem; there was no sound other than her own breathing, her own heartbeat.

Instinctively, she knew that was not a good sign. This was not a situation that she could interpret or make any sense of. She was not unused to waking up somewhere strange, without any memory whatsoever of how she had arrived there. She would often see a man asleep beside her and have no idea who he was or where she had come across him. But she would find out eventually; she would talk to them and gradually she would get the gist of how she had arrived in their bed and, somewhere in the back of her mind, she would dredge up something to explain the events of the night in question.

This was different. She was tied up and she was in pain. Her arms felt like they were being wrenched from their sockets, and her ankles were tied so tightly she couldn't feel her feet.

She felt the fear rising inside her once again, and she fought it down; whoever had done this to her would never get the satisfaction of hearing her cry out into the darkness, or calling for help. She was shrewd enough to know that, wherever she was, crying out for help would be futile. If there was any chance of being heard her mouth would have been taped shut. The silence around her was complete, like the darkness; she was not somewhere random passers-by would stumble across, let alone somewhere that noise would cause people to panic or phone the Filth. She was being held captive for some reason – she just hoped that the reason would be explained to her sooner rather than later.

She was cold, and she could smell the mustiness of the mattress she was lying on – the place was damp, so she could even be underground. The silence and the stench made her think that might be the case. She knew, deep in her guts, that she was not here for any reason that might benefit her.

She closed her eyes tightly because, once more, she was feeling the urge to shout her lungs out, however futile. She needed to use the toilet, she felt a sudden urge to open her bowels; she was coming down fast, and she could feel it. She had not eaten properly for a few days and, now that she was sobering up, she was becoming even more afraid of the dangerous predicament she found herself in. She tried to bring her hands out from behind her back, but she couldn't. They were tied together so tightly, every movement caused a burning pain. It occurred to her suddenly that she was still fully clothed, so whoever had done this to her did not seem to have touched her in a sexual way. She was not sure that was a good thing either – that would have been something she could understand, could even control. Everything in her life until now had been about using her feminine wiles to get what she wanted.

She took a few more deep breaths, but the panic lingered close to the surface. She closed her eyes tightly and tried to relax her body, but it was hard. Her arms were screaming now; she had probably been tied up for a good few hours, and her trying to move around was causing the pain. She tried to wiggle her fingers – a voice in her head was telling her to keep the circulation going. Tears formed in her eyes, and she blinked them away furiously. She was not going to show her fear to anyone, that was simply not in her make up.

This had to be a kidnapping. The thought gave her a thrill of anticipation – if that was the case then her dad would pay them and that would be it. Though she also knew her dad would never rest till he had tracked them down – not for taking her hostage, of course, but for trying to have him over. She suspected he wouldn't actually bother to pay them if it was left up to him – it was her mum who would insist. Her mum was all he cared about really, and his grandson, of course. Her son was the only saving grace Jessie had; her dad couldn't control her life, so he was determined to control his grandson's. He loved him though. She saw that, and it hurt her.

She managed to turn over on to her belly, and that eased the pain in her shoulders. She had never in her life felt so vulnerable or so alone, and she was craving a drink. Not water – though even that would be welcome. No, she was craving a real drink. She needed a large vodka or a Scotch, just something to take the edge off. Valium at least would help her relax and work out what she was going to do. It occurred to her that for the first time in years she was stone-cold sober, without the crutch of either chemicals or alcohol.

She heard the scraping sound of a heavy door opening somewhere in the distance outside the room where she was tied up like a kipper, and she felt the unmistakable prickle of genuine terror.

Detective Inspector Timothy Branch of the Serious Crime Squad was annoyed even though he had always known that this day would come. He was not a fool – no matter what Michael Flynn might think. He had been aware from the first moment he had taken the man's money that he was, to all intents and purposes, now owned by him. He would be called on at some point to repay the favour; he had just not expected it to come so fucking soon. In fairness, this actually was a police matter – a missing daughter was not something to take lightly. He shouldn't feel so angry about being summoned into his offices by Flynn, or about the man demanding, in a loud and threatening manner, that he wanted results.

'Take the opportunity to earn your fucking keep, you useless fucking ponce!'

That hurt. Timothy knew when he was being taken for a cunt, and the man he was dealing with was not someone who could be palmed off with legal jargon, more's the pity. He knew he had to deliver, and deliver sooner rather than later.

Michael Flynn was like a man demented. 'She disappeared three days ago, Branch, and I have it on good authority that she was last seen in a pub in Upney. She scored some coke and grass, and she left around midnight, and no one has seen her since.'

Timothy Branch nodded, as if he was in full accord with everything he was hearing. His carefully modulated pseudo-posh voice was like a red rag to a bull, though he wasn't aware of that just yet. He was a snob, and a social-climbing arsewipe who had no qualms about taking money on the side to bankroll his wife's pretentious upper-middle-class lifestyle, and who had believed that his expertise would never be compromised by his association with a known villain. His stupidity and his arrogance were exactly the reasons why he was on Michael's payroll in the first place; without someone like Flynn on his side, he had no chance of hitting the big time.

'I will put out a missing persons report, Michael, but, in all honesty, she will probably turn up as per usual, we both know that.'

Michael looked at the man he had been paying handsomely for so long, and it occurred to him that he had been paying out a decent wedge to a complete fucking moron. Timothy *had* to have known that at some point he would be called on to deliver, that the day would come when he would be asked to do a favour of some description. Now he was being asked to do something that he should be doing *anyway* – look for a missing girl – but he was not really demonstrating the level of motivation that Michael's regular payments should have guaranteed. In fact, he was not showing the least bit of willing, and that alone was irritating. He was showing no consideration of how much he had pocketed over the last few years, or how his rise through the ranks of the police force had been orchestrated by the same man he was now attempting to mug off.

Michael Flynn was not in the mood for this kind of aggravation; the last few hours had been a revelation to him as to how deeply his daughter and her fucking lifestyle had impacted on him personally. He was now being treated like a fucking tourist by a no-mark who relied on him for a second wage, and that was not something he could allow. 'You useless fucking cunt! All the money I have slipped your way, and you treat me like a fucking greebo! Like a fucking no one!' He dragged the terrified man from his chair, savouring his fear, and his dawning comprehension of exactly who he was dealing with. 'I expect the best, because that is what I have paid for over the years, and you are two seconds away from making me regret my decision to put you on my payroll. A decision that I can easily rectify – and that, my friend, would of course mean that you would have to return every penny I fucking shoved your way over the years. You avaricious useless fucking ponce! I hate dishonest Old Bill more than anything. If I ever get a capture it had better be from one I couldn't buy off. That's an honest nicking, you see, and I could swallow that. But Filth like you are only there to do what I fucking request of them.'

Timothy Branch lay on the floor of his own office, with his arms over his head to protect himself from another onslaught from Michael Flynn. He was well aware that everyone in the station could hear the conversation and would know exactly what was going on. He was waiting for the beating that he was convinced was going to come. He had made a mistake of Olympian standards, and he could not rectify the situation because he had brought it on himself. He had honestly believed that being a policeman, a *senior* policeman, would have guaranteed him immunity from this sort of behaviour. He had assumed that Flynn, for all his money and reputation, would have thought long and hard before he raised his hand to a member of the police force. But he had been very wrong. Flynn's power went far deeper than he had ever anticipated. The fact that no one had come to his aid was a real lesson for Timothy Branch. The outer offices were now deathly quiet; everyone out there was listening to this exchange and he knew his humiliation was now complete.

Then the office door opened with a bang, and Chief Superintendent Dennis Farthing came into the room like an avenging angel, all cigarette smoke and false teeth. Timothy Branch felt relief washing over him, until he heard the man say with mock sincerity, 'A sorry business this, Michael, but don't you worry, my friend – I will have my best men on it, of that you can be assured. Jessie is a priority, I guarantee.'

Michael Flynn felt the anger seeping out of him. This was what he wanted – a promise that everything that could be done to find his daughter was being done. His wife needed that, she needed to know that Jessie was being treated as a priority, that he was using his considerable power to locate her child. But, deep down in his gut, he knew that something was not right, that this was far more serious than anyone really thought. Jessie never missed a pay day, and she never went twenty-four hours without ringing her mother. Even drugged out of her brains, she still rang her mum for a chat, because she knew that if she didn't get in touch Josephine would worry herself sick. Jessie knew that her mum needed to hear from her, that she wasn't a well woman in her own way. It was Jessie's only real saving grace that she rarely let a day go by without a call to her mum.

Now it was almost four days since anyone had seen or heard from her. If Michael was honest, he was feeling more uneasy by the hour.

Josephine Flynn was having trouble breathing. It was a warning before she got one of her panic attacks, so she sat down in her chair and tried to regulate her breaths. She hated herself for her weakness, but she had always suffered with her nerves. She could feel her heartbeat slowing down, and she closed her eyes in relief.

She savoured the calmness that washed over her, the feeling of normality and the knowledge that she had conquered her demons, if only for a little while. She opened her eyes slowly, and looked around sadly; she knew she should motivate herself, tidy up, *do* something constructive. But she wouldn't because she never did. No matter how many times she convinced herself that she was ready to finally do it, to finally take control of her life and her surroundings, when it came to the crunch, she *never* did anything that made a real difference.

She noticed that the curtains were open; Michael must have snuck in and opened them while she was sleeping. She knew that if he had not opened them she wouldn't have bothered. She liked them closed, she liked to shut out the world, the *real* world. Michael always argued that they had such wonderful views – all farmland and no other houses in sight. He thought that would make her feel better, make her feel easier in herself. But he didn't understand that the view outside the windows was irrelevant, she had no interest in it whatsoever. She had no real interest in anything other than her immediate surroundings.

She got up slowly, and went to her dressing table. Michael had left her a pitcher of fresh water, and she smiled at his kindness. She poured a glass out for herself, and then she meticulously counted out her medication. She swallowed the pills quickly, comforted by the feel of them in her mouth as she forced them inside her with huge gulps of the fresh water her husband knew she needed. She felt better immediately; she had taken her first step into the day, a day that was as fraught for her as every other day in her life.

She went back to her chair, and settled herself down again. Everywhere she looked was cluttered – piles of photographs, newspapers, or used jars. Shoes were piled in the corners, and her clothes were strewn all over the floor. Rubbish was kept in bin bags, and she had placed them lovingly against the walls. The clutter was her armour against the world – it made her feel safe. She could look at something that she had kept for reasons known only to herself, and she could smile in remembrance of a memory long gone – a memory no one cared about but her.

Now her Jessie was gone. No word at all, and Josephine knew in her gut that something bad had happened to her daughter.

She opened up her make-up bags which were never far from her side and, pulling a large mirror towards her, she began the long and painstaking artistry she used to create the image that allowed her to face the world as best she could.

Michael Flynn was tired. He had not slept properly for two days and, even though he had not believed it possible, he was deeply concerned for his daughter's safety. She was selfish, greedy, manipulative and devoid of any real morals, and that was exactly why she never failed to turn up for her allowance. She had very expensive tastes, and she liked to be able to indulge herself; she wasn't as low rent as she made out.

She was never off his radar no matter what anyone else might think or what he might let them think. She was always going to be his baby. She was a girl who made it very difficult to love her, who knew exactly how to rattle his cage. It was something she had made her mission in life; hurting him was something she enjoyed so much she had even left her own son behind in her pursuit of his unhappiness. He had taken on responsibility for the child along with his wife although, to his daughter's chagrin, it had not been a chore for them. In fact, it had been almost like a rebirth for them both, inasmuch as they had adored their grandson from the moment he had entered the world. Jessie, on the other hand, had not been miraculously changed by giving birth to her own flesh and blood, as her mother had been convinced would be the case. Instead she had abandoned her little son at the first available opportunity, and she had drifted in and out of his life ever since. Michael hated her for that, even more than he hated her for how much she had hurt her poor mother.

Jessie thought she herself was the only person worth a day's interest. But that was his daughter – an arrogant fucker, who had no moral compass whatsoever. She saw everyone around her as someone to be used for her own ends, and that included her own child, her own flesh and blood. Michael had been forced to accept that about her over the last few years and it had not been as easy as everyone had believed. It had been very hard for him. Because he had loved her with a vengeance. She was his baby girl, his only child. She was also a selfish, vicious, bitter, manipulative, avaricious, devious, two-faced ponce, whose only interest in life seemed to be getting drunk, drugged, laid, or a combination of all three. She had been the apple of his eye once, and now she was someone he had to live down on a daily basis. It was only his standing that stopped him from hearing the real gossip concerning her, and he knew that was a good thing because if she pushed him too far, he knew he might finally do something to get himself nicked.

He was staring at the phones in his office, hoping that whoever had her would just ring him up and let him know she was OK. Then, once he had paid them off, and his Jessie was accounted for, he would hunt the bastards down like the fucking rabid dogs they were, and personally make sure that they never again put any other parents through such agony. He would take great pleasure in ensuring they disappeared from the world around them in as much pain and terror as physically possible.

He was taking his daughter's disappearance personally; whoever was behind it was trying to prove a point. This was about him. It had to be. Inside his head, he could not help wondering if his daughter was a part of it all. She was capable of anything, as he knew better than anyone. But he hoped that he was wrong. For all that had happened, he hated to think she was capable of trying to rip him off and, if she *was* trying to do that, he would personally make sure that everyone involved would be made aware of how irritated their actions had made him, his Jessie especially. If she *was* involved, that would be the last straw, and he would have to take drastic action against her.

There were some things that could never be forgiven. Some things that could finally cause a body to turn on their own.

Jessie woke up once more, and she was immediately aware that there was somebody else in the room with her.

It was still pitch dark. Still cold and damp. She knew that she couldn't be the first to speak – her dad had always told her: when in doubt, shut your trap. If you kept your own counsel, eventually the others would feel the need to explain themselves, and he had been right. She had learnt that the hard way. So she didn't say a word.

She could hear the shallow breathing of whoever was now in the room with her and, more to the point, she knew that they could also hear her breathing. They would know that she wasn't asleep any more. She was very much awake. It was a terrifying experience. She had never once, in her whole life, needed to worry about someone else's reactions to her or her antics. No matter what had happened to her, no matter what she had said or done, she had always known that her father would be in the background, and the reason why she would ultimately be safe no matter what she did. No one was willing to confront her because that would mean they would have to deal with *him*. That was something no one in their right mind would even consider. It was her get-out-of-jail-free card, the reason she pushed everything as far as she could. It was why she had been able to fuck her father over again and again. He had always made sure that she was untouchable. She had thought she was invincible because of her father – it was something she relied on. No matter what she did, no matter how much trouble she had landed herself in, her father had always made sure that it had all gone away. It was something she had seen as another of his weaknesses, as another reason to do whatever she wanted. After all, no matter what she did, he bailed her out. He made sure that her actions did not infringe on his lifestyle in any way and that was what it was all about. She knew his reputation was everything to him. Well, she was his daughter, his only child, and she had made damn sure that his reputation as a parent was worth nothing. She had enjoyed that, enjoyed the knowledge that her actions had undermined him, and made him see that he was not worth anything really.

But now she didn't know what to think. She would have to play this one by ear. She was in serious trouble. Whoever was behind this was not someone who cared about her or her family name.

She was so scared. She wasn't alone in this darkness, and she knew that she wasn't going anywhere anytime soon.

Josephine Flynn looked at her little grandson and smiled. He was beautiful – dark-haired and blue-eyed – his grandfather's double. He even had Michael's mannerisms. It was uncanny considering Jessie had no idea who had fathered him. Josephine believed that Michael's genes were so strong they had cancelled out any that the culprit contributed. She hoped so, for the child's sake; his father could be anybody – that was the honest truth. Jessie had only had the child because an abortion was out of the question as far as her father was concerned. It was also the only thing that would make her mother turn against her daughter. Still, Josephine liked to think, in her lighter moments, that her daughter wouldn't have been capable of doing something so heinous.

Jessie knew how she had struggled to have *her*. She had lost all her other children – some even after Jessie's birth. A child, Josephine believed, was God's gift, and to refuse such a wonderful offering was beyond forgiveness. So Jessie had calmed down, stopped her drinking and drug-taking for a while, and she had brought this handsome gorgeous boy into the world. Jessie had then walked out of her own child's world when he was two days old; she had given him over to her parents without a backward glance. That had hurt Josephine more than anything else her daughter had done, even if she was happy to take him on. Jessie had only been sixteen, and Josephine had hoped that giving birth might have made her daughter grow up, start to understand that all actions had their own set of consequences. But she had been wrong, very wrong – if anything, it had just made her daughter worse.

Jessie had not even bothered to name her own child, and that, for Josephine, summed up the whole situation. So she had named him herself – Jake – and Jessie had not voiced an opinion either way.

Jake was six years old now, but he wore clothes for an eight year old. He was bright as a button, already reading and writing well beyond his years, and showing every sign of being academic. Well, he had not inherited that from his mother! Jessie had always been a poor student – not because she wasn't clever, but because she was lazy. Jessie had always taken the path of least resistance. Josephine blamed herself; they had waited so long for Jessie to come along, and she had ruined her from day one. She regretted that now. Her mother had been right all those years ago. She had warned her that Jessie was a girl who needed to be chastised, who had a strong will that needed to be curbed.

Michael, in fairness, had allowed her free rein with Jessie's upbringing. He had never forced his own opinions on her where the child was concerned, even when she had known he had every right to call the shots. Michael loved her too much – he always conceded to her and her wants. He adored her, and she loved him all the more for that, because she knew that her problems would have made a lesser man run away as fast as his legs would carry him. But her Michael had never once made her feel anything other than cared for and cherished.

She watched as her grandson looked around her cluttered bedroom, and she waited for what she knew was coming.

'It's very dark in here, Nana. Why don't you come into the garden with me? You could push me on my swing if you liked.' The hope was in his voice, as always.

Josephine smiled sadly. 'That's what we have Dana for, Jake. She's much younger than Nana and she can run after you. How about after your swing, we have dinner with Granddad, and then we can all play a game together?'

Jake Flynn shrugged; it was no more than he had expected. 'OK. Will my mummy be coming to see me soon?'

It was a loaded question, and one he asked occasionally when he remembered he had a mummy. Josephine swallowed down the sadness inside her as she answered him brightly, 'You'll see her soon. You know that she is *very* busy. But as soon as she gets some time off from work, she will come straight here to see you.'

Dana O'Carroll was a good nanny – she knew when to intervene and, grabbing the child's hand, she said loudly in her thick Irish brogue, 'Come on now, Jake, let's go and play, shall we? Your nana needs to sort out a few things.'

Josephine watched them as they left the room, and she closed her eyes in distress. Pulling herself from her chair, she looked at herself in the full-length mirror that Michael had bought for her all the way from France. It was very old, and had cost a small fortune. She loved it. She saw a very beautiful woman, well dressed with perfect make-up, and sad green eyes. She didn't look her age, and her figure was still to be envied. Her thick blond hair had to be coloured now; a girl came every month and saw to that, her nails, and her waxing. She had always been a woman who had looked after herself in that respect. She suspected she could still turn a few heads – that's if she ever left the house, of course – and she knew that Michael was proud of her. He had always made her feel like the only woman in the world, and he still treated her like a queen.

If only Jessie had tried to understand him, meet him halfway even, she knew they would not be in this situation. But Jessie always had to have the last word, and had understood that, because of her mother's problems, she had the upper hand. Jessie hated that her mother's world was so small, and she blamed her father for everything that had happened. No matter how hard Josephine had tried to explain the truth, Jessie had not believed her. Now she was terrified that her daughter had taken up with someone who had harmed her, hurt her little girl in some way.

Jessie had a knack for finding that type of person – men who used her, who treated her like she was nothing and discarded her without a backward glance. Men who she sought out, and who she paid for, bankrolled with her father's money, and who she knew would make him angry because she was throwing her life away just to hurt him. Now, it seemed she had finally picked the wrong one – a man who she couldn't control.

It had been too long. Her Jessie never went a day without talking to her – whatever she thought about her father, she loved her mother. They were very close, and it was only the knowledge that she would find it hard if she didn't see or hear from her little girl, that had stopped Michael from sidelining his Jessie for good. He felt it would do her good to have to earn her own keep, and see what the world was like without his name to protect her; Josephine had argued that if he did that she would be in danger of losing her altogether. Her real fear was that Jessie would end up on the streets, selling herself to whoever for enough money to get stoned. Now she wondered if he had been right all along, and a short, sharp shock, as he put it, might have done Jessie some good.

She picked up her favourite rosary. It had been a present from Michael on their wedding day – it was not expensive, it was very plain, made from olive wood, but it meant the world to her.

She kissed the Cross of Christ, and blessed herself quickly. Then she walked from her bedroom into her large sitting room. There she knelt down before the crucifix that dominated the room, and she began the first decade of the rosary. She normally enjoyed the Joyful Mysteries but, since Jessie's disappearance, she was now concentrating on the Sorrowful Mysteries. She could feel the despair that Mary, the Mother of Jesus, must have felt when her son had been taken from her. All she wanted, all she was praying for, was a phone call. Just something to let her know her daughter was safe.

'Is he fucking sure? How are we supposed to plot his daughter's last movements? I mean, in all honesty, where would we start? She could have been literally anywhere.' Marcus Dewer was genuinely perplexed. He was also feeling worried – like many of Michael's workforce, he was guilty of having known Jessie Flynn in a biblical sense. If he was honest, on more than one occasion. Now she was on the missing list, and he was terrified that Michael would find that out. Like most people, he believed she was on the nest somewhere, drugged out of her brains and oblivious to all the aggro she was causing.

Jamie Gore shrugged. 'It is what it is, Marcus. She likes this part of Brixton because she can score here. So let's get parked, and start asking round.'

Marcus sighed, and parked the BMW neatly. He looked at the photo of Jessie; she was a pretty girl, there was no doubt about that.

'This is fucking stupid! Everyone knows there's a price for information on her. The whole of the Metropolitan Police are scouring the Smoke. So what we are supposed to find out I don't know.'

Jamie Gore secretly agreed with his friend, but he was too

shrewd to say that. 'Marcus, do me a favour, will you? Shut the fuck up, and do what the man is paying us for. Who knows – we might stumble on to something accidentally. In fact, I think we should poke our heads into a few skag houses. You know what junkies are like – the fucking Third World War could erupt and they wouldn't even notice until they ran out of heroin. So there's a chance, albeit a very slim one, that they might not know about her being missing. And don't forget, Marcus, if we find out something important, we will be greatly rewarded.'

Marcus nodded, but he wasn't convinced. He was more worried that they would be the ones to find her, overdosed and dead as a doornail. *That* wasn't the kind of news he would relish giving Michael. It was what the majority of people believed had happened to Jessie Flynn – they were waiting for her body to turn up, and no one wanted to be the one who found it.

Jessie was weak. The man who was holding her only gave her the minimum of water; she was always thirsty, although the hunger wasn't so acute any more. She couldn't work out how long she had been down here in the darkness. She seemed to sleep a lot, so she guessed that he was putting something in the water to keep her sedated. At least he had untied her hands although she was still manacled around her ankles, and the chain was attached to an iron hoop on the wall behind the mattress. She was still in darkness – the only time there was any light was when he brought her water. He had a torch, but it blinded her, so she covered her eyes. She had a feeling he wasn't interested in her seeing him anyway. She played the game – that was all she could do.

He had still not spoken to her, and that frightened her more than anything else. She had threatened him, abused him, told him that her father would be searching for her, and he had not reacted in any way. He had shone the torch and shown her an old chamber pot where he expected her to do her business. She had railed at him, cursed him, but there had been no reaction.

She had woken up earlier because she could hear him moving around outside the door. She swallowed down the rising panic that was getting harder and harder to control. She didn't know what she was supposed to do, what he wanted from her. She could smell her own faeces, could feel the dirtiness of her body and clothes. She had waited for him to rape her, or assault her, but he had done nothing. He brought her some water at regular intervals, and he emptied the chamber pot at some point, and he had also left her a blanket. She could only assume he had kidnapped her, and he was waiting for her father to pay the money. He would pay it – her mother would make sure of that. But why was it taking so long?

She kept thinking of every serial-killer film she had ever watched, every book she had ever read about men who abducted young women, and tortured and raped them. Only in the books and the films, there was always a detective on their trail who you knew would eventually save the girl and kill the maniac; you knew that because the detective *always* solved his case no matter how obscure the clues. The maniac would also often be in direct contact with the police, would be taunting them and, as the reader or viewer, you would be cheering on the detective, knowing all along that he or she would eventually work it out. But that was not real life. She worried that he was going to come in at some point and really hurt her, and she was so terrified about that.

Her initial arrogance was gone; she was not only stone cold sober for the first time in years, she was also acutely aware that she wasn't ready to die. She loved her son in her own way, and she wanted to see him again, see her mum, be hugged by her once more. She had to wonder if this was something to do with her dad – he had stepped on a lot of people's toes. Surely she should have been out by now if it was about money? What if this man was holding her as a grudge against her father? Or what if he was a serial killer and her father's name and reputation meant nothing to him?

She pushed her fist into her mouth to stop herself from screaming; she still had enough strength left to make sure she didn't show him her fear. She wouldn't show him how scared she was until she absolutely had to. She would beg him on her knees if that was what he wanted, she would do whatever she needed to try and get herself out of this situation.

She pulled the blanket around her, and she forced herself to try and think rationally. But it was hard to concentrate – the darkness was so intimidating, so final. And the man who held her was still an enigma. Until he spoke to her or acknowledged her presence in some way, she knew she couldn't even begin to understand exactly what she was dealing with. She felt the tears running down her face, and she didn't even try to stop them.

'Come on, Jake, eat your dinner up.'

Michael winked at his grandson, as always amazed at the love the child could engender in him. Considering the circumstances of his birth, Michael had always been in awe of the feelings he had for this child.

'I'm eating my dinner, Granddad, so I can grow up big and strong like you.'

Michael sighed. He remembered when his Jessie had been like this little lad, innocent, trusting and eager for her parents' company. All that had changed when she was thirteen. Overnight she had become a different person – difficult, awkward, full of hate. Everyone said it was teenage angst, that she would grow out of it. But she hadn't, she had gradually got worse, and she had become out of control. Now she was missing, and he didn't know what more he could do.

Book One

We will either find a way, or make one

Hannibal

Do not trust in extortion or take pride in stolen goods,
though your riches increase, do not set store by them

Psalm 62:10

Chapter One

1979

Michael Flynn looked around the dingy offices with interest. This was where Patrick Costello, the legendary East-End Face, orchestrated the serious earns for the Costello family. Up to now, Michael had been working for one of Patrick's collectors – a ponce named Jimmy Moore – but what he really wanted was to be in the thick of the Costello business. He knew he could learn a lot from Patrick Costello.

Patrick Costello was now nearly fifty, although he looked younger than his contemporaries. He had done a nine-year stretch in his twenties, and he had used his time inside wisely. He had been in for murder and, as a lifer, he had been afforded the opportunity to better himself, and he had taken advantage of everything that was open to him. He had taken up body-building, and he had also gained himself a degree in English Literature, understanding, for the first time in his life, the power that education could bring.

Since his early release, Patrick had a different approach to the Life. He had done his time, and he was not about to make that mistake again. Now he made sure that everything he was involved in could never be traced back to him. He paid his people to ensure that they would take the fall if everything was to go pear-shaped, and he paid well.

His brother Declan was just five years younger than Patrick, but he was like a big, overgrown schoolboy, all jokes and friendly camaraderie. He had a wide, open face that screamed honesty and shielded from most of the world the fact that he was capable of great violence. Coupled with the fact that he never forgot or forgave anything he might see as an insult, he was a very dangerous individual.

Declan was the one that most of the Costello workforce dealt with on a daily basis, and that was how both brothers liked it. Declan enjoyed issuing orders more than planning operations, and Patrick was more than happy for him to do that, while Declan, in turn, was happy to let his older brother make the big decisions and decide where and how they would invest their money. *He* couldn't organise a Papal Mass in the Vatican on his own.

Patrick was the head of the family. He made sure that everything ran smoothly, orchestrating every move that the Costellos made. He had a few men on his own personal payroll too. They had started out in the family business but, seeing their capabilities, Patrick had offered them a new path. When they came into his *personal* employ, they then saw the side of the Costello family business that was as lucrative as it was dangerous. Patrick trained them up personally, and they answered to him and no one else. The main criteria for working alongside him was the ability to keep everything on the down-low and if the person *did* get a capture, for whatever reason, they were expected to take the consequences involved without question. They knew they would be well compensated for their trouble.

Now Michael Flynn was getting the chance of a face-to-face with Patrick Costello and he didn't intend to waste it.

He could hear Patrick coming up the stairs, back to his office, and he waited patiently for him.

Patrick came through the doorway beaming. 'Sorry about that, son, but you know the old adage – no rest for the wicked, eh?'

Michael grinned in response.

Patrick stood by his desk for a few moments looking at Michael intently.

Michael held the man's gaze easily, but it unnerved him nonetheless. Patrick Costello looked more dangerous than ever in his own domain. Michael could see that Patrick's reputation as a man who was not to be crossed was more than warranted. Michael had never in all his life felt so vulnerable or so nervous. But he kept his emotions in check.

Patrick smiled suddenly. 'Don't be nervous of me, Michael. I have been hearing good things about you, son, and I want you to come and work for me – personally.'

Michael was so amazed at what Patrick Costello had said he couldn't even answer him.

Patrick smiled at Michael. He could see not just the amazement but also the sheer *want* in the boy's eyes. He had chosen well. Michael Flynn was much younger than any of the other men he had taken on, but the lad had already established himself as a good earner. Even more importantly, he already had a reputation as a young man who never discussed anything with anyone.

Patrick had been impressed by Michael's dealings with Jimmy Moore. *He* was a useless cunt, who was hated by everyone he came into contact with – even his relatives. He bullied everyone around him, thinking he could get away with it because his uncle, Terry Gold, was a well-known Face. Yet Michael Flynn – who Patrick Costello knew was more than capable of taking care of himself, especially when it came to a runt like Jimmy Moore – had been sensible enough to keep his cool, do his job. He'd also kept his mouth shut about Jimmy Moore's skimming – something Patrick intended to have a word with Declan about putting a stop to quick-sharp – until he knew exactly what the score was. That was the type of person that Patrick Costello liked to have on his side. This lad would happily work for him and, if push came to the proverbial shove, he would do his time inside with the minimum of fuss.

'I don't know what to say, Mr Costello . . .'

'Before you answer me, Michael, you need to understand something. My half of the business is very clandestine. I make sure that the serious earns are not only fucking lucrative, but also so secret that no more than two or three people have any real knowledge of the actual scam they are involved in at any given time.'

He was watching Michael intently, so Michael nodded slightly as if in total agreement. He was being sounded out – how he reacted now would be the making or the breaking of him, and would either guarantee him a place with Patrick, or see him back with Jimmy once more.

Patrick sighed, as if he was debating within himself whether Michael was worthy of his attention. 'I believe that fewer people in the know ensures the absolute integrity that serious earns demand, and I only deal with serious earns. I *know* – within hours – if anyone on my personal payroll has spoken out of turn or been foolish enough to let their mouths run away with them. I'm explaining this so you know where I am coming from, and so you know exactly what is expected of you.'

Michael still didn't say a word. If truth be told, he didn't know what to say. Instead he waited patiently for Patrick to continue.

'Declan is a fucking star. He fronts the family businesses, as you well know. But what I say now is for your ears only.'

Michael nodded firmly this time; he was giving this man his word.

'Declan, God love him, couldn't work out how to find his own cock with a detailed map and a police sniffer dog. So I have a couple of men who do the actual money side of it all and Declan does what he's good at – making sure that everything runs smoothly. Now, I am telling you all this because I trust you. I run the family and Declan takes his lead from me. I work on the more dangerous enterprises, behind the scenes, so to speak.'

Michael watched Patrick warily as he walked to the large old-fashioned filing cabinet by the back wall. Opening up the top drawer, he took out a bottle of Johnnie Walker whisky. He came back to the desk and, settling himself into his large leather chair, he poured out two generous measures of the whisky into two chipped tea cups, before passing one to Michael. Then, taking a deep drink, he carried on talking as if there had been no interruption at all. 'I like you, Michael. I can see a great future for you. You're very young but, in your case, I see that as a good thing. I want to take you under my wing, and teach you the business that eventually you will be responsible for. I will guarantee you a fucking serious wedge, but that wedge is because if it should all fall out of bed, for whatever reason, *you* will be the one looking at a big lump. Do you understand that, Michael? If it all goes pear-shaped then you will be expected to take the fall. That is why you get the big bucks, son.'

Michael sipped at his whisky before answering. The chemical burn as it crept slowly through his body was almost welcome. He was finally understanding exactly what was being asked of him. Patrick was not even attempting to sugar-coat it. He was being brutally honest, and that meant a lot to Michael. He spoke, and sealed his fate.

'I understand what you're saying and, if you still want me, I'm in.'

Patrick grinned; it was what he had expected. He had chosen well as usual. If the boy had backed out, he would not have held it against him, but the people he recruited had to know the score from the off. He liked to be clear *exactly* what they were getting into, and *exactly* what he expected from them. Once they came onboard, he owned them.

'You're a good lad, Michael. I don't normally bring in youngsters like you, but I need someone who can understand this new world that's emerging. I hear great things about you, and I know personally that you can keep your trap shut. If you listen to me and use your loaf, the chance of getting any kind of capture is very remote. But the chance *is* there, as it is with any criminal enterprise. You need to understand that.'

Michael shrugged. 'I know the score. I appreciate that you have been so honest with me, but I knew from an early age that getting my collar felt was an occupational hazard. It goes with the territory. I am not a fool, Patrick. I know the downside to this business and, if for whatever reason I *do* get banged up, I know I will get my head round it, and do my time. As you know yourself, that's all you can do.'

If Patrick Costello had liked Michael before, now he found that he had a sneaking admiration for him as well. He had it all, this youngster – good looks and a seriously sensible attitude. Now he needed to make sure that Michael was tied to him for ever. He had to make him a party to something that would not only guarantee the boy's allegiance, but would also bind them together, give them a bond of sorts.

'Well then, Michael Flynn. Welcome aboard.'

Chapter Two

Josephine Callahan was dressed to impress; from her long, thick blond hair, styled in the latest fashion, to her high-heeled stiletto shoes, she looked every inch the part of the girlfriend of a man like Michael Flynn. He expected her to look good when he took her out, and she understood why. He was making a name for himself, and he needed a girlfriend who was his equal. She had been seeing him since she was fourteen years old. He had been nineteen then, but the age difference had never bothered anyone. Now, at seventeen, she was his in every way that mattered. They were a couple, and engaged to be married. She could not have asked for anything more. They were a match made in heaven.

Josephine's dad, Des Callahan, was a Face – not a well-known Face, not someone people were really scared of, but he wasn't a mug either. He had done seven years for a bank robbery, and he had done it without complaint which had earned him respect. It hadn't been easy for his wife and daughter when he'd been put away, though – without a regular income coming in they'd struggled, relying on the goodwill of his bosses. By the time he got out, Des had learnt his lesson. This time he planned for the future, putting his ill-gotten gains into legitimate businesses in case he was ever unlucky enough to get another serious capture. Her mum, Lana, now ran a café on the A13 and a betting office in Dagenham. They were both booming businesses these days, and her dad, although not exactly retired, was in a position where he could pick and choose his work.

Josephine was an only child, adored by both her parents, and now by Michael, who was everything they could have wanted for her.

Tonight he was taking her to a housewarming party at Patrick Costello's. Patrick was Michael's new boss and Josephine knew how important it was for her to be accepted by the Costellos too. She loved Michael so much – she was determined to make him proud of her.

Chapter Three

Declan Costello was already feeling drunk, and he was aware that his brother Patrick would not like it. He had been drinking since the early afternoon, even though he had known that he should have arrived at the party sober as a judge. But with the information he had learnt today weighing heavily on him, it was no wonder he felt the need to seek oblivion.

He could see Patrick's wife Carmel frowning at him with her usual disgust, so he studiously ignored her. She was a royal pain in the arse, forever acting like she was something special. If she wasn't married to his brother she would be in a council flat two minutes' walk from her mother's, like most of her mates. He had never understood what his brother saw in her. She was such a fucking snob and she had no real personality. Declan wasn't exactly Mr Charisma, but at least he worked for a living. Carmel had nothing going for her except a pretty face and a large pair of knockers, end of.

Feeling her eyes on him, he decided to escape the party and made his way to Patrick's office in search of his brother and another drink.

Opening the door, he was surprised to find Michael Flynn alone inside.

'All right, Declan? Have you seen Patrick yet? He said he wanted a quick word. What a lovely drum, eh? I don't think I've ever been in a place like this before in my life. It's like something from a film.'

Declan grinned amiably. He liked young Michael Flynn. He was a good kid and talented at his job. Anyone who could put up with that ponce Jimmy Moore without trying to bail out had to have something going for them. Michael was the only person so far who had worked for Jimmy and not requested a move. Declan wouldn't fancy Jimmy's chances if it ever came to a straightener between the two, but he admired the lad for not rising to the bait. He knew his place, and that Jimmy wasn't worth any aggravation.

His brother had great plans for this young man, and he was pleased about that. Patrick had a knack of finding people who were not only astute and willing to work, but were also willing to take the flak if the need should ever arise. His older brother had no intention of ever being banged up again.

'That's exactly what I was just thinking to myself!' he lied conversationally. 'It's fucking handsome all right, Michael. Too much space for me, mate. There's about twenty acres comes with this lot. I like to be in the Smoke personally. All this country air can't be good for you!'

Michael laughed. Declan was clearly very drunk. He was a dangerous fucker if you weren't careful but, if you used your loaf and kept on his good side, he was good company. Michael had learnt the importance of giving certain people their due. That was why he rarely drank more than a few drinks in certain company, and why he made it his business to always say something nice to the people who could influence his career.

He answered craftily, 'I don't know about that, Declan, but they do say the country air makes you randy. It's all those fucking farmers' daughters – all that space and not enough geezers.'

Declan roared with very loud laughter; he did like a dirty joke.

Unlike his brother, Declan had never married. He enjoyed plenty of female company, but never felt the desire for one woman above all others. He preferred variety. He used the women who came into his life, but he was good to them and, for the few weeks that they caught his attention, he lavished his money and time on them.

'I never thought of that, young Michael! I better get around the local pubs, have a look at the strange on offer. Now, where is that lovely little girl of yours?'

Michael was pleased at the compliment; she was a real looker was his Josephine. She was a cut above the usual girls and he knew that.

Before he could answer, the door to the office opened wide and Patrick Costello made a grand entrance.

'Hello, boys, how'd you like my new house then?' Patrick looked expectantly from Michael Flynn to his brother.

Michael was about to speak when Declan broke in furiously with, 'You had to do it, didn't you, Pat, eh? I asked you not to and you still did it.' Declan suddenly looked fit to be tied.

Patrick Costello didn't reply.

Michael just stood there, unable to say a word. He didn't know what it was about anyway. It was the first time he had ever seen Declan so angry, and it seemed that Patrick sensed that as well. This outburst had come out of nowhere.

'The whole Golding family are dead, burnt to death in their beds. Except for the son – it seems he was staying overnight at his mate's. Two little girls died though. Twelve and fourteen. How must you feel, Patrick? All that mayhem for five hundred quid.'

Michael Flynn felt physically ill.

'It wasn't anything to do with me, Declan. I can only assume the man owed other people money. Let's face it, he was a fucking ponce.'

Declan laughed at his brother's arrogance. 'Who the fuck do you think you are, Patrick, eh? Well, remember, things like this have a nasty habit of coming back on you. It's called karma. And no matter what you say, how much you might deny it, I know this was your handiwork.'

He stormed out of the room.

Michael Flynn looked at Patrick Costello. Michael was white-faced, ashen, knowing that *he* had been the one who had caused such carnage.

Patrick shrugged. 'Hard lines, son. Typical fucking Golding, though, lying about his whereabouts as usual.'

Patrick could see the terror on the lad's face and, pouring him a large brandy, he gave it to him, saying, 'Get that down you, son. You're in shock. But no one knows the truth except us. These things happen occasionally. Shit happens.'

Michael gulped down his brandy.

'The man lied to me, Michael. He said they were all going away for a few days.' He sighed heavily. 'What's done is done, son. Just make sure we keep it close to our chests, OK?'

Michael nodded. He didn't know what else to do.

'I have explained the downside of the business to you, and now you are finding it out for yourself. Take my advice, son: if you want to get on in this game, you need to learn how to tune out the shit you don't need. It's a fucking tragedy, but if Golding hadn't been such a lying cunt, none of this would have happened.'

Michael was nodding, desperate to believe what the man was saying.

Patrick looked into Michael's eyes, and he said warily, 'If this is all too much for you, tell me now. We can part company, and no hard feelings. But I need to know I can count on you, Michael.'

Michael Flynn wasn't going to lose this opportunity; it was what he had dreamt of all his life. 'You can count on me, Patrick.'

The man grinned. 'I had a feeling you were going to say that!'

Michael Flynn knew then and there that he had burnt his boats. He had come into this business with his eyes open, and he had always known that people were sometimes murdered. It could happen to any of them, for a host of reasons. Just like the big prison sentence was always going to be there, hanging over his head. It was the chance you took if you chose the Life. He couldn't let an accident, a fucking misunderstanding, cloud the rest of his life. He would put it out of his mind, force it from his psyche. After all, he had only done what Patrick Costello had asked of him – that was what he was being paid to do, and that was what he wanted to do with his life. He had made his choice.

Chapter Four

'Oh, for fuck's sake, Mum, it's just a telephone. Anyone would think we were living in the Middle Ages the way you carry on. I had to get a phone put in for work, OK? But you are more than welcome to use it if you want.'

Hannah Flynn could hear the underlying annoyance in her son's voice. In the three months since he had started working for Patrick Costello he had changed drastically.

'And who would I be calling on the telephone, I ask you?'

Her voice held a questioning note that irritated her son all the more. Anyone would think she had never seen or heard of a telephone in her life. It had never occurred to him until now how few friends his mother actually had. She was only forty-one; anyone would think she was in her dotage the way she carried on.

Michael sighed heavily, forcing himself to be pleasant. 'I really don't know, Mum. But if you need the doctor, for example, or the fire brigade, you can call them. Now, if anyone rings for me, just take a message. I've left a pad and pencil by the phone, OK?'

She nodded, rolling her eyes angrily. She could hear her son's growing impatience with her and it hurt her deeply. 'Are you coming home at all tonight?'

Michael shrugged before saying testily, 'I don't know, Mum. I keep telling you, it depends on what I have to do. But look on the bright side for once, I can always ring you now, can't I? Tell you not to wait up for me. I'm not a kid any more, Mum, for fuck's sake.'

Hannah knew when to back off. She had always prided herself on understanding her son better than he did himself. Since he had been working for Patrick Costello, Michael had become a different being. He had grown up and away from her almost overnight, and her hold over him was all but gone. He loved her, she knew that, but he didn't talk to her now, not like he used to. She knew hardly anything about his life outside the home, and that wasn't going to change. Working for Patrick Costello was like working for MI5 by all accounts. She was not happy, but she knew when to retreat.

Forcing a smile, she said generously, 'No, Michael, don't be ringing me at all hours. You get yourself off, son, and I'll see you tomorrow.'

That was what he wanted to hear. Hugging her quickly, he left the house. As she heard his car pulling away, she closed her eyes tightly in frustration. He gave her so much, and she knew that she should be grateful for that, but he was all she had. With no husband or lover, he was her everything. She had devoted her life to him, and she felt that he owed her.

Nowadays, she was nothing more than the woman who washed and ironed his clothes, and provided him with a meal whenever he wanted one. He kept his own hours, and she never knew when she would see him. This was not what she had expected from him, but she had to tread warily. He was determined to marry that young Josephine and, now he was starting to earn, she realised it wouldn't be long before he did just that.

She was losing her hold over him, and she couldn't let that happen. Not without a fight anyway.

Chapter Five

Patrick and Declan were holding court in a public house near enough to the docks to make a good meeting place, yet far enough away so the meetings didn't look dodgy. It was a great pub, and the Costellos were regular punters. Their main workforce were happy to hang out there and, as it wasn't that big, it was also easy to keep an eye on the clientele, watch the comings and goings.

Michael walked into the bar just after nine. He was well dressed for the occasion, in a slim-cut, dark-blue suit, an outrageous lilac paisley shirt, open at the neck, and chunky gold cufflinks that had his initials etched on them. They had been a present from Patrick Costello and he wore them at every available opportunity.

His thick dark hair was still long, but it was now cut and styled professionally. Michael had always been aware that his good looks made women love him, and men admire him. As well as the looks and the build, he also had the added bonus of a nice disposition.

He made his way to the bar, and he was gratified to see that Patrick Costello already had a drink waiting for him. He caught sight of Terry Gold watching him intently, but he didn't react in any way. Terry had not been pleased by the turn of events and Michael's inclusion in the Costello inner circle; his nephew Jimmy had been *his* boss after all. Terry Gold was well aware of Jimmy's business practices, robbing everyone he dealt with hand over fist. Michael knew that Terry Gold was probably wondering if *he* might have mentioned that to anyone of importance. He was insulted by the man even thinking that about him. As if he would do that! He wasn't a fucking grass.

'You're looking sharp lately, Michael, I didn't recognise you when you walked in.'

Michael laughed, but he was a bit embarrassed at Patrick's words. He had changed in a lot of ways, but now he had money he could afford to look good. He felt he needed to dress as befitted his new station in life.

'Do you like it? I got it in Ilford from some Jewish geezer. It's the most I've ever spent on clothes in my life.'

Patrick laughed loudly. 'You look the dog's knob! All that old bollocks in the Bible about clothes don't make the man – they fucking do! A nice bit of clobber makes you feel good about yourself. You can wear a suit well and all, boy, you've got the build for it.'

Michael didn't know how to accept the compliment, so he took a large gulp of his whisky and soda. He had started drinking Scotch because the Costellos were whisky drinkers. But, if he was honest, he didn't really like the taste.

'You did well this week, Michael – I'm pleased.' Patrick swallowed down his drink, and motioned to the barman for another.

The juke box came on suddenly, and drowned out the noise of the men talking. It was 'Unchained Melody' by The Righteous Brothers. Michael sighed with contentment; he loved this song. He guessed that one of the older men had put it on and, as he glanced around the packed bar, he felt a thrill that he was part of this world.

Patrick motioned with his head, and Michael followed him

through the throng to the men's toilets. Inside, Patrick waited patiently for the men using the urinal to leave. Michael noticed that they each did just that. He was impressed with Patrick's ability to get whatever he wanted.

Once they were alone, Patrick looked into the large mirror that took up half the wall and, as he smoothed his hair down, he said quietly, 'I need you to sort something out for me.'

Michael nodded. 'Whatever you need, Patrick. You know that.'

Patrick turned from the mirror. 'You're a good kid, Michael. You are going to go far.'

He faced the mirror once again, admiring himself from all angles. He had this young lad's total loyalty, he already knew that. The boy had a natural decency about him, he was a straight arrow there was no doubt.

'I need you to take out Terry Gold, Michael. He has to disappear off the face of the earth, and it has to be done as quietly and as unobtrusively as possible. No one can know that we were involved. This is just between you and me, no one else can ever know about it.'

Michael was shocked, but he knew better than to show that. Instead he looked into Patrick Costello's eyes. He could see the man searching his face for some kind of reaction. The air around them was suddenly heavy, full of menace. In this game, Michael was well aware he would be asked to prove his worth, his loyalty time and again. He couldn't lose his nerve if he wanted to be a serious player in the Life. He had to show that he was capable of *anything* that might be asked of him. So he shrugged nonchalantly, aware that he had just made a life-changing decision.

'Consider it done.'

Chapter Six

'It's got to be something you ate, Michael.'

Josephine was genuinely concerned, and Michael hated that he had to lie to her. But ever since he had agreed to take out Terry Gold, he had been throwing up.

'Yeah, you're probably right, love.'

Josephine placed a cold flannel on his forehead. It felt good, there was no doubt about that.

'I'll get you a cup of weak tea. You lie back and rest.'

He nodded, but as he looked around her bedroom, he fought down the urge to vomit all over again. It was such a girly room with its pink paintwork and flowery wallpaper. Her kidney-shaped dressing table was painted white, and she had made pink satin curtains for it which hung in regimented pleats around the outside.

She had actually done a really good job, but he hated it and the frills and the frippery that she lived with. She loved clutter – that was just one of her little foibles. He wasn't used to it. His mother was not a feminine woman in that respect – his home had always been clean, unadorned and, in some ways, quite masculine. It had never occurred to him before but, whereas Josephine and her mum could spend hours deciding on a colour scheme or choosing a particular material, his mother had never really bothered herself with anything like that. He thought it might be something to do with the lean years they'd endured when Des was put away. They'd had so little for so long now they seemed never happier than when they were buying new bits and pieces. But it was all a bit much for him.

As much as he hated Josephine's bedroom in its girly glory, another part of him loved that she cared so deeply about such things. Her femininity was something that she gloried in and was one of the things that had attracted him to her. Josephine was a man's woman. A natural carer, she wanted nothing more from her life than to be his wife, rear his children, and look after the home he would provide for them.

He closed his eyes tightly, determined not to think about Patrick Costello's request. It was one thing to kill without realising it – another entirely when you *knew* what you were doing.

He heard Josephine come back into the bedroom. Opening his eyes he looked into her beautiful face, and he knew then and there that if he wanted to provide any kind of a decent life for her and his children, he had to man up and follow the path he had been offered. The path he had chosen.

'Go and see the priest, Josephine, set a date for the wedding.'

Josephine's eyes were stretched to their utmost; he could see the joy that was such a huge part of her personality radiating from them. Josephine could find the joy in anything, she could find the good in any situation. She was a girl who always expected the best out of everything and everyone, and he wanted to make sure that was exactly what she would always get.

'Oh, Michael, are you sure? What about your mum? You know she thinks we should wait.'

Michael laughed. 'Oh, sod my mum. We know what we want, darling. Sort it for next year. Big as you like, where you like and no expense spared.'

Josephine sat on the bed beside him and, smiling happily, she sipped at the mug of tea that had been meant for him. This wedding was what she had been longing for, and now it was finally happening.

Michael adored her and, as he listened to her chattering on about the dress of her dreams and the cake she had always wanted, he was content. He had burnt his bridges, the decision was made, and he felt much lighter in himself.

Chapter Seven

Ever since Michael Flynn had been given royal status by Patrick and Declan Costello, Terry Gold had been feeling nervous. It was just a matter of time until his nephew's skulduggery would finally come to light.

The Costellos were men of the world – they knew that an element of skimming was inevitable, that any cash business was open to a bit of creative accounting. It was what made their world go round. But Jimmy had been stronging it. Terry had told him time and again that while a few quid was deemed acceptable, a serious rob would only be frowned upon by the powers-that-be. Jimmy, though, was not a person who took kindly to any kind of criticism; he saw himself as *entitled* to everything. It was his buzz word.

Terry had his own creds where the firm was concerned: he had always been a good earner, always played it straight, more or less. He was a hard man in his own right, and his uncle's reputation was something Jimmy had played on. And Terry had let him get away with murder, because he was family. He had never envisioned that Jimmy's gofer would suddenly become the man of the moment. No one could have seen that one coming – not even Doris Stokes – and, according to his old woman, *she* knew everything.

He had been a fool, he could see that now. He had let Jimmy go too far and had even defended him. Until Jimmy had come onboard, though, Terry had never once had his credibility questioned. Not that anyone had actually accused him of anything yet, but he knew that Jimmy's reputation was a reflection on him. He had brought Jimmy into the fold, and he had failed to keep the boy under control. No one had really given a toss, until that ponce Flynn had been brought in as a worker. Jimmy had loathed everything about him on sight, from the lad's good looks to his quiet demeanour, and Michael's rep as a fighter – a fighter to be feared – had not endeared him to Jimmy either.

In fairness, Michael Flynn had never retaliated even though Jimmy had treated him like dirt, but Michael's quiet acceptance of Jimmy's bad behaviour had only made matters worse. It was an insult in itself, as if Jimmy was beneath his notice. Then, as Jimmy upset more and more people, he wouldn't take onboard the fact that, in their world, you had to know your own limits.

Eventually the Costellos would be forced to do something about Jimmy. They would have heard whispers already, especially Patrick – he had eyes and ears everywhere. Patrick Costello was the brains of the outfit. Declan had his own creds and was respected and feared by the people who worked for him, but Patrick was in a different league. There was plenty of talk about him and his private band of workers, but no one had any real information. It was all supposition and rumour, but the fact that he had now taken Flynn under his wing meant he had watched him for a good while.

Still, it wasn't Flynn who he should be nervous of – it was Jimmy. Since Michael Flynn had been catapulted into the big leagues, it was eating at Jimmy like a cancer.

Terry Gold sighed heavily. He could hear his wife chatting away to his sister in the kitchen. He loved his sister dearly, although he wondered how the fuck she had given birth to a no-mark like Jimmy.

As he made his way to the kitchen, he caught the aroma of roast chicken, and he felt a little bit better. He loved his food and, if he had to confront Jimmy, he would be much happier doing it on a full stomach.

Linda Gold smiled at her husband as she busied herself with making the dinner. She was concerned about Terry though. He looked very worried lately, and that wasn't like him at all. She opened the oven and, as she lifted the chicken out, ready to baste it once more, she said quickly, 'Oh, I nearly forgot, Terry. Declan phoned. I said you'd call him back.'

Chapter Eight

Jimmy Moore was angry, and he wasn't a man who could hide his emotions. All this questioning of his business practices was getting on his nerves. As far as Jimmy was concerned, he did what the job required, and that was that. He might skim a little on the side, but that was just a perk of the job. At the end of the day, he still managed to deliver a decent wedge every week.

He poured himself a large glass of vodka. It had no real taste or smell, but it did the job required, and that was enough for him. He glanced around his office. It was a real shithole, but why would he care about that? It was no more than a base for him to work out of. His uncle Terry was always on at him to clear it up, make sure that there wasn't anything that could be seen as incriminating evidence hanging around. As if the Filth were ever going to come near here!

His uncle Terry was turning into a right tart lately. He couldn't see that it was the 1970s, not the fifties any more. He couldn't see that the world was changing on a daily basis. He had been Jimmy's role model all his life, but now Jimmy hated that the man he had tried so hard to emulate was, in reality, no more than a fucking dinosaur. *He* was young, he could see where the world was heading. From the punks to the skinheads, the message was as clear as a fucking bell: you had to look out for number one. There was no other choice.

He lit a cigarette, and pulled on it slowly, savouring the taste of the tobacco. He had a bit of coke in his wallet, and he was sorely tempted to have a quick toot. But his uncle would suss him out and they would end up arguing again.

Jimmy glanced at his watch; his uncle was late. It was after ten, and he had been the one to insist that Jimmy be there by nine-thirty at the latest. He sighed.

Hearing the outer door open, he downed his vodka quickly. It was strange, though – he had not heard a car pull up or seen any headlights. Normally his uncle parked right outside, it was impossible to miss him. The silly old fucker had probably parked up the road. He was paranoid lately, seeing skulduggery around every corner.

The office door opened, and Jimmy was startled to see Declan Costello's minder, Danny Briggs. Danny was a large man of West Indian origin, with dreadlocked hair, and a body-builder's physique. He was carrying a large machete and, as Jimmy registered the significance of that, he was too stunned to even try and defend himself.

Chapter Nine

'It's awful, isn't it, Mum?' Josephine was as shocked as everyone else about Jimmy Moore's death.

Lana Callahan sighed. 'Well, he was a fucker, Josephine. I hate to say it because his mum's lovely. But, be honest, he was a lairy little fucker.'

Josephine didn't answer; she was still shocked by the brutality of the murder. The local news had reported that he had received over twenty blows from a machete, and that the police were encouraging anyone who had been in the vicinity between nine and eleven p.m. the previous evening to contact them with any information.

Josephine's father had remarked at the end of the news bulletin, 'Well, that says it all, girls. The plod have more chance of arresting Bill and Ben for smoking Little Weed than catching the fucker responsible.'

'His poor mum, though.'

Lana lit a cigarette and, pulling on it gently, she inhaled the smoke. As she blew it out, she said honestly, 'It's a tragedy, all right. But he upset a lot of people with his bad attitude. Look at how he treated your Michael. He's a saint, that boy. Let's face it, Michael can have a row if needs be – and how he kept his hands off that little fucker God only knows. But that's the point, really, isn't it? Unlike Michael, Jimmy didn't have a sense of place, didn't have the savvy to know when to back off, he didn't have the brain capacity to realise that the only thing he had in his favour was his uncle. Michael swallowed his knob because he had enough sense to know that, until he earned his own creds, he had to take whatever Jimmy dished out.'

Josephine was staring at her mum now; the turn that the conversation had taken was scaring her. She didn't like Michael's name being used like that. She was frightened that Michael might be a suspect.

'Michael was with us, Mum, you know that as well as I do.'

Lana shook her head slowly in disbelief; sometimes her Josephine really was as thick as shit.

'No one's saying that, love. If you listened to me, you'd know that all I was trying to say is that your Michael has self-control. That is very important in his line of work. I think that his ability to keep his emotions in check is why Patrick Costello took him on. The Jimmy Moores of this world never really prosper, Josephine, whereas the people like your Michael are a rarity. They are reliable, dependable, see?'

Josephine smiled then, her relief almost tangible. 'I see what you mean now. For a minute there I actually thought you were going to say that Michael might have been in the frame.'

'Oh, for Christ's sake, Josephine, have a day off, will you!' Lana looked at her lovely daughter – she was a real beauty. But the girl's propensity for worrying about nothing bothered her mother. Josephine had never really come to terms with her father's sudden – albeit temporary – disappearance from their life. Though they had visited Des regularly, Josephine had never been comfortable in the prison environment. She had hated visiting him in Parkhurst and, even when Des had been sent to the open prison on the Isle of Sheppey prior to his release, she had still found it difficult to cope with her father's predicament.

Even worse was remembering how rough life had been without him. Oh, they'd managed to keep a roof over their heads, but times had been tight and Lana had had to budget down to the last penny. Now, luckily, their businesses provided the Callahans with guaranteed financial security, but Lana knew Josephine had never forgotten that time. She'd never take the relative luxury they lived in these days for granted.

Now she had fallen head over heels for Michael Flynn. And, if Lana knew anything, young Michael was going to rise up to the highest echelons of the Costello firm. Her daughter needed to understand that, when you tied yourself to men like Des and Michael, you had to accept the possibility that they might be put away, and Josephine could find herself exactly where Lana had been all those years ago.

It was an occupational hazard for them, but it was hard on the woman left behind, alone with kids and an empty bed. You had to learn to deal with it, and that was basically that. Perhaps it was time she opened her daughter's eyes to the world she had chosen.

Chapter Ten

Michael was tired, and he had to stifle another yawn. It was late; the weather had turned over the last few days, and the night air was heavy with icy fog. It was bitterly cold for early October, and the Indian summer they'd been enjoying had disappeared overnight. The weather report had even said there was snow in Scotland – the best fucking place for it as far as he was concerned. He hated the cold, always had. The long nights depressed him – even as a kid he had dreaded the clocks going back an hour. You got up while it was dark, and it seemed wrong somehow. Days shouldn't begin like that, days should begin with light and sunshine. Even a weak winter sun was preferable to no sun at all.

But tonight the fog would serve a purpose. He looked around him – all he could see were the dark shapes of the trees, and the muddy track he had driven over an hour earlier.

He had thought he would be nervous, frightened, but now he'd set things in motion he had no real feelings either way. This was something that had to be done, and he had no option other than to get it over with, and get on with his life. He had already killed – a whole fucking family – even though he had not known what he was doing at the time. But he had learnt how to deal with it. Once you accepted something it was so much easier to live with – no matter how bad it might be.

He had planned every step meticulously this time and, so far, it had all fallen into place. He hoped that everything else would be as easy.

He was not a fool, and he had made sure that he had every contingency in place. He had pondered this for hours on end, planned every detail, trying to work out as many different scenarios as possible. He was convinced that he was covered, no matter what might happen.

He glanced at himself in the rearview mirror, pleased at how calm he appeared. If the police should happen upon him, and ask why he was sitting alone in a car in the middle of nowhere, he had a perfect alibi ready. He had blankets, a flask of soup, and a pair of binoculars. He was a twitcher he'd claim; tell them he often slept in his car so he could get up at the crack of dawn and pursue his hobby. He even had a notebook prepared to show them, if necessary, filled with times, dates, places and what species of bird he had seen. It was probably a step too far, but he had been determined to make sure he had covered every angle. Now he just wanted to get it over with. He was bored, cold, and dying for a decent drink.

As he arched his back to loosen his muscles, and allowed himself a large, noisy yawn, he saw the glare of headlights as a car crawled slowly up the dirt road ahead of him. He relaxed back into his seat, took a long breath, and held it deep inside, until the car pulled up beside his, then he exhaled slowly.

This was it.

He got out of his car quickly, and the cold night air was enough to chase away the last vestiges of tiredness. He smiled amiably as he slipped into the passenger seat of Terry Gold's Mk IV Cortina. Michael was pleased to see that Terry had used his usual car. That would make things much easier for him.

'Brass monkeys out there, mate, I'm freezing.'

Terry smiled apologetically. 'I had a bit of trouble finding this place, Michael. Not exactly the A13, is it?'

Michael smiled, and Terry Gold was impressed at how straight and white Michael's teeth actually were.

'You got the gear then, Terry?'

Terry Gold sighed in mock exasperation. ''*Course* I have. Be a bit pointless coming all the way out here if I didn't, for fuck's sake!'

Michael laughed. Terry Gold had to be as thick as proverbial shit. There was no way in hell he would have fallen for any of this. But greed was a great incentive to so many people. When Michael had told Terry casually that, if he could lay his hands on a couple of keys of coke, he had a buyer who was new to the game, caked up with money, and who wanted the transaction to be as private as possible, Terry Gold had nearly bitten his hand off. Terry had always had one eye on the main chance, it was second nature to him.

It didn't matter that Terry suspected Michael had had a hand in his nephew's murder. Jimmy's death had been overlooked, but everyone in the know was aware that the Costellos had wanted it. Terry Gold had no choice but to swallow – what else could he do? And this was an opportunity he couldn't turn down.

'It's in the boot, Michael.'

They got out of the car together, and Terry lit himself a cigarette. Michael watched as he busied himself opening the boot, pulling up the carpet where he had hidden the three keys of coke in the space where the spare wheel should have been.

Michael shook his head. How fucking predictable could you get? The first place the Filth would look if they were to search your motor was the boot.

As Terry leant into the boot to pull the heavy bundles free, Michael slipped a small lead cosh from his coat pocket. The first blow was enough to subdue Terry and knock him out. The next fifteen blows were just insurance; there was no way this ponce was ever going to recover no matter what might happen in the next couple of hours. Michael pushed the body into the boot and slammed the lid shut. Then, whistling under his breath, he got into the driving seat and started the car. He drove it deeper into the woodland until it was impossible to drive any further.

Getting out of the car, he leant in from the driver's side and took the handbrake off. Then he used all his considerable strength to push the car, and its grisly contents, into a large, deep and extremely filthy lake. He had to wade into the freezing water and keep pushing until the car finally slipped down and disappeared out of sight into the murky depths.

Satisfied that it was gone, and that no one would know it was in there, Michael finally made his way back carefully in the darkness to his own car. His trousers and shoes were already hampering him and, opening the boot of his BMW, he quickly stripped himself. Once he had dressed in clean clothes and new boots, he got into his car, put the heater on full blast, and drove slowly back through the lanes. When he finally pulled out on to the A2, he put on his radio, and drove home at top speed, feeling good. He had achieved something.

Terry Gold's disappearance was a nine-day wonder. His nephew's bloody demise had been a violent lesson to anyone in the firm who harboured similar dreams of getting ahead by skimming. But the disappearance of Terry Gold, a happily married man who adored his family and always put them first, really frightened everyone who knew him.

No one was ever arrested or even suspected of having any involvement in Terry's disappearance. On the other hand the Costellos didn't ask around about him either. They didn't discuss it, let alone speculate as to what might have occurred and that, in itself, spoke volumes. Not that anyone said that out loud, of course, but it didn't stop people wondering.

Chapter Eleven

Michael glanced at his reflection in the mirror behind the bar, pleased with how he looked. He was a man to respect; having the Costello brothers' favour gave him the creds he needed to carry out his new businesses with the minimum of real effort. No one in their right mind was going to give him any kind of aggravation.

Since taking out Terry Gold six months ago, he now had his own personal earns. Patrick had given him the lion's share of three very lucrative pubs, and a new nightclub they had recently opened in East London. All he had to do was show his face on a regular basis and collect the takings from his managers – it was so easy it felt almost wrong. He was coining it in, and he had to do fuck-all. But he was shrewd; this was just the opener. Once Patrick had seen for himself how Michael coped and what he could earn from the venues, he would then be asked to do some real work. Patrick was thrilled with him, and he had rewarded him well for proving that he was a man who could be trusted. It was just a matter of time until the serious graft was offered him. Michael couldn't wait.

Josephine was standing at the far end of the bar, and he watched her for a few minutes. She was chatting away to her friends and, as he observed her, he couldn't help smiling. Everyone liked her – she had no side to her and that was her greatest asset.

As usual she was the best-dressed bird in the whole place. She had a knack for finding the clothes that really suited her figure. She always looked well groomed, from her hair to her make-up to her nails. Even if she was only popping to the shops for a pint of milk she made sure she had her make-up on and her hair done. It was all part of her charm. He loved her femininity. She was fragile, vulnerable and she needed him so much. He *wanted* her to need him, to depend on him. That was how it should be.

The music was blaring out, and he was pleased to see that the place was already filling with people. It was still early, and Friday night was ladies' night. The girls got in the club for free before ten thirty and, by the time the pubs turned out, the place was thronging with women and girls of every shape and size.

Catching her eye, he motioned to Josephine to join him and, as she walked towards him, he saw the bouncers giving her the once over. It was gratifying, but she was his – and everyone knew that.

'It's really taking off, Michael, don't you think? You must be well pleased.'

He grinned. 'It's all right, Josephine, we're getting there. Listen, darling. I have to go and sort a few bits out. You be all right with your mates for a while?'

''Course! You go and do whatever you need to.'

He kissed her gently on the lips. 'I won't be long, darling, promise.'

Josephine looked into his eyes; he was so good to her, always had her best interests at heart. 'You know where I am!'

He watched her as she went back to her little clique of mates, before making his way to his offices. He walked through the foyer of the club, pleased to see that there was already a big queue of people waiting to get in. He saw the doormen searching the ladies' handbags, not just for weapons – a girlfriend was the obvious choice to smuggle in a knife or firearm – but for alcohol as well.

As he slipped through the heavy brocade curtains that led into the offices, he was whistling under his breath. Life was definitely good.

Closing the heavy door behind him, he savoured the relative quiet. The music was now no more than a muted drone. He loved this office, it was his sanctuary. It had pale cream walls and expensive oak furniture. There weren't any windows, but that was a plus really – it added to the security that was necessary when large amounts of money were involved. The big, heavy safe was bolted to the floor behind his desk, dominating the room. It was not just used for the storage of the money that the club accumulated, but also for certain other items of value.

He sat down behind his desk, and busied himself going over the invoices for the alcohol and food. He had a good manager in – the guy was young, granted, but so was Michael – and he had known him for a long time. He trusted him implicitly, and knew that Paulie O'Keefe had the gift of numbers. He could not only keep two sets of books going – a must for anyone in a cash business like this – but he also had the added bonus of being big enough and ugly enough to ensure that people would think twice before they crossed him. Michael and Paulie were a good team. The only way he could survive was by surrounding himself with people he could trust. He had learnt that from Patrick Costello.

There was a gentle tapping on the door and, sitting back in his chair, Michael called out, 'Come in.'

As expected, Paulie O'Keefe entered the room. With the heavy build of an Irish navvy, he seemed to fill the room with his presence. Michael was a tall man, but Paulie was big everywhere, from his huge legs, like tree trunks, to his giant head. He had short, thick red hair and small piercing blue eyes. His mouth was thick-lipped, and he had a nose that seemed to have been flattened across his cheeks. He had the look of the fool about him, but Michael knew that he was actually a genius, especially when it came to numbers. He was perfect for the job in hand and, once people got over his appearance, they soon learnt that nothing got past him.

'Fucking hell, Paulie, you seem to grow bigger every time I see you!'

Paulie laughed. 'What can I say, Michael, I like me grub.'

Paulie sat down gently in the large leather club-chair opposite Michael and, taking out a pack of Benson & Hedges, he lit one leisurely.

'Well, we are well in profit, Michael. It's like printing dough, honestly.'

Michael nodded in agreement. 'I know. I went over everything last night. This place is already paying for itself. Everyone's happy, I can tell you that.'

Paulie smiled, acknowledging the compliment. Then, leaning forward in his chair, he said quietly, 'There is one bugbear though, Michael, and I can't do anything about it without your say-so.'

Michael frowned. There weren't many things on God's green earth that Paulie O'Keefe couldn't sort out by himself. Michael felt a distinct tightening in his guts, and prepared himself for bad news.

'Come on then, Paulie. Out with it.'

Paulie O'Keefe stared at his friend for long moments before saying angrily, 'It's that flash little cunt Rob Barber. He's been coming in here mob-handed, and he runs up huge tabs – never paid one of them to my knowledge – and he causes a fucking fight every time. Now, the bouncers are wary – after all, he is a Barber. No one wants to be the one to cause a fucking turf war.

But he has to be tugged, Michael. I kept this quiet because I knew you would go mad if you found out. But last week he went too far. He was coked out of his fucking brains and, to cut a long story short, he ended up smacking some little bird in the mouth. I told him to fuck off out of here myself, and he went without too much trouble. I think even he knew he had gone too far. But we have to make a stand, Michael.'

Michael sighed heavily. This was trouble with a capital T all right. The Barbers and the Costellos had always had an uneasy alliance. The Barbers were Notting Hill boys, and they had no interest in East London, or South London come to that.

Jonny and Dicky Barber were not men whose company was sought after. The Barbers were no more than violent thugs. Unlike the Costellos, they had not adapted to the changing times, they still ruled their little empire with only violence and intimidation. Consequently, although they made a living, they were hated. Their empire was also shrinking. The Jamaicans were not easy to subdue – anyone who had ever dealt with them knew that. Now they were a force to be reckoned with in their own right. They had the monopoly in Brixton, Tulse Hill and Norwood, as well as a strong presence in Notting Hill, Shepherd's Bush and the surrounding areas. They were the new Irish, for fuck's sake – everyone with half a brain knew that. They were happy to work beside you for the earn, had plenty to bring to the table and, most importantly, had the contacts needed to supply the product for the growing trade in cannabis.

Now Rob Barber, the youngest brother, an idiot with the IQ of a fucking amoeba, had the gall to come to *his* club, and try to fucking mug him off?

Paulie could see the anger building inside Michael. He had to be the voice of reason, but he had not had any other choice here. Rob Barber had shit on their doormat, and that could not be tolerated. Still, it had to be sorted with finesse. 'Listen to me, Michael. My first instinct was to take the fucker out the first night he rolled up here, but I knew that would only cause more trouble. So I swallowed because, as big a cunt as he is, there are still his brothers and their firm to deal with. Patrick and Declan have to be in on this, mate. You have to see the logic of that. They must have the final say.'

Michael knew that Paulie was right, but it was the principle as far as he was concerned. That little shit Rob Barber would have known that it was *his* name on the door here, that the Costellos had given the club to *him*. Rob Barber had really been challenging Michael, and that was hard to overlook.

He had earned his place in the Costello family, he was respected by everyone in his orbit. When Patrick Costello singled a person out, it was assumed – rightly – that the person concerned had done something very noteworthy indeed. Something that warranted their meteoric rise through the ranks. To be treated so disrespectfully by someone like Rob Barber – a man who was a laughing stock – was fucking outrageous.

He had to calm down; he knew that giving in to his emotions was a futile exercise. He needed to keep a clear head, think this through properly. 'You're right, Paulie, we need to sort this with care. But you should have told me the score from the off. It should never have gone as far as it has. And I can tell you now, mate, Patrick will already know everything there is to know. He has ears everywhere – I learnt that very early on. I left you to it, and I know you were only trying to sort it out yourself to save me any aggro but, in future, you tell me anything of relevance sooner rather than later, OK?'

Paulie nodded. 'I didn't want to bother you with it. I honestly never thought it would go so far. But you're right, Michael, in future I'll know better.'

Michael smiled then, a big, bright smile. 'Oh, and tell all the doormen he's barred on my express order and if Rob Barber wants to discuss it, he can come and see me – personally.'

Chapter Twelve

'Are you looking forward to us getting married, Michael?'

Michael opened his eyes slowly at Josephine's question. He was just about to fall asleep, he was so tired, even though it was the middle of the afternoon. It had been a long, stressful week.

''Course I am, you silly mare.' He tightened his hold on Josephine, pulling her naked body even closer to him. 'You don't half ask some daft questions, you know.'

Josephine laughed. 'I just love hearing you say it!'

She was lying against him; they were a perfect fit together and she lived for these stolen moments in her bed. Her mum and dad were at the betting shop today going over the books, so she and Michael were safe for a few hours. She suspected her mother knew they were sleeping together but she knew they wouldn't talk about it out loud. She loved to be alone with Michael like this. She knew that he loved her, and she understood that he had a lot of things to take care of when they were out. She was happy to stand with her friends, chat, have a laugh, and wait for him to come and claim her. But, sometimes, she wished that he would forget about his work just for one night, and take her out like he used to, just the two of them. Now they were either in his club or one of his pubs. He would be here, there and everywhere, and she tried not to mind too much, but it was hard sometimes.

He'd fallen asleep, was snoring now, and she sighed. She didn't really have that many friends, the majority of the girls were just hangers-on. They were nice enough, she supposed, but she was aware that the main attraction was that she was Michael Flynn's girlfriend. They wanted to be a part of *his* world; they all flirted with him when he was beside her, throwing blatantly provocative looks his way. She could see that he wasn't interested in any of them, though – he loved her, she was certain of that.

She was better looking than any of them anyway. She'd always been aware of her beauty – accepted it as a fact of life. One of her earliest memories was somebody saying to her mum what a beautiful child she was. She wasn't a bighead – she didn't use her looks for attention; after all, she only had eyes for Michael. One of the nuns at her school had said to her that she was a lucky girl because she was beautiful inside and out. The nun had also told her that beauty could be a scourge, and to remember that looks faded eventually, but the beauty inside her was for ever. She had liked hearing that. It had the ring of truth to it.

She remembered the first time she had seen Michael. She had been fourteen years old, and she had been walking home from school. She had looked across the busy high road, and seen the most handsome boy ever, standing stock still, and he had been staring at *her*. She had smiled at him suddenly, as shy as she was then, and that had been it. He had walked over the road, dodging in and out of the traffic, and she had waited for him as if it had been the most natural thing in the world.

Once they were married she would feel much better. It would be different then, she wouldn't have to go out with him, night after night. She would have a home to look after, babies to take care of. She couldn't wait. She wanted a girl first, a little girl who would help her take care of her siblings. As they were both only children, she and Michael agreed that they would have a houseful of babies. All gorgeous, and all wanted.

She fell asleep beside him thinking of names for her babies that were waiting to be born.

Chapter Thirteen

Patrick and Declan Costello were both listening intently as Michael explained the situation that Rob Barber had caused in the nightclub.

His voice expressed no emotion as he gave them both the facts. This was something that had to be decided by the Costellos; his personal anger would play no part. Still it was hard for him to keep his personal opinions to himself.

He made Paulie O'Keefe sound like the hero of the hour, careful to emphasise that he had only wanted to keep Michael out of anything that might cause unnecessary trouble with the Barbers and that was why he'd kept silent at first. He could see Patrick nodding his head as if he could understand that kind of logic. It wouldn't have been through any cowardice – everyone knew that Paulie O'Keefe was more than capable of standing up for himself should the need arise. Paulie had the reputation of a real marler, a fighter's fighter. Once he was set off, he would bite, kick, punch, head-butt, use any available weaponry, no holds barred. He was also known to easily take on more than one opponent if necessary. No, that Paulie O'Keefe had not demolished young Rob Barber was the feat in itself here.

Declan was annoyed, Michael could tell that much. He hated the Barbers with a vengeance. They had a history. Many years before, Declan had beaten Dicky Barber to the proverbial pulp.

Dicky Barber had been the one to insist on the fisticuffs; he had confronted Declan outside a pub in Woolwich of all places. He had challenged Declan to a fight and, once provoked, Declan had been more than happy to oblige.

Jonny Barber had taken no action at the time. He had enough sense to know that Dicky Boy had brought all the grief on himself. *He* had sought out the fight, and he had lost. There was nothing to be done. The fight had been in public, and Dicky had been the instigator. Jonny chose his battles shrewdly and he'd had a feeling that, if it ever came down to it, the Costellos would not be easy to topple. They were a bigger firm in every way, and they were well liked. It was better to retreat on this occasion, and Jonny had made sure that Dicky Boy had done exactly that. This was something Patrick Costello had known within days.

'Rob Barber has to be thirty-five if he's a day! "Young Rob Barber", my arse. He's a cunt. Even Jonny don't trust him, and he's his own brother! What does that tell you?' Declan's voice was laced with anger and disgust.

Patrick poured them a large whisky each. He stood by the windows, looking down at the empty warehouse, picturing it in his mind as it might have been many years before, packed to the brim with casks of brandy, or bolts of different coloured silks. It would have been a hive of activity then, the whole place ringing with noise.

'It's a piss-take all right, Declan. But I think that this is a job for Superman.' He turned back towards his brother and Michael. 'You want him badly, Michael, I can tell.'

Michael smiled grimly.

'He was after you, my son. *You're* the one he wanted, and you know that. He was stronging it in *your* club. Now, thanks to Paulie O'Keefe and his good intentions, that ponce probably thinks that you haven't got the bottle to face him. He thinks you've tried to swerve him.'

Michael stood up abruptly, and Patrick and Declan Costello were both suddenly reminded of how dangerous the lad could be if provoked. Michael's biggest asset was his ability to control his temper. Not many people could do it so well. Patrick himself could, but Michael was the only other person he had ever encountered who was able to do it so absolutely. It was a rare gift, and it showed a strength of will that was as powerful as it was unique. In the world they inhabited, the capability for violence was the norm, but very few could channel that violence and use it like a deadly weapon.

Michael was genuinely furious now. Patrick wanted him to show his real feelings, knowing that he needed to vent his anger. This was personal. Rob Barber had come looking for *him*. He had invaded his personal space. Michael was the new kid on the block, and people like Rob saw that as an invitation, a chance to enhance their own reputation at the expense of someone else. Rob Barber would never have fought him one-to-one; Michael knew that his reputation as a fighter would have put paid to that. No, Rob Barber would need a knife or a gun, a posse of people around him. He was a coward.

'I want him all right, Patrick, of course I fucking do! But I know enough to keep my private opinions to myself, and I have enough self-control to make sure that I don't cause trouble for anyone else. If I *had* gone after him, you both know that I would have nigh on fucking killed him.'

Patrick Costello started laughing, and Declan, swallowing his drink in one gulp, joined in.

Michael Flynn stood there as the Costello brothers roared with laughter and, despite himself, he started to laugh as well.

Patrick wiped his eyes on his coat sleeve. 'You are so like me, Michael. Always thinking of the big picture. You try and work out what might happen if you were to let your natural instincts run riot. I know exactly what it's like.' He was tapping a finger into his temple now, his face screwed up with seriousness. 'I knew as a kid that I had too much anger inside me, that I had to learn how to contain it. As young as I was, I had the ability to kill someone when the anger took over. You are the only person I have ever met who has the same affliction, Michael. And, like me, you have learnt to control it.'

Michael recognised the truth of the man's words. He could see Declan watching them both, fascinated as he listened to his brother explain himself as if it was the first time he had ever really understood him. The discomfort that Patrick's words had created was evident.

Patrick sighed heavily, as though he was tired out from all the talking. 'You can have Rob, Michael. Declan, you can finally finish off that ponce Dicky. And, as for Jonny Barber, I have wanted to take that ponce out for years. Now we have no other option. Rob has seen to that, the useless fucker.'

Michael smiled. His smile was so endearing. No one looking at it could ever have believed that it could hide so much hate and so much anger.

Patrick poured them each another drink and raised his glass in a toast. 'We need to plan this well. Do it quickly and quietly.'

Michael nodded. 'I agree. We need to let things calm down. Take them unawares.'

Patrick Costello was hearing exactly what he wanted. This was something to be done with finesse. Done properly, it was a message for everyone out there with dreams of the big time. He said quietly, 'On the plus side, boys, once the Barbers are out of the frame, we will be without any natural predators!'

Declan nodded his agreement as they clinked glasses. 'Couldn't have put it better meself, bruv.'

Chapter Fourteen

Hannah Flynn watched her son as he ate his dinner. He had always attacked his food, and she enjoyed watching him eat. He savoured every mouthful and, like any mother, she loved to watch her child devouring what she had provided. Not that she had ever cooked elaborate meals on a daily basis; she didn't enjoy cooking so she had never bothered with anything fancy. Until now it had never really mattered. Now that her son was so embroiled with the Callahan family, she was making an effort to keep him around.

Lana Callahan, on the other hand, cooked meals as if her life depended on it, and she was teaching young Josephine the finer points of Irish cuisine, as she called it. A contradiction in terms if ever Hannah had heard one. Lana Callahan cooked all the old Irish recipes Hannah's granny had cooked. It annoyed the life out of her. *She* was actually far more Irish than any of them. She had been born in Ireland for a start – and she still had the accent to prove it. Second-hand Irish, that's all *they* were. They had no knowledge really of where their family had come from originally, and had no contact with people there. They'd never even been to Ireland.

According to Michael, Lana was a really good cook, and Josephine was following in her mother's footsteps. She was a veritable fecking saint, if her son was to be believed – the Holy

Mother of God should watch herself. There was a serious contender for the crown of Queen of Heaven in Josephine Callahan.

They were taking him over, and that he was *letting* them was apparent. Michael acted like he was already a member of the Callahan family, he spent so much time round there. Hannah didn't know how she could compete but even after nearly four years, and a wedding all planned and paid for, she still couldn't accept the girl as a permanent fixture in her life.

Instead, she was determined to spoil him while she could. She was on the offensive now, cooking for her son and giving him the benefit of his Irish heritage herself. 'You're enjoying that, son. I can see that.'

Michael smiled, his mouth full of stew. It was rare for his mum to cook something so delicious. Other than Christmas dinner, his old mum wasn't known for her culinary skills. Breakfast had always been cereal and cold milk – winter or summer. She'd never once made him a packed lunch – just given him money to go to the local chippy. He never complained; what he didn't have he couldn't miss. But the Callahan family had opened his eyes and he liked the way they lived. Meals were something to be enjoyed in their house, something to be shared together as a family. It was an alien concept to him at first, but now he found that he looked forward to it. The way they talked about their day, and sat there when they were finished eating, just enjoying being in each other's company, was something he wanted for his children.

'It's lovely, Mum. I was absolutely starving as well, so it's much appreciated!'

Hannah was suddenly struck with pangs of guilt. Michael wasn't averse to cooking for himself if the need arose. Eggs and bacon were his forte. He had cooked that for them both most Sundays after they had been to Mass. She had let him do it – eventually, she had even expected it. Now she was sorry. She had always prided herself on her feminist beliefs, even though, if she was truthful, she was just lazy. She had not even bothered to get up and see him off to school once he was old enough to look after himself. He had been quite happy so she had always felt that it was pointless both of them getting up when she was so tired. After all, she had always worked so they could live. She had expected him to do his bit from an early age, and he had never questioned her methods. Until now. Hannah realised her son was very old-fashioned in some respects. He liked having a decent meal waiting for him when he came home; he expected his laundry to be hung up in his wardrobe, crisply ironed. That was how things were done in the Callahan household. He didn't even bother to give her a thank you for her trouble any more; he seemed to think it was expected of her. It was as if he had taken a step away from her; she was frightened that, if she wasn't careful, he would step away from her for good.

She gazed at him, still amazed that she'd produced such a handsome man. He was really a looker, he could actually have been a male model if he had been that way inclined. There were plenty of them now, on TV adverts and in all the magazines. They were real men too – not like the nancy boys of old. Her Michael could have been in films, he was *that* fecking handsome. He had the rugged good looks that most men would kill for. He could have *any* girl he wanted, yet he had eyes for no one except Josephine Callahan. He was throwing himself away, but he could not see that. He was obsessed with her.

She decided to change the subject. 'How's it going with the Costellos, son?'

Michael shrugged as usual. She knew he was not going to give her bell, book and candle. He never discussed anything with her any more.

'Great. There's a party at Patrick's house tomorrow, why don't you come? It's his wedding anniversary. It will be a great night, Mum. Plenty of drink, great food, and a live band as well. You should really think of coming along with me and Josephine.'

Hannah grimaced. She had known about the party for weeks, but he'd said not a word to her about going with him. 'Oh, you and young Josephine wouldn't want me with you.'

Michael shook his head. His mother was such a bitter pill these days. He knew that Josephine had asked her to come with them ages ago but, as usual, she had totally blanked her.

It was starting to irritate him. She still treated Josephine as if she was no more than a casual acquaintance of his, even though they were on the verge of getting married. He had tried to keep the peace, tried to pretend that there wasn't any problem, but it was getting harder and harder to keep up the pretence. His mother went through stages of acknowledging Josephine existed. Then she would revert to ignoring her, and Josephine would allow her to treat her like shit. It wasn't on. He had really had enough.

'Josephine would love you to come with us, Mum, as you know.'

Hannah sighed and, looking at her son quizzically, she said haughtily, 'Oh, I don't think that's really the case now, Michael, do you?'

Michael hated her when she was like this. She had always acted as if everyone that he liked or he wanted to be involved with had something chronically wrong with them, and as if he was too young or too stupid to see that for himself. He had always backed down, feeling guilty for wanting other people in his life. His mother had been enough for him when he was a kid, but he saw that he had never made friends unless his mother had given them her seal of approval. Now he was a grown, successful man, but she still expected him to choose her over everyone else in his life.

'Why do you do this, Mum? Why do you always have to try and make everything such a fucking drama? You were invited, you know that.'

Hannah could sense the anger that her son was trying so hard to contain. She had pushed him too far. If only she could stop herself, enjoy his company while she had it, without trying to force him to prove that she was the only person he would ever love. But she couldn't do that. He was *hers*, her only child, her only boy, and she was not able to let him go. He *owed* her. The few years with Josephine were nothing compared with the lifetime with her. He would see that at some point.

'Josephine is forever inviting you out somewhere, Mum, and you are always saying that you can't make it. Well, listen to me. One of these days she'll finally take the hint and blank you, and who could blame her, eh?'

Hannah wanted to explain that she could not help herself. Josephine was like a thorn in her side. The day he had met that little bitch had been the beginning of the end for her and her son. Now with the wedding nearly upon them, she knew that she would have to accept her, at least on the surface. She had no choice. But it was so hard. Josephine Callahan was like a big balloon; bright and beautiful on the outside, but if you popped the fucker with a well-aimed dart, just hot air inside. Why could her son not see that? Josephine was not woman enough for a man like her Michael. He would tire of her eventually, that was a given.

'Listen, Michael, I don't accept her invitations for the simple reason I don't want to spend a whole day looking in clothes shops! Jaysus, Michael, you tell me one time you ever knew me to go shopping for a whole fecking day! I'd rather boil me own shites.'

Michael had to laugh; in fairness, she was telling the truth. But it wasn't about that – it was about showing willing, about accepting Josephine as her future daughter-in-law, as a part of the Flynn family. She knew that as well as he did.

'But you have money to spend now, Mum! You're not that old, you still look pretty good. Shopping is what women do these days, Mum, they like to keep themselves looking nice. Lana looks fantastic for her age, she dresses so well that sometimes people think that her and Josephine are sisters!'

Hannah laughed in derision. This was too much for her now. 'So who thinks that then, eh? Did this person happen to have a white stick and a fucking dog by any chance? *Sisters!* Now I've heard fecking everything.'

Michael pushed his plate away angrily, knocking over his glass of Guinness in the process and revealing the bitterness he tried so desperately to keep in check.

'Do you know what, Mum? Josephine's right about you. You are so fucking *negative*. No matter what she tries to do, no matter what she says, you never give her a chance. She got tickets for that West End show you said you wanted to see, and you turned her down flat. You actually sneered at her as if anyone wanting to go was a fucking moron.'

Hannah shook her head in self-righteous denial. 'You are wrong there, son, I'm telling you.'

'I was there, Mum, remember? I *saw* the way you reacted and I swallowed my knob because Josephine asked me to. I was all for having a fucking straightener once and for all. I tell you now, Mum, if it had been left to me, this would have been over a long time ago.'

Hannah was watching her son wide-eyed. She was aware that

she had to try and rein herself in, but it was too late. Michael was so angry and disappointed in her, she had no option but to let him vent his spleen.

'Then she got tickets to go and see The Dubliners, and you still fucking blanked her. I grew up listening to you telling me how The Dubliners were the greatest Irish band of all time. You have every album they have ever made, yet you passed up the chance to see them live. I thought you would have snatched her hand off, but, oh no, you were too busy making sure she knew her place in your fucking world. The Dubliners were the soundtrack of my childhood, Mum. I know every word to "Danny Boy", "Boolavogue", "Four Green *fucking* Fields", "Kevin Barry" and "The *fucking* Galway Shawl". The one chance you had to go and see them in the flesh, and you said no because poor Josephine asked you to go with her. She is a nice girl, Mum, because anyone else would have told you to get fucked years ago. You sit round her mum and dad's, and everyone knows you don't really want to be there. You act like you are doing us all a favour or something. Well, don't bother in future. If you can't get along with my *wife*, then I have no option, do I? If I have to choose between you, I'll choose my Josephine.'

Michael could see the genuine hurt on his mother's face. He was all she had, but that had been her choice – she had never wanted anyone else. And, even though he loved her with his entire being, he knew he had to put a stop to this. She'd had it her own way for far too long. Josephine had done everything physically possible to try and find some kind of common ground, find something that might bring them closer. It was clearly never going to happen. He could see that now. His mother was just too Irish, too focused on him and too proud. If she had her way, he would still be living at home with her when he was forty-five.

Michael was a man in his own right, a man to be reckoned with. He was not a kid, and he was not going to humour her. It stopped now.

Hannah just stared at her son, unable to believe that he had said such awful things to her. She knew he had meant every word. She had asked for the majority of it – even she could see that. But he was her only child. She had reared him single-handedly, and devoted her whole life to him. What else did she have?

The doorbell rang loudly, shattering the silence that lay between them. She felt the urge to scream in anguish, to give her pain an outlet, make her son understand how much he was hurting her, see his disloyalty before it was too late.

Michael was out of his chair like a bullet out of a gun, evidently relieved to get away from her. It was as though he wanted nothing more at this moment in time than to be as far away from her as physically possible.

Hannah was fuming. She knew who it was. Trust Josephine Callahan to turn up now. If she didn't know any better, she would think she had planned it.

Chapter Fifteen

Jonny Barber was nearly sixty years old. He had pretty much looked that age since his early forties. At only five feet eight inches, he wasn't tall; but with his barrel-chest, and bow legs he made quite an impression. His thick black hair had started to go grey in his late twenties, and he'd worn it as a steel-grey crew cut ever since. It was the only haircut that suited him. He was not a handsome man but his eyes were unforgettable. Like both his brothers, he had inherited his mother's big blue eyes framed with long, dark eyelashes. These were so striking that people always gave him a second look. He couldn't blame them – he knew they were wasted on him. His eyelashes were the envy of many a woman, and they also explained why he had been married three times. His eyes had the power to make a certain kind of woman forget about the rest of his face, though his reputation and large bankroll were also a great help.

These days, Jonny was a worried man. He had heard that his youngest brother Rob had been making a nuisance of himself as usual. Only this time it seemed he had been foolish enough to take his anti-social personality outside his home turf and all the way across London to the East End. He had decided to go and pick a fight with young Michael Flynn, a lad who had a good reputation and never looked for trouble, but was more than capable of looking after himself if it should find him. He was also one of Patrick Costello's workers. Patrick, as everyone knew, let his brother Declan run the main business, while he dabbled in everything and anything that was illegal and lucrative. He wasn't only talking drugs. From acquiring prestige cars for the booming Arab markets, to firearms of any kind, including sawn-off shotguns for the bank-robbing fraternity, and army-issue heavy artillery, you named it, Patrick Costello could get it. Jonny Barber had even heard a whisper that the man could procure Semtex if the price was right.

Over the years, the Costellos had made a good name for themselves; they out-classed the Barbers in every way, and that they had never once encroached on the Barbers' turf was something Jonny really appreciated. The Costellos had integrity. They still lived by the old code, and that meant that you never trespassed on anyone else's pavements. Jonny knew that if they had wanted to procure his family's turf, they were more than capable of doing it. The Costellos had the manpower and the money. He should have followed their example, but he had never bothered to look outside of his own front yard. Now it was too late.

Dicky had tried to take them on years before, and failed dismally. Declan Costello had hammered the fuck out of his brother, and there was no way he could have retaliated. Dicky had been in a pub in Woolwich, drunk as a skunk. He had eyeballed Declan in the same drinking establishment and, in a moment of utter fucking alcohol induced lunacy, had challenged him.

Jonny was well aware his brother Dicky could have a row – there was no doubt about that – but Declan Costello was another matter. Once riled he had no off button. However many times he was knocked down, he got back up, and kept coming. Not that he had ever been knocked down by a single man – it took a good few to achieve that. Declan could take on the entire British

Lions rugby team, and still be the only one standing at the end of the fight. *No one* who knew Declan would ever be stupid enough to take him on. Even Roy 'Pretty Boy' Shaw, the bare-knuckle boxer and a seriously hard man, had joked that he would fight any man alive except Declan Costello.

Jonny had heard at the time that Declan had tried everything in his power to get out of having the fight, but Dicky, being Dicky, had been like a dog with a bone. Eventually, Declan had lost his cool. The rest was history.

Now Rob had seen fit to pick a fight with Michael Flynn, a man who everyone knew was destined for greatness, who always treated the people around him with the utmost respect, but who had proved himself on more than occasion as a vicious fucker if roused.

Jonny sighed in exasperation. This was not something he had expected. He had assumed that even a fucking moron like young Rob would have had enough sense to keep away from someone like Flynn. With relatives like his, who needed fucking enemies?

He had to take action so he'd called a family meeting. As usual his two brothers were late. It was a fucking farce. He might as well be pissing in the wind. Dicky would take Rob's side, he was prepared for that. But he was going to make sure that his brothers were left in *no* doubt that, if they didn't comply with his demands, he would personally take them out himself. *He* was the head of this family and he was fighting for the whole firm – for everything that they had worked for. They were not strong enough to take on the Costellos. So they were just going to have to use their powers of persuasion to try and defuse the situation before they found themselves in the middle of an all-out war.

Chapter Sixteen

Father Riordan had always liked young Michael Flynn. He thought of him as a kind-hearted lad. Considering the fact that he had been brought up by that Hannah, a woman who had the face of an angel and the personality of a Doberman pinscher, he thought the lad had turned out very well. He was delighted to be performing the wedding ceremony for young Flynn and his lovely fiancée Josephine Callahan. He thought they made a wonderful pair.

Oh, he had heard the gossip, of course. Michael Flynn worked for the Costellos, both of whom were regular churchgoers and men who were generous to a fault. Father Riordan had only to mention the missions and they were putting their hands into their pockets. He wouldn't mind a few more like the Costellos in his parish, if he was to be brutally honest, as long as he didn't know too much about what they got up to. They were like so many of the second-generation Irishmen – they did what they needed to feed their families, and who could blame them? It was a hard world, all right; he knew that himself.

'So, Michael, are you excited about the big day?'

Michael grinned happily. 'I can't wait, Father. It can't come round quick enough for me.'

Father Riordan was thrilled at the lad's devotion; so few wanted the church ceremony these days. When he looked around the church on a Sunday he nearly fainted at the sight of the young girls, dressed like whores, with no bras, thick black eyeliner and faces liked a smacked arse because they had been dragged to the service by their parents. Parents who were as bewildered as he was by this new generation. It wasn't Ireland, that was for sure.

'Well, not long now, Michael, and Josephine will not only share your name, but she will share the rest of your life with you. The sacrament of marriage is a serious event in anyone's life. It's pledging your love and your allegiance to each other in the eyes of the Lord God Himself.'

Michael bowed his head. 'That's the plan, Father. She is everything to me.'

As they sat side by side in the church, Michael felt a peace settle over him. He loved the church and the solitude that it afforded him. He had often come here as a child to sit and think. For him there was nowhere else in the world where a body could be so utterly alone as in a Catholic church.

He was a believer, of course, in his own way. He had a deep respect for his religion, and he knew that it was something that would always be a part of his life, even if there were a lot of the teachings he couldn't help question. That was just part of growing up; all in all, he still needed the stability it afforded him.

Josephine shared his beliefs and it was something they would pass on to their children. It was important that they learn that they were a part of something so big and powerful, that would be with them for their entire lives.

'You ready to make your confession, Michael?'

'Yes, Father, of course.'

Michael knew he had to make a good Act of Contrition before his marriage. He wanted to be able to take Communion on his wedding day without any blemish on his soul whatsoever.

A Catholic marriage was a blessed sacrament. There would be no divorce; his marriage was for life and for the life thereafter. Michael knew how serious it was.

Father Riordan wished with all his heart that he had more young men like Michael Flynn in his parish. Decent young Catholics were getting rarer by the year.

'Come on, then.'

Michael followed the priest into the confessional box. He knelt down immediately, appreciating the softness of the leather beneath his knees. It was quite dark inside. He knew that the priest was now his conduit to the Lord Himself, and it was something he had never taken lightly. This was so powerful a thing that even the laws of the land had no authority in the confessional box. Whatever he told the priest could never be repeated and, as long as he was truly repentant, his sins would be forgiven and his soul would be once more without blemish.

He blessed himself quickly, wanting to get this over as soon as possible. 'Forgive me, Father, for I have sinned. It has been over two years since my last confession.'

Father Riordan blessed him, taking his time over it. He always enjoyed hearing confession. It was such a personal, private thing, the opportunity to talk to God Himself in person. You could unburden yourself of your sins and worries, and ask His forgiveness, knowing He would not refuse you. He would not stand in judgement of you or turn away from you. Father Riordan believed that this was the mainstay of the Catholic religion – the concept of the power of forgiveness and the knowledge that if you made a good confession you would be cleansed of your sins. You would be without stain, have a pure soul – for a short while anyway. You could take Holy Communion with a light heart, knowing you were in a state of grace. It was a very powerful thing to the true believer.

Michael bowed his head, and he started to speak quietly and respectfully. 'I have sinned, Father. I have used profanities, taken the Lord's name in vain. I have also had bad thoughts, terrible thoughts. I have not always honoured my mother.'

Father Riordan had expected as much. He smiled to himself. He had heard much worse than that over the years. 'Go on, my son.'

'I have also taken Josephine into my bed on more than one occasion. I know that I should not have done that. I should have waited, treated her with more respect. And I will do that now. I will wait until we are married in the eyes of the Church. I will make sure that our children are born in holy wedlock.'

Father Riordan already knew all about this. Josephine had been confessing that sin regularly for a long time, and she had not felt the urge to stop doing it. He understood that the weakness of the flesh was the scourge of youth, but he kept his own counsel. He was more astounded at Michael's honesty. The lad was being far more truthful than he had expected. He was also being so humble and painfully honest, that it was making the priest feel almost as if he was eavesdropping. It was years since he had heard such old-fashioned terminology; it was as unexpected as it was welcome. He could hear the total commitment in Michael's voice as he promised to wait until his wedding night so he could take his bride without sin.

There was a silence then. A long silence. But he could hear Michael's breathing – it was shallow and fast.

'I also have to confess to something else, Father. A mortal sin. A sin that I know will be difficult for you to understand.'

There was an edge to Michael's voice now. Father Riordan could feel a distinct change in the air around them. He knew, immediately, that whatever Michael was going to say to him, he did not want to hear. But he had no choice. He had to hear the confession, it was out of his hands. He was filled with a sense of trepidation, of the fear that always accompanied the unknown. He felt hot suddenly, sweaty. He knew he had to do his duty, to listen to Michael, and not judge him – no matter what he might say. He took a deep breath to steady himself before saying, 'You can say anything in here, Michael. Remember, you are not talking to me, you are talking to the Holy Father Himself. You can tell Him anything. I can never repeat anything I hear in the confessional. You know that. It's not for me to judge. I can only offer you an Act of Contrition.'

Michael sighed gently. Then, lifting his head up, he said softly, 'I have killed, Father.'

Chapter Seventeen

Patrick Costello was tired. He had been up since early morning, and now he was knackered. His anniversary party was about to start and he was fed up with it already. He loved his wife dearly, but she was what was known as 'high maintenance'. If anyone else gave him the grief that she did, he would have shot them in cold blood without a second's thought. Luckily, Carmel was a good girl, a great mother and, he had to admit, he loved her. But she had been on his back for the last few days about their wedding anniversary. It was like talking to the Antichrist; *everything* he said was wrong. She had decided that *he* had insisted on having an anniversary party, and he had been intelligent enough to go along with everything she said without a word. She could make him feel that he was in the wrong even when he knew, without a shadow of a doubt, that he was totally in the right. If truth be told, he actually admired her for that. She was one of the few people in his world who was not scared of him, and that was why he loved her so much. If she had feared him, he would have walked all over her. They both knew it. Declan had hated her since day one, but he had accepted that she was what his brother wanted. As Carmel also hated Declan with a vengeance, it had made no odds.

Tonight, Patrick had to entertain everyone in his world, and make sure that they enjoyed themselves. It was part and parcel of being the main man; every person he had invited into his home was not only grateful to be a part of his celebration, but the invitation conveyed the message that they were doing a good job. Patrick had always understood the need to make everyone on his payroll feel that they were appreciated. Declan might be who they dealt with on a daily basis, but Patrick made sure that everyone in the firm knew that he was aware of them and what they did. It was important to remind people that they were valued.

He poured himself a large brandy from the bar in the room he'd commandeered as his hideaway. It was the only room in the house that his wife had not been allowed to decorate. It was a man's room. The walls still had the original wood panelling and the flooring was a dark oak. He liked wood – it was honest, uncomplicated. He had two chairs – one on either side of the original Adam fireplace – both battered looking. They were as old as the hills, but the antique leather had cost a small fortune. The only other piece of furniture was a large bookcase he had picked up at an auction, which doubled as a bar, and there was a set of French doors that led out to the garden. He had no photographs or knick-knacks, nothing of a personal nature, but he liked it like that.

He settled himself into a chair, waiting for Michael and Declan to arrive; they needed to talk before the party got into full swing.

Declan arrived first; he was dressed to impress, and Patrick could not help laughing at him. He was wearing a bespoke suit, dark-blue with a pale silver pinstripe, a deep blue shirt, and handmade shoes. For the first time ever, Declan actually looked smart.

'Look at you!'

Declan grinned, but he was clearly embarrassed. 'I know! I went to see the bloke that Michael uses. He is a fucking magician I'm telling you, bruv.' His big head was bright red, even his ears were flushed. Patrick felt a rush of affection for his brother. He was pleased to see him looking so good.

'I can see that. I have never seen you look so smart! Fuck me, I never thought I would see the day!'

Declan went to the bookcase and busied himself by pouring a drink. 'I see Michael has already started on a new earn. He has a real knack for sniffing out the money shots. I only heard about it through one of my blokes. He mentioned that he had seen Michael over in Ladbroke Grove. He was drinking with that Winston Oates – he's the main man where drugs are concerned, as you know yourself. I assume he is making a point to the Barber brothers as that's their turf, so to speak.'

Patrick was startled; he had heard nothing about Michael having a new earn. He had always prided himself on knowing everything about everyone around him – even his brother Declan was not immune. He had always believed in the adage that knowledge is power. Now he was wondering if he was getting lax in his old age, if his affection for Michael was clouding his judgement. He had not even asked about the boy's movements recently; he had trusted him implicitly. Patrick had always been in possession of a healthy but suspicious nature – it was something he had always prided himself on. He trusted no one, and that was why the Costello brothers were so successful. But it seemed that Michael Flynn had achieved the impossible. For the first time ever, Patrick had not thought to have one of his main earners watched. He couldn't believe that he had been so remiss. He trusted Michael – of course he did – but large amounts of money could be a terrible temptation to even the most loyal of men. History was filled with examples of how money – second only to a seriously good shag – could turn the most level of heads.

Declan observed his brother's reaction and couldn't help

feeling a small twinge of satisfaction; it was very rare that he knew something of interest before his older brother. He had only found out about Michael's meeting by accident but, unlike Patrick, who had a pathological fear of taking anyone on face value, he really did believe that Michael Flynn was as straight as a die. He hoped that he had not caused the boy any unnecessary aggro – he knew from bitter experience that Patrick could turn on a coin if he felt that he was being mugged off in any way. He was dangerous was Patrick, especially if he felt he had been overlooked in some way. He always had to be the fucking main man. He decided to backtrack.

'Listen, Pat, I might have that all wrong, mate. I heard it from Cecil Thompson and, let's be fair, he was never the sharpest knife in the fucking drawer, was he? His wife had more cocks than a geriatric chicken, and he never had a fucking clue – it was only when his youngest came out blacker than Nookie's knockers that he suspected there might be skulduggery afoot!'

Patrick laughed and the tension eased. He knew that Declan was trying to smooth it over, sorry that he mentioned Michael. He sussed out that Declan enjoyed telling him something that he was not aware of – it was a rare enough occurrence and, for Declan, it was like winning the pools. Still, he was on his guard now.

'Michael will be here soon. Let's just see what he has to say, shall we?'

Chapter Eighteen

Josephine was wearing a cream-coloured silk dress that fitted where it touched and, even though she had no skin on show other than her arms, it showed off every curve she was in possession of to its full advantage. She looked stunning and she knew it.

She had added cream leather high heels, and a thick black belt that emphasised her tiny waist to complete the outfit. Michael liked her to look good, because he loved showing her off. He was proud of her and appreciated how she looked after herself, and he especially loved it when she dressed herself up like this. There was no cleavage on show – just as he wanted it – nothing that could be seen as provocative, yet she looked sexier than if she was wearing a micro-mini skirt with thigh-high boots.

Her hair fell down her back; it was lightly curled and lacquered. It looked natural, even though it had taken her hours to perfect it. Her eye make-up was not too heavy, but she was wearing a deep wine-coloured lipstick as her only splash of dramatic colour, which finished off her whole look perfectly.

She was pleased to see the reactions from everyone at the party as she'd walked into the room with Michael. He wanted her to be noticed and she was more than happy to oblige. She loved getting dressed up, it was something she knew she was good at.

Michael handed her a glass of champagne, and she took it from him carefully. Michael was considered an important man, and she had to make sure that she was seen as worthy of his attention. After all, they were going to be married soon, and that fact alone guaranteed her respect from the people around them. Still, a man like Michael was seen as fair game by most of the women in their world, but she had sworn to herself that she would make sure that he never had any reason to look anywhere else for attention. She herself had seen the women who had married their men, had a few kids and then let themselves go, got fat and frumpy. They stopped wearing make-up and taking care of themselves. It was easy to let your guard down with a wedding ring on your finger and believe that having a man's kids was enough to keep the man of your dreams beside you, loyal to you because you had produced their flesh and blood.

As if! It was the seventies, and the power of marriage was slowly being eroded. Divorce was no longer for the rich and famous, it was now becoming a part of everyday life. Josephine was determined that her Michael would always see her as the girl he had met and married, not as the woman he had tied himself to. She would not become a whining, overweight baby-maker who lost the knack of enjoying the life that was on offer. Those were the women she secretly despised. She believed she was too shrewd to fall for all that old fanny.

For now she intended to warn off any women who saw themselves as contenders for her position as Michael's girl. If she had to fight them off physically, if that is what it took to keep him beside her, she would, though she hoped it never came to that. Instead, she was making a name for herself as a beauty, as a fashion plate, and she wanted everyone to remember how good she looked each time they saw her. She was going to make sure that nothing interfered with them or their lives together. Still, she'd be a fool not to be a bit intimidated by just how important he was becoming, and how his status would make him even *more* attractive to certain women. Her mum had made sure she understood the ways of their world. There were pug-ugly men who, without their status as hard nuts, would be hard pushed to pull a muscle – let alone anything else. She knew that a lot of those men had walked out on their families for the lure of youth. It was pathetic, but it was a fact of the life they lived with. But it was not going to happen to her. Michael loved her and, if she used her loaf, that would never change.

She gulped her champagne down quickly, suddenly gripped by a feeling of anxiety. She swallowed hard and took a deep breath. Calm again, she lapped up the attention, which served to remind Michael of just how good she was for him, and how wonderful their life together would be.

She saw Patrick's wife Carmel beckoning her over; as usual she was surrounded by the other women at the party. Patrick's wife was never alone. Carmel's so-called 'friends' agreed with everything she said and waited for her to take the lead on all matters. It was almost embarrassing to watch at times. Carmel Costello loved being the queen bee, and she played the part to perfection. If she decided to dance, then they all danced. If she drank shots, they each followed suit. And if she decided that one of the girls had offended her in some way, they immediately became persona non grata to everyone, pushed out of her circle brutally and very publicly. Carmel Costello made her wishes very clear.

It was childish really, but Josephine knew that she had to follow suit and do what was expected as Michael's wife-to-be. She already had a level of security because of Michael's position in the firm as Patrick Costello's boy wonder. Michael was not going to fuck *that* up; he'd worked hard to get where he was and he would do whatever was needed to keep himself on the up and up.

This was the game they were both having to play. Josephine had joined a group of women whose husbands' livelihoods were dependent on the Costello brothers, and that was something none of them, Josephine included, could ever forget.

Chapter Nineteen

Colin Dawes was a man who went out of his way to avoid trouble of any kind. He wasn't a coward – he could look after himself – but he had never seen the logic of going out and actively looking for trouble. In his experience, it eventually found its way to your door anyway. Now, he was in a quandary as he stood outside Jonny Barber's office. He had known Jonny since they were little kids and, as big a bastard as Jonny could be, Colin couldn't stand aside and see him taken out without giving him a heads up of some description. It was only fair.

The problem was, Jonny wasn't a man who encouraged friendly conversation; he had no time for anyone other than his brothers so approaching him wouldn't be easy. But Jonny had seen him all right in the not-too-distant past, and that counted for a lot where Colin was concerned. He was a decent man, or at least he tried to be anyway. He knew he had to do the right thing and he owed Jonny Barber.

Colin took a deep breath and pulling himself up to his full height – just over six feet one inch – he rapped loudly on Jonny's office door, before walking in to face him. He consoled himself with the fact that he was doing what he would want someone to do for *him* if the need ever arose.

Jonny Barber had never really liked Colin Dawes. He suspected it was because Colin had the knack of being popular by his very nature. Even at school, Colin had managed to make friends with everyone around him. Admittedly, Jonny couldn't really fault him for that, but he found Colin's obvious camaraderie with all and sundry very unsettling. He just wasn't comfortable with people like Colin Dawes; he always felt wrong-footed around him.

Nevertheless, Colin Dawes had worked for the Barbers for a very long time, and Jonny recognised that he owed him a private audience for that reason alone. His loyalty had never once been questioned, he'd never given them cause for any doubt, unlike the majority of the men on the Barbers' payroll, who Jonny personally wouldn't trust to look after his mother's mangy old cat without a written statement of support from the RSPCA. His brother Dicky had played a hand in that. He had picked fights with everyone at some time or another – it wasn't even personal, it was just his nature. In all honesty, Jonny wasn't entirely without blame. Just like Dicky, he had never been blessed with a sunny nature, and he had caused his fair share of bad feeling with the people he employed. Thanks to his brother's natural antagonism towards most of the human race, he had never been in a position to relax his guard and put his trust in the people around him. Dicky could have more fights than Joe Frazier in a twenty-minute timeframe. Dicky had made a career out of alienating everyone on their payroll at one time or another. Now Jonny was worried it might come back to bite them on their arses. His younger brother was basically a fucking moron.

'All right, Colin? What can I do you for, mate?' He was trying to be friendly, jovial even. It was hard though. He was still waiting for his brothers to make an appearance.

Colin smiled, trying to look relaxed. He was still a good-looking man, even at his age. Colin had always put his looks down to his aversion to alcoholic beverages of any kind. He had never liked the taste of drink, even as a lad and, seeing the trouble that it could cause, he was very glad about that. Give him a cup of tea any day. Alcohol not only reduced people's inhibitions – it was also a fuel for bad tempers. It fanned flames that caused serious damage to everyone involved.

He was nervous, and he took a breath to steady himself. 'Look, Jonny. I don't want to cause trouble, mate. You know me – I keep out of everything, but I can't stand by and see you made a mug of.'

Jonny Barber was looking at Colin Dawes as if he had never seen him before in his life. He had not expected anything like this – certainly not such raw honesty. 'What the fuck are you prattling on about?'

Colin had no choice, he had to tell it like it was. Jonny was not going to make it easy for him, but it was too late to back out now.

'Rob and Dicky have taken a few blokes, and they are on their way over to Patrick Costello's house where, incidentally, he is having a big fucking party to celebrate his wedding anniversary. Rob and Dicky seem to think that they can easily gain entry into Patrick's home, and then they plan to take out the Costello family en masse. I assume they didn't discuss any of this with you, because you would have told them that they were on a death wish. It's fucking lunacy, Jonny. But you know young Rob – he's got a serious fucking hard on for Michael Flynn, and Dicky has always wanted to pay back Declan Costello for past misdemeanours.'

Jonny Barber was unsure if he was actually awake. This could only be some kind of nightmare brought on by narcotics or some kind of serious illness. No one in their right mind would think – even for a moment – that they could take out the Costello brothers. And certainly not in their own fucking *home*, for fuck's sake! It was so blatantly outrageous a claim, yet so like something Dicky was capable of, he knew that it could only be the truth.

He understood that Colin Dawes was only trying to help, was doing him what he felt was a favour – being loyal and decent even. But he wished Colin Dawes had kept his big fucking trap shut.

Jonny wasn't sure if he was willing to get involved. He would rather have been able to say, in complete honesty, that he had known nothing about any of this, and that it was as big a surprise to him as it was to everyone else. Thanks to this cunt, he couldn't do that now.

There was no way in hell that his brothers would be able to walk away from this. It was never going to happen. The fucking Flying Squad would be hard pushed to infiltrate Patrick Costello's house, even with a warrant and a tag team from the SAS. Patrick Costello had always made sure he was well protected from any outside aggravation. He was a man who was always two steps ahead and who, therefore, had put in place security that might be needed should any threat arise.

Jonny felt faint suddenly. His head seemed to be filling up with hot air, he couldn't breathe properly. He felt himself choking; his mouth was so dry, he had no spit left. He had only the sticky dryness that came from extreme fear. His chest felt tight, as if a steel band was squeezing all his breath out of him. His heart was beating so loudly in his ears it was drowning out everything else. He knew that he was on the verge of collapsing. For the first time in his whole life he was experiencing acute terror on a grand scale, and it was coupled with the knowledge that there was nothing he could do about any of it.

He was clutching his chest, but he was dismayed because he wasn't having the heart attack he so dearly craved. He was aware that he was already thinking clearly again, and that his natural instinct for self-preservation was kicking in. Even as he realised that, he felt guilty because he knew that he should be at least *trying* to do something to help his brothers out. But they had already made their beds. They had not seen fit to tell him what they had planned, so he could do nothing for them now. They had undertaken this madness alone – and they would have to take the consequences alone.

He had been left out of the loop because they had both known he would have forbidden it. So fuck them for the treacherous bastards they were! He could only look out for himself now, guard his own interests, and try to salvage what he could from what was, in reality, a situation that was fucking unprecedented in the world they inhabited. He would have to make damn sure that the Costellos and that ponce Flynn were given every assurance that he personally had no knowledge whatsoever of his brothers' suicidal mission. It was about self-preservation. His brothers were as good as dead already; he had no option but to try and save his own arse if it was in any way possible. But he didn't really hold out much hope.

'How about a drink, Colin? And then you can tell me everything you know, eh?'

Colin Dawes was thrilled by the invitation, unaware that he was actually being kept there as Jonny Barber's alibi for the evening and that he was putting his own life in danger if it all went pear-shaped.

Chapter Twenty

Patrick Costello's wife Carmel was a woman on a constant mission in life.

She was confident she had her husband's affection – his love even – but it was something she had to work for all the same. And she did just that. He treated her like a goddess, and always made sure she was given her due as the mother of his children. No matter what might happen in the future, even if he ever did get a capture by the Filth for some reason, he had provided for his family. Not that anything like that was really on the cards. Her Patrick was far too big nowadays. But, if it *did* come to pass, she knew she would still be able to live the lifestyle she had become accustomed to. She had access to his offshore accounts – he had given that information to her to ensure that she felt safe – and she never worried about the future.

Patrick was older than her; he had married later in life and taken those vows seriously. Even so, Carmel was a realist. Patrick saw himself as a good husband, as well as a good Catholic, but he was also a man. And not just any man, but a Face in a world of permanent strange, where good-looking and very willing young women were plentiful. There were far too many girls in the Life just like she had been, with the same goal in mind, and the same determination to get what and who they wanted, whatever the cost. She knew men with second, third and even fourth wives. That would never happen to *her* – *she* would keep her status come hell or high water.

These young girls – who seemed to multiply every year – had the edge, because they were younger than her, fresher, without the scars of childbirth and without the curse of familiarity. She made herself known to each and every one of them so they would be in *no* doubt of what they would be up against should they decide to try and challenge her position. However much Patrick adored her, she would not let her guard down for one second. She was determined to be the *only* Mrs Costello, and she was not going to give that status up without a fight. His only way out of this marriage was death – and not hers either. She made sure that she was surrounded by her own clique of girls and women that she felt were not a threat to her or her lifestyle. She knew every female in her husband's orbit, and she made sure that she was a permanent fixture in every part of his social life. Patrick might think she was being paranoid – he was a great guy, a good father, and a loyal husband. But he didn't comprehend the lengths that certain women were prepared to go to in order to get what they wanted.

Carmel was not going to give any fucker the chance to try and muscle in on what was rightfully hers. She had always worked – and she continued to do so every day – to keep her home and, more importantly, her place in the Life. It was a good life in so many ways, but it was also very difficult because she could never let herself relax, could never take her eye off the ball. She was constantly on alert, and it was exhausting. But she had to protect herself and her children from being ousted by a younger model.

Now they were having an anniversary party and, even though Patrick had made sure it was a great night and was treating her like royalty, she still couldn't bring herself to truly relax and enjoy it. She had made him organise it. She might tell everyone that it was all his idea, but it was all hers really. Occasions like tonight made a point to everyone. The Costellos were together, they were happy and nothing could come between them. It was a moment of triumph.

If only she could enjoy it and her husband's company. But she couldn't relax any more.

She caught sight of Michael Flynn's fiancée, Josephine Callahan. The girl was absolutely stunning, there was no doubting that. She was also a really nice person, and Carmel hated that she was so jealous of her, but she couldn't help it. Josephine was not only gorgeous, she was *young* – as young and as innocent as the day was long. It was an irresistible combination to most men.

Michael Flynn, though, was all over her like the proverbial rash, and Josephine had eyes for no one but her Michael. They were a lovely young couple, and she had no reason for the jealousy she was feeling towards them. Nevertheless, Josephine Callahan was another one to be watched like a hawk, and watch her she would. Keep your friends close, and your enemies closer – what a true statement that was. Patrick had asked her privately to take the younger girl under her wing, to look after her and ease her into the fold so to speak; after all, Carmel knew the score from personal experience. Even though her husband had shown no interest in the girl other than the fact she was Michael's intended, Carmel still felt the ugly pain of jealousy, coupled with a feeling of fear. That fear was *always* going to be there. She might act like she had everything under control, that she was in charge of everything around her – from her family, to her home and the people she brought into her personal orbit – but it was all a sham. Deep inside, she had never really known a truly happy day since she had married Patrick Costello. Once she had landed him, she had spent every minute since trying to keep him. And it was not easy.

Carmel had too much pride to let anyone, especially Patrick Costello, kick her to the kerb. She had invested too much of her time and effort to end up a has-been. From the moment he put a ring on her finger, she had made it her mission in life to keep him by her side.

Chapter Twenty-One

Michael was in a good mood. His Josephine looked the dog's gonads at the party tonight, and he was excited about his forthcoming nuptials. He really was a man in love.

He'd been feeling very wholesome since his confession. He didn't like being with Josephine knowing he had committed murder. It felt a bit off, even though he had chosen to do it and had known it was expected of him. There was a part of him that was secretly unnerved that his initial qualms about taking someone's life now seemed completely out of proportion. He wasn't exactly *pleased* by what he had done, but there was no getting away from the fact that it had been much easier than he had thought it would be to actually do it. He could argue that he'd been put into an impossible position. When Patrick made the request, he'd had no choice but to agree.

Father Riordan had taken his sins and wiped them away. It had been so easy, and he felt much better in himself now he had atoned for it. He felt lighter, as if the weight of the world had been taken off his shoulders. He would never again underestimate the power of his religion.

As he went into Patrick's office he was smiling; he felt fantastic. 'Hello, boys, you will not believe what I have got to tell you.'

Patrick grinned before saying sarcastically, 'Well, let me guess.

Is it to do with you, a dealer in Notting Hill, and the possibility of a cannabis-based business?'

Michael just laughed loudly. 'Fucking hell, Pat! There was me thinking that I had manoeuvred us a right good earn, but I should have known better! You cannot be surprised, you're always a fucking step ahead. You're like Secret Squirrel. Un-fucking-believable!'

Declan was interested in how his brother would react to Michael's news. He almost wished he'd kept his trap shut earlier. He trusted the boy implicitly – he should have known nothing was certain with his brother. But Michael was his blue-eyed boy, for fuck's sake! Declan wasn't bothered by the favouritism. He was more than happy with his earns. Patrick's interest had never been in the bread and butter side of the business, he had always craved the more exotic earns. Declan was quite happy that Patrick left him to get on with it. His brother was a difficult man to work alongside, with a terrible need to control everyone, everything, and every deal that he saw as being within his personal remit. He was basically a massive pain in the arse. Declan loved him dearly, but he was aware that he had never been quick enough mentally for Patrick. He had always known his brother was the brains of the family, but he didn't feel inferior to his brother in any way. He was proud of him, and he was more than happy with his place in the Costello businesses.

Declan saw in Michael Flynn the same quick brain, and the same resolve that was so much a part of Patrick's make up. It was why his brother had taken to the lad, and why he himself understood the boy's importance to the firm.

Declan watched his brother as he flexed his muscles and made his point.

'You know me, Michael. I always like to know the score. I make sure that I am never in a position of weakness. It's nothing personal, Michael, I just feel that it's in my interest to know everything about everyone.'

Michael was not fazed. He would have done the same himself. 'I'm impressed, Pat. But I think you'll see the logic of it.'

Patrick sipped at his drink noisily before saying, 'He's Jonny Barber's boy, Michael.'

Michael shrugged nonchalantly. Declan was impressed with the boy's complete disregard of his brother. He had such confidence in himself, it was a pleasure to listen to him. He would not be another of his brother's yes men. But Michael Flynn was not arrogant – he genuinely wanted to bring in an earn.

'We want the Barbers out of the way, so what's the fucking difference? They're all cunts. Why do you think I cultivated Oates when I got the chance? He's an all right geezer, and the Barbers have treated him in a diabolical fashion. None of the people they have around them are even remotely happy with the circumstances of their employment. They shit on their own doorstep, rip off their own – they don't seem to understand that times have changed. I have done no more than open up a dialogue with Oates and he was thrilled, believe me. It's the next step, Pat.'

Patrick was listening to the boy intently. Michael had no side, he was as honest as he was loyal. He had proved that already.

'You're right, mate. But I wouldn't be the boss if I didn't flex my muscles now and then. It never hurts to show that you're aware of what's going on. It's the reason we are so fucking successful, son. Remember that.'

Michael knew he had been both praised and subtly warned. He wasn't too bothered about either. He had no reason to worry – he had done nothing more than set up a good deal. He knew how to play the game. People like Patrick Costello needed to be reassured, needed to know that the people he put his trust in appreciated him. Michael was more than willing to give him what he saw as his due. It was a small price to pay for what he was getting in return, and he did respect him.

'I won't ever forget that, Patrick, don't you worry. I want you to know that I am grateful for every opportunity and every penny that I have earned from being a part of the Costello family. I just wanted to bring something to the table. It's a big earn, Oates likes me and, to be honest, I really like him. He's a decent bloke. But I'm not a fool – I guessed you would already be two jumps ahead.'

It was exactly what Patrick wanted to hear. He relied on the network of people he had accrued over the years, people who were willing to give him the full monty about anyone and everyone around him. Even Declan wasn't immune to his interest – that was something Patrick was not proud of, but he couldn't help himself.

'You're a good kid, Michael. I know that.'

The office door crashed open, and they were all surprised to see Douglas Marshall burst into the room. Dougie was no more than a soldier, one of Declan's crew of heavies, and his interruption was not appreciated at all.

'What the fuck are you doing, Dougie?'

The words were spoken by Declan and the inference was that he had obviously lost his mind.

'I'm sorry about this, Declan, but the fucking Barbers have turned up looking for a fucking row.'

Chapter Twenty-Two

Dicky Barber was drunk enough to be reckless, but not so drunk he couldn't hear the warning bell that was clanging loudly in the back of his mind.

As he looked at the men policing the gates of Patrick Costello's home, he could see that they would happily die before giving the Barbers and their entourage entrance. They were just standing there, completely unconcerned at the turn of events, armed, of course, and adamant that the Barbers were not on the guest list.

Dicky knew they had made a colossal fuck-up. Neither of them had thought it through. Dicky wished he wasn't so drunk. The reality of the situation was dawning on him, and he knew he and his brother looked every inch the complete cunts they were.

Rob, however, was experiencing no such qualms. He was still determined to make his mark, make a public statement to the world. But, as a man who had never once had the nous to plan ahead, to try and cover any eventualities that might occur if things were to go wrong, he was not taking onboard that the men who had accompanied them were now backing away, realising they were outnumbered and outclassed. He was being treated as a minor irritation, and not as a serious problem.

Rob was quite affronted that they had not been granted immediate access to the Costello home. He had believed they would be ushered in like visiting royalty. But they were still outside the gates, and that was not going to change.

Rob was shouting now. 'Just tell him we are here, will you? It's a fucking party, ain't it? We are fucking guests.'

A heavyset man in his late fifties stood in front of the gates. He sighed. It was like dealing with football hooligans – all drink and bravado and not a brain cell between the lot of them.

'As I said before, you are *not* on the guest list. I would strongly advise you to put the weapons away and get yourselves home.'

The security was much heavier than they had anticipated. Dicky had counted at least seven men on the gates alone, and that was without the security for the cars that lined the country lane leading up to the property. These men were not about to be intimidated by anyone, and they were more than willing to do what they were paid to do.

Still, it was a shock to see just how Patrick Costello actually lived. Even from outside the electric gates, the house looked like something from a film set. It was lit up like Battersea Power Station for a start, and the drive – if they ever got past the gates, of course – appeared to be a good seven hundred yards long. The night air was filled with the sound of music, conversations and laughter. Everyone in that house was completely unaware that anything was amiss.

Dicky had already clocked the brick wall that surrounded the property, knew that it was as secure as Parkhurst. No one was getting in there without a fucking Sherman tank.

The only thing they had achieved tonight was signing their own death warrants, after showing the world just how amateur the Barbers actually were. It was a joke – a bad one at that.

Costello's drum was full of just about every Face in the Smoke and the surrounding areas. But not the Barber brothers. That said it all really. If they had any kind of status they would have been in there now, enjoying the hospitality like everyone else.

Dicky felt the cold fingers of fear envelop him as he looked around and saw the men they had brought with them reassessing their chances of getting away from here alive. It had already gone too far. *They* had gone too far the minute they had arrived on Patrick Costello's doorstep. It was the man's anniversary, a party to celebrate his family life. His kids were somewhere in there, for fuck's sake.

Dicky knew that even if they backed away now, they were still dead men. This was a real piss-take, an insult of Olympian standards. It was a drunken fucking faux pas that was so outrageous it could never be overlooked.

Jonny had been right: the Costellos *had* given them respect, and allowed them to work their own turf, even though they could have taken it from them easily. He could see that now. Fucking stone-cold sobriety and hindsight could often be a truly terrible thing. Drink was a fucking curse – it caused more trouble than it was worth. It gave people false courage and, even worse, it had the added bonus of fuelling the smallest of fires until it was suddenly a raging inferno of hatred and anger.

Rob already had his shotgun out; it was a small-gauge sawn-off, not really a weapon for something like this. Dicky Barber cringed with embarrassment. This really was fucking amateur night, and Dicky hated that he had, once more, let his hate rule his head.

But Rob needed to prove himself, needed to show that he was not about to cry off and walk away. He was going to make his mark.

'You don't fucking scare me, you cunts.'

Dicky saw his brother raise his firearm and knew he was going to use it. He watched helplessly as his brother was taken out within seconds by a crossbow.

It was as quiet as it was lethal. It was all over.

Chapter Twenty-Three

The party was in full swing and Josephine was watching Carmel Costello closely. She could see the woman was getting more and more irritated by the second, and she couldn't blame her. Patrick Costello had hardly shown his face all night and, as it was his party, that was not only rude, it was also worrying her personally, because Michael had not been near or beside *her* either.

The music was good, the food was fantastic, and the drink was flowing like water. All around her people were having a great time but, like Carmel, she couldn't help wondering where the fuck the men were.

She saw Carmel slip out of the large living room, and she followed her up the staircase and across the landing into the master bedroom. She could see how upset Carmel really was, and she couldn't blame her. It had to be a work situation of some description, but surely, on a night such as this, work could take a back seat?

She tapped gently on the bedroom door and then, without waiting for an answer, she slipped inside, closing the door quietly behind her. Carmel was sitting on a king-size bed and, for the first time ever, Josephine saw her with her guard down. She was wiping her eyes with a tissue, and she looked very fragile, very vulnerable. Josephine had never realised how thin Carmel actually was. Looking at her now, she seemed to have disappeared into her clothes. It was awful. She seemed older, defeated somehow. Her lovely face, always so perfectly made-up, and always with her trademark smile, looked haunted. It was a real eye-opener for Josephine.

Josephine went to her without even thinking about it and, putting her arm around the woman's shoulders, she hugged her gently, aware that Carmel needed comforting, needed someone to share her burden.

'Are you OK, Carmel?'

Carmel Costello looked around her sadly. The room was beautiful, it was something most women could only dream of. She had walked into this room once and felt that she had finally got it all, had finally made it. Yet it meant nothing to her now, at this moment in her life. It was as if the house, the cars, the lifestyle she craved were nothing more than an illusion because, until tonight, she had never felt such acute loneliness. Patrick had disappeared and left her alone at his own party, and that had hurt her more than she had thought possible.

Oh, everyone was enjoying themselves and they would assume that Patrick, being Patrick, had important business to attend to; it wasn't in any way a slur on her. But it had hurt. Being left alone for so long and putting on a brave face was difficult when all she really wanted to do was stab him through the heart. She had not realised how much she had wanted him to be beside her, how much that would have meant to her.

It was nice being comforted by young Josephine. She believed the girl meant well and wouldn't broadcast every word spoken by her to the nation. She could trust her, she felt that and, for the first time in years, she let herself say what she really meant – she needed to get it off her chest.

'I'll be all right in a minute, Josephine. It's just sometimes I could kill Patrick. He's left me out there on my own for hours.

It's our night – he could at least remember that. I feel such a fucking fool.'

Josephine sighed. 'Tell me about it, Carmel. Michael's on the missing list as well, and Declan too. It has to be work. Something that needs sorting sooner rather than later. You're right to be upset, but I bet you it's something *very* important. Patrick worships you, anyone can see that.'

Carmel could see the girl was trying to make her feel better, and she appreciated that. It was kind of her to try and lift her spirits. But Carmel was feeling truly grieved. Josephine was too young and too innocent to understand the life she was getting into. She would soon learn the reality. It was easy to be so cavalier when it wasn't *her* husband who had left his own party.

'Listen to me, Josephine. Michael is just like my old man – he will always put his work first. Unlike most men, the work they are involved in can't be left till the morning. The world they live in means they are on their guard every second of every day. Literally anything can happen and, when it does, they have no choice but to make sure any problems are sorted, pronto. It means you had better get used to being alone most of the time, get used to worrying that the Filth will somehow take him from you, get used to looking over your shoulder constantly because you never know what the future might hold. You have to learn to look out for number one so that, if the worst does happen, you have made sure you have covered your own arse. It's a world of illusion, a world of pretending and putting on a front. It's a world that I really wish I had never entered. It's a world I craved, and one that I now feel trapped in.'

Josephine was shocked at Carmel's words – at the vehemence and also the truth of them.

Seeing Josephine's face, Carmel felt awful, sorry now that she had ever spoken. 'I'm sorry, Josephine love, take no notice of me. I'm just angry, that's all. I have a houseful of people, and Patrick has bloody well left me to it, and on our anniversary, if you please.'

Josephine just hugged the woman tightly once more, aware that Carmel regretted letting her guard down, showing her weakness, admitting her unhappiness.

'Listen, Carmel, I know I come across as a bit wet at times, and I know you have just told me the truth. But I love Michael and, no matter what happens, like you with Patrick, I will always stand by him. So don't worry about me. I'm stronger than I look!'

Up close, Josephine could see the fine lines around Carmel's eyes, and she could sense the woman's sadness. For the first time ever, she had seen the real Carmel Costello, and it had been a real eye-opener. She felt desperately sorry for her, more so because she knew how much Carmel Costello valued her reputation as a woman always in control.

'Come on, Carmel, let's get back to the party, shall we? If I was you I would go in that office and give him a piece of my mind!'

It was the right thing to say and Carmel laughed. 'You're right, Josephine. Come on, let's get back downstairs.'

But her words stayed with Josephine; she knew that she would never forget them.

Chapter Twenty-Four

'What a fucking abortion that was! The Barbers have to be on something to actually think they could come here.'

Michael was as shocked as the Costello brothers at the turn of events. It was unbelievable. He turned to Patrick, saying angrily, 'Dicky's still breathing by all accounts, but Rob's on his last legs. Still, he is one strong fucker, I'll give him that. I've said to go and pick up Jonny. Then, when the party's over, we can finish this once and for all.'

Patrick nodded. He was absolutely outraged at the whole turn of events.

Declan was watching him carefully, and he could see the signs that denoted Patrick's true nature. His brother rarely allowed himself the luxury of giving his natural inclinations free rein, but he would now no doubt. Patrick would make sure that the Barbers paid for their sins a hundredfold, and who could blame him? It was a monumental piss-take but, worse than that, it was utterly fucking disrespectful. If the Barbers had planned it properly, and given them a run for their money, at least they would have had *some* respect. But to show up like that, without a fucking thought, was no more than a diabolical liberty. It had kept Patrick from attending his own party. It had caused him untold aggravation. A wedding, an anniversary, a birthday, a christening, or a fucking funeral – these were sacrosanct. They were private family functions and they were, because of their very nature, taboo. Anywhere wives, children or close family were all together was off-limits. This kind of action was something that only a fucking lunatic would even consider, especially when it involved a family like the Costellos.

Michael changed tack, trying to play it down when he could see that Patrick was becoming unhinged. *That* wasn't something that would benefit any of them.

'I've kept it quiet so far, Pat. No one here knows anything has occurred, but it will probably get out at some point. The Barbers' entourage are long gone – the fucking tossers were willing to serve up Jonny to get a pass. I've got people disposing of them as we speak. So, as fucking outraged as we are, everything is under control. It's sorted.'

Declan laughed suddenly, he had always had a strange sense of humour. 'Look on the bright side, Pat – saved us petrol money, eh? We've got them now. Jonny won't give us any trouble. From what I can gather he had nothing to do with the night's entertainment, but he'll know it's over for them.'

Patrick looked around him. He was still reeling from the shock of how close the Barbers had got to them. To his home. His family.

Michael had done well. He had organised the security with Declan, and he had not underestimated the need for men who were not only fearless, but who were also sensible enough to know that any trouble needed to be dealt with as quietly as possible. The use of a crossbow was genius.

'Imagine turning up somewhere like this with a fucking sawn-off! It just tells you how fucking ignorant and cheap they really are. Imbeciles. Fucking morons.'

The door opened then, and Carmel Costello stood there like the avenging angel. 'Patrick Costello, it's our wedding anniversary, remember? And you have spent most of the night in here! Are you thinking of joining your wife and guests at any point?' Carmel was fuming, that was evident.

Patrick immediately looked contrite. He knew she had a point, and she would be bringing this up till her dying day. His voice was soft as honey as he placated her. 'Look, Carmel darling, there's been a bit of aggro with your present, and I've been in here on the blower trying to sort it out. I'm so sorry, love.'

It was exactly what she wanted to hear, and she forced a smile on to her face. Patrick had apologised, and he was finally joining the party, so at least she might salvage something from the evening.

Chapter Twenty-Five

Jonny Barber was resigned to his fate. It was all over bar the shouting – the only thing he could do now was try and take whatever came his way with aplomb.

He was sitting in a damp, dark cellar somewhere, waiting for the Costellos to arrive and finish what his idiot brothers had started. Knowing Patrick Costello, he would want to finish this job off personally – and who could blame him? Jonny would have done the same thing himself.

He was cold – not that that mattered much in the grand scheme of things. He could hear his brother, Dicky, muttering away under his breath, and he guessed that he had come to the same conclusion as he had. They were living on borrowed time. Dicky had taken a beating; he had put up a good fight, but come off worst.

Jonny sighed heavily. He was still reeling from the turn of events. Rob, his baby brother and the bane of his life, should already be dead, but not him! The moron was fighting for every breath, lying on the filthy floor. The crossbow had hit him square in the chest, but it had obviously missed his heart. Jonny was surprised at the lack of blood, though he knew that a weapon such as a knife, or a crossbow dart in this case, stopped the bleeding if it was left in situ. If a knife was pulled out of a stab wound it brought tissue, muscle, guts, all sorts with it, and caused serious bleeding. If the knife was left in the wound, then it was unable to do any real damage – it stopped the bleeding for a start. Ironically, the dart was the reason his brother was still alive.

He could hear the conversation that was going on behind the door. The noise was comforting in some ways – there was a radio on somewhere; he could hear the music in the background. It almost sounded normal.

He sighed. He had tried to talk to Dicky, but he was already away with the fairies. Terror at the realisation of what he had brought on them all had robbed him of his reason. Lucky Dicky.

At least he was assured that his family would be all right. Patrick Costello was a lot of things but he was first and foremost a gentleman. Jonny thought back on the road that had brought him to this. He had been a man who had embraced violence; he had lived by it and, like his brothers, he had enjoyed it. The Barbers had been big fish in a very small pond – now that pond would be owned by the Costello brothers. Jonny had no doubt that all the people who had been forced to pay homage to *him* would be overjoyed at his sudden demise; there were very few who would have been willing to stand by his side. Oh, hindsight was a wonderful thing.

His old dad's favourite saying had been 'those who live by the sword, die by the sword'. He should know – the wife-beating ponce. He had finally beaten his wife once too often, and had then been taken out by his own sons. What goes around comes around, that was another of his old man's sayings.

Jonny Barber was astounded by how calm he was about his own situation, and how easily he seemed to have accepted his fate.

But when Patrick Costello was making him watch as Michael

Flynn tortured his brothers to death, and he could hear their screams of agony ringing in his ears, he finally snapped out of his stupor. There would be no mercy; they were sending out a message that would be heard and remembered by everyone in their orbit for many years to come.

Chapter Twenty-Six

'For fuck's sake, Mum, give me a break, will you? All you ever seem to do lately is moan. I can't be doing with it. Fuck the priest! Why would I give a flying fuck about what he thinks of me?'

Hannah Flynn watched her son warily. She had heard the gossip about him, and about his growing reputation as Patrick Costello's right-hand man. Part of him had been gone from her a long time ago – Josephine had seen to that. But now the Costellos had him too and, between the lot of them, there was nothing left for her.

She rolled her eyes towards the ceiling, trying her hardest to keep her temper under control.

'I'm just saying Father Riordan is a good man who's always liked you, Michael. So I know that somehow you must have offended him for him to be avoiding you. He hasn't said anything outright, but there's clearly something radically wrong between you two. You must have said or done something to upset him and I'm telling you now, Michael, I don't care how hard you think you are, you will always be my baby, my *only* son – that will never change – but I want to know what you've done.'

Michael was just as annoyed. Father Riordan had no right to react in any way about something said to him in the confessional

– that was supposed to be between him and God. The priest was irrelevant, he had nothing to do with any of it.

His mother, on the other hand, needed to be placated, and sooner rather than later. She set great store by the Catholic Church, and she saw the clergy as above everyone else because of their great faith. He actually agreed with her about that; it *was* something to be in awe of. To devote your life to Christ, and the good of others, was something he would never, ever understand, but that didn't stop him from having complete and utter admiration for the people who were willing to do it.

'Father Riordan caught me on a bad day, Mum. I might have fucked him off. I'll sort it out, OK?'

'Well, you'd better. I thought I had brought you up better than that. He's going to conduct your marriage ceremony, a holy sacrament which will bind you to that girl for the rest of your life. There's no such thing as divorce for us, remember.'

Michael nodded his agreement. 'I have no intention of *ever* getting divorced from my Josephine, Mum, so you can rest easy about that much anyway. And I will see the priest and apologise to him, so wind your neck back in, will you? He shouldn't be so fucking touchy anyway. I put more than enough poke into his bin, as you know yourself.'

That was true. Her son gave a lot of money towards the Church's charitable causes. He was more than generous and, until now, Father Riordan had been very vocal in his praise of her son's contributions to the parish.

Hannah was almost placated, but she couldn't shake the feeling of worry. The marriage was going ahead, and she had no option but to accept it. It was out of her hands, and her son had made his opinion very clear about that. He was besotted with the girl, and Josephine Callahan – soon to be Flynn – was as besotted as he was. Hannah should be pleased that her boy was settling down. If only her future daughter-in-law didn't irritate the life out of her.

The doorbell rang and she watched as her son nearly broke his neck to answer it. She could hear Josephine's voice in the hallway – it was like nails on a blackboard to her – but she plastered a smile on her face, and prepared to greet her son's intended with as much warmth as she could muster.

Chapter Twenty-Seven

Lana Callahan had heard the talk about the Barbers' untimely end; she knew enough about the Life to understand that, for the Costellos, the talk about the men's violent deaths could only enhance their reputation.

It was common knowledge that the Barbers had brought it on themselves; everyone knew that their bodies were never going to be found – not in this lifetime anyway, if ever. They were long gone, but the story of their demise continued to be whispered about. The police might have their suspicions, but there was nothing concrete for them to pursue – not that they would feel comfortable accusing the Costellos of anything anyway. Considering the Costellos paid the London Filth very generously to be left in peace, it wasn't in anyone's interest to rock the boat. Even the Serious Crime Squad had expressed little or no interest in the Barbers' sudden disappearance. Ultimately, *they* had wanted them off the streets and they weren't in the least bit bothered how that had come about.

But Lana was now finding herself becoming increasingly worried about her daughter's beau – and wondering exactly what he was capable of. She liked Michael Flynn a lot and she knew that he loved her daughter, but she couldn't help wondering how much her daughter really knew about the man she was marrying.

She herself hadn't fully comprehended, until this had

happened, that he had another side to him. He hid it well, but it was there nonetheless. He had a kink in his nature, she knew that now for a fact. He had the capacity to completely disengage with anything that he felt was necessary to his own wellbeing, his peace of mind.

Her husband had told her, on the QT, the true story about the Barber brothers' final hours but, unlike Des, who seemed to think that Michael's part in the brutal murders was something to be applauded, she couldn't help worrying about what kind of a man her daughter was tying herself to.

Since Des had regaled her with their soon-to-be son-in-law's violent exploits, she had found herself watching him carefully. She'd observed him smiling and laughing as if nothing had happened – as though he had not a care in the world. He was still carrying on as normal and, in her heart of hearts, she felt that was wrong – very wrong. She understood that violence was a part of his life – it was a part of life for anyone in the criminal world. For people like the Costellos, violence gave them the edge, made their names and guaranteed them their place in society. She'd found it easy to accept until it had suddenly appeared on her doorstep.

She had been so pleased that Josephine had found a man like Michael, who could look after her, provide for her and give her a good life. Now she wasn't so sure. If only she didn't know so much about him; but Des had been proud to tell her how her daughter's husband-to-be had proved himself to Patrick Costello as a man capable of anything. He had seen it as an achievement to celebrate, something to be admired. He thought Michael Flynn was a high flyer, and he was over the moon that he was going to take their only child to the top with him.

It felt wrong to her now; violence should not be treated so matter-of-factly. Michael actually frightened Lana. He was marrying her daughter, and Josephine might think she understood what she was getting herself into, but she didn't. Josephine was a kind, trusting, loving young woman; Lana was convinced that if she ever knew the real truth about Michael it would destroy her. She was madly in love with him, and Lana knew that, even if she told her what she knew about Michael, Josephine wouldn't believe any of it.

She wished Des had kept his big mouth shut; he might think Michael was the dog's bollocks but now, thanks to him, *she* thought Michael was a dangerous fuck.

Chapter Twenty-Eight

Father Riordan could feel the sweat dripping from every pore in his body as Michael Flynn watched him closely. He knew that he had no right at all to stand in judgement over another human being, but the knowledge of the young man's crimes was something he couldn't forget about. It was on his mind every waking hour. He had listened to adulterers and wife beaters, he had made himself listen to people's deepest, darkest secrets, and he had always been able to tell himself that they had not told *him* – they had been confiding in the Lord God Himself. But not this time. This was something he couldn't find it in his heart to overlook. This was murder. It could never be rectified.

Now here was Michael, with young Josephine Callahan, listening to him eagerly as he talked about the importance of the marriage vows, about it being a blessed sacrament, and how they were expected to always remember that they had been joined together in Holy Matrimony by God Himself, when all the time *he* knew that Michael Flynn was a killer. Even worse, thanks to him, Michael had no guilty conscience about his act. It was over with, he had been forgiven. And Father Riordan had been the one to hear his confession. It was torturing him.

'Are you all right, Father? You look a bit peaky.'

Josephine seemed genuinely concerned about him and, as the priest looked into her lovely face, he saw the kindness there. This was a girl who was going to marry a man he knew was a murderer. He forced himself to smile at her and act normally.

'I'm not feeling too good to be honest, Josephine. I think I'm coming down with the flu.'

Josephine was instantly contrite, sorry that they had bothered him when he was obviously feeling unwell. 'Oh, listen, Father, we can do this another time. You get yourself off to bed. You know that we are both more than ready to be married. It's not long now, is it? I can't wait.'

Father Riordan was still smiling. 'You're right, Josephine, I shouldn't be here at all tonight. The last thing you two need is the flu! I'll see you both soon, OK?'

Michael stood up slowly and, grinning happily at Josephine, he said jovially, 'You go on, darling. I want to talk to Father Riordan in private for a minute.'

Josephine nodded, then she kissed the priest gently on his cheek. As she left the pew, she blessed herself before the altar, and the two men watched as she walked sedately out of the church.

Michael Flynn looked at the priest for long moments; he could almost feel the man's fear emanating from him. He was annoyed that Father Riordan, his confessor, his parish priest, was acting so oddly.

'What exactly is your problem, Father?'

The man didn't answer him – he couldn't even meet his eyes. This was an outrage as far as Michael was concerned. He had confessed his sins, as required by his Church, especially before his wedding day. Who the hell did Father Riordan think he fucking was? The cheek of him.

'You can't stand in judgement of me, Father, and we both know that. You're acting strangely, and I really don't like it. I confessed to you so I could get married free and clear. That's the *Church's* teaching, not mine. I've repented for all my wrongdoings and, as far as I'm concerned we are square, mate. But if you don't sort yourself out, we are going to have a serious problem.'

It was a threat, and Father Riordan knew it. He had never thought for one second that his chosen life in the priesthood would eventually make him question not only his faith, but everything that he had ever believed in. This handsome young man, who came to Mass every Sunday, gave generously to the parish, who looked like any decent God-fearing individual, was about to marry a lovely young girl, and live happily ever after, was a devil in disguise. He had made a choice. He had known that he had committed a mortal sin, and he had only confessed so he could put it behind him and get married with a clear conscience. Father Riordan was well aware that Michael Flynn felt no real sorrow for what he had done – he was playing at being repentant. But true repentance was the whole point of the confessional – without being truly sorry for your sins, it was meaningless.

'Are you listening to me, Father?'

The priest looked into Michael's eyes; whatever he did now would lay the foundations for the future. He prayed silently for the strength that he needed.

'I'm listening to you, Michael. But I don't feel that I can see you again. I know that I am failing you as a priest, but I have to follow my own heart, my own conscience.'

Michael was very quiet. He could see that Father Riordan was serious. Michael knew that he wasn't being awkward or deliberately obtuse. This was a real dilemma – for both of them.

'I trusted you, Father. Now I feel that was a big mistake on my part.'

The priest shook his head vigorously. 'No, Michael, you

didn't make a mistake. Anything you might have told me in the confessional is sacrosanct. I can *never* repeat it to a living soul, and I wouldn't, I can assure you of that. But I can't act like it never happened, Michael. I have to go away from here.'

Michael sighed; he liked Father Riordan, he was a decent enough man. 'Look, Father, I'm sorry if my actions have caused you problems but, as far as I knew, I wasn't talking to you, was I? Anything that I *might* have said, was between me and my God. I think that you are overreacting. I mean, for fuck's sake, this is exactly what you lot sign on for, isn't it?'

The priest stood up. He could never hope to make this man understand how confused he was feeling, or why he felt the need to leave not only his parish, but his home and his whole life. Michael would never understand that just because *he* could live with his own actions, it didn't mean that everyone else could. It was a waste of time.

'Michael, look after young Josephine – she loves the bones of you. I'll talk to Father Barry. He'll be more than happy to officiate at your wedding. You've both known him since you were little children anyway.'

Michael nodded sadly. He held out his hand and Father Riordan shook it heartily. He didn't know what else to do.

Book Two

Pride only breeds quarrels, but wisdom is found in all those who take advice

Proverbs 13:10

Chapter Twenty-Nine

1989

'For fuck's sake, Josephine, anyone would think we were fucking hard up, darling!'

Michael was laughing, but Josephine knew that he was actually annoyed. He spent money like it was going out of fashion on all manner of frivolities, and she didn't mind that; after all, he was the one earning it. But she couldn't understand why he got so annoyed with her because she liked to budget, liked a bargain. She could see him eyeing the mound of toilet rolls that she had piled up in the utility room, shaking his head in mock despair. All of the spare rooms were filled with her bargains and bulk-buys.

He just couldn't see that it made her feel good about herself, made her feel secure. She held her temper. She knew from experience that anything she might say would fall on deaf ears, and today she was not going to get involved in any arguments. She poured them both mugs of tea. It was her way of ending any dispute they might have, and it had always worked.

Michael smiled to himself, understanding that the conversation was now over. He was happy to oblige. 'Thanks, darling. I need this.'

Josephine smiled gently, and Michael was, as always, taken aback at how deeply he loved his wife. It never failed to amaze him how even a smile from her could tear at his heart. He adored her, and he wished that he knew how to make her feel better.

'You out all day, Michael?'

He nodded. 'I'll be home for dinner though – I'm only meeting Patrick to sort out a few bits and pieces. Nothing really important. Let's watch a film tonight, eh? Open a bottle of wine.'

Josephine laughed at his deliberate nonchalance. He was trying to make everything better and she loved him for that. 'That sounds good to me, Michael.'

'It's a date, then.'

Josephine leant against the granite worktop, and sipped her tea. She was never happier than when they were like this, easy in each other's company, and without the spectre that she felt was between then. No matter what Michael did or said to reassure her, she knew that, as much as he loved her, they were both aware of the void in their lives.

She swallowed down the sadness inside her. Michael couldn't cope when she felt like this, and he wouldn't leave her on her own if he thought she was obsessing about their life together and how she had let him down. He was so good to her, and she knew how lucky she was to have a man like him.

'Go on, get yourself off, Michael. I'm cooking a lamb casserole for us tonight, so ring me and let me know what time to expect you.' She kissed him softly, and walked with him to the front door.

He hugged her tightly to him, and she could feel the love he had for her. But instead of making her feel secure, all she felt was her failure as a wife. As he pulled out of the driveway, she closed the door and, leaning against it, she exhaled wearily. It was getting harder and harder to keep up her act.

The house was huge – much too big for just the two of them – but when they had bought it, they had assumed that they would be filling it with their children. Sons and daughters that they could love, cherish. They had meticulously planned for the big family they had both wanted. They had picked out names for the children-to-be, even chosen schools. They had never once allowed for the fact that she might miscarry each of those children, one after the other, with shocking frequency.

But she had done just that, lost every one in a blaze of blood and pain. It was so unfair. She had seen every doctor available, they had spent thousands of pounds, and they were still childless. Josephine was unable to keep a child alive in her womb for any length of time.

Now she was pregnant once more and this time she wasn't telling *anyone* – especially not her husband. *This* time, when the child they had created was expelled from her womb, she would carry the burden alone. She couldn't bear to look at his face again, first seeing the hope for her pregnancy then, eventually, witnessing his disappointment when it ended prematurely, seeing his pity for her, because she couldn't do the one thing that came naturally to every other woman in the world. It was the pity in his eyes that she found the hardest to endure.

No, she would carry this baby alone, with no doctors, no family involvement whatsoever. She would just wait and see, and accept the outcome alone. The days of crying for hours on end were gone and she was not going to let Michael be hurt any more. She would shoulder this all herself. It was the least she could do. She couldn't get his hopes up again. It was cruel enough for her – she would protect him from it this time.

Chapter Thirty

Patrick Costello had been up half the night fighting with Carmel, and he was tired out. These days he was really feeling his age. His Carmel could keep a row going for fucking hours – she relished every second of it. Years ago he had too – the passionate fighting, followed by the even more passionate making up. Then it had been about making love for hours on end, picnics together in bed, champagne cocktails he would make for them, followed by more sexual gymnastics, and protestations of their undying love for one another. It was another lifetime.

Nowadays, as he tried to explain to his wife, he could only manage one or the other – the fucking or the fighting. Unfortunately for him, his Carmel was a born arguer, and she loved nothing more than a knock-down, drag-out fight on a regular basis. It had been nearly three in the morning before she had finally let him sleep and, the worst thing was, he *still* didn't know what the fuck they had been arguing about. He had to smile though, she was a game old bird, there was no doubting that. She never ceased to surprise him. She could pick a row with a deaf mute if the fancy took her. That had been what had attracted him to her deep down. Sure, she was a smashing-looking bird and good in the kip, but the fact she had never been in awe of him had stood her in good stead once upon a time. He had respected her for that. Now, he hated that she needed to have a tear-up on a regular basis; to prove that he still loved her he had to fight with her. He loved her as much as he was capable of loving anyone, but that didn't stop her getting on his nerves. Her constant need for attention was wearing thin – the dramatics that had once been so exciting were draining him.

As the mother of his children, Carmel would always have a hold on his affection. His daughters were not exactly kids to be proud of, though. They were such a disappointment to him, even though he loved them dearly. They were both lazy, lacking in intelligence, and unable to understand the concept of hard work, let alone the importance of actually getting a job. He had trusted her with the girls, and couldn't help feeling she had failed them.

He sighed, deciding not to think about any of that now – it already took up too much time, and it was a pointless exercise.

He glanced around his new offices; they were a bit over the top for his tastes, if he was being honest, but it was all about top show these days. He resented weighing out for it; he had eventually bowed to Michael's wishes, as he had known he would. The boy was more often right than wrong. But it still galled him – he paid more for these offices a year than he had paid for his first house. It was fucking mental but he accepted that to be seen as legitimate, they needed to *look* legitimate. That meant they actually had to run everything from the offices from which they ran the more legitimate businesses. It was sensible, but it was also against his natural inclinations. The fact that the businesses they ran from here were all very lucrative made no difference to him; Patrick was a born thief which was never going to change as long as he had a hole in his arse. He would always crave the illicit pound. He could have had a legal earn if he had chosen that route in life, but where was the real fucking profit for anyone with that old shite? Paying fucking tax for a start, employing accountants, and all the other old fanny that would have entailed.

This wasn't a country that had ever encouraged free enterprise. As soon as a profit was made, the government slaughtered you with taxes, and then they taxed your workforce to boot! The whole fucking concept of tax went against his beliefs. Nevertheless, Patrick was a realist, and Michael was right about making sure the legit businesses were seen to pay the taxes required of them and, more to the point, visibly profitable enough to explain away the cars they drove and the homes they lived in. It was a different world now; it was hard to launder the dead money – it needed to be absorbed into real businesses and, he had to admit, the lad had a knack for doing that. Times had changed all right, but he still bitterly resented every penny that he paid out to the government.

Michael breezed into the offices and, seeing Patrick Costello's dark countenance, he laughed loudly. 'For fuck's sake, Pat, you look fucking knackered, mate. Sorry I'm late. Traffic.'

Patrick smiled despite himself; only Michael would have the front to say that to him. 'Don't start me off. Carmel had the urge for a fucking all-nighter. If any man had a fucking reason to find a new bird, it's me.'

Michael had heard it all before. Patrick had always been very vocal about his wife's ability to fight him on a whim, and at any hour of the day or night, by all accounts. It sounded so tiring to Michael – he could never have lived a life like Patrick and Carmel Costello. She was a raving nutbag, and that was being nice about her. But she was not a woman who endeared herself to the people around her. She was arrogant for starters. She looked down her nose at basically everyone around her, and she treated the people who worked for Patrick and Declan with such obvious disdain that it was impossible for them not to see it. He would *never* have tied himself to a woman like Carmel, he knew that much.

She had delivered Patrick's children with the minimum of fuss, but that was as far as her usefulness had gone. That Patrick was not as enamoured of his wife – or her tantrums – as he had once been, was more than evident lately. But Michael knew better than to give an opinion either way. That was the easiest way to destroy a good friendship, and the easiest way to get himself killed. Women like Carmel were inclined to cause as much trouble as possible if they felt they were being ousted from their position.

'Well, that's your business, mate.'

Patrick laughed once more. He was well aware that Michael loathed his Carmel, and always had. She had that effect on most people. The only person his Carmel had ever liked was Josephine Flynn, and that was only because poor Josephine actually liked his wife.

'You're a diplomat, Michael. So, tell me, how is everything going?'

Michael was all business suddenly, glad to be away from the personal – and the dangerous. 'Well, it's good news about the mortgage businesses. I told you they would be a lucrative earn, and they are. Serious money is coming in now, Patrick, and best of all, it's being encouraged by the government. Buying your own house is available to everyone these days, and our brokers are doing well. It's such an easy fucking earn. It's also a good way of laundering money, Pat. Buying a house for cash and then remortgaging it, means the money from the mortgage company can then be put into legitimate bank accounts. It can be moved about, buying and selling other properties, for example, investing it into businesses, clubs, whatever. I've been moving a lot of the money into Spain, investing in the property market in Marbella and Benidorm. The good thing about Spain is there's no extradition so, for a lot of our investors, that's a fucking added bonus. They can get out there easily – it's a lot closer than South America, put it that way.'

Patrick Costello already knew everything that Michael was telling him. It rankled with Michael that, after all this time, Patrick Costello should still feel the need to keep an eye on him. But he would never change; Michael had no choice but to accept it. All of that aside, Patrick Costello still trusted him more than he had ever trusted anyone. It was just the nature of the beast.

Patrick was happy with the news. They were coining it in, making real money, getting a fantastic return for their initial investments, and that was only because of Michael Flynn. *He* had the foresight to see the opportunities that Spain and Portugal had to offer long before anyone else. He had been adamant about investing not just money, but their time and effort, into the new ventures. He had insisted, from the start, that they needed to not just make their mark but, more importantly, they needed to ensure that they put their own people in the key positions ready for the future.

It was already paying off big time – plus they had guaranteed for themselves the foothold that ensured that anyone else who might feel the need to invest out there had no other option but to talk to them first. Patrick Costello knew that this lad had sewn up Spain and the surrounding areas. He had also done it legally.

'The Spanish don't give a fuck about anything, Michael, they just want people to bring their money out there. Tourism has already fucked the economy. They are far too reliant on it already, just as you predicted. Whole communities are now dependent on the hotel industry. You were right about that, mate. I bow down to you, you're a fucking genius, son. But I always knew that, didn't I?'

Michael accepted the man's praise as his due. He loved Patrick

Costello; he had been very good to him, and Michael had made sure that he had earned not only his trust, but also his respect. That was why knowing that Patrick still felt the need to spy on him rankled. It offended him and his sense of loyalty. But he couldn't say a word – that would be tantamount to mutiny.

Michael could never admit to Patrick that he was aware of it. His position in the Costello family gave him not just a serious earn, but also guaranteed him a place in the London underworld that he could never have occupied without Patrick Costello taking him under his wing and giving him his personal attention. He could never, ever forget that; he would always be grateful for the man's interest in him, and the opportunities he had been afforded because of it.

'Listen, Patrick, I think we should go and have a couple of drinks, a bit of lunch, and discuss a few business opportunities that I think might be in our interests.'

Patrick Costello was more than game. He always enjoyed listening to the lad's ideas – Michael Flynn had the knack of sniffing out an earn before anyone else. But, more than that, Patrick Costello genuinely enjoyed his company. 'Lead the way, my son. I'm up for all that.'

Chapter Thirty-One

Declan Costello woke up with a blinding hangover. He opened his eyes warily – the sunlight was already giving him gyp. He squinted his eyes and attempted to look at his watch, but it was a pointless exercise. He brought his right arm as close to his face as possible – all he could see was a blur. His watch was a solid gold Rolex, with a gold face and gold numerals. He could see fuck-all, let alone the time.

He looked around him groggily; he recognised the bedroom at least. It was the boudoir of one Samantha Harker. He had found himself here on more than one occasion and, in his defence, he had never remembered actually arriving. He pulled himself up in bed and, putting the pillows behind his back, he leant into them, using the headboard as a backrest. He could smell himself – a mixture of sweat, alcohol and Samantha Harker. He scrabbled around on the bedside table and, as he knew he would, he found his cigarettes and lighter. He lit a Benson & Hedges, and pulled the smoke into his lungs lazily.

The room was actually very clean. Samantha was a good housekeeper – he remembered that from past experience. Her flat was spotless, and quite well decorated, considering.

She was a nice enough girl and a game bird. *Great* pair of tits, and not bad-looking. She was very young though.

He felt a sudden flush of shame wash over him – he was old enough to be her father. She was the only girl that made him feel like this. Yet here he was, once more in her bed. He closed his eyes in annoyance.

He could hear her moving about in the kitchen. Her flat was so small, it was like being in a fucking envelope. The bedroom door opened a few minutes later, and Samantha came into the room, smiling that big smile of hers, and bringing him a mug of tea. Her little girl was, as always, hot on her heels. The child was like a miniature of her mum. She had the same blue eyes, the same thick blond hair, and the same wide smile. She stood at the end of the bed, and he could sense her watching him.

'Here you are, Declan, a nice cup of tea.'

He took the steaming mug of tea carefully. Samantha always acted as if he didn't owe her anything, and why wouldn't she? He owed her fuck-all.

Samantha sat on the bed beside him. She was devoid of make-up, and her dressing gown hid the killer body that he knew so well. 'What a great night again! Honestly, Declan, I really did enjoy myself.'

He smiled, unsure what to say to her.

Samantha looked closely at the man she had spent the night with on more than one occasion and seeing the way he was acting – as if his being in her bed was something to be ashamed of – she felt the burning anger that only humiliation could bring. He was the only man she had ever allowed into her home, into her bed, since she had given birth to her daughter. She had felt such an affinity with him from their first meeting, she had truly believed they had made a genuine connection. He was much older than her, but that didn't bother her at all. She had been attracted to his personality, his strength, and his kindness. She had felt all of that straightaway. She had also felt a deep physical attraction to him that she had never felt for anyone else before. He had sought *her* out after their first meeting; she had never once looked for him – she had too much pride in herself for that. He had pursued her, as she had known he would. Now he was suddenly acting like she was beneath him, and that hurt.

She opened her arms, and pulled her little daughter on to her lap, hugging the child to her. Declan watched her warily. He could feel the atmosphere changing, knew that he was naked, and had no option but to wait for his opportunity to get his kecks on, and run like the fucking wind as far away as humanly possible.

Samantha looked into his eyes for long moments. She was still hugging her little daughter tightly, and he could see how the child enjoyed her mother's embrace, and how much affection there was between them.

'Listen, Declan, I don't like you treating me like this. You act like this has never happened before, but it has – many times. I've fallen in love with you, Declan, I think you already know that. But I will not let anyone treat me like a whore. If you don't want to see me again, then you can fuck off, OK?'

Declan wanted to hold her, tell her it was going to be all right. But he couldn't. 'You could be my daughter, Sam. I'm far too old for you. I'm trying to be the good guy here.'

Samantha smiled sadly. 'Well, it's a pity you didn't think about that before we got so involved. It's OK to sleep with me in secret, then? Thanks a bunch, Declan. You know where the door is.' She stood up and, with as much dignity as she could muster, she carried her daughter out of the room.

Declan lay there in Samantha Harker's bed, wishing with all his might that he was anywhere else in the world. He could hear Samantha in the kitchen, chatting away to her little girl, pretending that everything was fine, but beneath the love he could hear in her voice for her child, there was a deep abiding sadness.

Declan Costello had never felt so guilty about anything in his whole entire life.

Chapter Thirty-Two

Carmel Costello watched her two daughters with growing irritation. They argued constantly with each other and with her. They treated her like she was no more than a servant. Assumpta, the eldest, had become her nemesis; she would argue that black was white if it meant going against her own mother. Gabriella, too, would gladly pick a fight with her own fingernails – she was as spoilt as her older sister, and even more inclined to argue just for the sheer hell of it.

Patrick always tried to insinuate that they took after her! As far as she was concerned, they were their father's daughters. They were completely spoilt – they had never once had to do anything for themselves, and they never *were* going to do anything for themselves. She had given them everything they had wanted, and they repaid her by demanding that she give them even more. To be fair, she had used them to make Patrick do whatever she had wanted him to do. The girls had been her bargaining chips, her way of making him toe the line, and he had done everything she had asked of him.

Now the girls were completely out of her control. They were both without a conscience, without any moral compasses whatever. They were as spoilt as she was but, unlike her, they didn't have the brain capacity to understand that it took more than a temper tantrum to get what they wanted from a man like their father.

Patrick was disappointed in the girls and she was as disappointed in them as he was. The girls' education had cost a small fortune, and they didn't have a single qualification between them. She had been so sure that they would both be achievers, would both make their parents proud of them. It had never occurred to her that they would end up no better than if they had been brought up on a council estate. She had assumed the fact they went to a very expensive private school would have at least guaranteed them a place in society, would have given them something that could have helped them to get on in life. But it had been a waste of time and a waste of money.

She was also becoming aware that her husband saw these daughters of his as the product of *her* machinations, *her* insistence that he let her sort it all out, because he was incapable of understanding the economics of a female's education. But she was not to blame – it was her daughters who had failed them both, who had not understood that they were in a position to make something of themselves, who had both left a very expensive education with no more than a backward glance, and nothing whatsoever to show for any of it. Even she had read more books than they had, and that was saying something. She had simply assumed the school would see to everything they needed for a decent education – they were getting paid enough money after all. It had never occurred to her that the school would take the money and run.

Patrick saw his daughters as no more than the spoilt brats they were. He was absolutely right about that, of course. Now she had to break the news to him that Assumpta was pregnant. She was losing him, she knew that much; he already saw her as the architect of everything that had gone wrong with the family. This could be the final straw.

The girls were still at it. It was amazing really to see them in action. When they were fighting they really didn't have any care for anyone else around them.

'Assumpta, shut up for five fucking minutes and talk to me, will you?'

The girls both looked at their mother with abject shock at her words.

'Your father is going to go fucking ballistic when he finds out you are in the club. So, if I were you, darling, I would think long and hard about his reaction to your news. I would also make sure that the father is on hand, or at least give him a name. By Christ, I never thought that I would look at you two and feel such shame!'

Assumpta and Gabriella exchanged glances. It suddenly occurred to them both just how serious the consequences of their lifestyles might be.

When Assumpta looked at her mother, Carmel saw the fear on her eldest daughter's face. She had finally broken through to both of her girls.

'Your father is going to want to kill whoever is responsible, take my word on that. So, please, Assumpta, use your brain for once, and try and make this as painless as possible for everyone concerned.'

Carmel Costello had finally won her daughters' full attention and, even though she knew it was only because they needed her to stand between them and the man who had fathered them, it was still something of a coup for her.

Chapter Thirty-Three

Michael had just come through the back door of his house and, as he was taking his sheepskin coat off, he called out loudly, 'Oh, Josephine, you're not going to fucking believe this, darling. It's so fucking mental.'

Sitting in her daughter's kitchen, Lana Callahan was all ears; she knew a serious bit of gossip when she heard it. She shook a warning finger at her daughter, and Josephine smiled. She always told her mother everything eventually anyway.

Michael bounced into the kitchen, all dark good looks and natural confidence. That was his way. He always seemed to be happy with his surroundings; no matter what the situation might be, nothing ever seemed to faze him. He sounded shocked, though, about whatever he had heard. Lana suspected that this was one of the few times he had let his usual guard down.

The sight of his mother-in-law, however, sitting to attention at his kitchen table, stopped him in his tracks. She wasn't his biggest fan, he knew that, but she was a woman who liked to know what was going on first-hand. And she was like the grave.

So, grinning nonchalantly, he said in a pseudo-dramatic voice, 'This is something you might regret hearing, Lana, I'm warning you now.'

Lana laughed. She loved to hear the latest gossip, but she was more than capable of keeping it to herself; she knew the danger involved in repeating things she heard in this house, especially when it concerned people like the Costellos and their ilk.

Josephine opened the fridge and took out a can of lager and, as she opened it, she looked at her husband craftily, and said, 'Come on then, Flynn, don't keep us in suspense.'

Michael took the beer from her and, after taking a deep drink, he wiped his mouth carefully. Then he waited for his wife to sit back down at the kitchen table before he said seriously, 'Assumpta Costello is pregnant. Patrick is going off his fucking nut.'

He waited for the reaction he expected, but it didn't arrive. Instead, his wife and her mother didn't act even remotely surprised at his news. He had expected them to have been agog, as shocked as he was at the news.

'Has she named anyone yet, Michael?' Josephine kept her voice as neutral as possible.

He shook his head, unsure now if this news was actually as secret as he had first believed. Patrick had not said a word to him personally about any of it, he had heard it from Declan. Now he had a good idea why Patrick was keeping this news so close to his chest. If his own wife and her mother were not shocked at the news of Assumpta being pregnant, that could only mean they knew something that he obviously didn't.

Michael shrugged carelessly, but he was a bit miffed. 'I don't know about that. Declan only told me because of Patrick's extremely erratic behaviour of late. He has been so unpredictable, so fucking angry with everything and anyone. Patrick is obviously keeping all of this well under wraps, and who can blame him? But he is like a bear with a fucking sore arse and, when he finally does fucking let rip, God help the poor fucker responsible. He is like a man possessed. He's ashamed into the bargain – I bet that's the real fucking problem actually. After all, she's still a kid, really.'

Josephine and her mother still didn't say a word to him about Assumpta or her predicament. That was irritating him. He felt pushed out, as if he was a mug or a fucking outsider, who wasn't deemed fit to know anything of importance. His good mood was slowly evaporating, and he was regretting his eagerness to discuss any of this with his wife or her mother. His amiable demeanour was gone in seconds and the women were immediately alerted to his changed mood. His voice was flat now, his irritation more than evident as he said sarcastically, 'I am now assuming that you two ladies know more about this drama than I do. So come on – spill. I'm all ears.'

Josephine really didn't want to be the one who told her husband about his closest friend's daughter – well, *daughters* if all the talk was true. They had certainly kept it in the family anyway. If they had not been Patrick Costello's daughters, their antics would have been the talk the town for a lot longer and with much more graphic detail. As it was, only a few of the women who were married to men with access to the inner circles had felt safe enough to discuss it amongst themselves, and they had never talked about it to anyone outside. It was far too dangerous. No one would want to be the person who informed Patrick Costello about his daughters' private lives.

But both of his daughters had been putting themselves out there for a long time, with anyone and everyone who would have them, if the gossip was to be believed. Now Assumpta was pregnant, and it was going to be a whodunnit, there was no doubt about that. If there had been a regular bloke involved, then Patrick might have swallowed it, but that wasn't the case. Assumpta had been taking on all-comers for a long time, and she was as brazen as she was available. It had been common knowledge amongst the women in the Costello world but, as always in these situations, the men had no inkling whatsoever.

Josephine could not help resenting the fact that girls like Assumpta managed to get a child without even trying, and grow it inside them without any problems whatsoever. If they didn't choose to abort the poor child, they just pushed it out with the minimum of fuss. They treated childbirth and pregnancy without any kind of respect, they had no concept of the importance of what their bodies had achieved. Pregnancy was no more than a problem for them. It was just something they could choose to either continue with or, the more likely scenario, remove from their bodies, and then carry on their lives as if none of it had ever happened, as if they had never been lucky enough to have a baby inside them. A little baby that was healthy and snug inside a womb that would not let them down, would not suddenly expel the poor child from their bodies, leaving them not only devastated but, with each painful, bloody failure, feeling less and less of a woman, unable to do the one thing that was expected of them. It was so fucking wrong. *She* wanted, *needed* a child more than anything else in the world, yet she had miscarried one after the other. The only baby she had managed to carry longer than a few months had died inside her, and she had gone through the whole pain of early childbirth knowing she would get nothing at the end of it.

She realised that her mother was talking to Michael. She forced herself to listen to their conversation, but she was so hurt, so angry at life.

Michael was shaking his head in amazement now, his earlier annoyance with his wife and mother-in-law gone. He listened closely to Lana as she told him the score about Patrick's daughters; she was very knowledgeable about them, and their lifestyles – that much was obvious to Michael. It seemed that the women knew far more than the men around them about what was actually going on.

He found himself believing everything that Lana was telling him about the Costello girls and their carryings on. There was a ring of truth in what she was telling him which he couldn't ignore. He felt the same burning heat of humiliation and anger that his friend would be feeling at his daughters' shame, and he was sorry to the very heart of him.

'If Patrick knew that his daughters were laying down with all and sundry on a regular basis he would go off his fucking tree. The men who they have been with can't have known whose daughters they were cavorting with, surely? No one would dare to touch them knowing they were Patrick Costello's girls.'

Lana shrugged, irritated now. She had not trusted her daughter's husband since the night the Barber brothers had gone on the missing list. He was a dangerous man, who acted like he was normal, but it was all a sham. If she had had her way, her daughter's wedding would never have gone ahead. Her husband loved him, though; he saw him as the son he had never had, thought the sun shone out of his arse, as did her daughter. But she had sussed the real Michael, and his complete ignorance about men and the lure of girls like the Costellos incensed her. It just proved to her how foolish these men could really be.

'You listen to me, Michael Flynn. You'd be surprised at just how low some men are willing to sink. From what we've heard, those girls have been at it for years. Carmel Costello might not be my favourite person, but she didn't deserve what those girls have done. She tried to give them a decent start in life. Patrick Costello, the big-headed bully that he is, has to come to terms with his daughters' actions. It won't be easy for him, but he has no other option. So remember this for the future, Michael – it takes two to tango. If she can name the father of Patrick Costello's first grandchild – and that is what her child is, remember, *his* grandchild, his flesh and blood – I will eat my fucking knitting.

'And another thing, Michael, while we are all being so honest. I would lay good money on the child being black, or at least dark-skinned. But I expect you and the Costellos will sort it out. "Who would sleep with Patrick's daughter?" This from a man who knows first-hand what men are capable of, who prides himself on his knowledge of the world around him. Patrick Costello is going to get the shock of his life, and do you know something? I'm glad. It's about time you realised that you are not the be all and end all. There is always someone who will sneak under your radar, and take what's yours, destroying everything you hold dear without you even noticing it.'

Michael was utterly taken aback at his mother-in-law's vehemence. He had only sought to give his wife a bit of gossip, as he usually did when he came home. He told her everything about his life, his work – he always had done.

Josephine, however, had been very quiet throughout this conversation. She had left her mother to tell him what they knew about Assumpta and her unfortunate situation. In truth, he had heard *far* more about the Costello girls and their sexual gymnastics than he felt comfortable with. He could *never* let Patrick know that he was aware of any of this.

Lana, he realised, had enjoyed giving him the truth about the situation. Lana had never really been right with him since before his marriage to her only daughter. She had seemed to change overnight. He had put it down to his own mother's interference, and Lana's natural concerns for her only daughter. Now, though, he couldn't help wondering if she just didn't like him. She had once been his biggest fan – now she had no real care for him at all. Every time Josephine had lost a child, Lana had been there, holding her daughter's hand, and he had seen her watching him closely, as he grieved the loss of his child with his wife. He had felt her blaming him for each one, even as he guessed that she didn't want her daughter to carry his spawn.

While they were childless, Lana felt that she had the upper hand. As though the marriage wasn't really consummated and, therefore, it could be dissolved. She didn't understand that, as much as he wanted a child, he would always want Josephine more. She was everything to him, and she always would be. It was Josephine who craved a child. He didn't care any more one way or the other. He just wanted his wife, his Josephine.

He smiled amiably, unwilling to let this woman know that she had affected him in any way. 'Well, Lana, that's told me, all right. In future, I will keep my fucking trap shut.'

Josephine could sense the animosity coming not only from her mother, but also from her husband. He had every right to feel aggrieved. Her mother had no right to treat him as she did, to show her contempt for him, and the life he lived. He provided her with everything she could want and more. Josephine knew that she had to say something to her mother. She had to show Michael that she understood how he was feeling, that she was on his side, as she always had been and always would be.

'That's enough, now. I think it's time you went home, Mum.'

Lana looked at her daughter in disbelief. She was being asked to leave, *told* to leave. It wasn't a request, her daughter was aiming her out the door all right. It was a dismissal.

Michael smiled genuinely then. He was pleased that Josephine could see his point of view, understood how he hated it when her mother treated him with such contempt in his own home.

Lana felt her face flush with humiliation. Josephine treating her so shabbily hurt her deeply, but she couldn't retaliate.

'Come on, Mum, Dad will be wondering where you are.'

Lana walked out of the room with as much dignity as she could muster. In the entrance hall of her daughter's home, she picked up her coat from the arm of the large leather sofa that was all but lost in the huge space that Lana had always admired. Her daughter's home was not just big, it was also very beautiful, Josephine had the money needed for such a property. Michael had always given her daughter whatever she wanted but, even knowing that, Lana still couldn't bring herself to forget what he really was or what he was capable of.

Josephine held the front door open, and Lana walked out of the house quickly. But she couldn't resist one last jibe; she was so offended at the treatment she'd received, which she felt was so unfair. She wanted nothing more than her daughter's happiness. Josephine was a lot of things, but she wasn't happy. How could she be with a violent thug like Michael?

'I can't believe you are really doing this to me, Josephine. I would give you the world on a plate if I could and you know that.'

'Oh, I do know that, Mum, I always have. But Michael is my husband, and he has already given me the world on a plate, in case you haven't noticed. He has also given you and Dad a good earn. You've never been so well off. And if I have to choose between you both, you know it will always be him, Mum.'

Lana walked away. As she got into her car, she heard the front door close loudly behind her.

Michael hated seeing his wife so torn. He wanted to protect her from anything that might harm her. It was his job as her husband. He opened his arms and pulled her into them. He could feel her body relaxing into his, knew that she was where she wanted to be.

'I'm so sorry, Josephine. I don't know what that was about.'

She hugged him tightly, enjoying the feel of him, the smell of him. He felt so safe, so strong. 'Oh, forget about it, Michael.' She wanted to change the subject. Make it all go away. 'How much does Patrick know about his daughters, do you think?'

He sighed in consternation. 'I really don't know. Declan told me about it in confidence. Patrick hasn't said a dicky-bird – now I know why. If what your mum said is true, and I think it probably is, Patrick will have a hard time taking all that onboard. Who wouldn't? He thought the sun rose and set with his girls. They were his reason for living. His kids, his flesh and blood.'

Josephine didn't answer that. She hoped that *her* flesh and blood, this pregnancy, would finally come to fruition and give them the one thing they couldn't buy. Just one child would be enough – that's all she wanted.

'I tell you this much though, Josephine. Whoever Assumpta names as the culprit will wish they had never been fucking born.'

Chapter Thirty-Four

Patrick Costello was practically hyperventilating, such was the vehemence of his anger. He knew he had to be alone for a while, so he had come into his office and poured himself a very large whisky. He sipped it slowly, savouring the strong taste, and the burn as he swallowed it down. He needed the alcohol to give him at least a modicum of inebriation, to take the edge off feeling too much.

This had never happened to him in his life before. He was never unable to control his emotions. His daughter's pregnancy was bad enough but, coupled with her bare-faced refusal to name the culprit, his usual aplomb was rapidly deteriorating. He took another large sip of the whisky, praying for it to calm him down and give him some kind of peace. He needed to deaden his emotions for a short while, until he could once more control himself – and his actions.

He was going to kill someone soon – that was a given – and, if his daughter didn't answer his questions, there was a good chance that the dead person might actually be *her*. It was her reluctance to name anyone as the father which had finally convinced him there must be more than one person in the frame. If it had been a love job, she would have come clean. He could have accepted that, could have understood the power of youth, of being in love for the first time. He wasn't a complete fucking moron, he could have overlooked such behaviour if it was down to love. He would still have been angry, but he would have allowed for his daughter, his baby, to have been caught up in her hormones.

But it wasn't like that at all. This was devoid of any romance and, therefore, of any reason he could have found to forgive her. She had no idea who was the father of her child and she didn't seem to care either. It was as if the child she was carrying inside her was nothing more than an inconvenience. She just wanted it gone from her, aborted, taken away as soon as. It was actually her complete disregard for the child inside her that really concerned him. His Assumpta, his lovely girl he had adored, was treating her pregnancy as simply a problem to be solved. She did not seem to comprehend the enormity of what was happening to her, that she was now the guardian of another human being, a child that *she* had created. She didn't understand that, as Catholics, they had no option but to bring the child into the world, and love it unconditionally, no matter the circumstances of its conception. That was the whole ethos behind being a fucking Catholic in the first place – especially an Irish Catholic. You sinned, and you then lived with that sin. You *loved* that sin, and you cared for that sin until it wasn't a sin any more – it was the best thing to have happened to you, a gift from God Himself. It was given to you for a reason – to make you a better person, and show you the miracle of life, and how it can bring you peace, and more love than you could ever imagine.

Assumpta just wanted it gone from her, as if she was drowning an unwanted kitten.

The door of his office opened quietly, and he stood still as a statue. His daughter was there. He could smell her, the perfume she wore, the heavy scent of her make-up. She had always worn far too much make-up. She was a beautiful girl, and he had never understood her fascination with painting her face. But he had allowed it. He had given his wife the final say on the girls and their lifestyles. Now he was sorry, even though he knew that his Carmel had done her best by the girls. She was as baffled as he was about Assumpta and her predicament. He stood stiffly, looking out of the window, seeing the beauty of the view, all the while forcing down his anger, his disappointment and his shame that his daughter had really thought that he would not have a problem arranging for her to have her child scraped out of her. One wrong word from his daughter now, and he would likely seriously harm her.

Assumpta looked at her dad. For her whole life he had only been there as a provider – her mum had been the main carer. She had done her best, but she had always been more interested in how she herself looked, or in how they were dressed.

Assumpta had been sexually active since her early teens. Her reputation meant nothing to her. She was a Costello and *that* had given her the power over everyone in her orbit since she could remember. Everyone was nice to them because they were Costellos – no other reason. She had started sleeping around to prove to herself that she could transcend the Costello name. If only she knew then what she knew now.

She was already four months gone, and all she wanted was for her dad to make it go away and let her start her life again, properly this time, sensibly, with the gift of hindsight. Now she knew the pitfalls, she was more than willing to learn her lesson. Whatever it took, she would do it.

'I'm sorry, Dad.'

Patrick closed his eyes in distress. She sounded so young, so innocent. This was his baby, his first-born. This was the girl who adamantly refused to give him the name of her child's father.

He gulped at his whisky. Then he said as calmly as humanly

possible, 'Just tell me who the father is. That is all I want to know.'

Assumpta swallowed down her annoyance. If he only knew the circumstances, he might understand her reluctance to broadcast it to the nation. But if he did, he would realise that she couldn't say exactly who the father was. She had a vague idea, going by the dates, but that wasn't going to be enough for her father. 'I wish I could turn back time, Dad. But I can't, no one can. I just want the opportunity to put this behind me and start again.'

Patrick turned around then, and looked at his daughter. She was so pretty, all tits and teeth – a real brahma. Her hair was thick and shiny, her eyes were deep blue, and she had his mum's high cheekbones. She was a Costello all right – physically, anyway.

'You're having this fucking baby, Assumpta – get that through your thick head. As a Catholic, I can't believe that you ever thought otherwise. If you *don't* have your baby, Assumpta, I will cut you off from this family without a second fucking thought. I swear that to you in the name of the Christ Child Himself. I will never forgive you as long as you live. You will be as dead to me as the child you murdered.'

It was over. Patrick Costello looked at his daughter and knew that he had finally beaten her. His threat to cut her off had frightened her more than anything else. That troubled him, but he firmly believed that the child would be the making of her. It was the only thing left that could redeem her in his eyes.

Assumpta knew that she had no option but to do as her father insisted. He had shown her how serious he was, and he was not going to change his mind. This child she was carrying meant more to him than it could ever mean to her. She hadn't thought for a second that anyone in her family would welcome her pregnancy; she had banked on her parents wanting the child removed as quickly and quietly as possible. That *her* father, Patrick Costello, really believed in the sanctity of life had been something she had never thought possible. But she could not have been more wrong. The stories she had heard about him all of her life suggested the opposite. His capacity for great violence, the myths about his involvement in the death and the disappearance of people who had thwarted or challenged him, implied that her father was a murderer.

To now find out that this same man was adamant that abortion was unacceptable, was a sin against God, scared her. She had always assumed that his churchgoing was just another scam, nothing more than a public show, a pretence to make him look like a good, decent man. That her father *actually* believed in the Catholic Church, and its most basic of beliefs, forced her to reappraise her position.

But she had one last argument up her sleeve. One she hoped would cancel out everything else her father had said.

'Dad, I have to tell you something.'

Patrick shrugged. He could be magnanimous now – he had won the war. 'Go on, then.'

'This baby I'm carrying might be black.'

Patrick could hear the hope in her voice. She genuinely thought that a black child might be enough to make him turn against everything he had ever believed in. This daughter of his would never cease to amaze him.

'And?' He made sure his voice was as nonchalant as possible.

Assumpta was rattled by his reply. 'I just thought you should know, that's all.'

Patrick laughed. 'The fact you said "might" tells me all I need to know about you. But I couldn't give a flying fuck if it was sky blue with pink spots. It's going to be born and it will bear the

Costello name. It will be my first grandchild and, as such, it will be given every opportunity I can provide for it and, hopefully, unlike its mother, it will have the brains to make something of itself.'

Assumpta turned to leave, and Patrick fought the urge to kick her arse out of the door. She had disappointed him in more ways than one. It wasn't the pregnancy itself – he would have come to terms with that eventually – but his daughter's disregard for her own child's welfare, and her complete indifference to it had really shown him how selfish she was. He had to admit that he was ashamed of his daughters – both of them. They were cut from the same cloth, and so self-absorbed they couldn't see further than their own needs and wants. He had grown up with nothing; they had been given all they could desire from an early age. His girls knew the price of everything, but the value of nothing.

There was poor Josephine Flynn, who had more right to motherhood than this whore of his, and yet she had lost child after child, denied the one thing that she craved. Well, his Assumpta was finally going to learn the harsh realities of life. She was going to have her child and, if she had any nous whatsoever, she would finally understand about consequences.

He had heard all the tales about his daughters. Declan had given him the gossip, so he wouldn't hear it from strangers. He had been shocked but, more than anything, he had been so hurt. That he had unknowingly harboured such poisonous vipers, such vacuous females, had really shown him the truth of his life. Carmel, God love her, had trusted them implicitly. She was even more outraged than he was about their exploits.

Everyone around him had known about his daughters, and the lifestyle they had chosen to pursue, while he was left in the dark. It was the worst kind of betrayal for a man like him who prided himself on never being taken unawares. He had no option but to face it, hold his head up, and front it out.

But if anyone *ever* had the nerve to say anything to his face, he would kill them without a second's fucking thought. He was going to find out who the father of his grandchild was, and the names of every single man who had taken his daughters to bed behind his back. Patrick's reputation was everything to him; it was something he had to fight for, and he would do exactly that.

Chapter Thirty-Five

'Listen, Pat, this has all got to stop, mate. You are making a fucking fool of yourself.'

Michael Flynn was asking for trouble, but he had no choice. Patrick was out of control, he seemed to have completely disconnected from reality. He had never seen anything like it in his life.

Declan stood watching him. Michael knew that he had not really believed that he would actually say anything to Patrick, even though they had planned this together. Patrick wasn't a man who encouraged any kind of criticism about himself, in fact he had a serious problem dealing with it. But something had to be done, and Michael was the only person with the balls to do it.

Patrick looked at Michael. The contempt in his voice was evident. It was not something he had ever thought he would hear directed at him, let alone from young Michael.

'I don't give a flying fuck what you might think, Michael. You need to remember that you work for me, mate, not the other way around.'

Michael steadied his voice, aware that he had to try and defuse the situation. But, by the same token, this had to be sorted, things had to be said. 'And you need to remember who *you* are, Patrick. If you have any brains you will stop this fucking witch hunt. Think about it. If your daughter actually ***knew*** who had knocked her up, don't you think she might have fucking mentioned it by now? I really do understand how you're feeling, but you are making a laughing stock of yourself. It's a joke, Pat. You're not the only man whose daughter is having a baby on her own. It's the eighties, it isn't even a fucking big deal these days.'

Patrick recognised that, on one level, Michael was speaking the truth. He was chasing after nothing. But he just couldn't stop himself. He hated that his daughter had let herself down so much and that, at the same time, she had let him down, shamed him in the worst way possible. He blamed Carmel. She was a fucking disgrace, she had failed him miserably. She was another trollop, another user. It was a family trait, by all accounts, and his daughters had not inherited it from him. That's if they *were* his daughters, of course. He was wondering about that now. He couldn't eat or sleep. His whole life was consumed with thinking about his daughters, the lives they had led, and his complete ignorance of it all. He couldn't believe that he had been so naïve. He had always told his girls how lovely they were, how beautiful they were; he had treated them like princesses, totally convinced of their goodness. He had assumed they understood the importance of decency, had cherished their virginity, known the value of self-respect. But that had been a complete fucking myth on his part. They had apparently lain down for anyone who gave them the time of day. He had never once even suspected them of anything untoward. Now he could only wonder what else he had missed, what else had been going on beneath his nose. Every day he was finding it harder to believe they were his flesh and blood.

Even Declan and Michael were suspect to him now. He had given them the same trust, and now he could only wonder at his own foolishness. His Carmel was the most suspect, as far as he was concerned. She had been in charge of the girls after all.

Now he was constantly reminded of Carmel's past. She had hardly been a wilting fucking virgin when he had met her, but she had been much younger than him, and she had pursued him with a fucking vengeance until she got him. He had happily signed on for life, for a family and a home. She had supplied the family, he had supplied everything else. He had given her and his girls everything that money could buy, contentedly settled down with Carmel, and he had never once given her cause to doubt him or his loyalty. But could he really say the same about her? He wasn't so sure any more.

Michael sighed; he could see that Patrick wasn't listening to him, was unaware that he was even in the same room. 'Are you even listening to me, Pat? I'm talking away to you and you're off with the fucking fairies again. Get a grip, will you? We are already haemorrhaging fucking money. You keep missing meetings, and when you *do* bother to turn up you pick fights with men you have known all your life – men who rely on you because they trust you, because you have always been so reliable in the past. If you don't fucking sort your head out, Patrick, we will be seconded. We are already losing custom but, worst of all, we are losing face. Our credibility is shot thanks to you.'

Declan could see that his brother was too far gone to listen to reason. Patrick was already tuning Michael's voice out. When he had these episodes, he had the knack of only hearing what he wanted to hear. In truth, his brother rarely listened to anything he didn't want to hear anyway. It was part of Patrick's psyche, his inability to ever be wrong. It was this unpredictability that gave him the edge over everyone else. He was not going to listen to anything unless it suited him, unless it was directly concerned with this latest fixation. Michael had never really experienced Patrick like this before; Declan knew how dangerous it could make him.

He had always accepted that his brother lived outside normal human parameters. It had once been his strength, the reason he instilled fear into everyone without even trying. Anyone with half a brain could see that Patrick Costello was marching to a different beat to the rest of the world. Now his brother had descended into utter chaos. This latest episode went far deeper than ever before. Declan had seen him paranoid, but never against his own. Who would ever have thought Patrick could have been brought so low by his own children?

Assumpta had destroyed her father. She had unknowingly unearthed the man's only known weakness, and Declan, like Michael, could see that, if they weren't careful, someone else was going to step up and take over the businesses. This kind of weakness was treated with the scorn it deserved in the world they inhabited. Patrick was far too influential to let something so personal take precedence over anything else. This kind of trouble was sorted quietly, and that suited everyone concerned. It was the law of the pavement, and was how it would always be. It was how the Costellos had made their mark, how they had taken over someone else's business. The trick was to make sure that the same thing never happened to you.

Declan shook his head, and said quietly, 'Leave him, Michael. You're wasting your fucking time.'

Michael knew that Declan was right. Patrick was oblivious to them. It was frightening, but Michael couldn't help his morbid fascination at the man's obvious lunacy. Patrick looked wrong; he was not just manic, he was without any kind of boundaries or guidelines. Everything that kept them at the top of their game was now going to destroy everything they had worked for. It was unbelievable, and Michael was well aware that he had to be the one to take control, because Declan wouldn't.

Chapter Thirty-Six

Josephine was happier than she had been for a very long time. She was still pregnant, and she was still the only person who knew about it. She was not going to tell anyone until she had to. She had let everyone down so many times in the past, she wasn't going to chance it again. The pain of each loss became more acute – it never lessened. Everyone she saw would give her clichés and pity. It was the pity she hated the most. She could feel this baby inside of her every minute of every day. She felt different this time, she was convinced of that. It felt right somehow. It was her secret to keep, this was her own private happiness. Her silence meant no one was watching her every move, questioning every expression on her face, asking if she was feeling ill, or if she was off-colour, telling her to sit down or lie down as if she was dying or something, searching her face constantly for the first signs of pain, followed by the miscarriage they had been expecting all along. No one forcing her to rest, or sitting with her so she never had any time on her own. It was wearing having so many people caring for you, tiring trying to be upbeat and constantly pretending that you weren't terrified of losing yet another baby down the toilet. This was so much better for her. This was far more relaxing.

She rubbed her belly gently, caressing her child and hoping that this time she might actually get the chance to hold this one in her arms.

Michael's mother was the real bugbear; she felt the woman almost wished the losses on her daughter-in-law. She was a vicious old bitch who saw Michael as hers and no one else's. A child, a *living* child, would cement their marriage and she believed that was something Hannah didn't want. She felt awful even thinking it, but it was the truth.

She heard Michael's car as it crunched on to the driveway. He was early; she had not even thought about any dinner for them – not that he would care, of course.

She could hear him as he walked around the side of the house – he always came through the back door. It was a running joke between them. He said it was his council-house upbringing: out through the front door and in through the back.

Josephine automatically put the kettle on. He always expected a cup of tea. They had become so predictable. She wondered if that was because they had not been blessed with a child yet. A child didn't allow for such routine. It was the reason why people could never make plans, or guarantee their days. A child was also the reason why people like them got married in the first place.

'Good girl, I'm dying for a cuppa.'

Josephine plastered a smile on her face. Then, turning to her husband, she said as gaily as she could, 'Name me one time you have ever come in this house and not had a welcoming cup of tea. It's me job, isn't it? It's what I live for, Michael, catering to your every whim!'

He laughed with her and felt himself relax. It was hard sometimes; Josephine could be sensitive. He adored her with a passion, but he knew that she felt the absence of a child acutely. She would never believe he didn't care either way. She was a very beautiful woman, and she was the only woman he had ever wanted – ever would want. If only she could believe it.

'I want my whims catered to, Josephine. I think you can cater to them tonight, actually,' he said teasingly.

She poured them both out mugs of tea and looked at him assessingly. 'I think I can just about manage that, Michael, if you're good.'

Michael grinned, happy his wife was so cheerful. He wished he felt the same, but all the worry about Patrick was getting to him. He sat down at the kitchen table wearily, and waited for Josephine to bring him his tea. She sat down beside him, and he smiled gently at her. The kitchen table seated eight people comfortably, it could accommodate ten at a push. It was scrubbed pine and, like everything else in the house, tasteful, expensive, and underused.

They had bought this house with such high hopes and, gradually, those hopes had been shattered. Now the house felt too big for the two of them. It seemed to scream loneliness, and it never felt cosy any more. But it was the only home they knew, and leaving it would be like admitting they had failed, and accepting they would never have a child. If, and when, they moved out it would have to be Josephine's choice – never his. It could only be her decision.

She was so pretty, he never tired of looking at her. Suddenly, he noticed that she looked different somehow. 'You look like you're putting on a bit of weight, girl.'

Josephine was pleased at his words. It meant she was doing everything a pregnant woman should do. She really wanted to share the news with him, but she knew she couldn't. They had been there so many times before. If she lost this baby at least he wouldn't have to grieve with her again.

'I think I have actually, Michael. But I'm pleased about it. I lost so much weight after the last baby. I think this means I am finally getting back to normal, eh?'

Michael felt so sad. He understood how hard it was for her to mention anything about the babies she had lost.

'You always look good to me, Josephine, you know that. But I think you're right, mate.'

Josephine sipped her tea, then she changed the subject quickly. 'Did you manage to talk to Patrick?'

Michael scowled angrily. 'Don't go there, Josephine. He's lost the fucking plot. He's always been a bit touched, as you know. That is why he's so successful. He has an air of controlled violence, and no one in their right fucking mind would ever want to cross him. But that's gone now. He is fucking strange. Even Declan is fed up with him.'

Josephine had expected as much. She had seen Patrick for herself, and she had sussed out that he was not firing on all cylinders. He was acting stranger by the day. Carmel was at her wit's end. She wasn't able to cope with the man he had become.

'Carmel told me that he doesn't ever sleep now. He paces the house all night long. The girls are terrified of him. Poor Assumpta feels responsible. Carmel told me that two nights ago he was nearly arrested. He walked into their local off-licence and threatened the bloke behind the counter – accused him of following him. It was only the fact that the local Filth were aware of who he was that saved him from being nicked. They rang Carmel and she had to go and get him. She said he was like a maniac. She's scared of him, what he's capable of.'

Michael had already heard that story from Declan. Patrick had never been the full shilling, but he was now ninety pence short of a fucking pound. It was amazing how much he had deteriorated in the last few weeks. 'Declan told me the story. But he also said that Patrick has lost it before. He's had what the doctors called a "psychotic break" on more than one occasion, just never as pronounced as this. In fact, according to Declan, Patrick has been under a fucking shrink since he was a little kid! He has been as mad as a fucking brush since junior school. As you can imagine, I was thrilled to bits to hear about that at this late stage.'

Michael was baffled by Patrick, and he didn't know what to do about him. This was something that no one could ever have planned for. Now, though, it was here, and it needed sorting out. Declan, as per usual, was leaving the real work to Michael. He didn't want his brother's latest escapade to become common knowledge. He also didn't want to have to sort his brother out personally. He didn't want any responsibility at all – especially the kind that involved him having to make decisions about his older brother. But that was understandable in a way.

'Patrick needs to be put away somewhere – for his own good, let alone everyone else's. He is so fucking far gone, Josephine, I've never seen anything like it in my life. People are already talking about him. He has picked fights with men who we have dealt with for years, accused them of all sorts. These are hard men, but they're not fucking stupid. They can see first-hand that Patrick Costello is a dangerous fuck. He always was – granted – but now he looks and sounds like a fucking card-carrying looney. It can't go on, can it? I have to do whatever is needed to sort this situation out.'

Josephine understood that Michael was unloading his worries on to her. He had always used her as his sounding board – she knew she was the only person he trusted enough to speak so openly to. It helped that she often told him what she knew he wanted to hear.

Josephine shook her head sadly. 'No, you're right, it can't go on, Michael. Patrick needs someone to take the reins for a while, give him time to sort his head out, look after everything so no one can take advantage of him. Only you can do that for him, Michael. You run everything anyway – everyone knows that.

Patrick obviously needs specialist help, and I know Carmel would welcome any support she could get. Reading between the lines, I think she would leave him if it was possible. But you and I both know that is never going to happen. He would see her dead first.'

Michael nodded his agreement. Josephine spoke the truth: Carmel was living on borrowed time. He pulled her from her chair, and on to his lap. He squeezed her to him, enjoying the familiar feel of her body against his. He loved the smell of her hair – she was always so fresh and clean. Even now, without any make-up on, she was still a really good-looking woman. He could feel the extra weight she had gained, and he was happy about that. She had been so thin after losing the last baby. He had been worried about her, but he had known from past experience that she didn't need to be constantly reminded of what had happened. Or question if it could have been avoided somehow. She just carried on as usual – it was her way of coping. But he knew that she grieved inside, that she hurt much more than she would ever have admitted to him or anyone else. He just respected her wishes, and he let her cope in the only way she knew how. If she cried in the night, he held her, comforted her. But, other than that, he played along with her, and pretended nothing had happened.

'I can feel love handles, Josephine! I think you might be getting fat!'

She laughed delightedly at his words. 'I eat lots of chocolate when I'm on my own. I put on a nice sad film, and then I break out the Cadbury's Fruit and Nut!'

He liked hearing her sounding so happy again. It felt as if she was almost back to normal again. He hoped so. He missed her when she was grieving. It was mad really – all the money he earned, and all the love she had inside her, and they couldn't have the one thing that they really wanted. The one thing *she* really wanted. Then there was Assumpta, who was carrying a child she really didn't want. Any other father would have seen it aborted, for no other reason than the girl was a fucking idiot and no one in their right mind would trust her with a baby. She had enough trouble stringing a coherent sentence together. It was so unfair.

He sighed, and hugged his lovely wife tightly to him. As his mum always said, if it was meant to be, then it would happen for them. He wanted it to happen not just because his Josephine deserved it, but because he would finally feel she had everything he had promised her all those years ago, when they were just starting out and life still held endless possibilities. She had never asked for anything, she had always been there for him, and he knew how lucky he was in that way. Nothing he could ever do would change her feelings for him, she loved him without any strings, or any kind of expectations.

She was his world, and that would never change.

Chapter Thirty-Seven

Carmel Costello looked awful, but for once she didn't care. This wasn't about her – this was about her husband.

'Assumpta, will you please shut up! If he hears you carrying on again he will be up here on top of us. Just ignore him.'

Assumpta knew that her mother was talking sense, but her father's shouting was getting too much now. It had been going on for hours. 'Just make him shut up, Mum, please make him stop! He's giving me a headache.'

Carmel grabbed her daughter's wrists tightly. The girl was getting hysterical, and she didn't blame her. Nevertheless, this was something her daughter had brought on herself – had brought on them all with her behaviour. Carmel's job was to emphasise to her daughter the seriousness of what was actually going on.

'Listen to me, girl, and you better listen good. That man down there is not in his right mind. He is capable of *really* hurting us. You know that he cannot be talked to when he is like this. If I thought I could calm him down don't you think I would have been down there hours ago? I'm the one person who has ever been allowed to disagree with him, and that's only when he lets me. Right now, he is beyond reason and if you don't shut the fuck up, he will be up here like an avenging angel and then we will really be in trouble.'

Assumpta was truly terrified now. Her father had been ranting without pause for hours on end, and it wasn't going to let up any time soon.

'Just keep quiet, let him get it out of his system, and hope to God that it's sooner rather than later.'

Chapter Thirty-Eight

Declan was tired out. It was the third time in twenty-four hours that Carmel had rung him to come and help with Patrick. If only Patrick would agree to go into hospital. But he was adamant that he was not going to do *that* again.

He was so fucking paranoid. He was convinced that everyone was plotting against him. It was like dealing with a six-foot toddler, who had no intention of doing anything other than exactly what they wanted.

'Please, Patrick, will you just let me speak for a few minutes?'

Patrick was still manic. Declan could see the toll the lack of sleep was having on his brother. He had seen him like this before, but never this bad. He was all over the place, unable to relax for even a few minutes. It was pitiful to watch him.

'I don't need to do fucking *anything*, Declan. I know that you will just talk shite to me again. I'm telling you what I've told you over and over: I am *not* going into a hospital. I don't *need* to go into a hospital. What I need is to sort things out. What I *need* is to fucking finally remove the people who are standing in my way. Don't you get it? I am surrounded by cunts, absolute cunts.'

Declan sighed. This was going to go on for a while. Carmel wanted to have him sectioned but she was too frightened to be the person to orchestrate that. She wanted Declan to do it and who could blame her?

He knew he *should* do it. It was in all their interests – especially Patrick's – but he couldn't. He couldn't bring himself to put his brother away. It was never going to happen. But seeing him like this was almost as bad. All his life Patrick had been on the borderline, but he had always managed to eventually control himself. His strength of mind was awesome. Patrick had always been very unpredictable but, in the past, he had accepted that about himself. He had understood his own weaknesses and fought to bring them under some kind of control.

It was finding out about his daughters that had tipped him over the edge this time. Declan had heard the rumours about them – especially Assumpta. More than a few people had seen fit to put him wise about his nieces and their lifestyles. The men who had approached him had been sensible enough to know that if Patrick ever got wind of his daughters' antics there would be hell to pay, and they had wanted Patrick to curb his girls before something like this happened. Declan had listened to the gossip, but he had no intention of telling his brother anything.

Carmel hadn't connected with her girls once they had grown up. In Declan's opinion, she was incapable of any real connection with anybody – she was too selfish, too self-absorbed. As long as the girls were well dressed, and their make-up was perfect, she didn't care about anything else. It wasn't that she didn't love them in her own way, it was more down to Carmel's inability to show interest in anyone other than herself. He had never liked her, but he had to admit she did do her best for Patrick. He believed that, in her own way, she loved him – at least as much as she was capable of loving anyone other than herself.

His brother was talking to himself and some of his mutterings were sending chills through Declan's body.

'I know that we have got to take Ozzy Harper out, Declan. We'll go over to his house tonight, and just shoot him, end of.

Quick, clean and neat. It will send a message to everyone then. All the people who have been running me down, slagging me off, taking me for a cunt, will know that they are living on borrowed fucking time. They'll realise that, eventually, I will get round to them as well – and I will do just that, Declan. I swear on our mother's fucking grave. I will take them out, each and every one.'

Patrick was deadly serious, and Declan was appalled. He smiled at his brother, aware that he had to talk him out of this lunacy. It was getting far too fucking dangerous. He was actually contemplating killing a man they had known all their lives, who was a real friend, a decent bloke – and a hard man in his own right.

'I think Ozzy is away, Patrick. I heard he was in Spain. He has a gaff out there, remember? In Marbella. We've stayed there many times.'

Patrick's eyes were darting everywhere. Declan knew his brother was now wondering if *he* could be trusted. Patrick's paranoia was getting worse by the minute. He had to sort this out before Patrick really went postal. Imagine if Patrick had decided to kill someone, and no one was with him to talk him out of it! It could literally cause fucking murders. Or what if his brother took against Carmel or his girls again? He was more than capable of killing them – he had killed before, after all. Only then, he had planned it out beforehand, and it had been nothing more than a means to an end. Now it was just an idea that popped into his head, and he felt honour bound to see it through to the bitter end.

Patrick was confused. 'Are you sure that Ozzy is away, Declan?'

Declan nodded. He glanced around his brother's office, saw that the door was closed and the French windows locked tight. He knew Carmel and the girls were upstairs, prisoners in their own home.

'Why don't we go and meet Michael? He will know for definite where Ozzy is. That way we can be sure, can't we? Michael always keeps tabs on everyone, it's in his nature.'

Declan picked up the phone on the desk casually, and rang Michael's house. He explained quickly and loudly that Patrick wanted to kill Ozzy, but no one was sure if he was in Spain at the moment, so could Michael please meet them at their old offices at the scrapyard. That way they could talk it over together, and plan what they were going to do about it. The scrapyard was the best place because, as Patrick said, all their other offices were bugged.

At the other end of the line, Michael listened to Declan quietly. He could hear the desperation in his voice, and understood that Patrick was obviously completely out of control now.

He kissed Josephine gently on the lips and left her curled up on the sofa watching TV. 'I won't be long, darling. I have to pop out for a while.'

Josephine was used to her husband's odd hours. She smiled her goodbyes. 'See you later, Michael. Try not to be gone all night.'

He didn't answer her.

Chapter Thirty-Nine

Patrick and Declan arrived at the scrapyard and, as expected, Michael was already there. The lights were on in the Portakabin that passed for office space, and Declan noticed that the night watchman and his Doberman were gone. He understood the significance of that. He could not change anything that was going to happen. It had gone too far now.

Patrick didn't seem to notice anything out of the ordinary, however, and he walked quickly towards the offices.

Declan followed his brother slowly into the Portakabin, sorry that it had to come to this, but knowing that there was nothing else to do now. Patrick was a liability, and that could not be tolerated.

Chapter Forty

Michael had planned for this and was leaving nothing to chance. He had given the nightwatchman a decent few quid, and he had willingly gone home with his Doberman who was his closest friend. She was in whelp so, as far as he was concerned, she had earned a few days off. It wasn't the first time he had been asked to leave his post for unexplained reasons. As he was a man who had no interest in anything or anyone – which was exactly why he had been given the job in the first place – he left without question.

As Patrick walked into the offices, Michael was already in place. He was clear that Declan shared his opinion about Patrick and his latest escapades. The fact that Declan had arranged for the meet to be here said it all. This was the only place secure enough to do what was needed. It was quiet, it was dark, and it had the added bonus of being somewhere that Patrick Costello would feel safe.

'You all right, Michael?'

Michael nodded. Even now, Patrick Costello was impressive. He seemed to fill the space with his personality, with his natural charisma. So few people displayed that kind of edge – it was what separated the men from the boys, the real criminals from the wannabes. Even now, completely off his fucking tree, the man still had more nous than most of the people around him. It was such a shame that the man's mental capabilities had finally let him down. The same capabilities that had given him the lead role in the criminal underworld for so long, were now the reason he couldn't ever be trusted again.

Michael walked towards his friend with a smile of greeting on his face, holding out his right hand. As Patrick gripped it, ready for the handshake he expected, Michael pulled him towards him quickly and with his left hand he plunged an eight-inch blade into Patrick's heart.

It was over in seconds.

Michael held Patrick as he crumpled in his arms, and carefully lowered him to the floor, giving him as much dignity as possible. He stood over him with his brother Declan as he bled out. He hoped that the man had not suffered too much.

'Oh my God.' Declan was nearly in tears. He knelt beside his brother's lifeless body.

Michael shrugged. 'My old mum used to say, Declan, I'm glad you think of Him as yours as you will need Him one day. She is a good Catholic, I'll give her that.' He poured two large brandies and, passing one to Declan, he said gently, 'You know this had to happen, mate. It's better this came from us than from someone else, someone who could use it to their advantage. It was quick, and almost painless. We did what was needed and we did it for the right reasons. Remember that.'

Declan knew that Michael was right, but it still felt wrong. For all Patrick had become, he was still his brother. 'I know you're right. But I wish it hadn't come to this.'

Michael didn't answer him. There was nothing he could say to make Declan feel any better. This was one of those things that happened in their world. It wasn't malicious, it was just necessary.

'I want it to look like a robbery, Declan. No one will believe that, of course, but it will satisfy the Old Bill and Carmel will get the insurance.'

Declan nodded. It occurred to him that with his brother's demise, he now, to all intents and purposes, worked for Michael Flynn. Michael was now the new king on the block. Not that he cared – he wouldn't want that kind of responsibility for all the tea in China – or should that be all the heroin the Chinese could supply? He knew Michael was thigh-high in that kind of shit.

Michael was already the go-to man, and Patrick's untimely departure would only give him more power. He wondered if Michael knew just what he was taking on. Without Patrick behind him, Michael Flynn would have to prove his own worth in more ways than one.

It didn't occur to Declan that Michael had always prepared for any and every scenario. He was a man who never once left anything to chance, who thought everything out from every angle possible – that was the reason Patrick had taken him on in the first place. And he had taught him well. Patrick had seen a kindred spirit in Michael Flynn. He had passed on the knowledge needed to be a part of the world Patrick had so carefully created. It was a world of extreme violence, where *everyone* was suspect, where money was made in huge quantities by people who needed not only Patrick's permission but also his know-how. Patrick Costello had never offered an earn until he had worked out every scenario humanly possible. It had been why people saw him as a safe partner. He never took risks, he would lose money before he would ever put himself or anyone he was involved with in any danger. It was what he was good at and why he was so well respected. Now he was gone and, like everyone in the world they inhabited, people would mourn his passing but, other than that, once the shock wore off, he would become just another story people told. It was brutal, but true. Patrick had one flaw: his natural capacity for lunacy. It had been his downfall. It had happened to many men before him. It was also the reason they eventually died violent deaths.

Michael Flynn was always going to get the top spot, it had just been a matter of time. In fairness, Declan knew that Michael would never have sought it unless there had been a good reason. He had thought the world of Patrick, and he had appreciated the man's interest in him and his trust. Declan knew that Michael had only done what was needed, but it still left a bitter taste.

Michael was more than ready to take control of the Costello business – in all honesty, he couldn't wait to get started. After a decent period of mourning, of course.

Chapter Forty-One

Michael felt fantastic. Everyone was giving him their condolences, while letting him know, at the same time, that they were willing to carry on as usual. *That* was the important thing – he needed to be seen as capable of taking over Patrick's role.

He was aware that his hand in Patrick's death – albeit without any hard proof – was already being accepted as a fact of life. Patrick's behaviour before his demise had been seen, noted, and, therefore, his untimely death had been judged a necessary evil.

Now at the man's funeral, Michael Flynn was being fêted as Patrick Costello's natural successor by everyone who mattered. It was more than he could have hoped for. He had been quite happy to fight his corner if needs be – he had worked hard enough for it, after all. But, in reality, he knew that Declan's acceptance of his leadership had been what had really sealed the deal. For all Declan might act the fool, he was far more on the ball than he let on. That he had stood back, today of all days, and let Michael take centre stage spoke volumes. He would always remember that, and appreciate it. He knew that Declan really missed his brother, and so did he. He had loved Patrick Costello – he had been the father he had never known. But Patrick had been the one to teach him the number-one rule – sometimes things had to be done and, as hard as it might be, you could never let emotions cloud your judgement. He had understood that from day one and, like Patrick, he had been determined never to allow his emotions to let him down.

Carmel Costello sat through the service, pleased at the turn out for her husband, but even more pleased that he was gone. She could breathe again, and her daughters could relax. Thanks to Michael, they were safe in every way. Assumpta had got rid of her child already, and now they were all going to move to the house they owned in Spain. For the first time in ages she could actually breathe easily, and relax like a normal person. She finally had Patrick off her back. Not that she hadn't loved him – she had in her own way, and she had lived with his strangeness when necessary – it had been a small price to pay for everything else she had got from the relationship. But, as the time had gone on, he had become a difficult man to deal with, and this last lot had really made her realise just what she was actually dealing with. He had terrified her and the girls, and she had known there was no talking to him, that he was beyond her control.

Carmel had wanted Patrick because of his money and what he could offer her. His reputation had given her security, and that had been his big attraction for her. She had believed that her tantrums and his allowing her to have her say, demand what she wanted, had been because *she* had some kind of control over the life they led. But that had been a sham. Providing she ultimately did what he wanted, he tolerated her antics and that was all. The last few months had opened her eyes, shown her exactly what she had tied herself to, and how precarious her life with him actually was. Patrick was dangerous.

Michael had given her not just her freedom, and her daughters' freedom, but he had also given her the one thing she had never really known existed until now. He had given her peace of mind.

She had watched the way that everyone had gone to Michael, offering their condolences – and their fealty. She hadn't cared that she was relegated to second place. None of that mattered – that was poor Josephine's problem now. She would soon see how difficult it was to be with a man who had to fight every day of his life to keep what he had and who saw skulduggery at every turn. It was hard work.

Chapter Forty-Two

Father Riordan was watching the congregation with a heavy heart. He had tried to leave this parish, but he had been made to stay, against his will. He looked at Michael Flynn, and he wondered at a God who could let a man like that loose on the world, a man who paid his dues to the Church, and who actually believed that he was a good Catholic. It was against everything he had always believed. Oh, he knew of priests back home who had happily heard confessions from the men in the IRA, who saw them as no more than products of their environments, but that could never be him. He believed that the fact that poor Josephine had not been given a child was his God's way of making sure people like Michael Flynn didn't bring any more of his ilk into the world. But that didn't explain why so many other violent men in the parish seemed to have child after child, year after year.

He waited patiently as the coffin was carried from the church on the shoulders of men who were all as violent as they were fêted. He would give Patrick Costello the full funeral Mass, as was his right – he was a Catholic and he was entitled to it. But Father Riordan was also aware that the man was another violent criminal, and he had died by the sword, or by the knife, which was the same thing really. It stuck in his craw. He had no option but to do as he was asked – he had to do as his religion commanded him. Jesus had been a prisoner, unfairly captured, tortured and humiliated. Finally he had died on the cross for the sins of the world – for men like these. His job was to never have an opinion or judge anyone, but it was hard, knowing what he knew about them.

He saw that Michael Flynn and Declan Costello were the lead pallbearers, and they did what was expected of them both with the maximum of respect for the man they were burying. It was the least they could do for the man they both loved in their own ways and, if the gossip was true, who they robbed of his life. It was an open secret, and it would never be questioned. Michael Flynn was too powerful for that now. He was untouchable.

In their world, Patrick Costello had been given a good send off. He had been given his due, for what that was worth.

But Father Riordan hated that he was again a part of it, and he could not do anything about that. He hated that this was what his life had become.

Chapter Forty-Three

'That went well, Michael. Patrick would have been happy with the day.'

Michael smiled sadly. 'I hope so, Declan. None of us wanted this.'

Declan was aware Michael was only speaking the truth even if it hurt. 'Well, Carmel's happy, anyway!'

Michael laughed – Declan had got that much right. Carmel was over the moon at her husband's death, and who could blame her?

'In fairness to her, Declan, she did what she could for him. Somewhere nestled between those expensive tits of hers is a heart. I feel sorry for her, but even she knew it was all over for him.'

Declan sipped his beer. The wake was being held at Michael's house. No one seemed to think that was strange – it was common knowledge that Declan wasn't in a position to host such an event, and the word on the street was that Carmel and her daughters didn't want the responsibility of such a huge undertaking.

It was a big funeral. People had come from all corners of the globe, as was expected. They were not just paying their respects to the man they knew and loved – they were also making sure their earns were safe.

Josephine had done a fantastic job. The whole thing was perfect. The food had been catered – it was expensive and plentiful and she had arranged for waitresses and bar staff to serve the drinks. Now everyone was happily drunk and reminiscing, as was expected at a funeral such as this. Michael's house was plenty big enough to hold such a huge party, and he knew that the fact it was at his *home* would just reinforce his credibility, as well as giving him the opportunity to prove how successful he was. He knew how important it was for him to be seen as a man of means with money behind him. The lifestyle was everything; it was what would define him to the people he'd be dealing with. This was a win-win situation for him, but he was glad that it was nearly over and he could finally get back to normal.

Still, it was nice to see his house full, and watch his wife play the hostess; she did it so well. He was going to make sure that the men he dealt with got the personal touch. He would invite them here with their wives for dinner. He would bring this house to life, and give his Josephine the opportunity to shine. He was so proud of her today. She had taken the onus off Carmel and, at the same time, she had made sure that people saw that he was the real deal. He couldn't help feeling as he looked around him that he was where he deserved to be. He had worked for this. He had learnt from the master, and now he could feel pride in what he had achieved.

He was still a young man, yet he had just inherited the biggest prize of all. He had taken on Patrick Costello's mantle, and no one had questioned that. Michael knew he had his creds, but he had still expected at least one person to challenge him. He planned his defence down to the last detail – he was not going to give anything away without a fucking fight. He was prepared to wipe out anyone who even looked like they might want to try it on. Yet he had been wrong. It seemed that everyone accepted his new role. Personally, he would have been straight in there, sooner rather than later; if he was in their shoes, he would have done everything in his power to take him out. This was the only chance anyone was going to get to push themselves ahead in the game for a long time, Michael was determined about that.

Declan brought him over a large whisky, and he took it gratefully.

'Old Joey Murphy is on top form. He loves a fucking Irish funeral. He wants to sing.'

Michael laughed. It was the icing on the cake. He dragged Declan over to the old boy; he was eighty if he was a day, and an old IRA man. He could cause a fight in an empty house with a drink in him. He had buried his children – three handsome sons. Two had been murdered, the youngest had died in prison of cancer. He was a real character, and he was always given the respect he was due. He was a great singer of Irish songs.

'Come on, Joey, how about "The Wild Colonial Boy"? Patrick always loved that one.'

Joey was thrilled to be singled out, and he sang the song with real feeling, knowing that everyone would join in the chorus.

Michael saw Josephine watching him, and he winked at her, before opening his arms wide. She walked into his embrace unhesitatingly; this was where she always wanted to be.

As the singing swelled around her, Josephine laughed delightedly. The baby was hanging in there, and she felt wonderful. Michael was so caught up in the aftermath of Patrick's death, he still hadn't noticed anything. That was what she wanted. She didn't want anyone to know about her pregnancy – all she wanted was to be left alone long enough to know if this baby was going to be there for the duration. Patrick Costello had inadvertently given her the time she needed to carry this baby inside her without a fuss, and she would always be grateful to him for that. Michael hugged her tightly suddenly, and whispered in her ear, 'I love you, Josephine Flynn.'

And, looking up at him and smiling brightly, she mouthed back, 'I know.'

Chapter Forty-Four

'It's a lot of fucking money, Declan, and I think you deserve to know about it. Now Patrick's gone, it's my call. I never understood why he kept you out of the loop anyway, to be honest. It didn't sit right with me but, while he was alive, I had no option but to let it slide.'

Declan didn't answer Michael. He recognised that Michael was trying to be fair and give him an in. He looked at Michael in his expensive suit, with his perfect haircut; he knew how best to present himself to the world. Men like his brother and Michael Flynn would always want more – it was what made them get up in the morning. They couldn't settle for anything other than being the best, being the main man. They were incapable of ever being content with what they already had. But that wasn't Declan.

'Look, Declan, I just want us to be clear about everything. You are a Costello after all, and I want to bring you into everything so we are both aware of what is going on.'

Declan saw his reflection in the window; he had never liked these offices any more than Patrick had. This was all Michael's idea. Michael had brought them into a new world, and given the Costello name a polish that had been sorely needed.

'Look, Michael, I appreciate what you're trying to do but, honestly, I never wanted anything to do with Patrick's side of the business. I chose to take a step back a long time ago. I only ever partnered him in the day-to-day. I know you mean well, but I have no interest in any of his other businesses – I never did. That was why he wanted you onboard. So do me a favour, mate – leave me out of it.'

Michael was silent for a long while as he digested what he had been told. He had half expected something like this, but he had also wondered if, now that Patrick was out of the frame, Declan might want to be more involved in the real money side of everything. Michael knew that Patrick loved his brother, but didn't exactly consider him as an equal, as someone to respect. Now he saw that Declan was genuinely happy to leave him to it, he was quite happy to do just that. In fact, this suited him down to the ground.

'If that's what you want, Declan. I just wanted you to know that the offer was there.'

Declan grinned. 'I know that, mate, but I am fine as I am. You know something? You're much more like Patrick than you admit. You have the same drive that he had. I never had that myself. I'm easily contented, happy with what I've got.'

Michael knew Declan was speaking the truth. He admired his honesty, but another part of him abhorred the man for his weakness. He had just offered him an in to a world of real money, of real power, and he had refused it point blank. Well, Michael had done what he felt was the right thing, and now he had no option but to carry on by himself.

'I just felt that I should give you the opportunity, that's all, Declan. If you're happy for me to carry on as before, then that's what I'll do.'

Declan shrugged nonchalantly. 'That suits me, Michael.'

Chapter Forty-Five

Josephine was listening to her mother with half an ear. She was already regretting inviting her round. Her mum resented her life with Michael, and that bothered her more than she liked to admit.

'. . . That is what everyone thinks, anyway.' Lana was watching her daughter warily. She had expected a reaction to her words, but it seemed that her Josephine was either unwilling to say anything, or she hadn't been listening. 'Have you bothered to listen to a word I've said?'

Josephine snapped back to reality as she heard the anger in her mother's voice. 'I'm sorry, Mum, I was miles away. What are you on about this time?'

Lana sighed in annoyance. 'I was just saying that people are talking about Patrick Costello's death. No one thinks it was really a mugging.'

Josephine looked at her mother, and felt the urge to slap her face. She knew what she was insinuating, and this wasn't the first time she had tried to bring this conversation up. Josephine stood suddenly. They were, as always, in her kitchen. She had made them both a lovely lunch, and she had tried to pretend that she was enjoying it. But she wasn't. Her mother had been a pain in her arse for a long time now. Well, she was fed up. She couldn't allow her mother to get away with this, not again. 'Just what are you trying to say, Mum?'

Lana could see the bristling anger that her words had caused. It just added fuel to her belief that Michael Flynn had been behind Patrick Costello's death. Everyone thought that, except this daughter of hers.

'I'm not trying to say anything, love. I am just telling you what people are whispering.'

Josephine gave a deep low chuckle as if she was really tickled about something. 'Do you know something, Mum? I couldn't give a flying fuck about what "people" are saying. What I *do* know is my Michael had better not hear it. He wouldn't like to think that "people" are accusing him of murder, because that is what you're trying to say, isn't it? At least that's what you seem to be insinuating anyway.'

It finally dawned on Lana that her daughter would stand by her husband no matter what, even knowing what her husband was capable of. It didn't bother her at all. 'I never said anything of the kind.'

Josephine flapped her hands in front of her mother's face. 'Oh, Mum, will you stop it! It's all you go on about. Now, I am telling you for the last time, any more of this and I will aim you out the door. I mean it.'

Lana knew that her daughter was more than capable of doing just that. 'I wouldn't hurt you for the world, Josephine.'

Josephine looked at Lana, so upset at her mother's words that she was nearly in tears. 'But you *do* hurt me, Mum, you know you do. Every time that you try to say something bad about Michael, you hurt me. I can't do this any more, Mum. It has to stop. What you don't seem to understand is that I don't *care* what he might have done. I don't *care* what you or anyone else thinks. I love him, and he loves me. Nothing else matters.'

Lana was heart-sorry to see her only child so distressed. If only she would see Michael as he truly was. But that wasn't ever going to happen, she knew that now. Even if Josephine did know the whole truth about her husband, she wouldn't care – she had just admitted that.

'I'm sorry, love. I won't ever say another word, I swear. I just worry about you.'

Josephine sat back down, the fight was gone from her. 'Well, don't. Me and Michael are fine. He takes good care of me, Mum. If you bothered to take any notice you would see that for yourself.'

Lana sighed. 'I *can* see that, Josephine. I know he loves you. I know he provides for you. But I'm your mum, it's my job to worry about you. If you had a child of your own you'd understand what I'm saying.'

It was the final insult, and Josephine hated her mother for bringing that up, using motherhood to gain an advantage over her. Well, she had a baby inside her now. But not for anything would she share that with her mother. Instead she walked out of the kitchen leaving her mother sitting there, and up the stairs to her bedroom where she felt no one could hurt her.

Chapter Forty-Six

'This is completely unbelievable. Do you know how much money this is potentially worth, Michael?'

Michael Flynn was smiling. ''Course I do, Jeffrey. More money than you could shake a fucking stick at. But it's dangerous. It'll mean a serious fucking lump if it ever comes to it.'

Jeffrey Palmer laughed. 'I'd already worked that one out. But it's got all the hallmarks of a classic earn. Right up my street.'

Jeffrey Palmer was in good shape for his forty-five years. He had classic good looks too. Men liked him – he was a man's man – and women loved him, which he used to his advantage at every opportunity. He had a good reputation, and he had worked hard for it. He had been a grafter all his life, but he had gone as far as he could. He had accepted that – he'd basically had no choice. Patrick Costello had taken against him, and he had never been able to find out why, but the man had never offered him as much as a crumb from his table. On the rare occasions they had been in the same place, Patrick had barely acknowledged him. Jeffrey didn't know why – what he *did* know was that it certainly wasn't because of anything he had done. He had racked his brain for a reason why the man treated him like a leper, but he could not come up with a thing. He had always given Patrick Costello the respect he commanded, never once said a word about him that could be misconstrued in any way. If Costello had wanted a straightener with him, it had to come from Costello himself. He had more sense than to go looking for trouble. It had rankled though; he had felt slighted, humiliated. But he had eventually accepted it was just one of those things. Patrick Costello was well known for his ability to take against a body overnight. He was a dangerous fuck, and Jeffrey Palmer watched his back; Patrick Costello had not been averse to making people he didn't like disappear if the fancy took him. He was known to get others to do his dirty work – not just as proof of loyalty to him but, more importantly, to make sure the person in question was capable of doing whatever he might ask of them. His death had been tragic for many people, but there were many more who could suddenly breathe a lot easier.

This offer from Michael Flynn was not only going to ratchet him up a notch, it was also going to bring him into the world of serious villainy, and all that entailed.

Michael Flynn was watching Jeffrey closely. He was pleased to be bringing him onboard. Patrick had always taken against the man and Michael knew why. He had taken a real dislike to him for no reason other than he had a thick head of hair, and three strong sons. He was also one of the few men that Patrick Costello couldn't intimidate. Michael knew that the man was wondering why he was being given such an in suddenly. Why he, Michael Flynn, had not respected Patrick Costello's wishes, and kept him outside in honour of the man everyone knew treated him like a son.

'You're very quiet, Jeff.'

Jeffrey Palmer shrugged, but he didn't answer him. He was waiting to hear what the score was, and that was something Michael could understand. Patrick had always told him to let other people talk to find out what you really wanted to know.

Michael spoke. 'I know you're wondering why I've offered you this opportunity, especially as Patrick wasn't exactly your biggest fan. But, for all that, he did admire you. He admired that you never challenged him, or bad-mouthed him. He was a funny fucker. He didn't like you, but he's gone now, and I think you are perfect for what I want.'

Jeffrey Palmer looked around him. He was in Michael Flynn's home, in his private office, and he was impressed at the way the man lived. It wasn't just about having money. Michael lived like a real businessman and his home reflected that. It wasn't the usual mix of expensive shite and ostentatious furniture. Michael's home was like his own – on a larger scale, of course. Like Michael Flynn, Jeffrey had married a decent girl, with a bit of savvy, and the intelligence to grow into the money that was coming in, who read the right magazines, and educated herself about how the other half lived. It was only a shame that Michael and his wife had not been blessed with a child to complete their family.

Jeffrey looked at Michael, and said seriously, 'I never knew why Patrick treated me like he did. I resented him for it, but I also knew there was nothing I could do to change it. The fault, whatever that might have been, wasn't on my side. But I can tell you now, Michael, you won't regret bringing me onboard. This is perfect for me, mate. I have already dipped me toe in, so to speak, and I am aware of the main players we will have to deal with. But I assume that's why you want me.'

It was what Michael wanted to hear. 'I know you're up to speed on the people concerned, but you must remember that this time you will be dealing with them on my behalf. That means you will be the main man – none of them can shit without your say-so now, and they will accept that. They need me to smooth their paths for them, and I will do that as always, but remember, like you, they are still working for me. You will be required to remind them of that, yet oversee everything personally. This will also give you not just added status, but more money than you can imagine. It's already up and running, Jeffrey, all I want from you is to take it over, and then report to me. I'd advise you to put someone in place to oversee your usual earns. This lot is going to take up all your time, believe me.'

Jeffrey Palmer was impressed, but not really shocked; he had expected nothing less. He knew that Michael Flynn would insist on his total dedication to the cause he had offered him, and he was more than willing to do that. This was the opportunity of a lifetime. 'That is a given, Michael. When do you want me to start?'

Michael laughed loudly, with genuine humour; he had known from day one that Jeffrey Palmer would bite his hand off for this opportunity. Getting up, he poured them both large whiskies and, when they were once more settled, he said seriously, 'I will walk you through it, from start to finish, do the introductions to the hierarchy – that's who you will be dealing with from now on. I know you have already tapped into them for your own gain, and that is a big plus as far as I am concerned. Just keep in mind that you are there for me in the future.'

It was a warning.

Jeffrey Palmer smiled. He had good teeth – teeth that he had inherited from his mother, and his sons had been lucky enough to inherit them too. His mother was Irish, strong as an ox, and he could see himself in her. His father, on the other hand, had never been more than a distant memory. He had been murdered when Jeffrey was two years old, shot to death over a game of poker. It wasn't a death worth commemorating; the man had been a piece of shit. Jeffrey had always sworn that his life would amount to something, that he would not be the kind of man his father was – an East-End bullyboy, whose only aim in life was to drink, gamble and engage in small-time villainy to achieve those ends. Jeffrey had made something of himself, lived down his father's name, and his father's memory. Now, thanks to Michael Flynn, he would be able to reach his full potential.

'Listen, Michael, I will do whatever is needed. You know that. I have to ask, though, how much product are we dealing with?'

'A lot more than anyone realises, Jeff. We are shifting about ninety keys a week, and that's just the cocaine. It's big business. We supply everyone who's anyone. Nothing moves without my express say-so.'

Jeffrey Palmer was suitably impressed. He was also working out his cut of the take. 'I understand. It's a big responsibility.'

Michael nodded his agreement, before saying sarcastically, 'I know.'

Michael finished his drink, enjoying the burn as the whisky went down. He was pleased with Jeffrey Palmer. He would do a good job but, more than that, everyone would know that if Patrick Costello was still in the mix, Jeffrey Palmer wouldn't have got a look in. It was Michael's way of letting everyone know that he was his own man. He would make any changes he thought necessary, and on his own terms. He had to make sure the people around him were all *his* men. Patrick Costello had taught him the importance of loyalty, and how giving certain people not just your trust, but also the chance to earn from that trust, was worth more than anything. He knew the truth of that first hand, and now he was going to use that knowledge to his advantage. In his own way, he had loved Patrick Costello; he had been like a father to him. But, like Patrick, he knew that, where business was concerned, emotions had no place. He had the capacity to overlook such trifles; he had understood that when Patrick had insisted he carry out murder for him. He knew now that if he had failed, he would still be no more than a drone, a nobody, and that was something he would always thank Patrick Costello for. He had educated him on the finer points of being a player in the Life. Without him, Michael would be nothing.

Chapter Forty-Seven

Josephine was busy; she had cleaned the house from top to bottom, and now she felt she could face the task of clearing out her overfull wardrobes. She was piling clothes up on the floor, trying to decide which to take to the charity shop, but she was finding it hard, she needed all of them. She was happy, still pregnant, feeling good, and that was what she was focusing on. Michael was so wrapped up in his new role, he didn't have time to think about her. That suited her, she was quite happy enjoying this by herself. This time it was going to be different, she felt that in every way. She felt stronger, more in control of everything this time. It was scary and exhilarating keeping such an enormous secret to herself.

She caught a glimpse of herself in the mirrored wardrobes. She could see the swelling under her clothes and she wanted to cry with happiness. She had to do it this time if it killed her. Unlike with the other pregnancies, she felt full of energy, without the familiar dragging feeling inside her belly, or the constant tiredness. She woke up feeling rejuvenated, ready for each new day. She had gradually lost contact with all her old school friends – they had all had babies, and she had not been able to stand it in the end. She still saw them socially, but that was about it. She had hated herself for the jealousy she had felt every time she had seen them hold the babies they had produced, hated herself for not being happy for them, for the bitterness she felt. It was nature, a natural thing that was expected of any woman, and yet she had been denied it over and over again. But not this time.

She heard Michael bounding up the stairs; as always he had come in search of her. It was so touching. She felt a rush of love wash over her. He stood in the bedroom doorway, and she marvelled at the sight of him. He was such a good-looking man, and he still had the power to excite her, make her want him.

'You having a clear out, then?'

She smiled at him, happy to see him. 'Not before time, Michael. I'm starting on your wardrobes next.'

He grinned. 'Go for it. I'm enjoying seeing you so lively.' He was quiet for a few moments before saying softly, 'It suits you.'

Josephine laughed. 'What suits me?'

He was beside her now, and pulling her into his arms. She loved the feel of him, he made her feel so safe and secure.

He kissed her forehead gently, before saying, 'Being pregnant, Josephine. It suits you, darling. But when were you going to tell me?'

She pulled away slightly to look into his eyes, and she could see the sorrow there, mixed with bewilderment and happiness. 'How long have you known, Michael?'

He hugged her to him closely. 'A while, Josephine. I've been waiting for you to tell me yourself.'

She wanted to cry, but she couldn't. He knew, and now she felt a fool – of course he would have known. He wasn't stupid. But she had really believed she had kept it secret, and that she had done so for his benefit, not hers.

'Oh, Michael, I didn't tell anyone, not a soul – no one knows. I thought if it all went wrong, I wouldn't have to live with the feelings of inadequacy. I wouldn't have to listen to the well-meaning clichés. If no one knew I could deal with it all myself.'

Michael felt the tears come into his eyes at her generosity of spirit. She wanted to save him hurt, and that was such a selfless act on her part. 'You silly bitch! I sussed a while ago. I wish you would listen to me, Josephine. If we have a baby I will be made up, but for you more than for me. As long as I have you I don't need anyone else. I swear that on my immortal soul.' He hugged her even tighter, raining kisses all over her face.

Josephine knew he was speaking the truth, but it still didn't make her feel any better. 'I'm so sorry, Michael, I just wanted to do this by myself. I would have told you eventually. I'm amazed that you noticed, to be honest.'

Michael was offended. 'Of course I did, Josephine! You're my world, for fuck's sake.'

Josephine looked into the handsome face she knew so well. She could see his anger, mingled with his despair, and she hated herself for causing it. He had only ever loved her, given her his love and his protection no matter what. 'Can you do me one favour, Michael? Keep this between us, please. I don't want anyone to know about it. If I lose it, I don't want it to be common knowledge. I couldn't go through that again.'

Michael sighed heavily. ''Course, darling. Whatever you want to do is fine by me.'

'Thanks, Michael. It's just I can't pretend any more. Your mum is always making remarks about how we should have a family by now, and my mum acts like miscarriages happen to everyone. It's too raw for me. Every time it goes wrong I feel such a fucking failure. I feel so bereft. If I do lose this baby, Michael, I want it to be a private grief this time. I want it to be our sorrow, no one else's.'

Michael could hear the longing in his wife's voice, the need for a child, and the fear that once more she would be denied that, because her body would let her down as it always had. He would gladly hand over every penny he had if it would give her a child of her own, and the peace it would bring to her.

'I promise you, Josephine, I won't say a word.'

She nestled into his arms, and he felt the overwhelming love for her that had never changed. He loved her unconditionally. 'How are you feeling, though? Do you feel all right in yourself?'

She nodded and, pulling away from him again, she looked up into his face. 'That's just it, Michael, I feel great. I feel better than I ever have before. This time it feels so right. I can't explain it. If it's going to happen for us, I think it will be this time.'

'Oh, my darling, I hope you're right.'

As he pulled her into his body once more, he was praying that she was right this time. But whatever happened, he knew he had no choice; he had to look after her as best he could.

Chapter Forty-Eight

Declan was tired out. He had a new little bird and she was more than willing in every way possible. She was only twenty-two, and she was built for pleasure. She had a lovely little face, blue eyes, thick blond hair and creamy skin, coupled with a pair of thirty-six D cups. She was also gifted with a mouth like a docker, and that, unfortunately for her, coupled with her desire to be married, was her main drawback. Declan was already on the look-out for a new conquest. Deirdre, though, was not about to be sidelined.

He had been here before – many times – and he had always managed to extricate himself from the lady in question. He wished they would listen to him from the off; he *told* them he wanted nothing from them other than a good time. He would always give them a nice parting gift – generally a few quid – or, if they were a bit posh, an expensive piece of jewellery. Deirdre, though, seemed determined to be around for the duration.

As he stood by the bar in the nightclub he had just opened with Michael, he felt irritation wash over him. Girls like Deirdre were born to be used – it was their lot in life. He could see her out of the corner of his eye – she was wearing fewer clothes than a professional athlete, and she was giving him the evil eye as if he might actually give a fuck. He was glad to see Michael walking over to him and, as they shook hands, he turned his back on his offending girlfriend with relief.

'What a fucking success, Declan! It's fabulous. Well done.'

Declan was pleased. He had worked hard on this place. He had acquired it as payment for a long-term debt. The man involved had a real passion for the gee-gees; unfortunately, the gee-gees didn't have a passion for him. Declan had given him a good deal on the loans, and a generous time span for paying him back. Neither had been appreciated, of course, but that was a compulsive gambler for you. The man in question had eventually been given no other option than to sign the place over and walk away, debt-free.

Declan had revamped it, renamed it, and now all he had to do was sit back and coin it in. It was a gold mine. It was located in East London with plenty of pubs and restaurants nearby and, best of all, it was now licensed for everything from live bands to boxing matches. The Costello firm, run by Michael Flynn, still owned enough Filth to guarantee anything they might feel they wanted. This was going to be a real earner; it had five bars over two floors, a huge dancing area, a glitterball that could pass for a spaceship and, like all their premises, the only people who could deal drugs were in their employ.

'I think it will pay us well, Michael.'

Michael grinned. 'I don't think you need worry about that, mate. I would worry about that bird behind you, though – I think she's out for a fight.'

Deirdre was tapping him on his shoulder, as if she had every right to be there. He rolled his eyes at Michael, who he could see thought this was absolutely hilarious. He turned slightly towards her and, opening his arms in a gesture of supplication, he said, 'What now?'

Deirdre looked at him with barely concealed malice.

Michael could see that Declan was not in the mood for a drama; this was *his* night, and he was clearly embarrassed because it was happening in front of him. Since Patrick had gone, Declan treated Michael with the same respect he had always given his older brother. It was instinctive. Although he had refused Michael's offer of a partnership, he still treasured his own place as a Costello, and the respect that demanded.

'What do you mean by that?'

Michael looked at the girl properly; she was a looker, but then all Declan's amours were lookers. He wouldn't bother otherwise – womanising was his hobby. This one had a mouth on her, though, and she wasn't going without a fight. Declan was willing her to take the hint and go away. But Deirdre was far too drunk, and full to the brim with righteous anger. She was going to have her say publicly and as loudly as possible.

Michael stepped forward and, grabbing her arm roughly, he said quietly, 'If you don't fuck off, you filthy little skank, I am going to get my blokes to drag you out of here and then I will personally see to it that you can never show your face within a ten-mile radius. I can do that. Declan can do that too but, unlike me, he's a nice guy. Now do yourself a favour, and fuck off.'

Deirdre was frightened now. This was Michael Flynn, and he was a Face, a real Face. That he had threatened her was something to be taken seriously, and she knew it. His words had sobered her up and, when he pushed her away from him, she nearly lost her balance.

Michael put his arm around Declan's shoulders, and she saw him pull Declan around till they were both facing the bar which meant they had their backs to her. It was the ultimate insult. Michael Flynn would not be in any company that reflected badly on him, or his world, he had made that more than clear. She walked away quickly; all she wanted now was to go home and lick her wounds.

Declan watched her walk away in the mirrors behind the bar area and, shaking his head slowly, he said gratefully, 'Michael, that was fucking priceless.'

Michael laughed. He knew they were being observed, and he played the game, but was annoyed that the situation had ever arisen, especially on a night such as this. They were being watched by everyone, which was all part and parcel of the world they inhabited. People knew who they were, and they wanted to be a part of it, no matter how small that part might be. They were interesting because of *who* they were. They were the people who between them ran more or less everything around them, including this new nightclub. He certainly wasn't about to let a slag like that make a scene, and show him up. He would cut her fucking head off first and ram it down her neck.

He was smiling jovially though as he said, 'You, my old friend, need to fucking grow a pair, and grow them fucking soon. Never, and I mean never, let a cunt like that think she has the right to cause a scene. It's a sign of weakness but, worse than that, it's a reflection on us. We are men who rely on our reputations – without them we are nothing. The fact she thought she could cunt you in front of me is fucking outrageous. Like I am going to swallow that, for fuck's sake! I wouldn't take that shit off my Josephine and I'm fucking married to her.'

Declan didn't answer for a while, he didn't know what to say. But he knew that Michael was right. Deirdre would have caused the Third World War if Michael hadn't stopped her, and she would have loved every second of it. He should have nipped it in the bud. 'I'm sorry, Michael. You know me – I like the lairy ones. But you're right. It will never happen again, I will make sure of that.'

Michael gestured for two more drinks, and the barmaid was there in nanoseconds. 'Good. I'm glad to hear it. Now, let's enjoy the night. We have to mingle with the punters, give them their money's worth, but I need a few more drinks first!'

Declan laughed. 'Welcome to my world!'

Michael was pleased to see Jeffrey Palmer and his crew making their way across the dance floor. He felt himself relaxing. He knew that, by the end of the night, everyone who was anyone would make their way over to him, and he would give them free drinks, and listen patiently to their life stories. It would guarantee the club's success, and he would have done his bit for public relations.

The music was loud, the place was packed out, and his expert eye was making sure the bouncers were all where they should be, and the bar staff were fast and efficient. It was second nature to him now, making sure everything was running smoothly, looking out for flaws, and working out a solution to any problems he might encounter. Patrick Costello had taught him well, and as he listened to yet another tale of derring-do from a wannabe Face intent on impressing him, he realised just how much he actually missed him.

Chapter Forty-Nine

Jermaine O'Shay was a very large Jamaican – he was into body building, and he spent at least two hours a day in the gym. He was not a handsome man, but he was imposing, standing at over six feet tall and naturally big-boned. He was a man who looked dangerous. His size guaranteed that, as did his bald head, along with his permanent scowl. Women, however, loved him. He was a man who knew the power he wielded, and who used it to his advantage. In reality, although he was capable of great violence should the situation merit it, he was actually a nice guy. Like Michael Flynn, he understood the need to exude a persona. And, like Michael Flynn, he ruled his little empire with a mixture of fear tempered with kindness. He surrounded himself with people he trusted, who he could relax and be himself with. Patrick Costello had offered him a partnership, and that had been a defining moment in his life. He had known how to import drugs, and he had made a good living from that. Patrick Costello had then entered his life, and shown him how, not only to utilise his contacts, but how to maximise his return. With Patrick Costello's backing, he had become a big player almost overnight.

Now, though, he was in a quandary. Michael Flynn was a perfect replacement for Patrick Costello, he could never refute that. Nothing had changed – it was as if Patrick Costello was still alive. Jermaine had dealt with Michael Flynn, as per usual, and everything had been fine. But now, Michael suddenly wanted him to deal with Jeffrey Palmer, and he wasn't sure about that. He liked the way things were – he wasn't a man who relished change.

He was sitting in the bar of his private club, nursing a rum and Coke. His club was just off the Railton Road, and only accessible to certain people. It was small, but his clientele liked that. It was a place where people could relax without worrying about what they might say or who they said it to. He catered for people like himself, who needed to keep a degree of privacy, and who were also willing to pay for that.

He heard Michael before he saw him. He was greeting the doorman as usual and, as he walked down the stairway into the bar, he was laughing. Jermaine stood up, and Michael shook his hand firmly. He then stood aside and Jermaine found himself shaking Jeffrey Palmer's outstretched hand.

There wasn't anyone tending the bar so early in the day, so Jermaine walked behind the counter himself. 'What can I get you?'

Michael Flynn sat down on the banquette in the corner. It was newly re-covered in gold and green brocade. Jeffrey Palmer sat beside him, looking around him with interest. Jermaine was glad he had upgraded the place. He had a sneaky feeling that this wasn't Jeffrey Palmer's usual kind of drinking establishment.

'A couple of whiskies, mate, and not any of that fucking knock-off either! I nearly lost the enamel off my teeth last time.'

Jermaine laughed. 'I told you, man, if you're putting Coca-Cola in it, you don't deserve the good stuff. My old dad would turn in his grave if I allowed a decent Scotch to be diluted with that shit.'

Michael nodded. 'He has a point, in all fairness, Jeffrey. But, when I come down here, I have to put something in the drinks – otherwise I would be flat out in no time.'

Jermaine grinned. 'Call yourself a fucking Irishman?'

Jeffrey laughed with them. 'Was your dad Irish then, Jermaine? I mean, with your name being O'Shay? It don't get more Irish than that, does it?'

Jermaine brought the drinks to the table and, sitting down beside them, he answered, 'My great-granddad was Irish, but it's been all black since then.'

Jeffrey wasn't sure how to react, and Jermaine could see that. He liked that he didn't want to offend in any way. That showed him the man wasn't racist – not outwardly anyway. Only time would tell.

'If you go to Jamaica, everyone has some Irish in them somewhere. Some even have blue eyes. It's fucking surreal. There are Patricks and Seans everywhere. We also like the Guinness – my mum used to call us the sunburnt Irishmen.'

Michael laughed loudly; he had heard this before, many times. He knew that Jermaine was proud of his Irish heritage, and even more proud of his Jamaican roots.

Jeffrey sipped his drink, and was pleased when he realised it was a good Irish malt. Like Jermaine, he had not been looking forward to this meeting; he had only dealt with the men who worked for Jermaine until now. A few keys here and there, mainly cocaine, and a lot of grass. When possible, he scored some Blond. Lebanese Gold was a really sought after product. Unlike the Black, that came from Afghanistan, the Gold always guaranteed a mellow buzz. There was a lot of Blond coming in from the States – Acapulco Gold – but it was the Lebanese that people were willing to pay for.

Michael was quiet, watching the two men as they circled each other. He knew that neither man wanted it, but both these men would do their best to accommodate him. He supplied their wages because, without his permission, they basically couldn't operate. He was in the wonderful position of allowing people to earn without hindrance. If he was involved, he could guarantee the minimum police interference, and the opportunity to work with like-minded individuals, giving them the chance to not only expand their businesses, but also their earnings.

'Jeffrey, if you do take over from Michael, we will have to meet regularly, at least twice a week. I need to know everything at least a month in advance. I'm sure Michael has explained all that.'

Jeffrey was surprised to find he was almost enjoying himself. Jermaine O'Shay was a man much like himself, aware of his own capabilities, and who disliked change. Like himself, Jermaine had no option but to work with whoever Michael Flynn told him to work with. That was a difficult thing for men like them, who were the head of their own firms, and respected by the people they employed. He was now on Jermaine O'Shay's turf, in the man's own drinking club, so he had to be the one who bent over. Like Michael Flynn, Jeffrey knew the value of humility, how it could be used to gain an advantage. It was a deadly weapon if employed properly. It could mask the violence that lurked underneath.

'Oh, yeah, I understand how this needs to work, mate. I just hope you are OK about us working together. I've been in touch with some of your boys for a while now, as I'm sure you already know. Now that Michael has given me this opportunity, I just want to make a success of it.'

Michael was impressed. He had hoped that Jeffrey Palmer would understand the situation with Jermaine, and work with him, but he had not expected Jeffrey Palmer, who could turn on a coin if the fancy took him, to humble himself for the greater good. It pleased him; he felt he had chosen wisely.

Jermaine O'Shay walked back behind the bar and, bringing back the bottle of malt, he poured them each another large drink, before saying sincerely, 'To us. The new order.'

Michael grinned. 'I'll drink to that.'

He was tired out. He had never completely understood just how much Patrick Costello had actually done until now. He had assumed that Patrick had given *him* the lion's share of the work. Now, though, he realised that the real money was what Patrick had concentrated on, and that was a full-time job in itself. Michael was having to work day and night to keep on top of everything and, even though he was given the same respect as Patrick Costello, he didn't have a Michael of his own, so he was having to gradually farm the lesser work out. He had not been too bothered at first, knowing that he just had to find the right people for the right jobs, and that might take time.

Josephine being pregnant again had changed everything. He needed to get things in place as soon as possible so he could concentrate on her. She was a diamond, never complaining about his late nights, always ready to listen to him. He knew she would stand by him through anything life might throw at them. Now it was his turn, and he wanted to be there for her. He would do anything to see that this child came into the world. She deserved a baby so much, and her craving for a child of her own was painful to watch. He owed her this, and no matter what happened, he was going to be there beside her.

Chapter Fifty

'Michael, will you go out, please? I am *OK*.'

Her husband was starting to get on Josephine's nerves now. He was always asking how she was, staying in with her, offering everything from back rubs to cups of tea. It was wearing her out. All this attention was really irritating, and he watched her like a hawk.

'I just want to help you, darling.'

Josephine sighed. 'You want to help me, do you?'

Michael nodded. He looked like a lost Boy Scout. 'Of course I do.'

'Then go out, will you? I know you have loads of stuff to sort out. I also know you want to help me. But all I want is a bit of space. I am OK! I feel good. But you're making me feel nervous, like you're waiting for this to go wrong.'

Michael was devastated. He was trying to be the good guy. He was worried about her, and he *was* worried that she might lose the baby. It would obliterate her, as it always had. 'Oh, darling, I just want you to know you are my priority. I spend so much time out and about. I love you. I want to be there for you.'

Josephine smiled sadly. 'I love you, Michael, you know that. But you are like a fucking bad smell lately, hanging around here. You're normally out all hours of the day and night. I've never once questioned that, have I? I accept that it's part and parcel of your job. Now, though, if I even fart, you're standing behind me. It is driving me mad. I can call you if I need you.'

Michael was looking at his wife, saw the way she was trying to keep as calm as possible, and knew he was getting on her nerves. He was getting on his own fucking nerves! But his real fear was that, if she lost this child too, she would not cope with it as well as she seemed to think. She was convinced this time was different somehow, but he wasn't so sure. He felt it might be wishful thinking on her part, and who could blame her? She saw the doctor regularly, and everything seemed fine, but that was how it had been in the past. He would gladly give ten years off his life, if it meant she could have a child of her own.

'Look, Josephine, I know what you're saying, darling. But I care about you, and I worry about you.'

Josephine closed her eyes in distress. Sometimes men were so thick! It was all about Michael really, but he couldn't see that. He was waiting for her to fail again. Oh, he never said that, of course! But she knew him better than anyone else in the world. He was scared for her if this all went pear-shaped again.

'Well, do you know what, Michael? Don't worry about me, OK? Just let me be. You're stressing me out, can't you see that? I have sat here night after night, all on my Jack Jones, for years, and I have learnt to live with that, live with your work, and the odd hours. I even have a routine. Bet you never knew that. I watch certain programmes, I have a nice bath, I go to bed and I read. I've learnt to cope *without* you and I like a bit of peace in my own home. So I am begging you, Michael, *please*, will you stop treating me like a fucking invalid? I know that this child might not come to term, I know that better than anyone, believe me. Been there, done that, remember? Many times. Go out, do your job, and let me do mine.'

Michael could see that Josephine was serious, and she had a

point. He was letting the business slide, and that was not good for either of them. He should be out there, sorting out the mess that Patrick Costello had left behind. But he also felt he should be there for his wife.

'All night that phone has been going in your office, Michael, but you won't answer it. You just sit here like a nun at a stag do. You make me nervous. Answer the fucking thing, and do what's needed.' She grabbed his hand tightly. 'I know how difficult it's been for you. Patrick left a big hole. You have a lot to contend with, so will you just get on with it? I feel like I'm keeping you from your business. I don't want that, Michael, and, if you're really honest, neither do you.'

The office phone was ringing again, and she could see that Michael was torn once more. 'Answer the fucking thing, will you, Michael? Put us all out of our misery.'

He laughed despite himself. He knew how lucky he was to have her. She never asked anything of him, she just accepted him for who he was. She wasn't a fool either, she knew the score – knew what he was all about. He stood up, and walked from the room to answer the phone.

Josephine laid back against the sofa cushions, and sighed in relief. She cupped her belly with her hands, content with the new life she had inside her, and the promise of some well-needed peace and quiet. Michael had to let her deal with this in her own way. She didn't need a babysitter, she just needed to feel in control of her own life. She closed her eyes, tired out. She just wanted her bed and some sleep.

Michael came back into the room a few minutes later, and she could see he was worried about something.

'I have to nip out, darling.'

She smiled gently. 'All I can say is, thank fuck for that!'

Chapter Fifty-One

Declan was seriously worried. *He* had never had to deal with a situation like this before – his brother had made sure of that. Patrick knew the value of speed in these kind of situations. Michael was finally on his way, but it just wasn't good enough. He should have been here ages ago, and he would tell him that as well. Michael was like a fucking ghost these days, drifting in and out at his leisure. It was a travesty. He was supposed to be the big boss now, and it seemed to Declan that Michael Flynn had dropped the fucking ball. He needed to up his game, because the people he dealt with looked for weakness and, if they found it, they went in for the kill.

He sat down. The Portakabin was too hot, stuffy, and it fucking stank. He lit a cigar, and puffed on it deeply. The smell of his big Churchill would mask anything and, as this place stank like a Turkish wrestler's jockstrap, he welcomed the tobacco's distinct aroma.

He could hear the swearing and threats coming from the other room, and he closed his eyes in annoyance. This wasn't his gig – this was Michael Flynn's territory. He didn't like being dragged into it all, but he had no choice in the matter. Someone had to do something before it got out of hand. This was the kind of situation that could easily cause a war.

He saw the headlights of a car as it pulled up outside, and he waited patiently for Michael to join him. He was really aggravated, but he knew he had to keep a lid on it until this was all sorted out. One thing at a time, had always been Patrick's mantra, and Declan chose to live by it.

Michael opened the door and, as he walked in, Declan saw that the man was already angry. 'Tell me this is a fucking joke, Declan.'

Declan shook his head, nervous suddenly. Michael Flynn looked fit to be tied, and that wasn't a good thing. 'Like I'd bring you out at this time of night for a fucking laugh. I've been trying to get you all evening. This is your fucking business, Michael, not mine.'

Michael knew he was right. He should have answered the phone – no one rang the house unless it was important. Josephine was his only weak spot, his Achilles heel. He had fucked up big time.

'So, come on then, what fucking happened?'

Declan realised that the man in the next room had suddenly gone quiet. He assumed that he had heard Michael's voice, and was now rapidly sobering up and wondering how he could get out of the situation he had caused.

Declan puffed on his cigar for a few moments. 'Jeffrey Palmer was in the new club having a few drinks, and who should turn up there mob-handed, full of drink, drugs and God knows what else? Only Kelvin McCarthy. He homed straight in on Jeffrey. It was fucking outrageous, Michael. Jeffrey was good in all fairness, he swallowed a lot. More than I fucking would have if it was me. But it got out of hand. Jeffrey was going to give him a well-deserved slap, and Kelvin pulled a gun on him – in full view of everyone. Thank fuck we were in the top bar. Most of the people there know the score. But it was fucking hairy, I tell you. He would have shot him and all, but young Danny

Kirby wrestled the gun off him. He is worth watching, that lad. He saved us all a fucking serious nightmare tonight. Anyway, to cut a long story short, I have got Kelvin in there.' He gestured towards the door that led to the other room in the Portakabin. 'We bundled Kelvin out of there as fast as we could. But Jeffrey Palmer is not going to let this drop, and who could blame him? It was a public humiliation. It's just that Kelvin's father is a different kettle of fish as you know. Christie McCarthy is a fucking known Face, and he has a big crew behind him. He also has a son who is about as much use as a nun's cunt. The bugbear is he is *still* his son.'

Michael looked around him quickly, his mind working overtime. This was a real problem in more ways than one. He admired and respected Christie McCarthy. He was one of the few people they didn't do business with although they had requested his services on occasion. Christie McCarthy was actually the only person capable of taking him on. He was also one of the few people that Patrick Costello had genuinely liked. They had grown up together, and they had always had a good relationship. Christie McCarthy pretty much kept himself to himself. He had long-term businesses that were not just very lucrative, but were also specialised. He was the go-to man if you needed someone to disappear permanently but, for whatever reason, you couldn't be seen to be involved. He was also a very experienced mediator who could not only solve certain problems between the warring factions, but who was also guaranteed to be without any bias whatsoever. That was his expertise. He had made his living from his ability to facilitate any kind of meeting, even between sworn enemies. He would then act as the mediator for their talks, and no one had ever dared to take advantage of him, use the meeting for their own ends or for payback. Christie McCarthy wasn't a man who would allow anything like that to happen; after all, this was his bread and butter. He could also provide any service that might be needed, from a getaway driver to a bent barrister. His forte was his wide range of contacts and his reputation as a man who delivered.

But now his son had been the catalyst for a situation so serious it could easily deteriorate into a fucking war.

Michael walked into the other office. Kelvin McCarthy was sitting on an old typing chair tied up like a kipper. Michael could see the fear in the boy's deep-blue eyes. He was his father's son, there was no doubting that. He had the same arched eyebrows and thick black hair and, like his father, his face had the dark shadow of a man who needed to shave twice a day. He was Christie's living image – a handsome fucker – but that's where the similarity ended. Personality-wise, he was the antithesis of his old man. He was a weak-willed, vicious bully, who traded on his father's name, and his father's reputation. Well, he had picked a fight with the wrong people this time.

Declan walked into the room behind him, and Michael knew he was wondering, along with Kelvin McCarthy, what was going to happen. His incarceration had clearly thrown Kelvin off kilter. He had not expected to be treated so roughly, nor so carelessly. Never before had anyone ever dared to bring him to book. He had always been given a pass, and his father had smoothed things over.

'How old are you, Kelvin?' Michael's voice was casual, even interested.

Kelvin could detect no real anger, and he felt himself relax a little. The fact he had been brought here worried him. He knew enough about the Life to realise that Michael Flynn wasn't a man to be crossed lightly and that even his father would balk at a face-to-face with him.

As he was sobering up, and coming down from the pills he

had popped like sweets, he understood for the first time in his life that he was in real trouble.

'I'm twenty-six.'

Michael didn't answer him immediately. He just stood there looking at him. Under the man's gaze, Kelvin felt the first flush of shame wash over him.

'Did you hear that, Declan? He's twenty-six years old, for fuck's sake.'

Declan Costello knew how to play the game, so he said nonchalantly, 'I heard him all right.'

'Fucking amazing though, isn't it, Declan? Twenty-six, and a completely fucking useless cunt. That has got to hurt your old man – he has to be ashamed of you, Kelvin. Can I call you Kelvin, by the way?'

Kelvin McCarthy nodded his agreement. He didn't know what else to do; he had never been in a situation like this in his life. ''Course you can. It's my name, after all.' He tried to lighten the heavy atmosphere that permeated the room, acting like he wasn't bothered about being trussed up like a chicken and unable to move.

Michael Flynn stared at him for long moments. Kelvin McCarthy watched him warily. His eyes were ice cold; he looked capable of anything. Kelvin knew instinctively that he *was*. He possessed no fear of anyone or anything.

'You can call me Mr Flynn.'

Kelvin McCarthy was suddenly feeling very frightened, and that was an alien concept to him. All his life, he had been cushioned by his name. Now he was feeling the terror that being at the mercy of a man like Michael Flynn could elicit. Kelvin McCarthy was a coward really. He had always traded on his father's name, and that had been enough to get him what he wanted, and guarantee him a level of protection. He wasn't so sure about that any more. But he still believed that, whatever happened, no one would harm him because his father was Christie McCarthy, and that alone gave him the criminal equivalent of diplomatic status. His father's name and his reputation was like money in the bank. He had worked with everyone who mattered, from Jack Spot to the Krays and the Richardsons, and had carved for himself a unique place in the world of villainy. He provided a service that no one else could even attempt to emulate. His word was his bond. His whole business relied on his reputation as a man of the utmost integrity, who could be trusted without question. That was his father's main strength, and why his father was so respected in his world. It was also why he felt that even someone like Michael Flynn would think twice before he did anything that might cause a rift between them.

Kelvin watched Michael warily. The man was completely relaxed, and that alone was unnerving. He was acting as if this was an everyday occurrence.

'So, Kelvin, what do you think I should do with you?'

Declan Costello walked from the room, and busied himself pouring them both large whiskies. He had a feeling they were going to need them. Michael was baiting the boy, and he hoped that Kelvin had the brain capacity to give him the answers he expected. He didn't hold out much hope though – he could see the boy was rattled.

Michael accepted the glass of whisky from Declan, and took a large gulp. He was enjoying Kelvin's fear. He needed to be made aware of his actions. 'I mean, think about it from my point of view. You came into my club, and you then caused a big fucking scene. You even had the fucking audacity to pull a gun on a very good friend of mine. I mean, think about it logically, Kelvin. I can't let this go, can I?'

Kelvin McCarthy was hurting everywhere. He was bound

tightly, and he couldn't move his arms at all. He was also tired out. He had the hangover from hell, and Michael Flynn was treating him like a fucking no one. He was threatening him, and Kelvin McCarthy felt that he should remind the man of who he was actually dealing with. He was scared, but he was also aware that his father would not allow anything to happen to him. His natural arrogance was coming to the fore. He was safe as the proverbial houses. Michael Flynn wasn't going to really harm him – he wouldn't dare. His dad had always stepped in and smoothed everything over. He had stepped over the line, and he would have to pay dearly when his dad learnt the whole story. But that was the point – his dad would ultimately be the one to punish him for his sins, no one else. That is how it had always been.

He sighed theatrically. He could feign abject contrition in his sleep; he had been doing it since he was fifteen and his dad had found out he was a thief. 'Look, Mr Flynn, I admit it. I fucked up big time. It won't happen again, believe me. I have learnt my lesson the hard way. But this is dragging on too long now, OK? My joints are screaming with pain, and I can't feel my hands. I've been tied up like this for fucking hours. My dad will be wondering where I am. The people I was with last night will eventually have to tell him what happened – that's if he hasn't heard already, of course – but I will explain to him that it was all my fault. I swear to you both, on my mother's life, that I will walk away from this without any malice towards you whatsoever.'

Michael Flynn listened to him intently, but he showed no reaction to his speech.

Declan walked from the room slowly and, once more, seated himself behind the big old desk that his brother had bought at an auction years before. He picked up the bottle of Glenfiddich and poured himself out another generous measure. He knocked it back quickly, and immediately poured himself out another large glass. The dawn was breaking. He could hear cars in the distance, the sound of people going to work, to jobs that paid the same wage week after week, year after fucking year. It was completely alien to him, that kind of life. But, as Patrick had always said, without people like them, Britain would be fucked. They were the people who kept the country going, who worked in the industries that made Britain great. They were the backbone of the country; without them and the work ethic they possessed, Patrick had always said Britain would die on its feet. There was a beautiful logic in there somewhere, a brutal truth that couldn't be denied. He sighed heavily, and looked at Michael warily. He was still standing there, not even a movement or a word to indicate he had heard anything that Kelvin McCarthy had said.

Michael could see the confusion on Kelvin's smug face. He had expected a reaction to his little speech. But Michael knew, deep in his heart, that he was never going to give this ponce a swerve. He looked at the man once more. He had everything a man could want. He was big, handsome, he had a fuck-off head of hair, and a father who would have gladly given him the earth on a plate. But he viewed his own father as nothing more than a fucking weapon, used him as a guarantee so he would never have to pay for his mistakes personally. That a man like Christie McCarthy could produce such a fucking weak-willed, avaricious, lazy, vicious, useless ponce like this was beyond Michael's ken. He would rather be childless than have to own up to fathering someone as heinous as Kelvin McCarthy. Even now, the man thought his name could excuse everything he had done. Michael was so disgusted, and so ashamed for Christie McCarthy, a truly great man. To know that he had produced such a fucking ingrate must be the worst thing a man could experience.

Michael went into the office where Declan was sitting quietly and, pulling out an old chair from the back of the room, he sat opposite him, and held out his empty glass. Declan filled it for him, and they both smiled suddenly.

'Patrick would never have sat there like you. He just couldn't have done that, Michael, you know? He had to be in the position of power always. This is the first time I have ever sat behind this desk! What does that say about me?'

Michael laughed. 'I know that better than anyone, believe me. It wasn't deliberate, Declan. It was just his nature. He had worked hard for his position in life, and it meant a lot to him.'

Declan could see the truth of that, and he was amazed that Michael had understood his brother so well, and what made him tick. 'You're right. Patrick always wanted more. Nothing would ever be enough for him. Like you!'

'I suppose so.'

Michael got up and, walking to the main door, he picked up a crowbar that was always there in case of emergencies.

Declan shrugged. 'This will cause a lot of trouble, Michael, but you know that, don't you?'

Michael was busy feeling the weight of his chosen weapon, moving it from hand to hand. He grinned. 'I know that, Declan. But even Christie McCarthy will have to accept that this time his boy has trodden on the wrong fucking toes. I can't swallow this, and neither can you. It was a blatant fucking public outrage. I will sort Christie McCarthy out, if necessary. But, whatever happens, that cunt in there is on his way out.'

Declan shrugged. He had expected this from the off. It was why he had brought the man here, and sent everyone involved home. This was not going to end happily for anyone concerned.

Michael went through to the back office a few minutes later. He had finished his drink first.

The first blow split Kelvin's head open, the second exposed his brain. He was dead almost immediately, so then Michael concentrated on the man's body. He was going to make an example of him. No one was going to be in any doubt about what was in store for them if they dared to cross him.

Chapter Fifty-Two

Josephine woke up slowly, and smiled lazily. Michael was asleep beside her, his arm around her waist. She felt her baby move inside her, and she felt a rush of happiness. Every time she felt it moving, she knew that it was still alive. She closed her eyes and said a quick prayer of thanks. She had been saying the rosary every day, the Joyful Mysteries, mostly. She wasn't comfortable with the others, least of all the Sorrowful Mysteries. She had also been saying the Thirty Days' Prayer, and the Creed. She had always loved the Creed. It was so beautiful. She prayed to Mary, Our Lady, a mother herself, to please protect her child, and guide it safely into the world. She was sure that her prayers would be answered. If it didn't happen this time, she was never going to try again; she would accept her barren state, and get on with her life.

She crawled out of the bed, making sure she didn't wake Michael up. He worked so hard, and she had forced him out of the house the night before. Now she felt bad about that. He was only trying to protect her.

She walked down to the kitchen, and put the kettle on. As usual, she opened the back door to let the air in. She loved that she had such a huge garden, and that it was so beautiful. The gardener came three days a week, and he kept it pristine. She had her own little herb garden, and a small patio that allowed her to sit outside and enjoy her garden at her leisure. She knew how lucky she was to have so much, she really did appreciate what her Michael had given her. She knew just how hard he worked for his family, and how lucky she was to have a man like that.

She made a cup of tea, and sat down at the kitchen table. She caressed her belly; it was really starting to show now. Her mum had to have guessed, but she had not said a word. Josephine loved her for that. Her mum had been her best friend, until she had taken against Michael practically overnight. They were suddenly at loggerheads, but her mother had the sense to know when to retreat, and she had done just that. No one was going to say a word against her Michael without a fight. If she had to make a choice, there would be no competition – Michael would win hands down. Every time her mother tried to slip a criticism in, she turned on her without hesitating. It had worked too. Her mother's complaints were now few and far between, thank fuck. Her dad loved him at least! As Michael always said, two out of three wasn't bad.

She sipped her tea. She would kill for a cup of coffee, but apparently it wasn't good for the baby, so she had stopped drinking it. She heard a car crunch to a stop on the drive. It was only eight a.m. She yawned noisily. Who could this be? It must be one of Michael's workers. They all seemed to have the code for the gates.

She went through the reception hall, and opened the front door. Two men pushed past her, knocking her backwards.

'Where is he?'

Josephine looked at the men in her entrance hall, absolutely terrified. They were huge and very aggressive. She recognised one of them, but she couldn't place him.

'He's not here. He hasn't been home all night.' She was not

going to let them get any advantage over her husband, she knew that much.

'Look, love, don't fuck me about. I ain't in the mood for games. Where the fuck is he?'

Michael was at the top of the stairs, and she looked up at him fearfully. She couldn't believe it. He didn't seem to be the least bothered about them coming to his house, her home. He walked slowly down the stairs, saying, 'Have a bit of respect, lads. My wife's pregnant.'

Both men looked at her, and she pushed out her belly to emphasise her condition.

'I expected you at some point, but I thought you would have the decency to come to my offices. After all, I didn't bring my grievances to your front door, did I?'

No one said a word, and Josephine waited with baited breath, wondering what the next step would be. Michael was beside her now and, smiling pleasantly, he said gently, 'Put the kettle on, darling. Make us all a cup of tea.' Then he walked into his office, and the two men followed him, like lambs to the slaughter.

Chapter Fifty-Three

Michael closed the door to his office quietly. He gestured amiably to the two men to take a seat and when they were both settled comfortably – though looking thoroughly chastened at learning of his wife's condition – he bellowed at them loudly, 'How dare you! How dare you bring your fucking grievances into my home! My home, where my wife resides, and where I expect her to be safe and left in fucking peace. You dare to fucking come here like the avenging angels, and then expect me to swallow such outrageous fucking behaviour without retaliating?'

When Michael was really angry, he was formidable. He concealed his temper beneath the usual friendly countenance he showed to the world most of the time, whilst maintaining his reputation as a man whose temper, when roused, was without equal. He had nurtured this unpredictability over the years, ensuring that his reaction to any situation could never be guaranteed. That had stood him in great stead – it was the reason why these two men were unsure now of what he was actually capable of. Oh, he remembered the guilt he had felt over the Goldings' death and the angst he had felt over his first kill. It had all been easier than he had ever believed. He had been given a baptism of fire all right – Patrick Costello had ensured that. But it had shown him how simple the kill actually was. Now his reputation was set – his reaction to any given situation, on the other hand, was something no one could ever foresee. It was why these men were suddenly so fucking subdued. He had not been even remotely bothered by their presence on his doorstep; they had assumed it would give them the edge – instead, it had given him the advantage. They had come to his home in anger without taking the time to think it all through. That alone was a fucking insult in itself.

Michael Flynn genuinely felt for Christie McCarthy. The man's anguish was evident and he had every right to feel as he did. He had lost his son and that was a terrible thing for anyone to endure. But all that really mattered in their world was righting a wrong – that was the bottom line. Kelvin had pushed his fucking luck big time, he had taken a dirty great liberty, and he had been punished for it. That was it, as far as Michael was concerned, but he was willing to try to build a few bridges.

'Look, Christie, I know how you're feeling, mate, I respect that. But you know, as well as I do, that Kelvin was long overdue for a fucking hammering of some sort.'

Michael waited for a reply. He wanted to give this man a pass; he had no argument with him personally. But Christie's silence was making it difficult. Well, fuck him! He needed a fucking lesson in etiquette.

'Do you know what I really think? I think that *you* should have reined your boy in a long time ago. I mean, I couldn't believe my fucking ears! He actually pulled a gun on Jeffrey Palmer, in *my* fucking club! In full view of the paying public, I might fucking add, disrespecting me and my premises.' Michael was getting even more annoyed now at having to explain himself. 'Do you honestly think that I should have swallowed my fucking knob? Done nothing? Your son baited that man for ages, he insulted him into the ground, and the only reason Jeffrey Palmer didn't retaliate and kill the cunt there and then, was because he was on *my* premises. He knew if he entered into the fray – bearing in mind that he had every right to sort that lairy little cunt out – he would now be in the same condition as your boy: dead as a fucking doornail. I cannot, and will not, allow such behaviour on my premises. I don't care who it is.'

Christie McCarthy knew that Michael had only done what he would have done himself in the same position. But this was still about *his* son. As useless as the boy had been, he was his own flesh and blood.

Michael was leaning on his desk, with his arms folded across his chest. He looked every inch the main man; he had something about him that told people he was not to be underestimated. Like Patrick Costello, he had an edge to him. McCarthy had dealt with dangerous men before – it was par for the course in the world they lived in – but, occasionally, the world threw up someone like Michael Flynn or Patrick Costello. They were few and far between, and the fact that they lived by such a completely different code was the reason they were so successful.

Christie McCarthy was a man who had his creds, and he had come here for a fight – not just to avenge his son's death, but to show people that some things needed to be redressed.

He glanced at his close friend, Sam Dunne, his sister's husband, and a man who he knew would always be there if needed. Like him, Sam was subdued.

'He was still my son, Michael, my boy, and you fucking murdered him.'

Michael shrugged nonchalantly. This was starting to irritate him now. It was all going on too long. 'Well, you know what? He didn't give me much fucking choice, did he? I'm not going to enter into a big discussion about this. I had to do what I did, and you both know that. I'm sorry to the heart of me for offending you, Christie. I have the greatest respect for you, but this was just business. It wasn't personal. If I had let his actions slide, you know I would never have lived it down!'

Christie was shaking his head in denial, so Michael bellowed, 'He asked for it, and he fucking got it! Not before time, either. You should have seen this coming, mate. He used your name, and he lived off your reputation like a fucking leech. I'm only saying to you what everyone else has been saying about him for donkey's years. I didn't want to do anything to him. As you know yourself, this kind of thing is a last resort, for fuck's sake! But it happened. Whatever you might think, I did what I had to do.'

Sam Dunne couldn't look Christie in the face. He was with Michael Flynn every step of the way. He loved Christie McCarthy like a brother, but that son of his had always been trouble. It was awful to know Kelvin was dead, for a father to know that his son had been murdered, but it had to be a relief for him in some ways. Christie had been plagued by the lad's antics for years. He spent money like water; he couldn't hold a job down, he had stolen from his own family. He had been devoid of any kind of decency whatsoever, he had lived his whole life believing he was entitled to everything. Now he had been taken out by Michael Flynn, and Sam Dunne was seriously regretting his impulsive actions in coming here. But family was family.

Michael could see how hurt Christie McCarthy was about his son. He didn't like to see the man so upset, but he wasn't going to sugar-coat everything; the man knew he had spawned a fucking moron of Olympian standards. He attempted to swallow his anger once more, and said gently, 'Look, Christie, I can't really apologise for what I did, all I can say is, I hope you can let this go. I don't want to fall out with you about it. I have no fight with you – I had no fight with him till he brought one into my club. But if you can't get over this, then tell me now.'

It was a threat, and Christie recognised it. Michael Flynn was getting bored, he wanted this over. He had apologised in his own immutable way, had tried to explain his action, and given Christie the respect he was due.

Christie had far more sense than his son – he knew when to let things go. Michael Flynn was also the main employer for many of the men he had to deal with on a daily basis – he was his bread and butter, really. It rankled – the death of a child wasn't something to be forgotten overnight, even if that child had been on a death wish for many a long year – but his earlier anger had diminished.

'I don't want to carry this on. You're right, Michael – my son should have known better. I knew he was a fucking waster. He broke my heart. I gave him every opportunity to work for a living, to have a life in the real world, but he fucked it up every time. I don't want to fall out with you over this. It is hard to say it, but he ain't worth all this. He never was.'

Michael smiled widely. He could be generous now, magnanimous. He had got what he wanted. 'I'm glad to hear that, Christie. I would have hated to have us at each other's throats. When I saw you two in my hallway, and my poor wife looking so fucking frightened, I was all for killing you both, just for the piss-take. I really didn't think we would get this far. It shows you how wrong first impressions can be, eh?' He held out his hand and Christie McCarthy shook it heartily. Then Michael turned to Sam Dunne, and did the same. It was all friendly now, the atmosphere lighter, and both Christie and Sam knew they had dodged a bullet. Michael was relaxed, acting like he was relieved that they had understood his terrible predicament and forgiven him.

'Let me pour us a drink. I'm so pleased we managed to get past this shit.' He poured them large brandies, personally serving them, making sure they were comfortable, offering them seats and cigars, treating them with the utmost respect, making them feel valued, acknowledging their status in his world.

'A toast. To the future.'

They all raised their Waterford crystal glasses, knowing that Michael Flynn had won the day. Everyone would find out that they had folded, that Christie had been forced to overlook his son's demise, and accept Michael Flynn's actions without any recourse whatsoever.

'I never wanted to fight with you, Christie.'

Christie McCarthy took a big gulp of his drink to steady his nerves. 'I know that, Michael. I know you had no choice. I can see that now.'

Michael was still smiling his big friendly smile, as he said nonchalantly, 'By the way, Christie, just one last question. I will never mention this again, but it's important that I know. Which treacherous ponce gave you the code to my fucking gates?'

Chapter Fifty-Four

Lana was on her third glass of wine. She was what she called 'merry' and, as Josephine topped her glass up, she laughed loudly. 'Oh, thank you, darling! This is just what the doctor ordered!'

Josephine laughed with her. This was the mum she loved, the mum she had grown up with – full of fun and mischief, always up for a good laugh. She had missed this. She hated them being at loggerheads, especially when it was over her Michael.

Lana looked at her daughter with her usual critical eye. For all her traumas, her Josephine was still a lovely-looking girl – well, woman now. She had kept her natural beauty, even after all the miscarriages and the stillbirths. The only real change had been her daughter's quietness; with every loss she had gradually lost her natural ebullience and her lust for life. Over the last few years she had become like a recluse – she rarely left the house now.

She still shopped twice a week, and that was it. But how she shopped! Talk about bulk buying! Everywhere you looked there were boxes, all piled up on top of one another. She used to keep them out of sight – now the whole place looked like a warehouse. Who the fuck bought twenty-four cans of soup at a time? There was only the two of them. As Des joked, if the bomb dropped, they could live round Josephine's for a year, and never eat the same meal twice. She had laughed with him, pretending everything was all right, but it worried her, as a mother. She knew that things were not OK with her daughter; her girl wasn't right in her mind.

This house had once been spectacular. Tastefully decorated, each item of furniture had been agonised over, carefully selected, and put into place with love and pride. Now, though, every room had boxes piled up everywhere. Josephine shopped like she was feeding the five thousand. A case of this, two cases of that. What really bothered Lana was that Josephine acted like it was perfectly normal. This was a very big house, yet her daughter was having to use *every* room to store her purchases. But Lana knew better than to say anything – she was not going to rock the boat in any way now that they were finally back on track. She kept her own counsel where Michael was concerned too. Josephine was not going to listen to anything detrimental about him, but Lana knew she must have heard the rumours going round. Look at all this about Kelvin McCarthy for a start – it was the talk of the town.

There was something she needed to pluck up the courage to ask her daughter though – something she couldn't let go. It was far too important. She gulped down her wine for more Dutch courage. It was really lovely; one good thing about Michael Flynn for all his faults – and they were legion – was he only bought the best.

'I'm a bit pissed, Josephine!'

Josephine laughed happily. 'I could have told you that, Mum!'

Lana laughed with her daughter, pleased to see the girl so happy for once. 'Josephine, my love, I have to ask you this, darling, as your mum – please don't be cross with me. Are you pregnant again?'

Josephine looked at her mother, sorry to her soul that her mum had not asked her the question straight out but had needed a few drinks to pluck up the courage. She knew that this was *her* fault. She had deliberately built a barrier between her and her mum. A barrier that had alienated her from her own mother so much she was too scared to ask her a perfectly natural question. She was nearly eight months gone now. She knew she should have told her mother already. She was an only child, she was all her parents had. She felt so guilty, and so disloyal. Her mum loved her more than anything, and she knew that without a doubt.

She was nearly in tears as she said brokenly, 'I didn't tell *anyone*, Mum. Neither did Michael – I wouldn't let him. I didn't want to get everyone's hopes up again. That way, if I lost this baby, I wouldn't have to face everyone, see their disappointment along with my own. I would have just coped with it myself this time. I didn't tell you in case it went wrong again. I couldn't bear to put you through it.'

Lana felt as if her own heart was going to split in two. Her daughter's words were so sad. But she could understand the girl's logic. It had been so traumatic for her, losing her babies time and time again. She had hated witnessing her girl's pain, watching her beautiful daughter die inside a little bit more with every failure. She had held her while she cried her heart out, wishing she could take her girl's overwhelming sense of loss and pain on herself, so her daughter wouldn't have to experience it. But that wasn't possible; all she could do was be there for her, and pray for the best.

'Oh, darling, I understand. But I want to help you in any way I can. I would have kept it to myself. I'm your mum, Josephine. I know we have had our differences, but never forget that you are everything to me. All I want is your happiness, darling.'

Josephine hugged her mum tightly, relieved now that she knew what was going on. 'I didn't even tell Michael at first, Mum. He noticed eventually, of course, but I couldn't bring myself to tell anyone else about it. As mad as this might sound, I feel different this time. I feel like this time I can do it. This baby moves about a lot. I can feel it's alive. I wish I had told you, Mum. I know I can always trust you, no matter what. I am so sorry.'

For the first time in ages, Lana actually felt close to her only child. She held her daughter tightly, marvelling at her firm, round belly, and the familiar feel of her daughter's embrace. It had been so long since she had held her in her arms. Her knowledge of Michael Flynn had caused the rift between them, and she knew now that she could not allow her personal feelings for Michael to cloud her relationship with her only child. She had no option – her daughter needed her, and that was enough.

'I can't even imagine what you've been through, darling. But I promise you, I will always be there for you, Josephine, no matter what.'

Josephine could feel her mother's tears mingling with her own. The guilt was completely overwhelming her now. She knew how much her mum loved her; never once in her life had she ever felt unwanted or neglected. Her mum and dad had lived for her, and she had always known that. She had chosen her husband over her mum, and that had been hard, but she knew she would do the same again, if needed. He was everything to her, and he always would be.

'Please, Mum, promise me you won't say anything bad about Michael again. I just can't stand it. He has stood by me and loved me through everything. He was happy to forget all about having babies, just so I wouldn't have to go through any more heartache. That is why I didn't tell him about this baby till I had to. I love him more than anything, and he loves me, Mum, I know that.'

Lana sighed gently. 'I won't say a word about anything or anyone. I promise.' She had learnt her lesson as far as all that was concerned. That her Josephine had chosen Michael over her had given her a reality check. She wasn't going to lose her daughter again, that was for sure. Michael Flynn was not someone she wanted in her daughter's life, she knew him for the man he really was. But her daughter didn't see him as anything other than her knight in shining armour, and she knew she would never disabuse her of that notion. It was pointless to even try. But she would watch him like a hawk, and pray every day that her Josephine would eventually see him for what he was.

Chapter Fifty-Five

Michael was watching Declan eat; the man was a veritable force of nature. He could consume his own bodyweight in steak, and still have room for a dessert. He was like a machine; he ate with a dedication that was almost inspiring, he enjoyed his food so much.

Michael was at the head of the table, of course, Declan was sitting to his right, and the other eight seats were taken up by people they worked with who were important enough to join them for dinner once a month. Declan couldn't see the value of it at all. He just saw a big bill at the end for Michael to pay. These people worked for them – surely *they* should be paying the bill? They gave them their earn, for fuck's sake! Yet Michael insisted that they wine and dine them. In Declan's mind, this was completely fucking ludicrous. But he couldn't see the money that they were bringing into the firm on a regular basis – Declan only saw the money they earned personally. He couldn't see the big picture – that these men brought in far more than they earned. But then, Declan didn't really understand the economics of the big earns. Michael made him come to these dinners, because he was his business partner. He had tried to educate him on the finer points of the businesses he ran, but Declan genuinely had no real interest whatsoever. Michael knew that these dinners were worth every penny. The men around him were all good earners, and they appreciated that he singled them out and showed them how much he valued them. He knew that, to keep people onside, you had to make them feel a part of everything, give them your time and, better still, your interest. It was a good night out for everyone concerned as well – good food, good wine and good company.

He sat back in his chair, feeling very relaxed. He had imbibed a few glasses of red wine, and he was enjoying the company. Jeffrey Palmer was on his left, in pride of place. He was always a good bloke to have around; Michael liked him a lot and, since the removal of young McCarthy, Jeffrey Palmer had done everything possible to show his appreciation. He was grateful to Michael Flynn for taking care of a very awkward situation for him, and he would never forget that.

Michael couldn't tell him that the main reason the boy had been dispatched was because he had dared to pull a gun on *his* premises. He could not let that go – no matter who might be involved. He would have taken out anyone, no matter who they were or who they worked for. It was the principle.

'What a great night.'

Michael smiled easily as always. He was good at that. 'I like it here, Jeffrey. It's a great place – a delicate mixture of bankers and wankers!'

Jeffrey laughed with him. 'That is a great analogy, and very true! But listen, Michael, I want to run something by you. I had a visit from an old mate this week. He did a big lump in the nick, but he has been out a good while. He now lives in Spain. He has a couple of nightclubs in the 'Dorm, and he has the contacts to procure any drugs required – in any quantity.'

Michael Flynn sipped his wine; he was not going to join in this conversation until he had to.

Jeffrey Palmer knew the game, but he had downed a few

drinks, and he felt secure. Michael Flynn had done him the favour of a lifetime and he wanted to return the favour. He grabbed Michael's arm roughly, pulling him closer. 'Look, Michael, from what he tells me, he can undercut anyone.'

Michael pulled his arm away roughly. Leaning forward, he looked into Jeffrey's eyes, as he said sarcastically, 'Well, fuck me, Jeff. Let's ring him now, shall we?'

Jeffrey Palmer was taken aback at Michael's reaction and, as far as Michael was concerned, so he fucking should be.

'Listen, Jeffrey. We deal with people who are well under the plods' radar, who can supply very good gear, and who have always proved themselves to be very reliable. Never once have we ever had even the threat of a tug. Yet you want me to wipe out a friendship *and* a business partnership that goes back fucking donkey's years – a partnership that I have recently given to you, remember, and for what exactly? An ex-fucking-con who lives in fucking Benidorm of all places – the arsehole of the world. What the fuck are you on?'

Jeffrey Palmer knew that he had just made a major fuck-up. He had listened to his friend's spiel and, as he had been promised a much bigger margin on what he was shifting on a weekly basis, it had seemed a far more lucrative venture for all concerned. He had foolishly assumed that Michael Flynn would bite his fucking hand off. But now he understood that he had not only discussed his dealings with an outsider but, to compound his offence, he had been willing to step over the man that Michael Flynn had introduced him to, who he had offered him a partnership with. A partnership he had accepted, and he had been so grateful for the opportunity. He was earning a fucking fortune, more money than he had ever earned in his life, and he was throwing it back in Michael Flynn's face. That was not a good move. He could see the disgust on Michael's face, and felt physically ill.

'I am a bit miffed, Jeffrey. To be brutally honest, I can only assume that you have discussed our arrangements with your fucking "friend" from Benidorm, and told him all our business – times, dates and, more importantly, weights. That's all private business, as far as I am concerned. I thought you understood the importance of loyalty and secrecy. I can't see any reason to discuss our business with anyone outside of our little circle. But from what you just said, you have obviously told your mate, Mr *fucking* Benidorm, everything about us, from delivery to distribution. Otherwise, how would he have known he could undercut us?'

Michael was absolutely fuming. Of all the people on his payroll, Jeffrey Palmer was the last person he would have believed capable of something like this. He sat back in his chair, concealing his fury, and smiled amiably at the men around him. The waitresses here were stunning-looking girls, and they were waiting for the dessert orders. The girls who waited on them knew they were guaranteed a big tip. The bigger the tits, the bigger the tips – it was another reason why they got such wonderful service.

'I think some cheeses for me, and a nice glass of vintage port. I'm not a dessert man, as you all know.' Michael was laughing and joking as if nothing untoward had occurred.

Jeffrey Palmer was devastated. He had ruined, in less than a few minutes, a reputation that had taken him years to build. He waited a moment, watching the men at the table laughing and drinking, before leaning towards Michael, seizing his opportunity for another private word.

'Look, Michael, I am so sorry. I just saw the money, I didn't think it through properly. My mate is a straight arrow, though – safe as houses. He did a sixteen. You probably know him – Charlie Carter? Out of Notting Hill?'

Michael shrugged his annoyance. 'Like I'd fucking care about all that. I couldn't care if he was Saint John the fucking Baptist. He still had no right to be told my business.' Bending forward once more, he looked into Jeffrey Palmer's face, searching it as if he was looking for another weakness.

'Look, Jeffrey, I am so fucking outraged, I can't believe what you said to me. It's not just the fucking disregard for everyone you are working with – me included – it's the knowledge that you felt comfortable telling a stranger how we all work. That is almost like grassing. Telling someone else about our business practices. You are a fucking liability. Can't you see that? I brought you in, trusted you, and paired you up with a man I have worked beside for fucking years. You were *my* replacement, for fuck's sake. You seem to have overlooked not just me, and what I gave you, but also the reaction of the people you have been dealing with on my behalf.'

All around, the men were telling jokes, and Michael sat back in his chair ready to join in. He had given Palmer enough of his time. He wasn't going to let him have another say now. As far as he was concerned he could go fuck himself.

Garry England, a young up-and-coming money launderer, was holding court. He was a really funny man – he could tell a joke like a professional comedian. Michael ignored his cheese board. He had lost his appetite. He busied himself lighting a cigar instead. He gestured to the maître d', and the man brought a bottle of Remy XO to the table, returning to place a brandy snifter in front of each of the men. The maître d' knew that the brandy that this lot would drink would cost more than the food. With the good wines and the aperitifs, this would be a serious bill. Michael Flynn was a valued customer in more ways than one. It gave them status to have Michael Flynn dine there on a regular basis. He was a good tipper, always made sure that everyone who waited on him got a decent wedge at the end of the night. He also made sure that none of his guests ever caused any disturbances, no matter how much they might have drunk.

Michael opened the bottle of brandy, and poured himself a large measure. Then he passed the bottle on to Declan. Michael sipped the liquid, savouring the taste. He did like a nice brandy. Patrick Costello had educated him, explaining the finer points of a good brandy and a good wine. Patrick Costello had told him, in confidence of course, how he had paid a mad French bloke – a sommelier from one of London's leading hotels – to teach him about wines, and how to appreciate them. Patrick had admitted to him that he had been amazed at the man's knowledge, and at how much he had learnt from him. And Patrick, in turn, had enjoyed passing his knowledge on. Michael would always thank him for that.

Garry England was telling everyone at the table a funny story about when he was a kid and he had gone with his mum on a visit to Parkhurst to see his dad. Declan was already giggling like a teenager; he had heard the story before. Michael couldn't concentrate though, he was still reeling from the shock that Palmer had actually attempted to replace the man he had introduced him to, a man he had worked with for years, who he trusted implicitly.

Jeffrey Palmer had been his choice. He had recruited him personally to be his replacement. He had trusted him to take over. That was the real bugbear – he had trusted a man who had not understood the enormity of what had been offered him, who had not had the intelligence to understand exactly what he was dealing with. It was a real melon scratcher, as his mum would say.

Chapter Fifty-Six

A very pretty girl carried their coffees into the spacious office that Michael used when he was in Canary Wharf. This was where the legitimate businesses were located, and where some of the more exotic business was also conducted. They were luxurious, and they were private. There was a whole workforce here who actually worked for their living.

Declan Costello was tired out and he sipped his coffee carefully.

Michael Flynn watched the big, overweight man opposite him with affection. Declan looked like a social worker, his suit was a tad too small, and his shirt was cheap. His whole look was unkempt and slightly soiled. But Michael trusted him. Declan Costello was a man who looked like an affable fool, but was actually a dangerous fuck when crossed.

'I need your advice, Declan. I know I can trust you, so please tell me what you think.'

Declan sighed. He knew that Michael was in a quandary; he had surreptitiously listened in to his conversation with Jeffrey Palmer and, like Michael, he had been mortified. More so because it had been Jeffrey Palmer talking such bollocks, a man who should have known better. But it was always the chosen ones who overstepped the mark.

'I did try and warn you, Michael. Patrick always said, the more you give people, the more they want. He was on the money. Why do you think he recruited you? As young as you were, he trusted you from the off, but you also had the added advantage that Patrick actually liked you. He saw your potential, and he was right. I know he made you prove yourself to him, prove that you were capable of what he asked of you – that was his way of sounding people out. But, on reflection, he brought you in out of nowhere, didn't he? He didn't bring up someone from the ranks, someone he knew, he had already worked with. He brought you straight in over all their heads.'

Michael digested the man's words; there was a logic there that couldn't be denied.

'You need to think long and hard about the people you put in place, Michael, and eventually you need to find yourself a number two. I've said this to you before. It's a big fucking responsibility for one person.'

Michael listened carefully. He respected Declan's opinion. He had a lot more going for him than anyone realised. Patrick used to joke that Declan was like a tree who didn't quite manage to reach the top branches, but he was a lot shrewder than people gave him credit for.

'I am aware of all that, Declan, but I'm asking what do you think about Jeffrey Palmer? I can't believe he opened up to Charlie Carter! The man's a fucking card-carrying, paid-up moron, who now knows *who* we deal with, *how* and *when* we deal with them, and *what* we earn from them. That is a dangerous fucking combination. What was that cunt thinking? I would have laid money on him having the nous to keep his fucking business to himself.'

Declan laughed. 'He was thinking about *money*, Michael. What else? You might guarantee him a good fucking wedge, but I bet Carter can offer him a better one. They are mates as well, and that is the danger, see? Jeffrey can't see that he is dealing with people you chose, who you know are safe, who have proved their worth over and over again. Jeffrey Palmer doesn't know anything about them, he's never even heard of them. He can only see his mate, and the benefits of working with someone he knows well. He has been told he can earn a lot more money if he can persuade you to change suppliers. It's the old story, Michael. Though I have to say, Charlie Carter will swallow a tug. He is a man who knows when to shut his trap.'

Michael sighed heavily. 'I know all that, Declan. You are hardly giving me a fucking lesson in life are you? What do you think I should do about it? That is the fucking question.'

Declan smiled lazily. 'You want me to suggest you take out Palmer, Carter and anyone else who you think needs to be silenced? Well, I won't, Michael. I think you need to give Palmer a good fright, and Carter as well. After all, they aren't going to confront you, or try and usurp your position, are they? I bet they are at panic stations already. But, remember this, if you stay your hand now, Jeffrey Palmer will never forget how close he came to dying. It's a learning curve for him.'

Michael laughed. 'If Patrick were here they would all be in blindfolds and smoking their last cigarettes.'

Declan shook his head. 'You're wrong. Patrick would have used this against them, and guaranteed their loyalty for life. Unless, of course, he was on one of his fucking mental half hours, then he would have killed everyone anyway, whether they had fucked him off or not.'

They laughed together then, knowing how true that was.

'Fucking hell. He could turn on a coin, could old Patrick.'

Declan nodded his agreement. 'You're preaching to the converted here, Michael. I lived with it all my life, remember? That is why I am telling you to think about this carefully. Patrick was a hard man, and he had a lot of respect, but he made a lot of unnecessary enemies over the years. He took against people on a whim, for no real reason, and that caused us untold aggravation at times, believe me. Ultimately, *you* had to take him out for the greater good.'

Michael closed his eyes; he hated to be reminded of his part in Patrick's death. Declan was right in what he was saying but, even though Michael knew all that, and agreed with everything the man had said, he still felt, deep down, that Jeffrey Palmer had crossed a line, gone too far. But he kept his own counsel; he had asked for Declan Costello's opinion, and the man had given it to him.

Chapter Fifty-Seven

Josephine was looking at herself critically in the mirrored wardrobes; she had a bump, but not a huge one. She caressed it instinctively, but the baby had not moved for two days, and now she was starting to feel panic rising inside her. Although she was eight months pregnant – the longest that she had ever carried a child – she was feeling nothing but dread. If this child had died, she knew she would never have another.

She was naked except for her dressing gown, a long flowing silk affair that had cost a small fortune, and it looked good on her. It was a pale pink colour, and with her thick blond hair and deep-blue eyes she knew that it suited her complexion perfectly. Even pregnant, she still wanted to look good for Michael. She took a step closer to the mirror and pulled the dressing gown around her, tying it loosely. Her face was pale, gaunt; she could see fear reflected in her eyes.

Turning away, she walked to her bed and, picking up the clothes she had laid out earlier, she slowly started to dress herself. Her doctor had told her that if she felt she needed to see him at any time all she had to do was call. Michael had made sure of that. He had probably offered the doctor what he would call a 'sweetener', but which was, in reality, a very large amount of money – hard cash and tax free. She wasn't complaining though. She sat on the side of the bed and, bending over carefully, she slipped her maternity knickers over her feet. Michael called them her 'passion killers'. She stood up and pulled them into place.

She was putting her bra on when she felt a stabbing pain shoot through her abdomen. It was so sharp that it immediately took her breath away. She waited for it pass, then she slipped her dressing gown on again. Sitting back on the bed, she waited nervously to see what, if anything, was going to happen to her next. She was not going to ring Michael or her mum or anybody until she knew what was going on. She would finish getting dressed, ring the doctor, and then she would drive herself to the hospital. She was determined not to panic; she was going to keep herself as calm as possible. Her doctor had told her that this was a normal pregnancy, and she was to treat it as such. There had been no bleeding or cramps, no feelings of illness or nausea. She had not felt her usual fragility, as if the child inside her womb was already too weak to go full term. There had been nothing untoward this time, and she needed to remember that. But until she held a baby of her own in her arms, she would not take anything for granted. She had suffered that kind of disappointment too many times before.

Chapter Fifty-Eight

'I hope she manages it this time, though why it was such a big secret I don't know. Let's face it, Michael, you could have told me! Anyone would think I was a stranger on the street instead of your own mother the way you treat me these days. I suppose the house is piled up with baby powder and nappies again. If she had a squad of ten, she couldn't use half the stuff she buys. It's ridiculous.'

Michael had heard enough. With Hannah, it was a constant barrage of complaints – then she wondered why they didn't want her around. Her snide remarks about grandchildren broke Josephine's heart. She made him feel guilty because he didn't seek her out every day, even though it was her own fault. She was so fucking bitter and twisted. As if he didn't have enough to deal with in his life without listening to her going on.

'Oh, for fuck's sake, Mum! Will you give it a rest!'

Hannah shut up. Her son's voice was full of anger and irritation. She pursed her lips together tightly, so she wouldn't react. Her son was worried about his wife, and that was natural. But he should still remember who had reared him, fed him, clothed him all his life.

Michael felt the urge to throttle his mother. She could make a saint swear. She was sitting there now, acting like butter wouldn't melt, while his poor Josephine was being examined by the doctor.

He made his way back to his wife, wondering why on earth he had bothered to go and update his mother on Josephine's progress. It was a complete waste of time.

He walked into Josephine's hospital room, a bright smile nailed to his face. He couldn't let her see how worried he was. If it went wrong this time, she would never get over it – he knew that much.

Lana was holding her daughter's hand, and he was pleased to see that Josephine was laughing at something her mother had said to her.

'Hello, Michael. The doctor said that everything is going fine! We heard the heartbeat, didn't we, Mum?'

Lana grinned. 'We did. Strong as an ox by the sounds of it.'

Michael sat on the bed. 'How long do they think?'

Josephine shook her head, and shrugged nonchalantly. 'Don't know. Still waiting for my waters to break. Could be here for ages!'

She would happily stay there for days if necessary and he knew that. All she wanted was for everything to be all right.

'Is your mum OK?'

Michael rolled his eyes. 'Same as always, Lana – about as much fun as a broken back.'

Lana laughed at him. 'No change there then!'

Josephine was watching her husband sadly. She knew how much he loved his mum, but she was not the easiest person to be around. Josephine was well aware that Hannah had never liked her much, but it had not mattered at first. If she had given her a few grandchildren, it would have made a big difference to their relationship. 'She doesn't mean it, Michael.'

Michael waved his hand impatiently. 'Sod her, Josephine.'

The midwife came in, and Michael automatically stepped away from his wife. He watched as she smiled and nodded, as always eager to please, to do the right thing. He prayed once more that this time God would bless them with a living child. He wanted a baby, of course, but if it wasn't meant to be, then, for him, that was that. He couldn't watch her go through this again. This time it seemed to be going normally but, with their track record, he wasn't going to let himself get excited about it.

The midwife was a heavyset West Indian woman, with a loud voice, and an infectious laugh. Josephine loved her, and he watched as the woman examined his wife, while chatting and joking with her, putting her at her ease. He was glad that he had paid to go private, it was worth every penny. Only the best for his Josephine. He loved her more than life itself.

'Did you hear that, Michael? My waters have broken! It's all go now.'

Carmen Presley was pleased with her charge's progress; the girl had been so unlucky in the past, and no one was taking any chances. But everything seemed to be going as planned.

Michael smiled happily, but he was relieved when Lana said pointedly, 'Get us a cup of tea, Michael, will you, darling?'

As much as Lana disliked her son-in-law, she felt sorry for him. She could see that he was terrified, and she knew that it was fear for her daughter. Whatever he was, she believed he loved Josephine.

As he left the room, she clasped her daughter's hand, and said another Hail Mary. Like Michael, she wanted this baby for her daughter more than she had ever wanted anything in her life.

Chapter Fifty-Nine

Declan Costello was in the top bar of their newest nightclub, The Gatsby. He was holding court, and enjoying every second of it. His latest amour, Sinead, a petite blonde with huge breasts and delusions of grandeur, was by his side. She was pretty enough, green-eyed with high cheekbones and full lips but, unfortunately for her, she had about as much personality as a tadpole. It had only been a week and already Declan was getting bored with her. The only women who lasted for a while with him, had one thing in common other than being good-looking – a sense of humour.

Declan looked around him. Everyone, from Jeffrey Palmer to Jermaine O'Shay had turned out to wet the baby's head. Even the Notting Hill lads had come over to the East End – an almost unheard of situation. But Michael Flynn was popular and everyone wanted to congratulate him on the birth of his first child. Christ Himself knew they had waited long enough for it.

Jermaine was drinking whisky and, as usual, he had women lining up to talk to him. Tonight, though, he wasn't interested in the strange around him; he just wanted to share Michael's night with him.

The club was packed out, and the music was loud and pumping, the beat resonating through the floor.

Michael Flynn finally arrived just after midnight and, as he walked up the stairs to the top bar, Whitney Houston's 'I Wanna Dance With Somebody' came on. Laughing excitedly, Michael made his entrance by dancing erratically, and singing the lyrics at the top of his voice.

'Fucking hell, Michael! You pissed already?'

Michael was so happy, it was almost painful to watch him. After all these years, poor Josephine had finally managed to produce a child for them.

'Drunk? Am I fuck, you cheeky bastard! I'm happy. Get me a large Irish, mate.'

Everyone was clamouring to congratulate him; he was shaking hands and hugging people all around, his happiness infectious.

'So, come on then, what did she have?'

Michael looked at Declan in disbelief. 'Didn't you tell them?'

'No, I kept schtum. That's for you to know, and for that lot to find out! It's your news, mate. Not mine.'

Michael felt almost tearful at Declan's generosity of spirit. He understood how big this moment was for him and, even though he would not have minded Declan telling the people around them his news, he appreciated that Declan had left it to him.

'Come on then, Michael, what you got? It can only be one or the other!'

Michael was laughing once more. Then, standing up straight and clearing his throat theatrically, he announced, 'Jessica Mary Flynn was born today on the tenth of September nineteen eighty-nine weighing in at six pounds, five ounces. She is her mother's double, and she's fucking gorgeous.'

The cheer that went up from everyone was so loud it drowned out the music. Declan pushed a glass of whisky into Michael's hand, and he downed it in one go. Then, giving Declan his empty glass, he shouted, 'More!'

Michael had already noticed that Jeffrey Palmer was there

with some of his crew, looking very sheepish. He had clocked Jermaine O'Shay too. Michael smiled at the people there; it was a great crowd, and he knew that they were there for him, to celebrate his good news with him. Almost every Face in London was in this bar tonight and, as he looked around him – at young Danny, as always telling jokes and making people laugh, and at Orville Cardoza, a Rastafarian of advanced years who was capable of extreme violence at the least provocation – he suddenly felt at peace with himself, and with his life. His little daughter was a miracle. She had arrived with the minimum of fuss, and he had never seen Josephine more beautiful – the look of triumph on her face had said it all. She had finally achieved the one thing she craved more than anything else in her life. As she had cradled her daughter in her arms, he had closed his eyes tightly and thanked God for finally answering their prayers.

He had another large whisky put into his hand and, once again, he swallowed it down quickly. 'Keep them coming, boys. Tonight I am going to get fucking plastered.'

The men around him were cheering him loudly. Arnold Jameson, a young Jamaican guy with a bald head and a taste for outlandish shirts, hugged him tightly. 'I remember getting my first baby. Your own flesh and blood. It's a real trip, ain't it, maw?'

Michael hugged him back. Until now he had not thought of it like that. His little girl, his brand spanking new little baby, was his flesh and blood.

Chapter Sixty

Josephine lay in the hospital bed, tired and sore, but also elated. She watched her little daughter as she slept in the Perspex crib beside her bed, fascinated by each breath and each snuffle. She was still worried that this was all a dream, and she would wake up in her own bed, covered in sweat and silently crying into her pillow.

She looked down at her body; already her belly had gone down – she didn't look like she had just given birth. She had laughed about it with the midwife, and another new mum who had popped her head around the door asking if it was OK to come in and say hello. She had really loved that. Talking babies with another mum was something she had never thought she would ever do. It was so natural, and they had chatted together for ages. Then she had fed her little Jessica – already she was Jessie, Michael had seen to that. Her mother had never allowed her name to be shortened – she was Josephine, never Jo. Yet she had already accepted Jessie for her daughter; it suited her somehow, she looked like a Jessie.

Even Hannah had not been able to ruin this day for her. Unlike her mother and father who had held the baby, cooed to her, and shared in her first few hours in the world, Hannah had refused the offer to hold her grandchild, and she had left without even saying goodbye. Michael had not even noticed his mother's absence; he was as besotted with Jessie as she was. He just gazed at his new daughter with complete and absolute awe. She was a lovely child already; she had been born pink and creamy, not even any blood or vernix on her. She could see herself in her daughter's features. Her mum had said Josephine had been *her* double, the image of her as a baby, and she was going to bring in the pictures to prove it. Michael was so dark, Josephine had thought the child would resemble him, dark-haired and apple-cheeked. But she wasn't – she was fair-skinned, and honey-blond, just like her mum.

Josephine knew she should try to sleep – she was whacked out – but it was impossible. She wanted this day to last for ever. It was the best day of her whole life. She felt truly alive for the first time in years. Michael had been so good, pretending he didn't care if they had children or not, but she believed, deep inside, that he *did* care. She hugged herself with glee. She was finally a mother, she was someone's mum, and that felt so good. She looked at her little daughter, lying there so defenceless, so vulnerable, and she whispered softly, 'I promise you, my little Jessie Flynn, that I will never let you down. If you need me I will always be there for you.' She meant every word. It never occurred to her that sometimes you couldn't protect your children, no matter how much you might want to. Life just didn't work like that.

Chapter Sixty-One

Michael took a deep breath, and counted to five slowly in his head. Josephine was feeding little Jessie, and he had walked into his kitchen, barefoot, in only his boxer shorts, gasping for a cup of coffee, and stubbed his toe on a new pile of boxes that seemed to have appeared overnight. He had hopped around in agony, while cursing under his breath.

Instead of laughing as expected, Josephine had deliberately ignored his pain. He had hoped that now she had a baby to care for the bulk buying would stop. He had always thought her need to buy so much was because of her failure to have a child of her own. He had ignored it, telling himself that if it made her happy then that was enough. But now it was starting to annoy him. In the last six months, she had got worse not better. He glanced quickly at the boxes as he sipped his coffee. More fucking food – like they didn't have enough already! Twenty-four tins to the case, and there were five cases. Two were full of baked beans, one was spaghetti, and the other two were chilli con carne of all things. She cooked wonderful food for them – they rarely opened a tin of anything. It was getting beyond a joke.

He sat down, and smiled at his wife and daughter. Little Jessie pushed her bottle away, and gave him a huge gummy smile. She was absolutely gorgeous, there was no doubting that. Her eyes were a deep blue and framed by long, dark eyelashes. Everyone commented on her eyes – even complete strangers, they were that remarkable. She seemed to look into your soul, she peered so intently. Even his mother had eventually succumbed to her charms.

'Morning, my darling.'

She started to crow at him, grinning and grabbing her own feet, and he laughed as Josephine tried to get her to finish her bottle. He kissed his wife on the forehead gently. 'Morning, my other darling.'

Josephine smiled at him, but she could sense his frustration, and she hated it. She knew that, on one level, he had a point about her buying, but it wasn't as if they couldn't afford it. Possessing the things that she purchased made her feel secure somehow. It had started so long ago, it was normal for her now. And if things were on special offer, she just saw it as a way of saving money.

'She is looking happy enough.'

Josephine grinned. 'She's already had her breakfast. She loves her food, Michael.'

He felt his heart constrict with his love for her. If only she would admit that her compulsive buying was getting out of hand. The house they lived in was huge by anyone's standards, but she was gradually filling it up with more and more boxes of food, talcum powder, even bloody dried milk. She bought stuff they would never even use, like the tins of chilli con carne, and the boxes of dried fruits. It was completely without logic. If they lived to be a hundred, they could never use it all. In the spare bedroom, she had piled up box after box of cereals, every kind. Big packs that were all out of date, along with tins of tuna and tins of pilchards.

'She'll need a big appetite won't she, Josephine? There is more cereal in this house than in fucking Tesco.'

He saw the hurt on his wife's face and immediately felt bad, as though he was in the wrong. Her eyes were filling up with tears, and he sighed. 'I don't want to hurt you, Josephine, but surely you can see that this is getting out of hand? Look around you, darling. This place is like a fucking warehouse. We don't even eat any of it. I tried to use a tin of beans the other week and you nearly bit my head off.'

Josephine rolled her eyes in exasperation. 'There were tins in the cupboard. You didn't need to open the case up. I explained that to you.'

He picked up his daughter, pulling her from his wife's lap. 'Listen to what you're saying, Josephine. Who gives a flying fuck where a tin of beans comes from, I ask you? And, as we have more beans in this house than a fucking army canteen, I would have thought you'd have welcomed someone actually *eating* the fuckers. They aren't ornaments, are they?'

Josephine was nearly in tears now. He forced himself to lower his voice, calm down. 'I've got a couple of lads coming round today. They are going to move all the boxes into the garages, OK? I want this place clear when I get home tonight. It's not a fucking depot, all right? It's our home.'

She didn't answer him, just looked at him with those huge pained eyes.

'I'm sorry, darling, but it's arranged now.' He stood up, playing with his little daughter, determined not to look at his wife and cave in as per usual. This time the house was being cleared, he was going to make sure of that. One of the rooms off the kitchen was a spacious old-fashioned larder. There were over sixty jars of jam on the shelves, forty jars of honey and, more worryingly, he had counted thirty-two tin openers in one of the drawers. Everywhere he looked, there was evidence of her hoarding, and it scared him more than he liked to admit. It wasn't normal. He had seen her wiping the tins over with a damp cloth, and placing them back into the boxes they had arrived in. Who the fuck did things like that? He had to put his foot down. They had a child to look out for now. She needed to start getting with the program. He had hoped that her finally having a baby would have sorted out her eccentricities, but instead it seemed to have exacerbated them. He loved her more than life itself, but he knew that things were not right.

'She's getting to be a right lump, isn't she?'

Josephine nodded. 'She is. Like I said, she loves her grub.'

'Well, she won't fucking starve in this house, will she?' He laughed as he spoke, trying to lighten the mood, but Josephine didn't react in any way at all.

Chapter Sixty-Two

Declan was extremely irritated – almost fuming, in fact – and that was a very unusual occurrence for him. He was a man who rarely let anything throw him off kilter. He saw that as a weakness, a character flaw – not that he had ever said that out loud. His brother and Michael were his polar opposite in that respect. Chasing the dollar was why people like them got up in the morning.

Well, he liked the world he had created for himself. He ran a good business, and he ran it very well. Declan believed wholeheartedly that he had more than enough for his needs. He earned a good wedge, he had shagged more women than he could shake a tenner at, and he genuinely liked his life. He didn't want marriage or children really. He was happy enough playing the eternal bachelor. What he didn't like was discord, especially among the ranks. He was very easy going, but the people who worked for him knew that, if they pushed their luck, he was capable of great vengeance if the need should arise.

But now Michael Flynn needed a serious fucking talking to and he was going to give it to him, please or offend. This should never have been allowed to go so far, and Michael knew that better than anyone. It took a lot to make Declan angry but, when he finally succumbed to anger, he could be a very dangerous individual. Michael would do well to remember that.

He glanced at his watch. Michael was already over an hour late, and that added to his irritation. Tardiness was the greatest insult of them all; arrangements were made to suit those concerned – it was the height of rudeness to overlook other people's needs.

He heard Michael arrive; he hailed people as always with his usual bonhomie and smiling face, but Declan knew Michael Flynn was not the amiable, hail-fellow-well-met cunt that he pretended to be. He was a vicious fucker, who could pass in company as a well-heeled, well-dressed businessman. And that was fine, so long as he remembered that, while he had been playing happy families for the last six months, he had inadvertently dropped the proverbial ball. He had a fucking seriously damaging break in his ranks, and it needed to be addressed sooner rather than later.

Josephine's problems were common knowledge and as much as everyone felt for him – after all, no one wanted a fucking nutbag on the team – Michael needed to remember the golden rule: family life came second to everything else.

As Michael made his entrance into the office, it took all of Declan Costello's willpower to stop himself from smacking him one. If ever a man needed to be brought down a peg, Michael Flynn was that man.

Chapter Sixty-Three

Hannah was holding her granddaughter on her lap, amazed at the love she felt for the child. The only other person to ever make her feel such overpowering love had been her son, and where had that got her? But little Jessie had crept into her heart, and now the thought of being parted from her was a real torment. She had even tempered her usual sarcastic remarks, frightened that if she pushed too far the child would be taken beyond her reach.

She could see herself in her, although no one else would admit that. She had her eyes, and her own mother's cupid bow lips. It was unbelievable really, the child's hold on her. Hannah adored her, and that was something she had never envisaged.

Hannah watched surreptitiously as Josephine oversaw the removal of her boxes of crap from the house. Not before time either, as far as she was concerned; it was like an obstacle course to get in, and Michael should have put his foot down years ago. She could see the panic in her daughter-in-law's eyes as the house was gradually emptied of her purchases. Despite herself, she actually felt sorry for the girl. Anyone would think she was being asked to give her family away. For the first time, Hannah realised that her daughter-in-law had a real problem.

'Come and sit down, Josephine. I've hardly spoken to you since I got here!'

Josephine looked at her in distress. 'I'll be with you in a minute, Hannah. I just need to make sure that everything is put away properly, where I can find it . . .'

Hannah stood up with the child in her arms, and walked to where her daughter-in-law was standing. She was at the back door and, as she went to follow the young men out to the garage, Hannah grabbed her by the arm.

'Leave it be. I don't want to upset you, but you're acting strange, love. These young men Michael sent here to move everything out of the house can see how strange you're acting. People talk, love, you know that as well as I do. Don't give them the opportunity for a story. If not for yourself, then for Michael. He can't be seen as having any kind of weakness. Now, come and sit down, and I'll make a fresh pot of tea.'

Josephine knew that the woman was right; she wasn't acting rationally. She shouldn't care about what was happening. But it wasn't that easy. She couldn't help the way she felt. Watching everything leave the house was like witnessing the death of a loved one. She felt bereft and vulnerable.

Hannah pulled her gently away from the door. 'Sit down and nurse your baby. I can see how hard this is for you, Josephine, but you have to let it go.' She passed the child to her daughter-in-law, and watched as her natural maternal instincts took over.

Josephine sat down at the kitchen table and Hannah breathed a sigh of relief. Little Jessie was so good-natured, and she thanked God for that much at least. She wasn't a cross child and rarely cried.

'She is so contented, Josephine. I've never seen such a contented child in all my born days. That is all down to you, and your wonderful mothering.'

It was the right thing to say. Josephine smiled with pleasure at her words, and Hannah Flynn finally understood the reason her son loved this girl so much. She literally didn't have a bad bone in her body. She felt a moment's shame at the way she had treated her over the years. She had never given the girl a chance. She had always resented the way she had replaced her in her son's affections. It was only Jessie's birth that had softened her up. Now she saw the girl as she really was – a frightened young woman, who needed her kindness and understanding. She was a troubled soul, all right, and she needed help. Her Michael knew that and if Hannah had not been so selfish, so bitter, he would have turned to her for help. Instead he had protected the girl from her, knowing she didn't have a great opinion of her anyway. For the first time ever, Hannah felt truly guilty.

Chapter Sixty-Four

Michael held his hands out in a gesture of supplication. He knew that his late arrival would not be overlooked by Declan – tardiness was his pet hate.

'I'm sorry, Declan, but I had to sort some stuff out at home.'

Michael looked immaculate as always; the man had clearly spent a long time on his appearance. It was Michael Flynn's only vanity, he never looked anything other than perfect. Declan knew that his haphazard approach to life was the antithesis of Michael's. Declan was getting larger by the month and he had never been what anyone would call a looker. Unlike Michael Flynn, however, he didn't care about that. Michael, though, looked every inch the part of the well-heeled Face, from the expensive gold watch to his perfect haircut.

'You know why I called this meeting, so let's not fuck about, eh?'

Michael laughed at his friend's attitude; only Declan would dare to talk to him like that – only Declan could get away with it. He shook his head slowly in mock disbelief. 'OK, hold your fucking horses! It's sorted, all right?' He was being deliberately contrite, apologising without saying a word.

'I'm gonna need a bit more than that, Michael, and you fucking know it.'

The smile was gone now, and Declan was reminded of just

how hazardous confronting someone like Michael Flynn could be. Like Patrick, his late brother, the man was capable of literally anything if crossed. He would do well to remember that, even if he had the man's respect and his affection.

'I know what you're saying, Declan. Believe me, I've tried to build bridges. I've given them every opportunity to sort the situation out between them. Jeffrey Palmer was willing to swallow his knob. He knew he had dropped a humungous fucking bollock from the off. But Jermaine O'Shay has been a real pain. He just won't let it go – not even for me.'

Declan sat down suddenly, and looked out of the large picture window that had a really magnificent view over the river. It was a cold day, overcast, a typical March morning. The threat of spring was in the air, and London looked like shit. He sighed. He could already see exactly where this was going. If Michael Flynn requested a personal favour, he expected the person to agree immediately.

'So what are you saying, Michael?'

Michael dragged a chair over to where Declan was sitting, and settled in beside him. Then, after a few moments, he said quietly, 'I've thought about this long and hard. I even asked Jermaine, as a friend, to overlook Jeffrey's faux pas, put it behind him. They are both good men. But he won't.'

Declan looked at Michael, saw the suppressed anger in his face, and the way that Michael was trying to hide it. But Declan knew him too well. 'So what are you going to do about it?'

Michael grinned amiably, all white teeth and stunning good looks. 'What else can I do, Declan? I have been left with no fucking choice. They have to go.'

It was as Declan had expected. He couldn't change anything even if he wanted to. 'I see. Both men are well connected. It will be noticed.'

Michael smiled easily once again. 'I should hope so too! This is a fucking warning, mate. It's my way, or no way.'

Declan watched quietly as Michael picked imaginary dirt from his trousers using his manicured nails, pretending everything was normal.

'When are you going to do it?'

Michael looked over the river; he loved this view, he loved these offices. They spelt success to him. His legitimate businesses were booming, and that was important. He knew that if you earned enough legit money, it made it so much harder for anyone to find a reason to investigate your finances. He paid a lot of money out to keep his life on track – not just to accountants and secretarial staff, but also to the police, and the people the police dealt with. But it was worth every penny spent. He had more Filth and CPS on his bankroll than the Metropolitan Police Force. He paid off people all over the country. It made good business sense.

He looked at Declan, knew that the man was not sure about the latest developments. That wasn't unexpected, but he knew Declan would go along with him as always. '*We* are going to do it tonight, mate. I've arranged a sit down at the scrapyard.'

Declan nodded his agreement, as Michael knew he would.

'I think I've been good, actually. Normally, I would have taken them out much earlier. But now I've had enough.'

Chapter Sixty-Five

Jermaine O'Shay was wary. He didn't trust Michael Flynn as far as he could throw him. As far as Jermaine was concerned, Palmer should have been removed from the equation the minute he fucked up. But Michael Flynn had been determined to find a way to sort everything out. He had understood Jermaine's problem – had agreed with him, sympathised – but he had still wanted him to let it go. He had even asked him to swallow as a personal favour to him.

As if that was ever going to happen. Jeffrey Palmer wasn't a cunt, but by the same token, he had tried to treat Jermaine like one. Palmer had a good rep, was well-liked, but then so was he. This was about respect, and Michael Flynn needed to understand that. His assurance that he had sorted everything out just wasn't good enough. It had gone pear-shaped from day one. Palmer had tried to tuck him up and there was no way Jermaine O'Shay was going to back down. He was going mob-handed to this meet and, if it all went off, he would be prepared.

Chapter Sixty-Six

Jeffrey Palmer sipped his whisky, and felt himself relax. This had not been anything like he had expected. Declan and Michael were both friendly and chatty, making sure he was comfortable, asking if he needed anything else.

The scrapyard was legendary, and this was the first time he had been there. Everyone knew that this was where Michael and Patrick had conducted their real business. It was also a big earner in its own right; he had been told that over a million pounds worth of scrap went through the place every year.

'I hope we can sort everything tonight, Jeff. I don't like discord within my workforce. It causes unnecessary aggro for everyone.'

Jeffrey sipped his drink, savouring the taste of the whisky. 'You know I don't want it either, mate. I dropped a fucking big bollock, and if I could fucking take it back I would. I just got a bit overenthusiastic, that's all. I was blinded by the earn.'

Michael laughed at the man's honesty. 'Well, you will know for the future.'

The headlights from a car played over the ceiling, and Michael got up from his chair behind the dilapidated desk, and walked to the door. Opening it wide, he said gaily, 'Get yourself in, mate. It's fucking freezing.'

Jermaine got out of his car, and Michael saw he had two men

with him. They were both close to Jermaine O'Shay, had worked for him for years. Michael Flynn ushered them into the Portakabin, before closing the door. Then, rubbing his hands together noisily, he said jovially, 'It's fucking taters out there tonight, all right. Colder than a witch's tit.'

The Portakabin was warm and inviting. Motioning to Jermaine with his hands, Michael watched as he sat down in the only other available chair. His two minders stood awkwardly by the doorway. The Portakabin was already filled to capacity; none of the men there were exactly small.

'I thought I said to come alone, Jermaine?' Michael's voice was cold now. His face without his usual smile, without any emotion whatsoever, looked very different, like a mask.

Jermaine O'Shay was not going to be intimidated. He had two of his best men with him and he was here to fight his corner, and remind Michael of who he worked with, and why he was so well thought of. He was partner to some of the hardest men who walked the earth. This was not a fucking friendly sit down, as far as he was concerned. This was him, making a point, once and for all. This had gone on too long now, and he was bored with it.

'Well, as you can see, Michael, I didn't. I haven't come here to negotiate.'

Alarm bells rang for Jeffrey Palmer – there was going to be trouble. He swallowed the last of his whisky quickly. He could see that Declan Costello was as nervous as he was. This was not going to end well, he knew that much.

Michael laughed gently. 'Do you know what, Jermaine? I fucking knew you would come mob-handed. I said that to you, didn't I, Declan?'

Declan nodded his agreement. 'You did at that, Michael. That's why we made provision for just such a situation.'

Jermaine O'Shay frowned. This was not what he was expecting at all.

Declan got up and opened the door that led to the other office.

Michael Flynn called out happily, 'Come in, guys, your moment in the spotlight has arrived at last.'

When Jermaine O'Shay saw the Barker brothers enter, he felt his heart sink like a stone in his chest. There were four Barker brothers, they were each born within a five-year period, and looked like clones. They were all over six foot, heavily built, with a natural penchant for extreme violence. Born from a Jamaican father, and a second-generation Dutch mother, they were handsome fucks, with coffee-coloured skin and dark blue eyes. They were Michael Flynn's private army, and he paid them well. He had their loyalty but, more importantly, he had their friendship. They only worked for the people they *wanted* to; they were known throughout England as men of courage, men of good character who couldn't be owned. They had always stood alone, and that was why they were so sought after. Now they were standing there with machetes in their hands, and smiles on their faces, eager to get down to business.

'I think this is what is called in France, a *fait accompli.* Basically, mate, you're fucked.'

Jermaine looked at his men then, still expecting them to back him up. But they were both standing by the doorway, staring straight ahead.

Michael shrugged nonchalantly. 'I asked you to swallow, Jermaine, but you refused. Months of aggro you've given me.'

Jermaine O'Shay was still not going to be intimidated. 'You know I deserve better than this, Michael. Remember who I work for.'

Michael laughed again. 'Oh, don't worry about me, Jermaine.

I don't shit without planning it out first.' He put his hand on Jeffrey Palmer's shoulder and squeezed it. 'I never wanted this, remember that.'

He went to his desk and opened up one of the drawers, taking out a small axe. 'But I always do my own dirty work.'

He split open Jeffrey Palmer's skull with one massive blow. 'I think that is what the Jamaican Yardies call a permanent parting.'

No one moved, or batted an eyelid.

Jermaine O'Shay felt the spray of blood hit his face. It was outrageous. He watched in disbelief as Michael chopped the man's head off. Declan was looking at Jermaine with resignation and sorrow. He had tried to warn him, but he wouldn't listen.

Michael Flynn was drenched in blood now, it was like a scene from a cheap horror film. Jermaine tried to stand up, tried to defend himself, but his own men forced him back on to the chair, and held him in place.

Michael laughed once more. 'I hope you realise, Jermaine, that this is nothing personal. I liked you. I liked Jeffrey. But I will not be crossed. I will not be treated like a cunt by anyone. I gave you every chance I could. But you insisted on throwing it all back into my face. So fuck you.'

He took his time with Jermaine O'Shay, knowing that this night would be whispered about and remembered by all present. It was about credibility, about teaching people a lesson. It was about making sure the people you employed never forgot who they were dealing with. It was about making a point for the future. Even the Barker boys were impressed, Declan could see that. Like them, Michael Flynn actually enjoyed this.

Chapter Sixty-Seven

Josephine heard Michael come in and glanced at the alarm clock on her bedside table. It was four a.m. She had just fed the baby, and was settling herself into bed again. She waited a few minutes, expecting him to sneak into the bedroom as he usually did. But he didn't come.

Then she heard the shower turn on in the main bathroom. He always used the shower in their en suite, and she wondered why he would suddenly need a shower in the middle of the night.

She got out of the bed, and walked silently out of the bedroom, and across to the bathroom. She slipped through the bathroom door, shutting it quietly behind her. It was a large room, with black marble tiles from floor to ceiling, and an antique bath that had cost a fortune. The walk-in shower was big enough for five people. She saw his clothes on the floor. They were soaked in blood. She instinctively reached for them and saw Michael watching her from the shower as she bundled them up quickly.

'Bring the towels down when you're finished, Michael.'

His eyes followed her as she left the room, before he turned back to finish his shower.

When he came downstairs she was burning everything in the large fireplace in his office. He passed her the towels he had used, and she threw them on to the blaze without a word. She didn't want this mess in her home.

'Is that everything?'

He nodded.

'You're safe, then?'

He pulled her into his arms, and held her tightly. ''Course I am, you silly mare.' He kissed her hair. She was trembling.

'We've got a baby now, remember.'

Michael smiled as he pulled her away from him gently, and looked deep into her eyes. 'How could I ever forget? It's all for you and her now.'

She smiled back brokenly. 'I know that, Michael. I know.'

Book Three

He who brings trouble to his family will inherit only wind,
and the fool will be servant to the wise

Proverbs 11:29

Chapter Sixty-Eight

2004

'That is one lairy little mare, Josephine. Don't you let her get away with it.'

Lana was furious, and Jessie Flynn knew her nana had a right to feel like that. She was heart-sorry for what she had said to her, but she had been goaded.

Josephine didn't answer. Instead she kissed her daughter on the cheek, and walked her to the front door. 'Declan is dropping you off at the disco, and your dad or I will pick you up, OK?'

Jessie sighed theatrically, still ashamed about swearing at her nana, but at least her mum understood why she had done it. 'I know, Mum. Why change the habits of a lifetime?'

'Well, we worry about you, darling, that's all.'

It was said easily, but the underlying warning was there. Jessie was well aware that her father would never let her out of the house if it wasn't for her mother.

'I'm sorry for shouting at Nana.'

Josephine smiled sadly. 'I know that, lovely. She means well, try and remember that. She was the same with me.'

'I know. But I hate having to fight for my freedom, Mum.'

Josephine laughed delightedly at her daughter's dejected countenance. She was a real drama queen, a natural actress.

'Look, darling, if it was left to your father you'd never leave the fucking house. I've told you before, the best way to manage him is to let him think he is in control.'

Jessie rolled her big blue eyes with annoyance. 'I'm nearly fifteen, Mum, I'm not a child any more.'

Josephine pushed her away gently. 'Well, the jury's still out on that one, mate. Have a good night.'

She watched her daughter as she climbed into her uncle Declan's Mercedes. As she waved her off she felt a stab of fear. Jessie looked eighteen even without any make-up on – she was her daughter all right. Done up she looked like a grown woman. But she wasn't, that was the trouble. She was twenty-five in her body, but still a child in her mind. Older men looked at her with interest, and why wouldn't they? She didn't look like a schoolgirl; she had ripened far too early, bless her heart. It was a godsend that she was Michael Flynn's daughter, that alone gave her the protection most girls of her age didn't have. She was a beautiful girl, and that wasn't a mother talking. Her Jessie was a true stunner, in every way that counted for this generation.

She went back into the kitchen, prepared for the fact that her mother was going to give her an earful about why Jessie should never be allowed out without a chaperone. Her mum worried about Jessie looking so much older than her years, and she did too. But, by the same token, her Jessie had her head screwed on. It was strange because Jessie was much closer to Michael's mum than hers. Who would ever have thought that? Hannah seemed to understand her granddaughter in a way that Lana couldn't comprehend. If she didn't know better, she might actually think her own mother didn't like her only grandchild. Lana always seemed to be finding fault with her. It hurt Josephine because her Jessie was a good kid, but all Lana saw was the girl's appearance, and she seemed to insinuate that Jessie being well-developed was a black mark against her somehow. It wasn't something that anyone could have prevented. Nature had endowed her daughter with good looks, a great figure and a bone structure to die for. She was a sensible girl, who had never given them a day's worry, and that was the most important thing as far as Josephine was concerned.

Lana was still fuming at being called an old bitch. 'Did you hear the way she spoke to me, Josephine? Who does she think she is? You need to put a stop to that fucker's gallop, I'm telling you.'

Josephine looked at her mother, saw the way she was bristling with indignation, determined to make her point about her only grandchild, and suddenly she heard herself bellowing loudly, 'Oh, Mum, will you give it a rest, for fuck's sake? She's fourteen years old! Get off her back, and give her a chance.'

'You let her get away with murder. You are making a rod for your own back, madam.'

Josephine was trying hard to keep a lid on her anger. 'Do you know what, Mum? Jessie is a fucking good kid, she does well at school, she goes to Mass without a fight, she helps out around the house. She never pushes her luck. She is my baby and, unlike you, I don't look for flaws, or weaknesses. She's still a kid, Mum, so let her be one while she has the chance.'

Lana sighed. She couldn't help it but she didn't like the child – didn't trust her. She was still waters, deeper than the ocean, that fucker. She would be proved right eventually. She *loved* her granddaughter – of course she did – but there was no liking there. Jessie Flynn was so selfish, so arrogant, so self-assured it was sickening to witness. She wouldn't be a kid for long. Already she knew too much. She had never understood the word no but, then again, she had never heard it. Everything she had ever wanted, she had been given. Michael would pluck the moon out of the sky if she asked him to. She was the only child, late arriving, and she was treated like fucking royalty. But she was also sneaky. Even as a little kid she had known she possessed the upper hand in the relationship with her parents. She was an accident waiting to happen, she would not toe the line for much longer, Lana would put money on that.

She looked at her daughter, who she loved with a vengeance and, modulating her voice, she said carefully, 'All I'm saying, Josephine, is she plays you like a fucking banjo.'

Josephine laughed. ''Course she does, Mum! It's called being a teenager. It's what they *do*. But she knows that me and Michael wouldn't put up with too much nonsense from her. She is still young enough to listen to what we say to her. Now, do you want another glass of wine or not?'

Lana nodded. Josephine poured the wine, and Lana turned her thoughts to her daughter. Josephine rarely left her house now – more often than not it was Lana who did the shopping for the family these days. Josephine was becoming more insular by the week, and young Jessie wasn't a fool – she would be bound to use that to her advantage. It was human nature. She had a lot of her father in her; she was stubborn just like him, and she was prone to serious anger when thwarted. She was her mother's double in her looks, but she had inherited none of her mother's kindly nature. Like her father, she rarely showed anybody her real self. She had inherited Michael's temper too. It had occasionally surfaced over the years and, just like Michael's, when it did finally erupt, it was a powerful force in its own right.

Chapter Sixty-Nine

Michael was exhausted, but he had no choice but to carry on. He was negotiating a deal that would bring him millions over the next few years if it came off. He had planned it down to the last detail; it had taken nearly a year to bring to fruition. Now he was almost there. He was working with a huge Colombian cartel personally, and he was only too aware how dangerous that could be. *These* people were not impressed with anyone, anywhere, and it had taken him a lot of time and effort to convince them he was a viable partner. He had his own rep as a bad man in Europe, but compared to them and the world they moved in the Europeans were fucking amateurs. These men were a law unto themselves; they would shoot their own mothers if they deemed it necessary to the cause, and were more than capable of torturing and murdering a rival's child to prove a point. They inhabited a world where a human life was valued cheaper than a can of Coke. It was a different ballgame altogether.

Now he, Michael Flynn, was fronting one of the biggest deals ever negotiated on British turf. And, once it was in place, he would be the undisputed king of Europe. No one could have a shit, shave or a shampoo without asking his permission first.

He looked out of his office window over the Thames. He loved this view; it made him feel invincible. He surveyed his domain. London was all his. He had bought, fought and forced his will on everyone who mattered, and it had paid off.

The offices had been recently revamped, and he wasn't sure he liked the results. With the white walls and bleached oak flooring, there was nothing remotely attractive about it – it looked far too impersonal for his tastes. He missed his old desk – an antique captain's desk. It had been bulky and scuffed, but it had character. Now he sat at a very expensive modern desk that was basically two planks of highly polished wood, held together by willpower and two pieces of eight by four. It had six spindly legs, which didn't exactly fill him with faith it would stay up, and it was without even one single fucking drawer to give it an iota of usefulness. Even the chair he sat on was uncomfortable – yet it had cost more than his first car. But it was all about front – he knew that better than anyone – and it impressed people he dealt with.

He was getting old, he supposed. He was turning into the very people he had loathed as a young man. Yearning for the past; now, of course, he understood why they had felt that way. He still wouldn't let anything be done over the internet. He was classed as a dinosaur because of that, but he didn't care – he didn't trust it. They could shove cyberspace up their arses. For the right price, like most things in this life, it could be abused. He didn't trust anything that had the power to reach millions of people at a stroke. It seemed to him that computers bred laziness and apathy. People were too quick to trust in something that they couldn't build themselves, that they had to rely on other people to maintain for them, and at great cost as well. It was a recipe for disaster. He particularly worried about leaving a trail that could be discovered without the person involved even leaving their office. No, he wasn't prepared to join the cyber rats.

He worked in a world where the fewer people in the know the better. He still relied on private meetings and word of mouth.

Fortunately for him, so did the Colombians. Now they had finally agreed to meet him on his own turf. It was the last step. That they had felt confident enough to come to him was a coup in itself. They needed to show him that they trusted him, and he had to prove to them that he could guarantee them the protection needed. He had done just that. They had landed safely in England, and no one had questioned them.

It was dark now, the lights were on across London. It was funny, but he always thought that London looked more impressive by night. It looked more alive to him, full of possibilities and secrets. He glanced at his watch, a diamond Rolex with a platinum face. It was just after nine p.m. They would be here in the next ten minutes or so. He glanced around him. He had everything ready. The drinks cabinet – that he personally thought looked like a fucking cheap filing cabinet – had every alcoholic beverage known to man, and the leather sofas were placed strategically so everyone could interact together without having to move about too much. There was also food in the kitchen, should anyone request it.

Salvatore Ferreira was an extremely cautious man. Michael appreciated that trait. He rarely left his native Colombia. Michael had taken over a whole floor of one of the top London hotels to guarantee Salvatore his privacy, and also to give him the chance to enjoy the luxury such an establishment could provide.

He heard the soft thrumming noise that heralded the arrival of the private lift and, settling himself into his chair, he waited patiently to begin the meeting he had been waiting for for a year, and which would cement his legendary status in the criminal underworld once and for all.

Chapter Seventy

'Listen, Declan, I didn't want to be the one to tell you this, believe me, but what else could I do, for fuck's sake?'

Peter Barker, the elder of the Barker brothers, looked into Declan's face with its usual blank countenance. But his colour was high, he was flushed red. Declan could tell the man was angry, and so he fucking should be. This was a piss-take, especially now when everyone knew there was something serious in the wind.

'Look, don't shoot the fucking messenger, mate – I'm trying to do the right thing here.'

Declan shook his head. This was the last fucking thing he needed tonight. The music from the nightclub was loud, even through the heavy fire doors of the offices. He hated the music they had to play in the clubs these days; it was fucking abysmal – it sounded like electrical interference to him. Declan sighed and, as calmly as he could, asked, 'Who did you say told you this, Peter?'

Peter took a large joint out of his jacket pocket and, after lighting it, he puffed on it fiercely, before he answered his friend's question. 'I told you already, Declan – it was Jack Cornel. He was full of it. The stupid-looking northern ponce! I was all for hammering him, but my brother Billy stepped in. He reckons that this is about nausing up Michael's meeting with the

Colombians – though how they know about it is fucking suspect in itself. You and I know the Cornels have never been happy answering to him. Michael never gave them their due, and they fucking knew it. They are so fucking full of themselves. They still seem to think that the North is a fucking no-go area for us lot down here. The M1 passed right over their fucking heads, I tell ya.'

Declan laughed at the man's words despite himself. He could be funny, could old Peter Barker. He had a dry humour which wasn't everybody's cup of tea, but always hit the proverbial nail on the head.

'So they have come down south, determined to cause fucking havoc, have they?'

Peter nodded sagely. 'Basically, yeah. They think that if they cause problems for Michael, the Colombians will see the error of their ways. That's the real worry. Michael won't want any kind of issues, will he? That stands to reason.'

Declan let this information sink in. The Cornel brothers had been a thorn in everyone's side for a long time. They were without scruples, devoid of even the most basic of social graces, and they had taken over the North East almost by accident from the Dooleys. Jack Cornel had shot one of them over a debt and, as the older Dooley brothers were on remand, he had not yet been challenged about his foolishness. The Cornels were relatively new to the real game – up to now, they had been no more than cannon fodder. It had been assumed that they would be removed tout suite. But it had not happened. No one had ever seen the Cornels as a serious threat; now, it seemed, they were under the misapprehension that they were hard enough to take on Michael Flynn and the whole South East. What planet they were inhabiting was up for debate all right. It was ludicrous, and it could not have come at a worse time. Jack Cornel was a natural-born fighter, but his younger brother, Cecil, was a fucking looney. He was definitely two bob short of a pound note. He didn't fight as such – he just attacked with whatever weapon came to hand. Jack Cornel was a fucking exhibitionist; he would love nothing more than to cause a row with Michael in public. He was too thick to see the folly of his actions – all he would see was the glory of people knowing he had dared to do such a thing. As for Cecil, an original thought in his head would die of fucking loneliness; he would follow his brother's lead. It was a fucking abortion. Of all the times the Cornel brothers could have chosen to get themselves killed stone dead, they had to go and pick now, when Michael Flynn was negotiating the biggest deal in criminal history.

'Oh, Jesus Christ. Michael will go fucking apeshit when he finds out.'

Peter Barker grinned. 'I had worked that one out for myself, Declan.'

Declan Costello held his head in his hands; he was absolutely mortified. 'Round them up, Peter. But try and keep it on the down low.'

Peter took a deep toke on his joint before saying huskily, 'It will be a fucking pleasure, Declan, believe me. It's already in hand actually – I took it upon myself to presume!' He shook his head in wonderment. 'It never ceases to amaze me, Declan, just how fucking thick some people actually are. But as my old nan used to say, you can't educate a fucking haddock.'

Chapter Seventy-One

Jessie was pleased to see her mum waiting outside her school, and she jumped into the car happily. She knew how hard it was for her mum to drive at night; she had guessed far more about her mum and her problems than she let on.

'I thought Dad might be picking me up. You know what he's like about me getting home at a reasonable time!' She was genuinely amazed that her mum had come to get her. She rarely left the house these days if she didn't have to. It was something she knew was wrong, but no one would ever say it out loud. It worried her that her mother didn't go anywhere any more, and it scared her that everyone acted as if it was normal.

Josephine smiled nervously as she pulled away from the kerb tentatively. 'He was unavoidably detained, as usual! Work stuff. How was your night anyway, darling?'

Jessie laughed with delight. 'It was a good night, Mum, a right laugh.'

Josephine could hear the pleasure in her daughter's voice. 'That's how it should be at your age.'

Jessie didn't answer; she was still basking in the night's events.

'I thought Natalie needed a lift home?'

Jessie shrugged easily. 'No, she's walking home with some of the other girls.' She wished it was her – she would love to walk home with everyone, exchanging gossip, and talking about the next party on Friday night that they were all looking forward to. Jason Ford had asked her to go with him. But that was never going to happen – she was always dropped off, and then picked up and taken home safely. It was her life, and she had to accept that.

'By the way, Mum, I'm staying at Natalie's house on Friday night. We're going shopping Saturday early. I told her mum it was OK.'

Josephine yawned. ''Course it is! We'll get you picked up when you're ready to come home.'

Jessie grinned happily. 'Thanks, Mum.' She knew her mum would never question her staying over at Natalie's. They had been friends since infant school, and they lived in each other's pockets. Natalie was going to tell her mum she was staying at *hers*, and they would then be able to go to the party in peace. She couldn't wait. Jason Ford was going to get the shock of his life on Friday. She was determined to show him she was a lot more grown up than he realised. She had been mad about him for over a year, and now he had actually asked her out. If her mum or dad knew about him, she would be grounded until she was old and grey. Her dad was like her minder! Yet she knew that he was not lily-white himself. She had heard all about him and her uncle Declan, but when she tried to ask her mother about the stories she'd been told, her mum had been less than forthcoming. She loved that they cared so much about her, but she also resented that they never gave her any freedom. She lived so far away from her friends, and that alone made her feel like an outsider.

The name Flynn gave her a certain cachet. She was the daughter of a man who was feared and respected in equal measure and that was her cross to bear. She had been treated like royalty all her life, and she had known from a young age that was because of her father. Even her teachers were wary of her father; that had been a real eye-opener for her. She wasn't a complete fool. People called him the Crime King of England – and a violent thug. It was awful, especially as her friends knew all the gossip too. But he was still her dad, no matter what people might say about him. She had a good life, and she appreciated it. Whatever he might be, he was the man she looked up to, and who she adored.

Nevertheless, she was going to lie and cheat her way to the party on Friday night. She was going to have a good night out, by hook or by crook.

Chapter Seventy-Two

Salvatore Ferreira was not as big as Michael had expected him to be. In fact, he was quite short – only about five nine – but he was built like a brick shithouse. Anyone looking at him would know immediately that he was more than capable of great violence. It was there in his eyes. He had the look of the gutter; his eyes were without any kind of emotion whatsoever and that was the real giveaway. Michael knew he had the same look. It was why they had both advanced so far in their careers. It was what made most people take a step back from them.

Salvatore Ferreira was dark-haired, dark-eyed and dark-skinned and he possessed a very proud countenance. Michael understood that as well – without that innate arrogance neither of them would have achieved anything of note. Michael was pleased to see that the man was very well dressed in a bespoke suit, handsewn shoes, and without the usual South-American need for loud, garish jewellery. He looked just what he was: a well-heeled businessman.

They shook hands affably; each had a very strong grip. Sizing each other up, they were both pleased with what they saw in their prospective business partner. Michael knew his size gave him the edge, he was a powerful-looking man. Patrick Costello had told him many years before, 'Always walk into a place like you already own it, and the chances are that eventually you fucking will.' It was good advice, and something that he had never forgotten.

'It's an honour to have you here, Salvatore.'

His tone conveyed the respect the man required from him. After all, he was the main supplier, the benefactor – without him, Michael would never have been able to guarantee such huge amounts of drugs to the people he dealt with. This was something that had never been done before on such a large scale. Thanks to Ferreira, he had an endless supply of cocaine that was purer than anything else on the market. It could be cut over and over again, and still be purer than anything in Europe. Everyone was a winner.

'I am pleased to be here, Michael. My first time in London. Already I am in love with this country.'

Michael grinned. 'It's a funny old town, Salvatore. But it is also one of the biggest tourist destinations in the world. The Queen sees to that, mate. We may be a small country, but we are a rich one. Europe has always looked to us for guidance. We are the main players, as we always have been.'

Salvatore sat down on the black leather sofa gracefully. Michael knew he had come out of one of the worst slums on earth, that he had no real education – except what the Catholic priests had beaten into him on the odd occasion he had gone to school. Yet he was feared and respected by everyone he dealt with. There was more to this man than met the eye. He was not what Michael had been expecting. He had been told, on good authority, that the Colombians were basically fucking animals, without any social graces, but he had cast his net wider for information, and found out a lot more about the man by himself. You didn't live as long as Salvatore unless you had something going for you up top. Salvatore was already coming across as a man after his own heart, who had embraced the financial aspects that his career had provided for him, and who had then learnt how to carry himself in any company.

The two men had bonded immediately. They saw themselves in one another, and that was something they understood the value of. It was important to have trust – without it they were doomed. It didn't escape Michael's notice that Salvatore had left his men outside the door, and he was glad that his decision to meet the man alone had paid off.

Michael sat down beside Salvatore. 'I am so pleased that you came to England in person. I know how much that proves your belief in me. I wanted to show you that I have the money *and* the strength needed for such a venture – to not only finance this business arrangement, but also to police it and, more importantly, to guarantee you that there is *nothing* I am not prepared for.'

Salvatore nodded easily. 'I know this. I have done my homework, as you say. I would never have ventured this far from my homeland, unless I was sure of that beforehand.' He took a long drink of the brandy Michael had poured him, then he said honestly, 'But I have to ask you this, Michael, face to face – how are you going to deal with the Russians? They have always had the monopoly in Europe. The Russians, and their counterparts the Eastern Europeans, are like us South Americans in many ways. They come from countries that are more corrupt than you could even imagine. They are ruthless, and they are here in London already. They don't play by the rules. They also have their own suppliers. True, it's always shit stuff – as you know, they are better with heroin and it's a completely different market. That aside, I need to know that you can control them, and that you have already implemented plans to ensure that they can never interfere with our business should they decide to. This is not something I would enter into lightly, you know that. You have guaranteed that you have the monopoly in Europe, and I believe you. If I didn't, I wouldn't have journeyed all this way. I just want you to reassure me that nothing and no one can interfere with our plans.'

Michael was irritated. He had already proved to Ferreira that he had everything under his control – that was why the man had come over to England in the first place! The Russians were already on-side, as he had informed him; they were quite happy to let him supply whatever was needed. Once he was onboard with the Colombians, they didn't really have a choice. It was a done deal. There was too much aggravation in Afghanistan and Pakistan these days for the crops to be safe. It wasn't so easy for the Russians any more – they were not as welcome as they had been in the eighties and nineties. The Americans were all over them like a rash, and they were concentrating more on finance deals and investing heavily in property, especially Dubai, Croatia and Greece. Michael knew that Salvatore had been told this, and more than once. He also knew that Salvatore Ferreira would not have taken his word for it, he would have found out what he needed to know himself.

Michael swallowed down his frustration. This was nothing personal, it was just Ferreira flexing his muscles, and making sure that Michael understood exactly what was expected of him. He was warning him that any problems that might arise would be his alone, and he would be expected to sort them out quickly and with the minimum of fuss. The man was a businessman, and at least he had the grace to say this to him on the quiet, man to man, without an audience. Still it rankled. But Michael had listened to his mentor Patrick Costello well. He could hear his voice now saying quietly in his ear, 'Never let anyone know what you're thinking, Michael, never show them anything of importance. The earn is the prize, never forget that.'

Walking casually to the bar, he picked up the bottle of

Remy XO. Then, pouring them both another drink, he sat back down beside Salvatore Ferreira on the leather sofa, smiling as if he had just been blessed by the Pope himself.

'I can assure you, Salvatore, that no one will interfere with our business. I own fucking everyone of importance, from the police, to the Customs, to the fucking High Court Judges. I can access anyone needed.'

Salvatore Ferreira nodded; he had expected no less. He had made his point, he could be magnanimous now. 'I believe you, Michael. But I had to ask, you understand that?'

Michael took a large sip of his brandy and, shrugging nonchalantly, he said carefully, swallowing down the raw anger that was threatening to overwhelm him, 'Of course I do, Salvatore. I would do the same in your position. Now, I thought I would take you to one of my clubs in the West End.'

Salvatore was watching him closely, and Michael knew this was some kind of test.

'I like the English girls. Proper blondes!'

Michael sighed heavily, rolling his eyes in mock annoyance. 'I had a feeling you would say that!'

Chapter Seventy-Three

Jack Cornel believed himself to be an intelligent man – if he had been allowed to have a decent education, he knew he could have made something of himself. His biggest problem was his arrogance, which he had worn like a shield since childhood. All his life he had sought arguments with anyone that he felt might be looking down on him. He had a huge chip on his shoulder. He hated to be treated like a nobody. His father had been a well-known drunk and his mother an even bigger one. The Cornel boys had grown up in a filthy council flat, the result of haphazard parenting, and had to live with the stigma of having the Cornel name.

They had not just witnessed violence – they had been the recipients of it since they could remember. It had been a hard upbringing. Jack had tried to protect his younger brother from his parents' viciousness and their complete disregard for the two children they had somehow created.

His father had finally beaten his wife to death when the two boys were thirteen and ten respectively. They had then had to try and survive in the care system. Too old for adoption, and much too disturbed for fostering at a residential care home, they had eventually been placed in a lock-down facility that catered for children either sent there by the courts for serious offences or, like the Cornel brothers, because no one knew what to do with them. It was a severe and harsh environment, and they stayed until eventually the social workers released them one after the other on to an unsuspecting public. By then they were past redemption, inured to pain and, without the skills to adapt to society, they had lapsed into the world of petty villainy. Burglars, thieves and liars, they had simply existed, until Jack shot a Dooley. That one act had made him believe he was now capable of moving them up in the world, thereby making a real name for themselves. Jack Cornel saw this as his chance to shine, and he was determined to make the most of the opportunity. He had assured his brother Cecil that, with Dooley's murder behind them, they were finally on the road to public recognition and wealth.

Chapter Seventy-Four

Declan was watching the Cornel brothers as they drank themselves stupid in a private club Michael had acquired a few years previously, in lieu of a heavy debt. They were with a couple of young lads, both up-and-coming Faces, who knew exactly what was wanted from them. The Cornels had walked into the club with the lads, without a second's thought, and that alone proved just how gullible they were. They were not even on their own home turf.

It was pitiful. The Cornel brothers actually believed that Michael Flynn was going to arrive here at some point, with the Colombians in tow. As if that would ever happen! As if anyone truly in the know would think that a man like Michael Flynn would actually come to a shithole like this, and bring his overseas guests with him.

He had told the bar staff to give them what they wanted, and to make sure the drinks were large and plentiful – the drunker these prats were the better. The Dooleys had made a major fuck-up by not paying the Cornels out for their brother's murder. The fact that they were on remand didn't really mean anything – they were running everything from the prison, business as usual. Rumour had it that they had a problem with the brother who had died, but so what? No one in the world they lived in would swallow something so outrageous. It was their brother, for fuck's sake! And that needed sorting out. It was a piss-take, an insult to them as a family, and especially when it was perpetrated by people like the Cornels – a pair of prize cabbages, whose combined IQ was equivalent to a fucking mongoose.

Whatever the rights and wrongs of the situation, Declan blamed the Dooleys' tardiness for the Cornels thinking they were on course for the big time. Now the Cornels were *his* problem, and that wasn't something he would forget in a hurry. The Dooleys owed him. He was doing their dirty work for them after all, and he was going to make sure they compensated him for his aggravation. It was going to be a very expensive oversight on their part.

He stepped back into the office quickly. They were drunk as cunts, but Jack would know there was something amiss if he saw him there.

He had told the doorman to clear the club by two a.m. The Cornels would think they were getting a lock-in. His lads had already told them they had arranged it so they could be there when Michael arrived. They were drunk and vulnerable and, as far as Declan Costello was concerned, that was exactly as it should be. The treacherous pair of filthy, dirty bastards! Wanting to fucking shoot Michael Flynn dead, and then to assume that would be enough to give them credibility, turn them into real Faces, real villains. They thought he would allow them to step into his shoes without a fight? It was so demented, it was almost comical.

Declan Costello could feel the beating of his heart as his anger smouldered. If the Barkers had not given him the heads up tonight could have been a blood bath; it could have brought the Filth down on everyone concerned, including the visiting Colombians, and that was something, he had a feeling, that would not have been taken lightly.

He lit a cigarette, and pulled on it deeply. It was just coming up to one o'clock. Michael would be there within the hour, and that was when the Cornel brothers would finally realise the error of their ways.

Chapter Seventy-Five

Michael Flynn watched Salvatore Ferreira as he cheerfully succumbed to the charms of the beautiful Bella. She was one of his top-earning lap dancers. She wasn't as young as she looked, but that didn't really matter. She had the thick blond hair, blue eyes and creamy skin of a real English rose. She also had a very posh accent, and that went a long way with the clientele. She was really from Dagenham, but she had taken elocution lessons, ballet lessons, and had shrugged off the mantle of an Essex girl, creating a whole new persona for herself. He admired her. She had the sense to realise that this wasn't a job with a pension, she knew that her shelf life would be short, but could be very lucrative if she played her cards right. He had guaranteed her three grand, cash, to keep Salvatore amused: go home with him, and make him feel like a king. In fairness, she deserved a fucking BAFTA. What a performance! He caught her eye, motioned towards the door, and Bella was off her pole, and in Salvatore's lap within nanoseconds.

Michael Flynn walked them out to a private car five minutes later and, winking lewdly at a very drunken Salvatore Ferreira, he waved them off gratefully. He had done his bit, and now he could finally concentrate on the other business of the night. He was being driven by a young lad called Davey Dawkins, a good kid, who drove the car without ever trying to start a conversation.

Michael appreciated that tonight more than usual. He was so angry he was quite literally capable of murder.

Chapter Seventy-Six

Josephine couldn't sleep – it was a long time since she had slept through the night. Even sleeping tablets didn't work any more. She had her own bedroom now. When Michael was out all hours, she didn't have to go to bed without him and pretend everything was OK. She could come in here and watch her TV programmes, sit in peace surrounded by her private things – her 'knick knacks', as Jessie called them. Though they weren't really knick knacks as such. The boxes she kept in here were full of important papers and magazines. She also had all of her daughter's school work from the first day she had attended – all her pictures, drawings, report cards. She even had the wrappers from sweets her daughter had eaten over the years. She couldn't part with them. Michael didn't think keeping everything Jessie had ever touched was normal. She didn't care. He didn't understand the bond between a mother and her child. She had every item of clothing that her daughter had worn. It was boxed up now, of course, washed and ironed. She knew exactly where everything was – every Babygro, every bib, everything she had kept she could find should she wish to.

Her bed was a double, with an antique mother-of-pearl headboard, and crisp white linen. There was no other furniture in here now, except for her chair and her TV. She didn't need anything else; she was quite happy to give the extra room over to her boxes of memories.

Sitting in here she was surrounded by her whole life. Michael hated it. He felt she dwelt too much on the past, when she should be enjoying the present or looking forward to the future. It was hard for him to understand how attached she was to her treasures. He was different to her; his life was mainly lived outside the house – he was always off somewhere – and he wanted her to be the same. Her journeys out into the world were getting rarer and rarer; she preferred the comfort and safety of her own home. She didn't drive much any more either, she only got into the car if she had to for her daughter's benefit. She knew, deep inside, that she was gradually becoming even more of a recluse, but she didn't care. She had all she needed here in her own home.

She looked down at her legs; they were still shapely. She was a good-looking woman, and she took good care of herself – she always put on her make-up and dressed well. Michael still wanted her; he enjoyed her body as he had years before. She still wanted him, and loved the feel of his arms around her. But she had no desire to go out with him any more. She cooked him meals that a professional chef would be proud of, she always made sure the table was dressed with everything from the finest glassware to the best linen. She kept a home for him that was the envy of many a man. All she asked in return was that he allowed her to live her life her own way.

She walked over to the French doors and, opening them, she went out to the small balcony. Sitting at the table, she looked at the sky. It was a clear night, the moon was full, and the stars were glittering above her. She shivered in the cold night air and, picking up the glass of white wine she had left out there earlier, she took a deep drink. Jessie was asleep, and she envied her daughter for a few moments. It had been so long since *she* had really slept, she had forgotten what it was like. She wished she didn't suffer from insomnia, that she could get into bed and relax like everyone else. Just to lie down and drift off peacefully was a luxury she couldn't enjoy any more. Instead, she was wide awake, straining her ears for the sound of her husband's car crunching on the drive. Once he was home safe, she always felt better.

It was when she was alone in the night like this that she couldn't stop herself thinking about things she knew were better left alone. Michael's lifestyle frightened her; she remembered late at night that the world he inhabited was a violent, bloody world. It was a world that she knew he loved, and one that she had never truly understood until the night she had seen him as he really was, covered in blood, and calmly washing it away without any emotion whatsoever. She had helped him – it had been instinctive; she had done what a wife in her position was expected to do for the man she had married. But it was a moment that changed everything. After that night, she had suffered from violent nightmares for weeks, and that was when her insomnia had begun. She was afraid of sleeping, afraid of the nightmares that would take hold, and she had never recovered. His lifestyle, what she knew he was capable of, terrified her. She'd thought she'd understood; seeing it first-hand was completely different.

She knew he would never harm her or his daughter; he loved them more than anything in the world, but that, in itself, was part of the problem. She didn't feel she could live up to his expectations of her, she hadn't even been able to give him a child for years. Now she worried that he saw her need for staying at home as a flaw. It was, she supposed, but it was how she coped. Even though he never said anything to her outright, she knew that her refusals to accompany him anywhere hurt his feelings. She didn't want to do that to him – she loved him with all her heart. But it was getting harder and harder for her to venture outside her home. Just picking up Jessie tonight had been so nerve-racking that when she had finally got back to the house, she had been sweating profusely.

Every day, her world shrank a bit more. She could only ever really feel safe inside her own home, with all her things around her. This need she had to feel safe was powerful. She had to step away from the world that Michael inhabited. It was a world that had gradually crippled her.

She just didn't want to fight it any more. Tonight she had made her mind up, admitted the truth to herself at last, and made a firm decision not to leave her sanctuary again. She felt almost tearful with joy. Michael would eventually accept her decision. Michael would never risk her actually telling him the truth, the real reason why she was like this.

Picking up her empty wine glass she went back into the warmth of the house. She would have another glass of wine, and watch a nice DVD. That was how she passed the hours away, because sleep was a luxury that all the money in the world couldn't buy.

Chapter Seventy-Seven

Jack Cornel was drunk, and he was not a friendly drunk at the best of times. He was, in actual fact, a paranoid drunk, looking for problems where none existed, and willing to follow his hatred wherever it might take him. He was already looking for a row, a reason to kick off. He had been waiting all night for that ponce Flynn to arrive and now he was bored. He had come to London to take out Michael Flynn. Every time he thought about it he felt the excitement stir in his belly. This was going to give him and his brother the kudos that they craved. He wanted to step into the limelight, show people what he was capable of, convince the world that he was not a man to be ignored.

Cecil was also drunk. Unlike his older brother, though, drink mellowed him out. He loved the world, and everyone in it. Jack watched as Cecil staggered to the men's room, all smiles and camaraderie. He was disgusted by his brother's antics – he was like a fucking big girl's blouse, so gormless it was embarrassing to watch him. Jack Cornel had one thing in his favour: even as drunk as a skunk, he was shrewd, and he never missed a chance that came his way. He had an in-built cunning that copious amounts of alcohol seemed to bring to the fore; he was one of the few people who actually functioned far better while under the influence of alcohol.

Glancing around, he noticed that the club was already almost empty. When he saw the doorman watching him, he knew immediately, without any doubt whatsoever, that there was something radically wrong. Years of living round two hopeless alcoholics had prepared him for the worst, and it had also taught him the need to have an escape plan at all times. He had not trusted the two young fellows who promised him Michael Flynn on a plate. He had felt from the off that they were just stooges. But he *had* counted on them producing the man in question at some point. He would then have happily taken his chance and, as he was in possession of two firearms, he felt his chances were much better than average; all he needed was a decent shot. He wasn't about to play games – he just wanted to get in there, take the fucker out, and then bask in the glory.

Now, though, he felt the cold fingers of fear on his neck. There was something more going on here. He swallowed down his drink quickly, before turning to his young hosts and saying craftily, 'I need a piss, lads, and I need to make sure that my little brother is still capable of cognitive thoughts and behaviour! Fill us up again – the night is young.'

He walked towards the men's room slowly and carefully, knowing he was being observed from all angles. Inside the toilet, he looked at his younger brother, who was trying unsuccessfully to drain his bladder without soiling himself and his trousers too badly.

Cecil looked in the mirror at his brother and he grinned idiotically. 'What a fucking great night, bruv!'

Jack Cornel rolled his eyes. His brother was never a man who could hold a drink inside him – he either pissed it out, or spewed it all over the floor. It was a cross he always had to bear, but tonight it annoyed him more than usual. Ignoring his brother, he walked into the stall. There was a window in there. It took him two minutes to open it – someone had painted it shut, so he had to use his penknife to open it. Once it was open he stood on the toilet bowl and climbed outside, calling to his brother to follow him. They found themselves in a small alleyway. Scaling a three-foot wall that took them on to another level, Jack grabbed his brother none too gently by the arm and pulled them both up a flight of rickety stairs until, finally, they were out on the street.

'What's going on, Jack?'

Jack Cornel didn't even bother to answer.

By the time they were missed, the two brothers were long gone.

Chapter Seventy-Eight

'What do you mean, Declan? How could you have fucking lost them?'

Michael Flynn was genuinely perplexed. This wasn't happening, surely? The Cornels were fucking idiots. How the fuck had they escaped?

Declan Costello was mortified; this was like amateur night. 'Look, Michael, that Jack is a lot more fucking with-it than we gave him credit for. He followed his brother into the john, and they went out the fucking window. No one could have foreseen that.'

Michael Flynn was looking at Declan Costello as if he had never seen him before in his life. He was so outraged at the man's complete fucking dereliction of his duty, he wasn't sure he could be trusted not to hammer him into the ground.

'This is fucking unbelievable! I have been entertaining the Colombians all night. All you had to do was keep an eye on two northern fucking wankers, and you are telling me that they outwitted you? They scrambled out of the crapper window, and no one fucking noticed anything? Are you telling me no one was outside?'

Declan shook his head in abject denial; he was reeling with amazement. He had kept a low profile, waiting for Michael to arrive, and now it was completely fucking naused up in the worst way possible.

'Was he armed?'

Declan nodded once again. 'He had two firearms, a Glock, and a smaller handgun.'

Michael laughed sarcastically. 'Oh, that is just fucking great. Just what I need – a drunken fucking northerner after my blood, running the streets of London without a care in the fucking world. You useless crowd of cunts. If anything happens to cause problems with Salvatore, I will personally hunt every fucker involved down, and I will kill them myself.'

Declan looked around. Everyone in the club was looking at the floor; no one wanted to catch Michael's eye, or bring his wrath down on their heads.

Michael was in total shock. He was in the process of making a deal with one of the most dangerous men on the planet, and nothing – *nothing* – could go wrong. If Salvatore Ferreira thought that there was even a minuscule chance of aggro he would back off faster than a transvestite at a tractor pull. Salvatore had travelled to England because he had been assured that nothing could happen to him while he was here. If he was dragged into a police investigation because the Cornel brothers decided they wanted to chance their arm, it would cause murders – literally.

'Get out there, Declan. I want everyone we have on our payroll looking for them. There's a twenty grand bonus on each of the Cornels' heads. Find them, and find them soon. I'm going home. I assume you already have people watching my drum? The last thing we need is my wife and daughter put in the frame.'

Declan nodded. ''Course. Give me some credit, for Christ's sake.'

Michael stormed out of the club and, as soon as he was gone, Declan turned to the doorman. They were terrified for their lives, knowing they had made a major fuck-up.

'Patsy, get on the blower and get four of your guys over to Michael's drum sooner rather than later. I will organise geting everyone out on the pavements. We need to find the Cornels and, when we do, I will fucking skin the bastards alive myself.'

Chapter Seventy-Nine

Jessie Flynn woke up suddenly and, turning on her bedside lamp, she listened intently. Whatever had woken her from her sleep was still going on. She could hear her mother's voice shouting at someone. Her mother *never* shouted at anyone. She was one of the most inoffensive people on the planet. This was not something she had ever experienced before in her life. But she could hear panic and fright in her mum's voice.

Jumping out of bed, she ran from her bedroom, and across the large landing to her mother's room. 'What's happening, Mum? What's going on?'

Josephine was at her balcony doors and, at the sound of her daughter's voice, she turned quickly towards her, saying quietly, 'Go back to your room, darling, and lock your door. Don't argue with me, just do what I say.'

Josephine didn't want the men on her drive to know her daughter was in the house with her. They were after trouble. They wanted Michael, and she knew they were not leaving without a fight.

'Have you phoned the police, Mum?'

Josephine shook her head angrily. ''Course not, and don't you either! Just do what I said, will you!' She was almost shouting at her daughter now, and Jessie was getting more frightened by the second.

She could hear a man's voice shouting angrily, 'I'm warning you, lady, open the fucking door or I'm blasting my way in.'

Jessie watched in shocked amazement as her mother shouted back loudly, 'Go on then, I dare you. But it won't be easy. A fucking cannon couldn't get through there. My husband will fucking be here any minute, and he will kill you. He will fucking take you out, mate, and laugh while he does it.'

She shut the balcony doors and pulled the wooden shutters across, locking them quickly. Then, as she ran from the room, Jessie followed her mother down the stairs, and into her father's office.

'Mum, we need to phone the police!'

'No, we don't! They are the last people we want on the fucking doorstep!'

Jessie Flynn couldn't believe her ears. 'Mum! We need to get the police here now!'

Josephine was opening the large safe Michael used for his cash, and Jessie watched as her mother removed a large shotgun. Priming it expertly, she pushed her daughter out of the door roughly and, standing in the hallway with the gun aimed at the front door, she bellowed, 'For the last time, Jessie, will you do what you're told for once. We don't need the police, OK? I've already rung for help. Now will you just *move it*!'

Jessie heard the urgency in her mother's voice, and she ran up the staircase quickly, but she turned at the top of the landing, and watched her mother – her quiet, kind-hearted mother – calmly lock all the downstairs doors, before she once more positioned herself in the centre of the hallway, the gun cocked, her lovely face set into a grimace of hate.

This was unbelievable – it was like something from a TV programme! There were men outside trying to get in, trying to burgle them and, instead of phoning the police, her mum was preparing to take them on single-handed. It was wrong. It was terrifying. This was something that the police should be dealing with, surely? Her dad knew the police, they were always round the house having meetings with him.

She was shaking with fear now. She sat on the top stair and, pulling her nightdress over her knees, she watched her mother as if she had never seen her before. And she hadn't – not this mother, anyway. This was a woman Jessie had never met before. This was a woman Jessie was actually frightened of.

She heard glass shattering – the men had smashed through the back door. She saw her mother turn towards the locked and bolted kitchen door, the gun poised, and ready to discharge. This was a nightmare. None of this was happening.

'I'm armed, and I will blow you away, you bastards. I'm warning you now. Go while you still have a chance.'

The sound of cars screeching to a halt on the gravel drive was loud, and she saw the relief on her mother's face. Then she heard her dad's voice.

Her mother opened the front door quickly, and her father was inside the house. She could hear the sounds of his men's feet as they scrambled around. He was holding her mother to him tightly, kissing her hair and talking to her in a low voice, calming her down, making her feel safe.

Jessie watched silently, aware that none of them had even noticed her. She moved quickly and quietly, so she was out of view, tucked behind the banisters at the top of the stairs, and hidden by the darkness. She heard her father ask where she was, and her mother tell him she was locked in her bedroom. She saw him sigh with relief.

'Who are these people, Michael? What are they after?'

She saw her dad take the shotgun from her mother's arms carefully.

'I'm so sorry, Josephine. This was an accident. It should never have happened, darling. You didn't call the police, did you?'

Jessie saw her mother shake her head quickly. ''Course not. But I tell you now, another ten minutes and I would have. They were nearly inside our home! Our *home*, Michael! Jessie was terrified. *I* was fucking terrified.'

Michael was holding his wife tightly once more. Jessie could see the love they had between them, and she felt the tears come. It was so powerful to see them like that, holding each other so tightly, so attuned to each other's needs, and looking so perfect together. Then she heard her father chuckle, and she knew that the danger was over, that everything was going to be OK.

'You're a fucking diamond, Josephine, and no mistake. Fucking shotgun primed and ready to use just like I taught you. I am so proud of you, darling. Defending your home, your baby. I always knew I had picked a good one, and this proves it!'

Jessie was astounded to hear her mum laugh shakily at her father's words. 'I was scared to death, Michael, I can tell you that much.'

'I know that, darling. Now you go up and sort out our little Jessie. Tell her it was a robbery gone wrong, and it is all fine now. Bless her, she must have been terrified. I need to shoot out for a while, but I will leave some blokes here, so don't worry. This is a one-off, darling. A fucking complete outrage, caused by two fucking imbeciles known as the Cornel brothers who, for some reason, got the breaks they needed by complete accident. It should never have got this far! After I have dealt with them – and, believe me, they will rue the day they travelled down south to front me up – I will then deal with the men in my employ who let this fucking abomination happen.'

Jessie ran back to her room quickly and, locking the door behind her, she went to her bedroom window, watching as the men her father employed forced the two culprits into the back of a Range Rover. She could hear the two men protesting, and see the way they were being punched and kicked violently. She was still shaking with fear as she watched her dad walk over to the Range Rover, and take a piece of lead piping from one of his men, before dragging one of the robbers out of the Range Rover, and on to the driveway. She watched the man's head burst open as her father struck him over and over again with such force she could see the man's skull and his blood spraying everywhere.

She could hear her father screaming in anger, 'You dared, you *dared* to come to my home! My fucking home! I will kill you. I will fucking kill you stone dead!'

The other men just stood there, watching her father as if it was the most natural thing in the world. The violence was so matter of fact, and she didn't know how she was supposed to deal with it. The whole driveway was lit up like Battersea Power Station, so she watched it all in glorious technicolour.

She was still vomiting into the expensive porcelain sink in her beautiful en-suite bathroom when her mother banged on her door, demanding entry.

Everything she had heard about her dad was true. She had finally seen it for herself. But it was her mother's actions that had really shocked her. That had made her realise just how little she knew about the people she lived with. Suddenly, she felt she didn't know anything any more.

Chapter Eighty

'Listen to me, Jessie. I know exactly how this looks, but you're too young to understand the reality of what happened here tonight.'

Josephine was heartbroken. She had never wanted her daughter to have to experience something so frightening. She had made coffee for everyone, left them clearing up downstairs, and then brought her daughter into her bedroom. Locking the door behind them, she had tried to explain as best she could that sometimes things happened, and there was nothing anyone could do to prevent them.

Jessie was staring at her mum, her lovely, quiet, kind-hearted mum, who everyone thought was as soft as shit and treated with kid gloves. Her entire life, she had believed that her mum was weak. Jessie had always felt that she needed to be protected, and Jessie had been willing to do just that. But it had been a lie. Her lovely mum, who had her 'problems', was actually capable of literally anything. Her mother obviously knew all about her dad and his business. Jessie knew her mother would have shot those men without a thought if the need had arisen. She had handled that shotgun like a pro. She was a liar; like her dad, her mother was a great big whopping liar. Here she was, acting like butter wouldn't melt, when it was all an elaborate act. Everything in her life had been a big pretence.

'Please answer me, Jessie. Talk to me, darling.'

Her mum sounded so genuine. It was amazing – she actually sounded as if she cared. She was once more all nervous tension; she even looked anxious, her voice quivering with emotion.

'I don't know what you want me to say, Mum.'

Josephine was relieved to hear her daughter actually speaking. She had not said a word for so long. 'I just want you to understand that what happened tonight was a one-off. It wasn't supposed to happen. None of it. Please, Jessie, you have to understand that, darling. Your dad would die before he would ever have let you see that.'

Jessie nodded slowly, unsure what else she was supposed to do.

Josephine Flynn could understand the way her daughter was feeling. She had been party to something that she had no experience of, and Josephine remembered only too clearly how disturbing it was to witness it first-hand. But there was nothing anyone could do about that now. Most importantly, Jessie needed to understand that she could *never* discuss it with anyone outside their family. Here were some things that were best kept private.

Grabbing her daughter's hands in hers, Josephine squeezed them tightly, as she said huskily, her voice choked with emotion, 'Come on, Jessie love. You must have guessed that your dad wasn't the usual. I mean, I know you must have heard things about him.'

Jessie was sitting beside her mum on the bed, and she could feel the warmth of her mother's hands as she gripped hers tightly. It felt wrong. She wanted to pull her hands away, push her mother as far away from her as possible. But she still loved her mum more than anything. This made no sense to her. She was just a kid, only fourteen years old. She didn't know how to react to the night's events. She had been a witness to extreme violence and murder – something that would have frightened her had she seen it on a movie screen, let alone in real life. Now here was her mum, acting like it was nothing, as if it could be explained away and forgotten about.

Josephine brought her daughter's hands up to her mouth, and kissed her fingers gently, so desperately sorry for the girl's predicament. She'd do anything to take the pain away instead of having to make her daughter understand the importance of family loyalty, and how easily a careless word could destroy the life they had together.

'Look, Jessie, I know you can't understand any of this now, but you will one day. When you're older and wiser, you will understand why I am asking you to forget about tonight. I need you to promise me that you will never ever tell *anyone*, not even your nanas, about this. You've already guessed how serious this situation is. You're not a foolish girl. Remember, your father needs your loyalty now, and so do I.'

Jessie watched her mother carefully. She understood then that her mother would always put her father first, no matter what. She had sacrificed her own peace of mind for her husband many years before, and that was why she was so strange. Jessie did understand about the loyalty that her mother was asking of her. Family loyalty, along with being Irish Catholic, had always been seen as very important. Now her mother was asking it of her, and she couldn't refuse. No matter what she might be feeling deep down inside, she suddenly realised that she could never, *ever*, turn against her own family. It was a real moment of revelation for her. The knowledge that, even after all she had witnessed, all she now knew about her parents, if push ever did come to shove, she would never breathe a word to anyone. The fear that had overwhelmed her was suddenly replaced with another fear – the fear of losing the only life she had ever known. She had no other choice, and she would do what was expected of her.

Chapter Eighty-One

Declan Costello had been drinking heavily all day long, but he was still as sober as a judge. There wasn't enough alcohol in the world to get him drunk at this particular moment in time. He had really dropped the fucking ball. He should have had Michael Flynn's back from the off. He had happily taken a good wedge from Michael, he had been expected to sort out the minor businesses as he had always done, as well as any aggravation that might cross his path – especially any that might impinge on the serious businesses. He had become lazy; he had waited on Michael's word for everything, and that wasn't the deal – he knew that.

The Cornel brothers should have been taken out by him quickly and quietly, and Michael should never have had to be involved personally. Michael should have been told the details *afterwards*, secure in the knowledge that a threat like them had been dealt with. Instead, the Cornels had made it all the way to Michael Flynn's front door, and he had not even given the man's family any protection. The man's wife and daughter had been left hanging, vulnerable and defenceless, and that was *his* fault. The fact that Josephine had apparently turned into Bonnie Parker aside, Declan was aware that he had a lot to answer for.

He had fucked up. Michael was going to come for him, and he had no defence to offer. His brother Patrick, who had loved him dearly, would *never* have swallowed that – Declan would already be dead by now. Declan couldn't forgive himself for the trouble he had caused.

He looked across the bar; there were only two barmaids in – the club was very quiet today. The barmaids were both good girls. Estelle was in her fifties, but she looked good for her age – she could serve three people at once, and she was also adept at removing drunks if the need arose. She was all bleached-blond hair and long red nails. The other girl was a lot younger, perma-tanned, with thick, dark hair, heavily made-up brown eyes and impossibly pert breasts; she was on the look-out for a Face with a good few quid and preferably his own home. She had given him the nod more than once, but he could never remember her name for the life of him.

'Come on, girls, off you go. I'm locking up early today.'

Estelle had her coat on in seconds, and Declan watched gratefully as she steered the other barmaid up the stairs. He heard the door slam shut behind them.

He had sent all his workers out and about, and he was waiting patiently for Michael Flynn to arrive. He was not going to try and justify his actions, he was prepared to take his punishment. He loved Michael's daughter Jessie as if she was his own child, and that he had not even thought to see to her safety – or her mother's for that fact – was the biggest shame of his life. He had made two fatal mistakes – not only had he underestimated the Cornel brothers, he had let down Michael Flynn.

Chapter Eighty-Two

Hannah Flynn was worried about her granddaughter – not an emotion she had ever experienced before. Jessie, however, had managed to find her way into her heart. She loved the girl as much as she could love anyone. She saw herself in her at times. Hannah Flynn had always had a way of carrying herself – she walked tall, straight-backed, and with a natural grace. Jessie had inherited that along with her intelligence.

Josephine didn't have a brain in her head – she had the conversational skills of a twelve year old. All she had ever been interested in was fashion, clothes and shoes. She was a wonderful cook, though, and she kept a good table. Jessie, on the other hand, was very sharp, quick-witted. She was a girl who read voraciously, and to whom learning came naturally. She was capable of so much, and Hannah knew that whatever the girl decided she wanted to do with her life, she could do it.

But today young Jessie had looked seriously ill when she called at the house. Josephine had practically thrown her out, and Hannah wasn't going to forgive that in a hurry. She had not made it further than the entrance hall, before she was back in her cab and on her way home.

There was something going on in that house, and she would get to the bottom of it if it was the last thing she ever did in her life.

Chapter Eighty-Three

Every time Jessie closed her eyes, she relived the night's events. She felt physically ill, sickness roiling inside her belly, and breathless, unable to calm her fears.

Her bedroom was huge – bigger than most people's front rooms. It was very beautiful and she had always loved it. The walls were covered with a pale pink silk which had cost a fortune but from the moment her mum had shown it to her she had wanted it. Her double bed had been brought over from France – hand-carved, it would not look out of place in a palace. The curtains on her windows were a deeper pink than the walls, the floor was white oak, and every piece of furniture, from her bedside cabinets to the dressing table, was hand-picked and very expensive. Until today, she had never thought about the cost – suddenly it seemed to be important to her. She looked around her, saw the bookcase with her favourite books, the pictures of her life exquisitely framed, showing her smiling so happily – and completely unaware of the real world that she was living in. Unaware that, one day, that safe, happy world would explode in her face.

She closed her eyes, wanting desperately to blot it out. Her lovely bedroom that was the envy of her friends, which she once had loved so very much, where she had felt safe and secure, was where she now felt trapped.

The door opened and her mother came into the room quietly. She had a tray in her hands with a glass of milk and a plate of cookies. Jessie waited for her mother to come to her and, as she sat on the bed, Jessie saw the sorrow in her eyes, and felt the deep sadness that enveloped her mother.

'Try and eat something, Jessie. For me.'

Jessie sat up abruptly, knowing that her mother would have to move away from her.

Josephine stood up awkwardly and, when her daughter had finally settled, she placed the tray across her lap. 'Drink the milk at least, Jessie.'

Jessie picked up the glass, and obediently took a few mouthfuls of the milk.

'There's a good girl. You'll feel better now.'

Josephine was so worried about her daughter. It had only been a day, but she hated that her child had been traumatised by the events of the night before.

Jessie pushed the glass roughly into her mother's hand. 'I'll feel better now, will I?'

Josephine placed the glass on the floor carefully. Then, sitting down on the bed, she looked at her lovely daughter for long moments before saying angrily, 'No, Jessie. You *won't* really feel better, darling. *I* know that, and *you* know that. Last night was a fucking nightmare, darling, and I would give anything to change it. But I can't. We can't phone the police like normal people. We can't talk about it to anyone *ever*. We have to make sure that no one knows what happened. It's not ideal, but it's how things are for people like us. I'm telling you, from personal experience, Jessie, you just have to find a way to deal with it.'

Jessie knew that her mum didn't realise she had seen as much as she had. Her mother really did believe that she had locked herself in her bedroom, and that was something Jessie needed her to believe. Her mother could never know what she had actually witnessed, and neither could her father. She actually didn't want them to know. The less they thought she knew about it, the better for all concerned.

Chapter Eighty-Four

Michael Flynn was bone weary. He looked tired and gaunt, he needed a shave and a shower – his usual good looks had deserted him.

Declan Costello stood quietly before him, a broken and shamed man. He was also in need of a bath and a shave; his clothes, like Michael's, were soiled and wrinkled.

Declan opened his arms wide in a gesture of supplication, as he said sorrowfully, 'What the fuck can I say, Michael? I naused it up from the start. I don't know what I was thinking. The Barkers were trying to do me a favour. If I'd had any fucking sense, I should have told them to deal with it. Instead, I honestly thought you would want to sort it yourself.'

Michael was so angry at Declan's explanation that he was frightened to say anything to him until he had harnessed his anger.

Declan could see that Michael was fighting to control himself. 'I'll get us both a drink, Michael.' Once behind the bar, he poured them both large whiskies.

Michael was trying to control his breathing. He had every right to be angry, and every right to exact any revenge he felt was warranted. But he knew that Declan didn't feel any malice towards him, and that he had not expected the Cornel brothers to be such a slippery pair of bastards. Declan Costello had been guilty of nothing more than sheer stupidity and laziness.

Michael gulped his drink, savouring the burn as it hit his belly. He could feel the energy coming back into his body and, swallowing down the rest of the whisky, he placed the glass on the bar gently, before leaning his body over the counter and picking up the whisky bottle. He poured himself out another large measure of Scotch. His back was turned away from Declan, and his voice was rough, as he said disgustedly, 'Do you know what fucking annoys me more than anything about you, Declan? That you can stand there like the orphan of the fucking storm, all sad-eyed, and ready to take your punishment, yet you know exactly what you did wrong. You know why my fucking wife and daughter were terrorised in their own fucking home. So what I want to know is, why didn't you think this through before it got out of hand?' He turned to face Declan, to look him in the eyes.

Declan just shrugged his huge shoulders; he was as bewildered as Michael. 'I was already well pissed by the time Peter Barker came to see me. I can't condone my actions. I need a day or two so I can think things through properly. Why do you think I didn't want the partnership when you offered it to me? I can't think on my feet. I run the same fucking businesses I did when my brother was in the big seat. I thought I was doing the right thing. I didn't think of the consequences. I certainly never dreamt the fuckers would go on the trot. Fuck me, Michael, they could barely stand up!'

Michael finished his whisky in one gulp. Then, sighing heavily, he brought the whisky tumbler down on to Declan's head with all his strength, and began beating the bloodied man viciously and deliberately.

When he was finished, Michael went into the men's rest room and washed his hands carefully, before tidying himself up as best he could. He left the club quickly; his car and driver had been waiting for him patiently. There were also two of his doormen waiting outside. As arranged, as soon as he drove away, they slipped into the club and began the job of cleaning up the mess that Michael Flynn had left behind him.

Chapter Eighty-Five

Michael had showered, and changed into a pair of black jogging bottoms and a crisp white T-shirt. As he walked across the landing from his bedroom to his daughter's, he could hear his wife pottering about in the kitchen below. It was a good sound, the sound of a home, of normality.

He tapped gently on his daughter's door, before walking into the dimness of her bedroom. Her TV was on, providing the only light, but the sound was down. She was lying in her bed and, as she turned to look at him, he forced a smile on to his face.

He knelt down beside her bed. She could smell the shampoo and soap that he always used – it was a familiar scent, something that had always comforted her until now. She looked up into his face, as she had so many times before, only this time it was different. He wasn't the dad she had loved and adored any more. He was a stranger to her. This was a man she didn't trust.

'You all right, Jessie?'

She nodded. He put his arms around her and hugged her tightly. He could feel the stiffness in her slim body, knew that she was still traumatised by the events of the last twenty-four hours. He relaxed his hold on his daughter and, settling her back on to her pillows, he sat beside her on the bed. He could see that the fright lingered, and he knew she was never going to forget what had happened. But he continued to smile down at her, as she watched him warily.

'Listen to me, Jessie. That was never supposed to happen. It was a complete one-off. I swear that to you, darling. Burglars! Fucking creepers! They are the scum of the earth. Anyone who wants to nick someone else's hard-earned cash is filth. Never forget that, my little darling. But they weren't banking on your mum were they, eh?' He was trying to make light of everything, make a big joke of it. 'Did you see her, Jessie? With my shotgun! She looked like Calamity Jane!'

Jessie didn't answer, and that bothered him. She had always been able to say what she wanted to him – that was part of their closeness.

'She was only trying to protect you, darling. There are some bad people in the world, and sometimes bad things happen. But it's over now. It's all sorted out. Daddy's here.'

Michael could see his daughter's sad face, still full of fear. It was ridiculous. He was with her now – she had no reason to be scared of anything.

'I want to go to sleep.'

Michael watched his daughter closely. Her voice sounded different, there was no inflection in it, no emotion whatsoever. She had been truly affected by the Cornels. If he could, he would happily murder the fuckers all over again for that.

'OK, baby. But promise me you will try and put this behind you. You're a Flynn, and that means nothing or no one can ever hurt you.'

Jessie could hear the cold arrogance in her father's voice as he said his name and, without thinking, she said sarcastically, 'The name Flynn didn't seem to do us much good last night, did it?'

Michael was almost as shocked as she was by her words. He

stood up quickly. She could see the anger she had caused, but she didn't care any more.

'There wasn't any burglary, Dad. No police were called either – I know that much.'

Michael didn't answer her for a while. Then, smiling sadly, he knelt down beside her bed once more. 'You're nearly fifteen. When I was your age I knew a lot more than people gave me credit for. So I'll say this, Jessie – me and your mum love you more than anything in this world, and everything we do is for you. Never forget that.'

She looked him straight in the eye as she said quietly, 'I won't.'

He stood up slowly. Something had changed between them, and he knew that it wasn't for the good. 'If I could change the last few days I would, Jessie. You know that, darling.'

She did. He would do anything for her – last night's events proved it.

'But you can't, Dad. No one can.'

She saw the mask slip from her father's face; he was still very angry, she could see that as plain as day. He looked like he was going to explode, but within seconds he was smiling at her once again. The smile that she had always coveted, that had been such a big part of her daily life.

'What I *can* promise you, though, is that I will *never* allow anything like that to happen to you or your mum again.'

She was watching him carefully, and he sensed that she was still not convinced by his promise to keep her safe. She was so beautiful – she was Josephine all over again, from the thick hair to the arched eyebrows. It was uncanny, the striking resemblance between them. But one thing he realised now, was that she didn't have her mother's nature. Jessie was not as warm or forgiving as the woman who had birthed her. There was an underlying steeliness in his Jessie that was reminiscent of *his* mother. He could be wrong; after all, the poor girl had just been through a terrible ordeal, and he mustn't lose sight of that. But there was something else going on here, he could feel it. He bent down and kissed his daughter lightly on her cheek, aware that she didn't respond.

'You try and get some sleep.'

Jessie watched her dad as he left the room. A part of her wanted to call him back, wanted to tell him that she knew what he had done to that man, and she still loved him. But another part of her was reeling from what she had seen him do. At least her mum had tried to be honest with her. Her lovely mum, who looked like she wouldn't hurt a fly, who everyone thought was as soft as soap, but who was far stronger than anyone would have believed. Her whole world had been stripped bare, and she had been left with nothing. Her life had been a sham, built on nothing more substantial than lies and deceit.

Chapter Eighty-Six

Josephine was sitting at the kitchen table, a large glass of white wine in her hand and a cigarette between her lips, when Michael finally joined her.

She could see from his expression that his visit with his daughter had not gone well. She should have warned him, but she had not wanted to cloud his thinking. She could see Jessie had been seriously affected by the events of the previous night.

Michael sat down wearily, and she poured him a glass of wine. 'I made you a few sandwiches, Michael. I can cook you something if you want? A bit of egg and bacon?'

He shook his head slowly. 'These are fine, mate.'

He grabbed a cheese and pickle sandwich and bit into it eagerly. He was hungrier than he had realised. He took a large sip of his wine, and savoured the crispness of it.

'It's still early days, Michael. She'll come round.'

He nodded his agreement. 'I hate that she had to go through that. I hate that you did! For fuck's sake, Josephine, those fuckers got right the way to our door. I will never forget it.'

Josephine smiled weakly at her husband. She hated to see him like this. She always made sure that she never let him see her own fears. She was still shaking inside but she could never let him know that. It had taken everything she had to face those men and defend her home.

'I just want to forget it, Michael.'

'I should be in the West End now. Salvatore wants to be wined and dined every night. I've had to send young Alex Martin in my place. He's going to take him clubbing. He's a good lad. He'll keep him out till the morning, and give me a bit of breathing space.'

'Did Cecil tell you how they knew about the Colombians?'

'Did he fuck! He was clueless. Jack was the brains of that outfit, and that's a contradiction in terms, I can tell you. That Cecil was as thick as shit. I have never in my life met someone as dense as him. He made Trigger look like a fucking applicant for Mensa.'

Josephine laughed despite herself. 'Your mum turned up today. You know her – she's like a bloodhound. I had her out the door in record time though. She sussed that there was something going on.'

He finished his sandwich, not bothering to answer. The fact that someone like Jack Cornel had managed to get so close to him had really thrown him. It had shown him just how vulnerable he was, even now when he was such a major player. He had been foolish to think that his name was enough to guarantee his safety, but he had not allowed for nutters like the Cornels. The last few days had shown him the cracks in his armour, had forced him to re-evaluate everything he had believed in. Patrick Costello had once said to him that there was nothing lonelier than being a success. How true that was.

Chapter Eighty-Seven

Natalie Childs was looking at her oldest and best friend in abject amazement. 'You can't be serious, Jessie!' Her voice had risen until it was almost a screech, she was so shocked at her friend's words.

'Oh, yes! I'm very serious, Nat.'

Natalie was still reeling from the shock of Jessie's latest revelations. Jessie Flynn had become a completely different person recently. The girl she had known and loved was long gone. This girl – the new Jessie – was not just without shame, she was brazen. This new Jessie was already getting a name as a whore, and she seemed to relish it.

'If you don't watch it, Jessie, you are going to end up in so much trouble.'

Jessie just shrugged nonchalantly. 'I don't care, Natalie.'

Natalie was scared for her friend; she couldn't understand what had happened to Jessie or why she was suddenly acting so strangely. 'Your mum and dad will go apeshit if they find out.'

Jessie could hear the bewilderment in Natalie's voice, and she felt a moment's sorrow for her friend. But Natalie could never understand her life, no one could. Unless they lived in her family's chosen world, it was impossible for anyone to understand. She looked at her friend's lovely face, so full of concern for her, and she wanted so much to set her mind at rest, but she couldn't do that.

'How the fuck will they find out? If you do what I ask, and say I am with you, nothing can go wrong, can it?'

Natalie wasn't sure. She didn't like all this lying and scheming. It wasn't a part of her life and, up until a few months previously, it hadn't been a part of Jessie's life either. Now Jessie lied about everything.

'What if your mum rings the house to talk to you? She's friends with my mum, remember? Have you thought of that?'

Jessie just laughed; she didn't care either way, that was obvious. 'So what if she does? If it was left to my mum and dad I would never leave the house without an armed guard. If I get busted, that's my problem, Nat, not yours. Anyway, if my mum did decide to ring, she would ring me on my mobile.' Jessie busied herself lighting a cigarette; after pulling the smoke deeply into her lungs, she said dismissively, 'I really don't give a flying fuck, Natalie. If I did get a capture, you know I'd take the flak – you wouldn't be dragged into anything. If that's what's bothering you, then forget it. I don't need anything from anyone, mate.'

Natalie knew when she was beaten and, as usual, she would do exactly what Jessie wanted her to. It had been like that since they were little kids. Jessie had always been the boss of the relationship and Natalie had never minded until recently. Now all Jessie wanted from her these days was an alibi. Unlike Jessie, Natalie had no interest in pubs or clubs, in meeting men who were far too old, and who expected far too much in return for the drinks they provided.

Jessie Flynn was getting a real reputation, but that didn't seem to bother her in the least. She was fifteen years old, but with her make-up and her clothes she looked at least twenty-five. She also had a way with her that belied her youth; she seemed so much older than her years. Everything about her friend, though, was an elaborate act. No matter how much Jessie tried to pretend that she was a grown-up, Natalie knew different. But she was still her friend, and that counted for a lot more than Jessie realised.

'OK. So who are you meeting this time?'

Jessie grinned mischievously. She had got what she wanted. Stretching her whole body slowly and luxuriously, she laid herself across Natalie's bed like a cat. Every movement was sensuous, dripping with her youthful sex appeal.

Natalie had always been envious of Jessie; she had developed very early, and now she had a body that any woman would kill for. She was high-breasted, with a slim waist and long legs. With her good looks and her amazing hair, it was a dangerous combination.

Natalie was pretty enough, but she knew she wasn't in Jessie Flynn's league. Men had been watching Jessie since she was thirteen, and who could blame them? She was stunning.

'Come on, Jessie, spill!'

Jessie stretched herself once more, a deliberate, sexual movement that made Natalie feel uneasy. It was too calculated, too deliberate.

'His name is Bill, and he is a builder. He is really good-looking, Nat.'

Natalie was intrigued despite herself. 'How old is he?'

Jessie pouted sexily. 'Late thirties. I'm not really sure, to be honest.'

Natalie looked suitably scandalised, and that pleased Jessie. It was exactly the reaction she had wanted to create.

'You will be careful, Jessie, won't you? Promise me.'

Jessie laughed in delight. 'Don't worry about me. I'm always careful, Nat.'

Natalie Childs shook her head slowly in disbelief; she couldn't believe her friend was so willing to take such chances, knowing the trouble it could cause. Everyone knew her dad wasn't a man to cross – not that she would ever say that to Jessie outright, of course. Her family's name and reputation had never been spoken of outright, but it had always been there between them. Jessie's father was a dangerous man, and if he found out what his Jessie was getting up to, Christ Himself only knew what the consequences would be. Jessie just didn't seem to give a damn.

'You're mad, Jessie. You can't keep all this up for ever.'

Jessie laughed, a deep husky chuckle that sounded far too old and knowledgeable for her years. 'You're probably right, Nat, but I really couldn't give a fuck either way.'

Chapter Eighty-Eight

Terence Brown was not a tall man, but what he lacked in height he made up for in width. He spent a lot of time in the gym, and his body showed that devotion. He wore clothes to accentuate his build. He wasn't a handsome man, but had an interesting face, and he looked very amiable and friendly. People assumed he was approachable – his countenance led people to think he was willing to open up a dialogue with them. Unfortunately, that was not the case.

Terence Brown was a man who could pick a fight with a novice nun if the mood was on him. He saw the majority of the people in the world as no more than an irritation, none more so than the people who insisted on attempting to engage him in pointless conversations. He made his living by collecting outstanding debts; they were always for huge amounts of money, and employing Terence Brown was the last resort. He could track any debtor, no matter where in the world they might have travelled to. He was like a bloodhound. He could sniff the fuckers out, and track them down with an ease that was as fast as it was unexpected.

His reputation was his greatest asset, and he used it to his advantage. He took thirty-five per cent of the monies that he collected, plus the ten grand up front he insisted on, to be paid whether he collected the debt requested or not. It was for his expenses and his time, and he saw that as his due. He was known and respected as a man who did the job required of him, not only quickly but, more importantly, *quietly.* If Terence Brown arrived on a doorstep, the person concerned made sure that they found the money needed as quickly as humanly possible. He was known to dispose of anyone who was unable to pay him. He saw failure to pay as a grave personal insult to him, and his retaliation as a reminder to anyone he might call on in the future. Terence Brown had carved a good life for himself, against the odds, and it was something he was proud of.

He glanced around the pub. It was Friday night, and it was packed out as usual. He paid for his drink, and sipped it carefully as he scanned the bar. It was just after ten and the place was buzzing – the music was loud and the conversations were louder. A bird he hooked up with occasionally was already walking towards him, and he smiled widely at her. She was a great-looking girl, all blond hair, minimal clothes and fake tan. She was also a good laugh. That was the main attraction for him – so few people caught his attention, but her sense of humour impressed him. She was looking for a Face, he knew. He wasn't going to get caught up in that shite, though. If, and it was a big if, he ever did decide to marry, it wouldn't be to someone who had lain down with anybody who bought her a few drinks and paid for the odd meal.

'I thought that was you, Terence!' He grinned at her, happy that she never made the mistake of pretending they had a real relationship. So many girls in her position tried to manufacture a closeness that wasn't there.

'I was passing, so I thought I'd pop in, Jan, and see if you fancied a quick drink?'

Janice Evans smiled widely. She liked Terence Brown a lot, he was always so nice to her, and she had a feeling that he liked her much more than he let on. 'That sounds lovely, Terence. I'll have a JD and Diet Coke.'

He ordered her drink, and Janice was chatting away, laughing and joking, when she realised that Terence wasn't listening to a word she was saying. She followed his gaze, and saw that he was watching a couple at the bar with an interest that wasn't exactly healthy. She grabbed his arm tightly and, as he looked down at her, she said huffily, 'Are you all right, Terence?'

Pulling a twenty out of his pocket he gave it to her, saying, 'Get another couple of drinks, Jan. Large ones, eh?'

She took the money, and turned back towards the bar, but she was annoyed. The girl he was staring at was very young, and that didn't sit well with what she knew of Terence Brown. He wasn't interested in many women, she had worked that out herself. But she shrugged her thoughts away; Terence wasn't the kind of man she could ever question, he wouldn't allow a woman to feel she had any hold over him. But he had never looked at anyone else while he had been in her company and she had liked that about him. Seeing him staring so intently at such a young girl bothered her. Even worse, she was annoyed with herself for caring so much.

Terence Brown suddenly found himself in a very serious quandary, and he was not sure what he should do. This was a situation that he could never have envisaged happening to him in a million years, but it was something that he couldn't ignore and walk away from in good conscience. It was a fucking dangerous situation. A very *delicate* situation, that needed to be handled with tact and diplomacy. Luckily he was more than capable of doing that; the people he worked for used him because of his ability to keep his mouth shut. He saw himself as a man of principle, with old-style morals, which were very important to him. He had no choice – he had to do what was right.

Terence had worked for Michael Flynn on many occasions. Michael had always given him his due and he liked and greatly admired Michael. He had been invited into Michael's home and had broken bread there on more than one occasion. He'd spent many happy hours talking with the man who had always treated him with the utmost respect and never been anything other than charming to him.

Now, as he stood at the bar of this complete shithole of a pub – a place only the lowest of the low would frequent – he couldn't ignore the fact that Michael Flynn's young daughter was there, dressed like a pole dancer, and in the company of a man old enough to be her father.

He took the drink that Janice Evans gave him, and gulped it down. Then he pulled Janice towards him roughly, shouting to be heard above the music. 'Here, Jan, who's the bloke over there with the leather jacket and the Churchill shoes? Do you know him?'

Janice nodded quickly. If Terence Brown was asking questions there was a good reason for it.

'He comes in here all the time. Billy something-or-other. He's a builder out of Silvertown. A complete fucking waster, always on the pull – married with a couple of kids, by all accounts. The young girl he's with started coming in a few weeks ago. She's jailbait, if you ask me. She's already been with half the blokes in here from what I've seen of her. Anyone who buys her a few drinks is in with a chance!'

Terence Brown frowned at her words. 'Listen, I need to make a quick phone call. Do me a favour, Janice – will you keep an eye on them for me? I think he owes someone I know a good few quid, the treacherous cunt.'

Janice grinned happily, pleased that Terence Brown was asking her for a favour, happy to be a part of his life however small.

Chapter Eighty-Nine

Billy Thomas was drunk. It was late, and he knew his wife was going to give him grief for weeks, but he didn't give a toss. It was worth it. This little beauty was a real find; she was game for anything, as long as he supplied her with a good drink and a few lines. She was very young – younger than she let on – and he didn't reveal he knew the truth about her. She was fifteen years old at most – a real fucking draw for him; he liked them young and stupid. Treat them like grown-ups and they were so thrilled they would do anything he asked of them. She was his dream date.

He parked his work van neatly outside the flat conversion he was working on in Rainham. Jessie was nearly asleep, lying against his shoulder, and he kissed her gently, before slipping his tongue between her lips, licking the inside of her mouth roughly. She responded eagerly as he knew she would.

'Come on, mate. I've been waiting for this.'

As they got out of the van, Billy Thomas was already hard as a rock; he had been thinking about this all day, and he had planned ahead. He opened the front door quickly and, pushing Jessie inside, he didn't turn on any lights, just shut the door quietly behind them.

'Come on.'

He dragged her into the front room which was empty except for an old sofa. Pushing her down on to it, he kissed her roughly before getting up and walking into the kitchen. Jessie could hear him as he poured them both drinks.

She smiled happily. He had really come up trumps. She liked that he had planned – gone out and bought the alcohol, and then brought it here in readiness for the night's entertainment. The knowledge that he had done all that for her was a real power trip.

It was dim in the room with the only light coming from the lamp post outside, but she noticed that the walls had recently been plastered. The whole place smelt of damp and neglect. Even the sofa looked dilapidated. As her eyes adjusted to the dimness she could see it was filthy. It stunk of cigarettes and fried food. But who cared? It was comfortable, and more than adequate for what she wanted.

Billy brought the drinks in and handed her a plastic glass full of vodka and Coke. 'Get that down your neck. Plenty more where that came from.'

Jessie took a deep draught; it was nearly all cheap vodka, as she had expected. She lay back against the arm of the sofa, and she could see his excitement as she gave him her glass, and casually started to undress herself. She was not wearing that much anyway and, as she pulled her top over her head, and dropped it on to the floor, she heard his intake of breath. She was without underwear – she knew the power of that from previous experience. Billy was already putting the drinks on to the floor, his whole world focused on her and her body. Her breasts were heavy and well-shaped, enough to make any man fold, and Jessie enjoyed the power she had as she exposed them to the air. She lifted her skirt up around her hips, opening her legs wide, and she could hear the change in the man's breathing, feel his mounting excitement, as she pulled him into her arms, and kissed him deeply, pulling at his shirt, trying to rip it open.

'Come on, Billy boy, you know what to do.'

Billy Thomas was in a state of pure ecstasy. He jumped up quickly, tearing his clothes off with abandon. This was the best he'd ever had. This young girl was a fucking dream come true for him, and she was his – all his. It was as if all his Christmases and birthdays had arrived at once. He had never felt so aroused by anyone in his life. She was like a porn star, willing to do anything he wanted her to do. In this light, she looked her age – so fucking young and vulnerable. She was a schoolgirl in a woman's body, and it was a huge turn-on.

But as he finally thrust himself inside her, all hell suddenly broke loose.

Chapter Ninety

Terence Brown was more disgusted than he had ever felt in his life. Seeing a man like Michael Flynn shamed like this was unprecedented. The girl was screaming in terror, and he automatically grabbed her and placed his hand over her mouth. The noise she was making had to be stopped as quickly as possible – the last thing any of them needed was the fucking Filth arriving on the scene, all notebooks, bright eyes, and awkward questions.

Billy Thomas was being severely reprimanded by Michael Flynn, as he should be, the filthy piece of shit. He had more than earned this fucking hammering. He was a nonce, a fucking beast. The girl was only a kid for all her tits and make-up. It was a disgrace – what man in his right mind wanted a young girl? A child? Michael Flynn was really giving him the large. It occurred to Terence Brown that Billy Thomas was not going to leave this room alive. But that was his look-out – he had asked for it, and he was getting it.

Jessie could see everything that was happening around her and, as the reality of her situation sank in, she stopped trying to fight her way out, stopped trying to scream. Instead she closed her eyes tightly, and waited for it to be over.

Terence grabbed the nearest thing to him with his free hand, trying to cover the girl's nakedness with Billy Thomas's new shirt.

Michael Flynn was still beating the man with his fists and his feet, using all his considerable strength, but Terence knew the man was already dead. No one on earth could have survived that kind of a beating – it was impossible. The girl was quiet now, and Terence guessed that it had finally occurred to her that this was her fault – she was the instigator of everything that had happened. It was outrageous.

Michael Flynn continued kicking Billy Thomas long after the man had died. When his anger finally subsided, the man was no more than a bloody piece of meat, unrecognisable as a human being.

Michael Flynn looked at his only daughter for long moments before bowing his head in shame. '*You* did all this, remember that, Jessie. You caused this.'

Jessie Flynn stood up then and, dressing herself quickly, she said harshly, 'Oh no, *you* did this. It's what you do, Dad. Remember?'

Chapter Ninety-One

Josephine Flynn was absolutely devastated. Everything that she had been told about her daughter had hurt her like a physical blow.

'Oh, Jessie, what possessed you? For fuck's sake, have you no shame? Have you no fucking decency?'

Jessie laughed nastily. 'Oh, have a day off, will you, Mum? Acting all fucking shocked. I might have fucked a few blokes but, in the grand scheme of things, that's nothing really, is it? I never *killed* anyone, did I? I've never murdered anyone.'

Josephine stared at her lovely daughter; she saw the beauty she had inherited from herself, and she saw the coldness she had inherited from her father. Her Jessie was every bit as vicious as the man she seemed to hate so much.

Grabbing her daughter roughly by the hair, she forced her head back until she could look straight into her face. 'Don't you fucking *dare* try to bullshit me, lady. I'm warning you now, Jessie, don't push me too far. I might seem like a fucking push-over, but I'm not. Far from it. We *trusted* you, lady. Whatever you might think of us, we *trusted* you. So the real world has finally arrived on your doorstep – get over it. But don't you *ever* try and justify your own fuck-ups by blaming me and your dad. All we did was love you. We gave you the world, and don't you ever forget that.'

She threw her daughter away from her angrily, watching as she fell to the floor, unable to find it in her heart to comfort her child and make it better. At this moment she hated her – hated her for what she had done to her father, to them all. Her daughter had chosen her own road, and it was a road that she would find very lonely, and very hard.

'You broke your father's heart, I hope you know that, and I'll never forgive you for it. He loved you more than life itself. You stupid, stupid girl. You knew that we weren't like other families – don't pretend you didn't. You knew all about us, I know you did, so stop trying to pretend different. Your nana Flynn made sure of that. I know she's filled your head with her spite and her anger the last few months.'

Jessie pulled herself up slowly from the kitchen floor, grabbing at the black marble worktop to steady herself. She was in so much pain, hurting all over. She could see clumps of her hair on the flooring. That her mum could have attacked her like that was something she would never have believed possible. Even after everything that had happened, it was her mother's anger that had really been the eye-opener for her. Her mother had always been the one person she had felt she could rely on no matter what. She knew now, though, that her mum would always put her father first – he was her only real interest. It was a learning curve all right. She could see the truth of everything her mother really stood for now, and it was just another let-down for her, just another lie they lived with.

She had been brought up to believe that her family were blessed, and lived so well because her father worked so hard. She had never questioned that – why would she? The man she had loved was a thug who used violence to earn a living. His lifestyle had nearly caused the death of her mother and herself, but no one seemed to think that was of any importance. Now her mother was actually trying to tell her that she was disappointed in *her*? That *she* was the one in the wrong? It was outrageous. How could her mother not see her point of view?

'I saw everything that night, Mum. You with the shotgun, acting like fucking Calamity Jane. I saw everything that went on – I was watching. You hypocrites, telling me what to do all the time, watching me like a hawk, the *good* girl, the *good* daughter, pretending we were a *normal* family, when it was a lie. We could have died that night.'

'But we didn't, did we?'

Jessie sighed heavily, unable to believe her mother's attitude.

Josephine poured herself a large glass of wine and, taking a long drink, she sat down at the kitchen table. Lighting a cigarette, she puffed on it for a while before saying sadly, 'So you saw everything that night. I'm sorry, I really am. But you also saw a man murdered earlier tonight, a man you were sleeping with. Fifteen years old, and already a seasoned mistress! Yet that doesn't seem to be bothering you too much – in fact, if it wasn't for you, he would be alive and kicking, darling. So let me ask you this – how can you justify that? It seems to me you are more like your old man than you realise, lady.'

Jessie Flynn didn't answer her mother, she didn't know what to say to her. She just knew she wasn't the same girl she had been before those men had arrived on their doorstep, armed and dangerous. Her whole life had been like a dream until then, like a fairy tale, and it had been based on lies, built on quicksand. Everything she had ever believed in was without foundation, without substance. Even now, her father was out there, making sure that Billy's body was disposed of, taking care of business, and everyone acted as if it was the most natural thing in the world.

The truth was, she *didn't* care about Billy Thomas. She didn't care that he was dead. She had wanted to be found out from the start; she had never dreamt that she could get away with her behaviour for so long. But she had, and it was only because her parents had always thought the best of her. They should have known that something was wrong with her, none of them had noticed anything amiss. That wasn't right; she resented them for assuming she would just pick herself up and carry on as normal. It had shown her that she was really no more than an outsider, that her mum and dad didn't really give her more than a passing thought. All they needed was each other.

'I can't answer that question, Mum. To be honest, he meant nothing to me. I wish I had realised that before. But what I do know is you and Dad don't need me – you never did, Mum. I feel like you and Dad built this big lie, and it was all for my benefit. You never leave the house now unless you have to. I don't feel like this is my home any more. Overnight I went from convent girl, with a perfect life, to no one. Everything I had ever believed in was stripped away, was destroyed. Dad even attacked Uncle Declan and put him in hospital. In a matter of days, I was thrust into *your* world, your vicious, violent world. I'm fifteen years old, Mum.'

Josephine Flynn was heart-sorry for her daughter, she understood what she was saying. But it was too late now, she should have said all this a long time ago.

'I'm sorry to hear you say that, Jessie. You were always everything to me and your dad. I tried to be honest with you.' Josephine finished her glass of wine and poured herself another. 'When I was a kid, Jessie, my dad was put away for a long time. I spent the best part of my youth visiting him in Parkhurst. I didn't like it, but I got on with it. My mum and me made his time bearable. We wrote, we visited. I had so many Christmases, so many birthdays without him, just me and her. We struggled without him, but we just got on with it. I didn't rail at the world, but I missed him, God how I missed him. He was my dad. I remember the Filth coming round our house, tearing it apart, searching for evidence, being dragged out of my bed. They even slit open my mattress with a huge knife, in case he had hidden anything inside it. I can still remember the court case, my mum coming back from the Old Bailey every night, and pretending everything was all right. My heart was broken, but I knew, even then, as young as I was, that my mum needed me to be strong for her. So I was. But I know in my heart, that you knew about your dad, Jessie. You acting like it was all a fucking big surprise doesn't wash with me. All your mates know about us and, even though that doesn't make it right, it still makes me question why you would use it as an excuse to whore yourself out.'

Jessie pulled a chair out from under the table, and sat down beside her mother. 'I was scared out of my life, Mum. I can't believe you don't understand how much that affected me.'

Josephine looked at her lovely daughter and, getting up slowly, she went to the nearest cupboard and brought another wine glass to the table. She poured her daughter a small glass of red wine, pushing the glass towards her roughly.

'I *do* understand. I was there as well, remember? I protected us as best I could until your father arrived. You could have come to me at any time afterwards, but you didn't. I trusted you, as I had always trusted you, and I was wrong. I know that now. Drink your wine. From what I understand you aren't averse to alcohol.'

Jessie didn't want any wine. She pushed the glass away from her.

Josephine watched her daughter carefully, before saying sadly, 'Good girl. I knew you wouldn't drink that now you're sober. You're pregnant, aren't you?'

Jessie didn't answer her.

'Do you know whose it is?'

Jessie's usual arrogance came to the fore as she said haughtily, 'What difference does that make now? I don't want it. I'm only fifteen.'

Josephine sighed heavily. 'A word to the wise, Jessie love; your father is capable of a lot of things, as you know, but he would *never* be party to an abortion. You're carrying a life inside of you, girl, and we are Catholics. We celebrate a child. I think you need to remember that for the future. As the Bible says: as you sow, so shall you reap. The damage is done now, darling.'

Josephine opened up her arms and, as she hugged her young daughter tightly to her breast, she wondered at a God who could heap so much hurt on one household.

Book Four

Be not deceived, God is not mocked:
for whatsoever a man soweth, that shall he also reap

Galatians 6:7

For the wages of sin is death

Romans 6:23

Chapter Ninety-Two

2012

As Jessie Flynn walked out of a pub in Soho, the cold night air hit her. She staggered slightly in her high-heeled shoes, and leant back against the wall for a few seconds to steady herself. She was out of her nut, as per usual, and she was also bored – bored of the company she was in, bored of her life in general. Her father didn't seem bothered any more about her or her antics, something she was having trouble accepting. Even her mother was losing interest in her these days. After years of trying to buy her back into their life, controlling her with their cash, and attempting to make her take an interest in her son, her parents had suddenly stopped. She had a feeling she had won, but what she had actually won, she wasn't sure. In fact, she now felt much more like she was the one who had *lost* something important.

There was no more pretending from her father, no more acting like everything was OK between them. He wasn't rude as such, but he was clearly ashamed of her and the life she lived. That's exactly what she had always wanted; she had been determined to beat him, prove to him that she didn't care about anything, especially not him, or his precious reputation. Strangely, her dad turning away from her didn't make her feel as good as she had thought it would. In fact, her dad's attitude the last few times she had seen him had made her feel like *she* was the one in the wrong, that she was the bad bastard.

She sighed. She was too out of it to think about anything rationally. She rummaged through her handbag for a pack of cigarettes, and lit a Marlboro Light, toking on it deeply before blowing the smoke out into the night slowly. She was tired, but that wasn't anything new to her – she was always fucking tired lately. She spent more time out of her flat than she did inside it. She loved being in company, enjoying herself. Life was too short – her own father had shown her the truth of that. She had learnt at a young age the value of a human life. She was far too young to settle down anyway.

She was also far too young for the man she was with tonight. He was boring the arse off her – all he talked about was himself. She heard the door open and knew that it was Jonny Parsons looking for her. He was so sure of himself, it wouldn't occur to him that she was with him for no other reason than he was a lowlife piece of shit. She didn't have the patience for him now, he was getting on her nerves big time. The idiot. He looked baffled and sorry for himself. She could see the wrinkles around his eyes and the flakiness of his skin – he was a real prize. Lately, she'd noticed that the more out of it she got, the more she seemed to see the truth of her situation and the life she lived. She was feeling more and more disgruntled by the day.

'What's going on, babe? For fuck's sake, I turned around and you were gone.'

Jessie rolled her eyes in annoyance. He was a real prick. Why hadn't she admitted that to herself before now? He was on the wrong side of forty, he was overweight, he dressed like a fucking extra from *The Sopranos* and he talked like a fucking special guest on *The Jeremy Kyle Show*. He was a complete fucking embarrassment. She stepped away from him quickly, hating that he was too stupid to take the hint that she didn't want to associate with him any more. She had sussed out that her main attraction for him was her father – all he wanted from her was an in.

'I'm not your fucking *babe*, or anyone else's, you fucking moron. Who says "babe" in this day and age, for fuck's sake? Have you heard yourself? You sound like a reject from the eighties. Fuck off and leave me alone.'

Jonny Parsons was really drunk *and* stoned, although he wasn't capable of any kind of lucid conversation at the best of times. Jessie Flynn was starting to get on his tits. He had invested time and money in this arrogant little bitch, and she had the nerve to talk to him like he was a fucking corner boy? She was without any kind of reputation, she had fucked over more people than a high-street bank, and she had nothing going for her other than her name. Who the fuck did she think she was? She had a bad attitude and she talked to people like they were fucking idiots. She didn't seem to understand that she wasn't exactly a fucking prize herself. She was a whore – that was all she was and all she would ever be.

'Fuck *you*, Jessie Flynn. Just who the fuck do you think you are? I've fucking bankrolled you, lady, and don't you ever forget that. I won't be made a cunt of, especially not by a fucking no-mark like you.'

Jessie sighed dramatically; she was actually enjoying herself immensely. 'I think you and I both know the truth of this situation. We both know that I am far better than you, Jonny. That's what is bothering you.'

She could see her words hit home; she wasn't going to let him get the better of her without a fight. Well, that suited her fine. She liked a good fight, she liked to get a reaction. It just proved to her that she was right – all men were bastards and not worth her time or effort.

'If you really want to know the truth, Jonny, I think you're what is commonly known as a fucking moronic imbecile. I've had better conversations at bus stops with glue sniffers. So do me a favour and fuck off, will you?'

Jonny Parsons was not a man to take anything off a woman. A coward by nature, he didn't think twice about raising his hand to a female. Jessie Flynn's words were like a red rag to a bull – he was never going to let her treat him like a mug. Grabbing Jessie by her throat, he forced her up against the wall and, taking his fist back ready to use it, he said angrily, 'Don't you talk to me like that, you fucking whore. I don't take that shit off anyone, especially not from a fucking tramp like you.'

Jessie was laughing at him now, enjoying the drama and violence no end. 'Go on then, Jonny, I fucking *dare* you. Hit me. Go on, big man. Give it your best shot.'

Jonny Parsons could see the need in her face; she wanted a fight, she wanted a scene, and suddenly he wasn't sure he wanted to be a part of that. As drunk as he was, he knew this could only bring him untold aggravation. She was a Flynn, after all – Michael's daughter – and that fact alone was enough to sober him up, and remind him of why he had sought her out in the first place. She was even more fucked up than he had believed and, from what he had heard, she was a real fucking headcase. But she wasn't worth dying for.

He threw her away from him angrily, aware that she wanted him to hurt her. She would always insist on being the star of her own show. It was pathetic. She was a good-looking young woman, but she was dangerous and vindictive. A deadly combination.

'You destructive fucking bitch, you *want* me to hit you, don't you? You want me hurt you, stoop down to your level. But I wouldn't give you the satisfaction. You're not worth a fucking slap – you're not worth the aggravation.'

He walked away from her unsteadily, and Jessie watched him warily. She had asked for that, she had pushed him too far. It was what she did. She pushed everyone to the limit. She loathed people like him, who saw her as nothing more than a stepping stone into her father's life, who thought that, by fucking her, they would somehow get Michael Flynn into the bargain. It grieved her, knowing that her only real value as a person was her name. She leant back against the wall once more and, closing her eyes tightly, she breathed in the cold night air for a few minutes, steadying her heartbeat, and trying to calm her nerves.

If only they knew the truth – that she was the kiss of death where her father was concerned. He loathed the men that she attracted; he saw them for the pieces of shit they really were. She did too, if she was really honest with herself. Not that she let that stop her, of course. She went out of her way to humiliate her father – he deserved everything he got.

She looked at her watch, a gold Rolex that had been a birthday present from her *loving* parents. If anything, it had been a bribe. Her mum and dad had tried to make her feel they loved her and cared about her, but it was a crock of shit. As long as her son was in her mum and dad's care, she could do what she liked and, in return for her son, her old man would happily bankroll her and her lifestyle. Jake was her parents' second chance at parenthood. He was the son they could never have, the golden boy, the heir apparent. Her dad had forced her to have her baby. The big Catholic, who saw abortion as tantamount to murder – and who would know more about that than her dad? But what they couldn't do was make her settle down, embrace her role as mother and pretend that she had learnt her lesson.

She closed her eyes tightly; she mustn't think about any of that now. It was pointless. She didn't want to look after her little lad anyway, so why did she let it bother her so much? She had handed him over to them willingly, glad to have someone else take the responsibility for her. It had been a fair exchange.

It was just after eleven, and she wasn't going to waste the rest of the night thinking about things she couldn't change. Flagging down a black cab, she climbed inside its warmth eagerly, making herself comfortable on the leather seat as she travelled back to East London, glad that the cab driver wasn't the usual fucking chatterbox. There was nothing worse than a cab driver with a loose mouth and too many stories to tell. It was irritating, especially when they tried to tell her how they knew all the Faces in London, particularly her dad. She saw the way they watched her in the mirror and knew they couldn't understand for the life of them how her father could let her live the way she did.

She jumped out of the cab at a pub she frequented in Upney, pleased that she had made it there in such good time. All she wanted to do was score and, if nothing interesting was going on, she would go home and sleep.

Her father had presented her with a lovely flat in Canary Wharf; it was the envy of everyone she knew. It *was* gorgeous – it had fabulous views across the river, and it was furnished to the highest standards; she would have expected nothing less from her dad. Like everything else in his life, he thought that if it cost a fortune then it must be good. She hated the place. It was another reminder of her father's hold over her. It wasn't in her name so she was no more than a lodger. It was hers only so he would know where she was living, just like he paid her a weekly wage so he could keep her within his orbit. Everything her parents did had an ulterior motive.

She slipped inside the public house, breathing in the familiar smell of sweat and stale beer. She saw the dealer she was looking for standing at the bar, and she made her way over to him quickly. It was late, and the place was nearly empty.

Georgie Burns smiled at her, displaying his gold teeth. It had been a slow night, and Jessie Flynn was always a good spender. She bought in bulk and paid cash, and that guaranteed her a very warm welcome. With his gold teeth and expensive dreads, Georgie looked every inch the bad man. In the real world, he had a degree in Sociology and his parents were both teachers. He had grown up in a nice house in North London with two sisters and an overweight Labrador called Bubbles. Now he was a dealer because it was the only way he could earn himself a decent living, pay his mortgage, and cover his two daughters' school fees. His wife was a woman who needed a good wage coming in; she liked the finer things in life. She was also more than willing to turn a blind eye to her husband's activities.

'Hello, Jessie. You looking for me, girl?'

Jessie smiled. She genuinely liked Georgie – he was a nice bloke and one of the few men in her life who had never tried to take advantage of her.

'Of course I am, Georgie. I wouldn't come inside this shithole otherwise, would I?'

They laughed together, and Georgie motioned to the barmaid for drinks. 'Agreed. So, what you after tonight?'

'Just the usual.' She glanced around her. 'It's empty in here tonight. I'm amazed you're still here.'

Georgie shrugged with irritation. 'Nothing going on anywhere, girl. I was just on my way home.' He passed her a large JD and Coke, and she swallowed it down quickly.

'Soho is the same. Dead as a fucking doornail.'

Georgie laughed at her delightedly. 'You should have gone clubbing. It's a week night, for fuck's sake.'

Jessie grinned. 'I know. But I didn't feel like it tonight. How much do I owe you?'

Ten minutes later she left the pub, and made her way towards

Upney station. It was a few minutes' walk. There were usually plenty of minicabs outside the station, and she climbed into the back seat of the first taxi as usual, pleased that she knew the cab driver a little. He had driven her home before, so they chatted amiably together until they arrived at her apartment building.

She paid him, and then walked quickly towards her home. As she was about to unlock the main door that led into the lift area of the flats, she heard someone calling her name. Turning towards the sound of the voice, she expected to see someone she knew, someone like her who was always on the lookout for company, but the man she saw was a complete stranger. Before she could say another word, she felt something come into contact with her skull.

It was all over in seconds.

Chapter Ninety-Three

'Do you know what, Michael Flynn? If I didn't know any better I would think you were trying to annoy me now.' Josephine was joking, but the underlying question in her voice was clear.

Michael sighed. He hated all this ducking and diving, but it was a necessary evil – there was no other way to handle his wife. These days Josephine couldn't cope with the truth. She was quite happy living in her little dream world. Sometimes it could be very wearing. *He* had to live in the real world – it was how he earned his living.

'I just want to know if you think I should warn this Jonny bloke off, Josephine. I know that Jessie has been seeing him and, from what I can gather, he's another complete fucking waster.'

Josephine sat down on her bed. She wasn't sure what she should say – as much as Jessie's lifestyle disappointed her, she wasn't going to do anything that would alienate her daughter completely. She didn't want to be the bad guy – that was Michael's job.

She didn't look at her husband as she said quietly, 'What have you heard about this bloke, then?'

Michael snorted in derision. This was always the way – Josephine left him to find out everything of relevance where their daughter was concerned, then acted as if she was not expecting to hear what he told her.

'Well, for starters, he's forty-odd, has a wife and four kids and he's a druggie. A cokehead to be exact and a small-time dealer, who thinks he's a fucking big villain. And our Jessie is bank-rolling him.'

Josephine put her head into her hands; she wasn't shocked at her husband's words, she was just disappointed in her daughter's choice of man. Why she felt so dismayed she didn't know – it was the same old story time and time again.

'Oh, let her get on with it, Michael. Don't interfere. She's promised to come and have tea with little Jake on Sunday. I'll see how she is then.'

The subject was closed and Michael knew it. 'Well, I'll be seeing her tomorrow anyway, Josephine. It's pay day.'

Josephine didn't answer. She knew that Michael detested paying his daughter just to keep his eye on her. If it was left to *him* she wasn't so sure he would still bother. It was all for her, to keep Jessie as close as she could.

Michael put his arm around his wife's shoulders and hugged her to him. His daughter had broken his heart, but she had given him her son, he had salvaged that much.

'How is the little man, anyway? Did he enjoy his school trip? Where did they go? To a farm, wasn't it?' Michael's grandson was his life; he adored the child.

'Yeah, he loved it, Michael. He was full of it when he got home. He's clever, you know, a real shrewdie. Six years old and he can already read anything. His teacher reckons he's well ahead of the other kids in his year.'

Michael was pleased. He knew his grandson was a one-off, now it seemed that the school was of the same opinion. Jake was a right little character.

'I said that, didn't I? He is a real fucking brainiac. He's always been ahead of the other kids. Look at how early he was with his counting and reciting things.'

Josephine basked in her husband's joy. Jake had always been quick off the mark. She was pleased he was showing such talent. 'Well, the school thinks he has real potential, so we need to make sure that he gets all the encouragement he needs.'

'A done deal, darling, you know that. Why don't you come downstairs with me and have a glass of wine? I could do with something to mellow me out a bit. I'm tired, but I'm not sleepy, if that makes sense?'

But Josephine was already shaking her head at his words, and Michael swallowed down his annoyance. Josephine rarely left her rooms these days. She went to the kitchen to cook occasionally, or to see Jessie, if she deigned to visit, but that was about it. She spent most of her life inside her bedroom and she had not ventured outside the house for years. Even the garden was off limits to her these days.

'Bring the bottle of wine up here, Michael. I need to get myself sorted out.'

She looked around her, as if she had important things to do. It was her usual reaction, and Michael wasn't going to say anything to challenge her. He got up from the bed slowly, pretending, as always, that he didn't notice the clutter everywhere, the boxes of rubbish that she surrounded herself with. Smiling easily at his wife, he said gently, 'I fancy a nice glass of red. You OK with that, darling?'

Josephine smiled back, grateful that her husband was always so kind to her, so very understanding. She saw how hard it was for him. 'That sounds good to me, Michael. I love a nice red.' As he opened the bedroom door, she had a sudden urge to say something else. 'I'm so sorry, Michael. I wish more than anything that I could make everything all right for us. You do know that, don't you?'

He turned back towards his wife and saw the sorrow on her lovely face. She was still a real beauty, still the only woman he had ever wanted. ''*Course* I know that. You're the love of my life, Josephine, always will be. Now, let me go and get the wine. I feel like spending some quality time with my lovely wife.' He winked at her saucily, then he left the room.

She watched him go and sighed. She had never wanted anyone else since the first time she had clapped eyes on him. She had always put him before everyone else in her life, even her daughter, and she always would. He was everything to her, and that would never change.

Michael came back with the wine and two Waterford crystal glasses. She followed him obediently out to her balcony; she knew he liked to see her in the fresh air. She sat down at the wrought-iron table, and took a large sip of the wine her husband had poured for her.

'It's chilly out here tonight, girl.'

'I know. I was out here earlier on. It's always cold in the evenings.' Josephine looked at her husband; he was still a very handsome man. 'Will you do me a favour, Michael? Will you ask our Jessie if she is really going to come on Sunday? Only Jake is expecting her, and I don't want him to be disappointed. Waiting all day and then she doesn't bother to show up.'

Michael nodded. He knew only too well what his daughter was capable of. 'I'll ask, but you know what she's like. She's so fucking unreliable. The only time I can guarantee her presence is when she picks up her money. Funny how she never sleeps in on a Thursday, isn't it?'

Josephine didn't respond to that; she knew how angry Michael could get over Jessie.

Michael sipped his wine, savouring the taste. He was looking over the gardens; he had turned the outside lights on earlier, and he was enjoying the view. So much had gone into making the gardens look beautiful, but his wife didn't seem to notice them any more. It was so sad. She took no pleasure in anything these days. How could she? All she did was sit out the days – and that was *all* she was capable of doing. She was unable to sleep at night, unable to enjoy her life in any meaningful way. His lovely bride, his Josephine, had gradually lost the knack for living life, and she didn't seem to want to find it again.

Josephine sighed; she missed her daughter so much, but there was no way Jessie was coming home again. She avoided them all like the plague, especially little Jake. Josephine blamed herself for her daughter's actions. Jessie had needed her, and she had not been there for her daughter – she had put her husband first and done what *he* wanted.

'Do you think we were wrong to make her have little Jake? She was so young, Michael.' She watched her husband as he shook his head in swift and angry denial.

'How can you even think like that, Josephine? He is a lovely little lad. If we had let her have her way he wouldn't even fucking *be* here. For all her fucking antics, and her fucking determination to act like he doesn't exist, the day will come when she will realise that she did the right thing by having her baby, and that *we* did the right thing by making sure she gave the child a chance at life. She needed to understand the seriousness of what had happened to her. She needed to learn that having a child isn't a fucking game. As a Catholic, she had only one choice open to her. There would be no abortions in this fucking house, I made that perfectly clear to her.'

He was getting angry, so he drank some of his wine, and willed himself to calm down. His daughter's treatment of her son still rankled with him. 'The worst thing is, Josephine, I actually thought it might make her grow up, you know? I thought it might make her realise that eventually everything has to be paid for. But I was wrong. All it did was drive her further away.'

Josephine busied herself lighting a cigarette, even though she knew that Michael hated her smoking. She didn't know how to react to her husband's words. Michael was always so sure of everything, but she wasn't as sure as he was about her daughter. She leant forward in her chair and, looking directly at her husband, she said seriously, 'Do you know what I think, Michael? I think the night the Cornels came here ruined her. It was such a big trauma for all of us, but she never seemed to get over it, did she? She just went off the rails afterwards, and then with the baby on top of everything else, it was all too much for her. She was a mother at sixteen years old, that's a really big event for anyone, Michael, let alone a young girl like Jessie.'

Michael laughed sarcastically. He had no intention of making excuses for his daughter. She was the one who had got herself pregnant, and it wasn't even as if she had known who the culprit was. It could have been anyone. Josephine's problems had been made worse by her daughter's actions, and young Jessie was the main reason that Josephine couldn't bring herself to leave her home any more. There was no way he was going to sit here tonight and pretend anything different. He had seen first-hand the toll his daughter's lifestyle had had on his wife. Tonight he wasn't in the mood to overlook it.

'You listen to me, Josephine. I don't care what anyone says – she might have had a fright that night, and I get that – but that wasn't any reason to carry on the way she fucking did. She had never, *ever* in her life had anything other than love and care from us. There are kids in this world who are living in war zones, who have seen their families murdered, and they get over it. Our Jessie's fucking problem is that she let one fucking night cancel out all the years of love we had given her beforehand. I tell you now, and I'm being honest with you, I think she would have gone to the bad anyway. Look at how she's living now! How she's been living for years. Drink, drugs, fucking men. That is a *lifestyle*, Josephine, a fucking choice she's made. I was talking to Tommy Ambrose the other week, six kids he has, and one of his sons is a fucking heroin addict. It's breaking his heart but, as he said, there's nothing he can do about it. The kid's a fucking waste of space, end of. Tommy said a very true thing to me; he reckons it's a kink in the boy's nature. Nothing could have prevented it from happening. The boy was destined to be a fucking junkie. I think that applies to our Jessie. She would have found her level, eventually, I honestly believe that. She looked like a fucking paraffin lamp last week, when she came to get her money. I was so ashamed of her. Her breath was so bad, I could smell it from six feet away. Her clothes were dirty – she had obviously slept in them – her legs were scabbed over, and covered in fresh bruises, so I knew she had fallen over at some point. Then she had the fucking nerve to snatch the money out of my hand as if she was doing *me* a favour by taking it. I tell you now, Josephine, it took all of my willpower to stop myself from telling her to fuck off, and aiming her out the door on the end of my fucking boot.'

Josephine had never once heard her husband talk like that about their daughter, and she knew, then and there, that he had been thinking like that for a long time.

'Oh, Michael, I'm so sorry to hear you talking like that about our Jessie. But I do know what you're saying and, as much as it pains me to say this, I think you're right.'

Michael laughed in derision at his wife's words; he was angrier than he had realised. Without thinking, he found himself shouting with temper, 'Have a fucking day off, will you, Josephine?

For Christ's sake! She's a fucking walking nightmare. If it wasn't for you, I would have cut her off years ago.'

Josephine started to cry real tears then, her whole body shaking with her sobs. Michael was out of his seat and kneeling before his wife in seconds. Holding her to him tightly, he held her as she cried bitterly, knowing that this was something she should have done a long time ago. He hated himself for saying what he had. He knew that his Josephine didn't want to hear the truth, but sometimes he really felt that she *needed* to hear it, needed to be dragged back into the real world, no matter how much that might hurt her.

Chapter Ninety-Four

Declan Costello was laughing loudly; he liked a good joke, and he also liked a drink in the afternoon. The new barmaid was a real comedienne. She could make a cat laugh. Shame she looked like a fucking Russian athlete – if she had the looks he would have been on her in nanoseconds. He was getting older now, and was still overweight but that didn't bother him too much, he had never been what anyone would ever call a looker. Many girls had tried to tie him down, but he had never let himself get caught. After a few weeks they bored him, even the really good-looking ones. He didn't want a life partner, never had.

He was waiting for Michael. It was Thursday, and that meant Michael would meet him in the private club they owned in East London by one o'clock at the latest. It was something they had done for years. Michael always liked to hear everything that was going on first-hand, and Declan was more than happy to oblige. He always gave Michael the lowdown on everything and everyone he dealt with. After Michael had nearly murdered him all those years ago, no one had been more amazed than him when Michael had brought him back into the fold, treating him as if nothing untoward had happened between them. It had been a real learning curve for him, and he had never forgotten it. Michael had only ever mentioned their contretemps once, on the day he had come round to his house just after he had finally left the hospital. After enquiring about his health, Michael had looked at him sadly, before saying, 'I never want us to fall out again, Declan. All I want is for *you* to keep your eye on the ball in the future. You were supposed to have my back, you were supposed to be making my life easier.'

Declan had been so grateful to be given another chance, he had sworn to prove himself worthy of Michael's kindness. He had never once forgotten his role, and he relished his position, realising how easily it could be taken from him if he ever fucked up again. His laziness, combined with his refusal to think for himself, had nearly cost him not just his livelihood, but also his life. It was a mistake he wouldn't make a second time.

He took a deep gulp of his beer, enjoying the icy coldness as it slipped down his throat. He was a very happy man, and that was something that he really valued these days. He had lived through the humiliation of Michael's attack, and that had been very hard for him; without Michael Flynn he was basically worth nothing.

He held up his empty glass to the barmaid, and she took it quickly, filling it up once more for him. The bar was empty; they had just had the whole place decorated, and it was odd to see it so clean-looking. But it still had the old-fashioned vibe to it; the men who frequented this place would not be comfortable otherwise.

He glanced towards the stairs. He had heard the door opening, and he watched Michael Flynn walking down the stairway slowly. He was still a very handsome man. Michael had never put on any weight, he still had a good body on him. He would get better looking as he got older, the jammy fucker; some men were lucky like that.

'All right, Michael.' It was a greeting, not a question.

Michael smiled. 'All right, Declan. You're looking good, mate.'

Declan grinned with pleasure. 'I feel fine anyway. That's the main thing. Drink?'

The barmaid took the order, and Declan was amazed to see Michael Flynn drinking a large whisky so early in the day. '*Are* you all right, Michael?'

Declan's voice was genuinely worried, and Michael swallowed his drink down in one before answering him. 'It's my Jessie. She didn't turn up for her money. I know it's silly to worry, but she's never missed a Thursday before.'

He motioned to the barmaid for another drink, and she took his glass from him without a word. She refilled it and placed it on the bar in front of him. He smiled his thanks, noticing she wasn't the usual eyeful they employed.

'I don't know, Declan. It's not like her. I'm worried.'

Declan knew how fragile Michael's situation was regarding his only daughter. He suspected that young Jessie was probably shacked up with some piece of shit lowlife somewhere, but he knew better than to say that. Instead he took a drink of his beer, before saying easily, 'I'm sure she will turn up. You haven't got anything to worry about there, mate. She probably had a late night.'

Michael looked at his old friend. Declan was ageing before his eyes. It didn't help that he dressed like a fucking Nigerian refugee. He always looked like he had got dressed in the dark. 'I suppose so. But Josephine wanted me to report back to her, and how can I do that now? I've sent someone round to her gaff. She won't like it, but who gives a fuck? I need to know she's OK.'

Declan didn't say anything. Jessie Flynn was notorious in their world. Her name was a by-word for whoring. She had used up all her brownie points with her uncle Declan years ago. She disgusted him now. If she was *his* daughter he would have crippled her many moons ago, put a stop to her gallop then and there. She had slept with everyone they knew.

'Daughters, eh, Declan? A breed apart!'

Declan laughed gently. 'I wouldn't know, Michael. I never wanted kids, or a wife, come to that. You know me, mate. I never felt the urge to reproduce.'

Michael was laughing despite himself. 'I can't say I fucking blame you for that. Anyway, what's the score? I heard about the aggro in the lap-dancing club.'

Declan groaned theatrically, pleased to be changing the subject. 'If you had seen the bloke who caused it, you'd freak out. He was as old as the hills for a start, and the girl was all of nineteen. He had made the fatal mistake they make, of course – assumed that because he had been giving her money all night he owned her. Then, when her shift was over and she tried to leave, he kicked off. Typical city type, thinks the whole world owes him allegiance. Well, he got a fucking slap in the end – there was no talking to him. He's barred now, the wrinkled up old ponce.' Declan motioned for more drinks before saying craftily, 'I had to laugh, though, he was two grand down, and drunk as a coot, but he was a game old fucker, I'll give him that.'

Michael was laughing with him now. 'It always amazes me that they just don't get it.'

Declan picked up his fresh pint, drinking deeply, enjoying it. ''Course they don't get it, Michael. If they did we wouldn't earn a fucking bean!'

Chapter Ninety-Five

Hannah Flynn was listening to her arch enemy with interest. Lana wasn't her favourite person, but she did oftentimes have a good insight into her daughter's life.

'I tell you, Hannah, my Josephine is getting worse. If it wasn't for that little boy I don't know what she would do.'

Hannah nodded slowly in agreement. Her daughter-in-law was not a bad girl; as the years had gone on, she had become quite attached to her. Josephine was weak, that was her problem. She had no backbone. Jessie's antics had been the last straw really. Her pregnancy had knocked them all for six, but it had broken Josephine. She had never recovered.

She had made her way round to Lana's because, for the first time ever, Jessie hadn't turned up at her house for a late lunch. She always came to her on a Thursday. Jessie saw her dad first, picked up her cash, and then she came straight to her nana's. Hannah made them lunch, and they chatted together. It was the highlight of her week. But today she hadn't shown up; that wasn't right. Jessie never missed their lunch together. She had tried her mobile over and over again, and nothing – it had just rung. She had come round to Lana's house in the end, hoping to find out something about her granddaughter. But it was obvious Lana knew even less than she did.

'Has anyone seen Jessie today?'

Lana shrugged. 'Not that I know of, Hannah. When does anyone ever see the mardy bitch? I could smack her face at times.'

Hannah sipped at her tea. She was aware that Jessie didn't really bother with her mum's family, and that pleased her usually. Nevertheless she still felt uncomfortable about Jessie being a no-show. As unreliable as Jessie could be, she always came round to her house on a Thursday. It was their little secret.

Chapter Ninety-Six

Jake was so boisterous and loud, Josephine could hear him even through the tightly shut French doors in her bedroom. He was tearing around the gardens as usual and, smiling to herself, she made her way out on to her balcony to watch him. His nanny, Dana, was chasing him, and he was easily getting away from her. She could see the glee on his face as he laughed loudly. Jake had such a lust for life. She saw him standing on the lawn, his hands on his hips. He looked so much like her Michael, she felt the sting of tears in her eyes. She thanked God every day that her grandson didn't look like whoever had fathered him. It would have been very hard to look at the child if he had nothing of his family in him.

Josephine sat down on the nearest chair and wiped a hand across her mouth. She hated to think like that, but she couldn't help herself. Jake meant the world to her and, even though she couldn't bring herself to do much with him, she made sure that inside the house he spent quality time with her. He was already questioning her lifestyle, asking her why she never took him to school, or went for a walk with him. He was always asking about his mum; he knew she should be around more, that his friends' mums were always there. He didn't have his mum, and he didn't have his nana there for him either. She couldn't be there for him – she couldn't leave the house, not even for her grandson. Jake was getting to an age where he was noticing these things.

She saw Dana pick her grandson up and swing him around. The girl was so good with him. She genuinely did care for the child.

Josephine could feel the erratic beating of her heart and the shortness of breath that heralded a panic attack. She was sweating profusely, unable to prevent it happening. Closing her eyes tightly, she concentrated on her breathing, taking deep breaths slowly and evenly, like the doctor had taught her. She felt the panic subsiding, and the terror left her body as quickly as it had arrived. Then she heard her name being called and, standing up, she saw that Jake was now down below her, on the patio, looking up at her balcony, his handsome face cross. He had his hands on his hips; she had been away with the fairies, and had not heard him calling her name.

'Really, Nana, it's not good enough, you know! I've been calling up to you for ages!'

As he stormed off, Dana looked up at her and shrugged, before following him into the house.

Josephine closed her eyes in distress. This was happening to her more and more lately; she seemed to be losing all sense of time and place. She saw her pack of cigarettes on the table, and she lit one quickly, drawing on it deeply. Then she smoked it slowly until the trembling in her body subsided once again.

Chapter Ninety-Seven

'So you're sure she wasn't there?'

Daniel Carter nodded. 'I let meself in, Michael, as you told me to. I'm telling you, there wasn't a soul in that flat. I searched everywhere. Jessie had definitely left the building.'

Michael expected as much; his big fear had been that she would be in there, but dead as a doornail. With her lifestyle, that wasn't exactly unheard of. 'OK. Thanks, Daniel. I appreciate it.'

Daniel Carter was heart-sorry that he couldn't put the man's mind at rest. 'I can ask about if you want, Michael? See where she is?'

Michael laughed bitterly. 'I've already done that. Thanks anyway, mate.' He watched Daniel leave the room and, sitting down behind his desk, he sighed heavily.

No one seemed to have clapped eyes on Jessie since last night. She had scored in Upney, then cabbed it back to her flat. After that, no one had seen or, more to the point, heard from her. Her mobile was permanently attached to her lughole, yet she hadn't used it in the hours since. The piece of shit she had been hanging about with was shitting bricks now. He had been dragged from his bed, and questioned by three very large men. But he had been telling the truth – he had gone on to a club, which had been verified. Michael knew she hadn't been nicked or he would have heard about it by now. He owned the local

Filth, and they always contacted him immediately whenever she was arrested. Nevertheless he insisted that they check. But nothing. Jessie had disappeared off the face of the earth.

He tried her mobile again, but it just rang and rang. Where else could he look for his daughter? Jessie didn't know that her whereabouts were always reported to him; if she turned up somewhere, he knew about it. It was his way of looking out for her and checking out the men she socialised with. It was so fucking hard having to pretend to everyone around him that he didn't care about her life choices, knowing that if he interfered she would turn away from her mother completely and could cause problems for them and her little boy. She had him by the nuts.

Chapter Ninety-Eight

Josephine was listening to Jake as he chattered away to her. He was dressed for school, and she looked at him with pride; he was such a handsome boy.

'Dana's promised to take me to the park after school. I wish you would come with us, Nana. It's such fun. I like the swings best. But Dana says that's because I am such a fidget bucket!' He laughed with delight. 'I promise you, Nana, I will be a very good boy. I won't make too much noise.'

Josephine hugged him tightly and kissed his forehead. 'I think you and Dana will have a good time, Jake. You know your nana has lots of work to do. But I will see you when you get home, and you can tell me all about it.'

Jake looked at his nana intently for long moments, and Josephine could tell that he didn't believe her about having to work.

'OK, then. But I wish you would try to come with us sometimes.'

'I will, Jake. Now get along or you'll be late.'

He kissed her on the cheek, and she could hear him talking and fussing as he made his way down the stairs. She heard the front door slam, and sighed sadly; the house was so empty when he wasn't in it. It had always been far too big really. Michael loved it and, in her own way, so did she. It was a home fit for a large family; as Michael used to joke, many years ago, the Von

Trapps would get lost in it. That was back when they had thought they would be banging out babies as and when they desired them, before the pain of disappointment had settled over them. That was a long time ago.

She stood up slowly, and made herself cross the large landing to the bedroom she had once shared with her husband. As she walked into the room, she was pleased to see that he was already wide awake. He was sitting up in bed, watching the news on TV. He had a large mug of black coffee in his hands, so she knew he had already been up and about for a while.

'I didn't hear you come in last night, Michael.'

She sat on the bed beside him, and he leant over to kiss her lightly on the lips. 'I was late in, Josephine. I didn't want to wake you up, darling.'

'Did you talk to Jessie? She hasn't called since Tuesday morning. How did she seem yesterday? Did you ask her about Sunday?'

Michael Flynn looked at his lovely wife, who he loved more than anything else in the world. She was already in full make-up as always, and dressed in a very fetching cream-coloured silk dressing gown. It was expensive, he could see that, and it looked wonderful on her. Lana must have picked it out for her. She had always taken such good care of herself; the last few years, it was all she ever did. It was surreal, seeing her fully made-up night or day, her hair and her make-up perfect, as if she was going somewhere. His life was fraught with so many problems; sometimes, like now, he resented her for that. But he wouldn't say anything. It was too late.

'I didn't see her, love. I had a lot on yesterday, and I didn't hang about too long. To be honest, I wasn't in the mood for her anyway.'

Josephine smiled at her husband gently. 'I was hoping you'd seen her. But you know Jessie – she'll turn up at some point.'

Michael nodded his agreement. 'Like a fucking bad penny, she is. Anyway, we shouldn't let her bother us. She knows where we are.'

Josephine didn't like her husband's attitude but she didn't comment. 'I wish she'd call me though, Michael. We talk regularly, you know that.'

He grabbed his wife's hand, and squeezed it tightly. She had such small hands and feet, she was so fragile.

'Don't worry, Josephine. Knowing our Jessie, she's probably shacked up with some lowlife she met last night. It wouldn't be the first time, would it?'

Josephine didn't reply; this was upsetting her now. She didn't need her husband to remind her of her daughter's failings. She pulled her hand roughly away from Michael's, and he knew he had hurt her feelings. But he couldn't tell her the truth, that Jessie had dropped off the radar and no one seemed to know where she was.

'I better get myself back, Michael, I have a few things I need to sort out today.'

Michael felt his anger rising at Josephine's words, but he swallowed it down as always. All his wife actually did, day in and day out, was repair her make-up, paint her nails and re-arrange her boxes of crap. For the first time in years, he felt he needed her, wanted her to be like she was in the old days, when he could tell her anything, and she would advise him, listen to him. He didn't like having to admit to himself that his lovely wife Josephine was like a stranger to him these days. She would choose her old crap over him, over Jake, over Jessie, if she had to. He had done his best to see his wife happy; now he wasn't so sure he had done the right thing by her. All he had accomplished was to allow Josephine to live a life without any meaning. He had stood back and let it happen. The doctors had given her pills, but no one challenged her or told her that her life was odd, that *she* was odd. The psychiatrist talked to her for hours in her rooms; he paid the fucker a small fortune, but Josephine just got worse. Looking at her now, he wondered how he could have let it happen. When she had first started bulk-buying food, he should have put his foot down then. They rarely made love any more, and they talked only in generalities of things that were of no real importance. All they had in common was Jake.

He could see Josephine watching him warily, and he wanted to grab hold of her, drag her into bed with him, and give her a serious seeing to, like in the old days. But he didn't feel he could do that to her any more. She wasn't the old Josephine, the woman he had married – this was a woman who lived inside herself, whose every waking moment was lived in a vacuum.

'Are you happy, Josephine? I mean *really* happy?'

He could see the confusion on her face at his question, and he wanted to slap her, wanted to make her react to him without thinking it through first. 'Answer me! It's not a hard question, is it? It's a simple yes or no.'

Josephine looked down at her hands, unable to look her husband in the face. 'Of course I'm happy, Michael. What a thing to ask.'

Michael put his finger under her chin, and he made her look him in the eyes, before he said seriously, 'I don't think you are, Josephine. I don't think you have been happy for a long time. Not really.'

Josephine looked at her husband, saw the sadness in his expression, and the way he was waiting expectantly for her answer. 'I am happy, Michael.'

She meant it. He smiled because he knew she was telling him the truth – as she saw it. 'Good. That's all I wanted to know.'

Chapter Ninety-Nine

Jessie was frightened and cold. She was also starving, which amazed her because she didn't think food would be high up on her priority list. But it was. She didn't eat that regularly anyway but, for the first time in years, her stomach felt empty; the hunger like a gnawing pain inside her. Her arms and legs were tied, and it was so painful; every time she tried to move her body, a burning pain shot through her limbs.

She was terrified. It was so very dark. She felt tears running down her face, and she forced herself to stop them. She wasn't going to cry, that wasn't sensible; she couldn't afford to let her emotions get the better of her. She was going to keep her wits about her, and try and work out what the situation actually was. If this was a kidnapping, which she doubted, whoever had organised it had better take the money and run as fast as possible. Her dad wouldn't let something like this go unpunished – he would take it very personally, see it as an act of treason against him, and all he stood for.

The pain was shooting through her skull again, and it was so acute she closed her eyes and bit down on her bottom lip, trying to ride it out. It was a losing battle – the pain was too intense. She felt herself losing consciousness again, and she didn't try to fight it this time. Her head was aching so badly, but at least it had stopped bleeding.

She embraced the sleep that washed over her; she was glad of it, even though she knew it wasn't natural.

Chapter One Hundred

'I have already got people out there searching for her, the Old Bill included, useless fuckers that they are. But I swear on my fucking eyesight, when I find out what's gone down, I will fucking kill the bastards responsible with my bare hands. How dare they! How dare anyone think they could touch my daughter and live to tell the fucking tale!'

Michael was stalking around the office of the nightclub in Ilford. He was so angry he couldn't even breathe properly. There was no doubt in his mind now; his Jessie was missing. It was over three days, and that wasn't normal, even for her. She was a fucking nuisance, living her life like a fucking hippy but, as much as she thought she was some kind of enigma, she was actually very predictable. Not that he would ever explain that to her, the dozy little mare. It suited him for her to think she was a fucking maverick, a fucking independent woman. As if. Without him and his protection she would have gone under a long time ago. She had more problems than the euro and, in real life, if she had to sort things out for herself, she would be seriously fucked. But she was still his baby, and he couldn't turn his back on her.

Declan Costello watched Michael as he stalked around the small office; it was unusual to see him so flustered. He always kept his cool, no matter what happened. But this was different, Declan understood that; this was about his kid.

Declan sat back in his chair, heart-sorry for his friend. 'It can't be a kidnapping, Michael – you'd have heard from them by now. It's fucking mental! No one can just disappear like that.'

Michael sighed heavily. 'That's just it though, Declan – they can.'

Declan knew what Michael was trying to say, and he shook his huge head violently in denial. Who would bother to kill Jessie? People disappeared, that was a given, but there was always a reason.

'Fuck off, Michael! Will you listen to yourself? Why on earth would anyone want to kill young Jessie? It's ludicrous.'

Michael Flynn stood in front of his old friend, and he said honestly, 'Think about it, Declan. You know what she's like. I want to kill her myself half the time. She's got a fresh mouth on her, she talks to people like they're shit. I warned her time and again that, one day, if she wasn't careful, her big mouth would get her into real trouble. She pushes everything, pushes everyone.'

Declan laughed. 'Can you hear yourself, Michael? Ninety-nine per cent of the population couldn't kill a fucking earwig unless they had to. It's why people like us can do what we do. But you have to remember that there is no one on this planet who would dare to touch a hair on your daughter's head. She knows that herself – why do you think she acts like she does? For all her fucking arrogance, she knows that without your name she wouldn't last five minutes.'

Declan could see the real fear in Michael's face, could almost feel the worry the man had for his only child. It wasn't fair. He didn't deserve any of this. Michael Flynn, for all his faults, was basically a decent man, a good man where it counted. Even *he* acknowledged that, and he had been on the receiving end of the man's temper.

'You haven't even had a stand-off with anyone for years, Michael, so this can't be about payback, can it?'

Michael could see that Declan was speaking sense, but it didn't take the fear out of his chest. He had traced her calls, and there had been nothing for days to or from her number. Her 'friends' – and he used the word loosely – had been as baffled as he was about her whereabouts.

The office door opened, and Michael smiled nastily as Jonny Parsons was pushed into the room roughly. He tripped over his own feet, and just about stopped himself from falling flat on his face. He was absolutely terrified; that was more than evident to both the other men in the small room. The man looked what he was: a cheap imitation, a wannabe gangster, a fucking thug.

Jonny looked at Michael Flynn's hard face, and his heart stopped in his chest. He hadn't realised the power that the man radiated, the menace that surrounded him. This was what he had wanted: a meeting with Michael Flynn. It was why he had romanced Jessie, but he had not understood until now exactly what that entailed.

Michael Flynn towered over him and, in the confines of the room, the man looked almost demonic. It was easy to see why people were so wary of crossing him, why he had accumulated so much power over the years, why he was so respected by everyone around him. He was the main man throughout Europe, the boss of everyone around him, and that was not an easy task.

He could see Declan Costello sitting behind the desk like a big, overweight leprechaun, all smiles and expectation. Declan was watching him closely, waiting to see what was going to happen and, by the looks of him, he was going to enjoy it.

Jonny Parsons felt trapped. He just stood there like a fool, unable to talk or move.

Michael was looking at the man who had slept with his young daughter, his only child. He wasn't impressed with what he was seeing; in fact, he was disgusted. Jonny Parsons was forty if he was a day, his hair was cut like a teenager's, he was dressed in cheap knock-offs – even the man's Rolex was a cheap imitation.

Worst of all was that Jonny Parsons was without any kind of decency. The man was a complete and utter coward. Yet his daughter had taken this man into her bed. It galled him that she could lower herself to this level.

He poked his finger hard into the man's chest, making him lose his balance once more. He could feel the terror coming off him in waves, and he was glad. At least he had reason to let the man know what he truly thought of him.

'I'm looking for my daughter, Jessie Flynn. I assume you remember her? Do you know where she is?'

Jonny Parsons' mouth was so dry he wasn't sure if he could actually form any words.

Michael was enjoying every second of Jonny's discomfort, and he bellowed into his face suddenly, 'Are you fucking deaf? You useless cunt! I just asked you a fucking question.'

Jonny Parsons was shaking his head in denial, wondering how he had ever thought that, by using Jessie Flynn as a stepping stone, he could have somehow gained an entry into this man's world. He must have been off his head to have even contemplated it.

'No, Mr Flynn, I swear to you. I haven't seen her since last week.'

Michael sighed. The man was a fucking complete imbecile. What the fuck was Jessie thinking about? Didn't she even *look* at the men she slept with?

'You haven't spoken to her or called her – I already fucking know that. I just want to know if you've seen her, or spoken to anyone who has?'

Jonny Parsons was shaking his head vehemently. 'No. Nothing. Not a word. I ain't heard anything about her from anyone either.'

Michael turned around, and looked at Declan in abject disbelief. 'What a fucking Casanova this cunt is, Declan. He fucks them and leaves them by the sounds of it.'

Jonny was in deep trouble, and he didn't know what he could do to help himself. If he had any information about Jessie he would happily tell her father.

Michael shook his head sadly, and Declan knew what was coming next. The first punch lifted Jonny Parsons off his feet, and opened up a large gash in his right eyebrow. Michael watched the man go down. He collapsed on to the floor and, curling himself up into a tight ball, he tried to protect his head with his arms. Michael looked at the man for a few seconds, then used his feet and, as he kicked his daughter's bedmate over and over again, he was glad to be able to vent some of his anger. He had sussed Jonny Parsons out, knew the man had bragged about his relationship with his daughter, had seen her as his passport into the big time. He wasn't the first idiot to think that and, unfortunately, he probably wouldn't be the last. But it felt good hurting him, reminding the man of who he was dealing with.

Declan watched everything with his usual calm. He had been on the other end of Michael's anger himself, and he knew how violent it could be. Michael needed to vent his spleen – it would do him the world of good.

Declan waited until Michael's anger was spent before he stepped in. Jonny Parsons was a bloody mess and, pulling Michael away from the man firmly, he sat him down behind the desk. Then, going to the office door, he opened it and called in a couple of the bouncers. They knew the score as soon as they stepped into the room, and they picked up Jonny Parsons without any words needing to be spoken.

Declan shut the door behind them and, turning to Michael, he said carefully, 'Feeling better, are we? Now, we need to think about this logically, Michael.'

Michael sat forward in the old typist's chair and, holding his head in his hands, he said brokenly, near to tears, 'That's just it, there's *no* fucking logic to it, Declan. That's the problem. I know in my guts that this is fucking serious. This is fucking personal. This is not about my Jessie. How can it be? You said it yourself. Who would fucking dare to touch my daughter?'

Declan could see the man's point, but he still wasn't convinced. Michael Flynn had the Colombians behind him; there wasn't anyone who had the guts to take him on. He was too protected, too respected. He ran his empire fairly and squarely, and he made sure that everyone he was involved with earned so much they were loyal to him. Michael Flynn entertained some of the most dangerous men in the world. It was terrible to see him like this, so vulnerable, so worried.

'Look, Michael, what if she's shacked up somewhere, oblivious to all that's going on? You know what she's like.'

Michael looked at his old friend, and he sighed heavily. 'I hope you're right, Declan, I really do. But something is telling me, inside, that's not the case. She's in trouble. I just know it.'

Chapter One Hundred and One

Jake was all smiles, his happiness contagious. Josephine was watching him drawing pictures and, as he finished each one, he showed them to her with a flourish.

'That's you and Granddad eating your dinner!'

Josephine couldn't help but laugh – he had captured them perfectly. She looked at the drawing and saw herself and her husband sitting on her bed together, with plates on their laps. Then she saw that Jake had drawn himself on a chair all alone, watching them. He wasn't smiling. He looked sad.

'Why do you look so sad, Jake?'

He shrugged nonchalantly. 'I'm waiting for my mummy, of course. But she didn't come.'

Josephine felt so sorry for her little lad. 'I told you, Jake. Your mummy has to work a lot.'

He carried on drawing, but he didn't answer her. She could slap her daughter sometimes for the worry she caused. And now she was missing, and it was worrying them all. She had heard nothing from her daughter for nearly four days and, like Michael, Josephine was beginning to be seriously concerned.

Dana came into the room beaming, and when Josephine saw the way that Jake reacted to her, she felt a stab of jealousy.

'Come on, you. It's your bath time, mister.'

Jake got up from the floor, abandoning his drawing without a thought. 'Can I play with my toys?'

Dana picked him up effortlessly. He was a big child for his age, but Dana didn't seem to notice that; she still treated him like a baby. ''Course you can! They are all there waiting for you!'

'See you later, Nana!'

Josephine waved to him, and watched as they left the room together. She knelt down on the rug, and busied herself tidying his paper and pencils away. Then she carefully picked up his sweet wrappers – fun-size Snickers and a Milky Way – and folded both of them neatly, before placing them into one of the boxes scattered around the room.

Glancing at herself in the mirror of her dressing table, she checked over her appearance. She looked perfect, which pleased her. She picked up her lipstick from the dressing table, and ran it over her lips quickly. The action alone calmed her, made her feel better in herself. She gained a lot of comfort from doing familiar things. Her doctor said it was about control, but she couldn't see that herself. She just liked the feeling of ease it gave her; there was a lot to be said for order, having a routine. She couldn't cope without it.

She sat down in her chair once more and glanced around, mentally counting the boxes in her room, and running through their contents in her head.

She picked up her glass of red wine from the small antique table beside her chair and sipped it, savouring its warmth. She didn't see clutter around her or chaos – what she saw was her possessions, things she loved and needed. Today she needed the comfort more than ever. But no matter how hard she tried to calm herself and tell herself that Michael was right, she didn't need to worry, her daughter's disappearance *did* worry her – greatly. She knew that Jessie wouldn't do this to her mother without good reason.

Chapter One Hundred and Two

DI Timothy Branch was annoyed. He had been told in no uncertain terms to use every resource at his disposal to locate Michael Flynn's daughter. Easier said than done – the girl had been around the turf more times than a Grand National winner.

He had put the word out, but she was nowhere to be found. He wasn't relishing telling that to Michael Flynn – the man seemed to think he could somehow conjure the girl up from thin air. If only it was that easy. He now had the unenviable task of admitting to the man who had been paying him shedloads of money for a lot of years, that he couldn't help him. Jessie Flynn was, without doubt, a missing person.

Michael Flynn's minions had already questioned everyone in his daughter's orbit – and not in a nice way. Branch's men had been called out to disturbances by concerned citizens many times over the last few days. He had been expected to ensure that the people concerned didn't have to deal with the police on top of everything else. Not that any of the victims were willing to press charges, but it was still very stressful. It had been a hard few days for him in particular. He had been forced to show his hand as a bent copper. He hadn't meant it to be common knowledge. But what could he do about it? As Michael Flynn had so forcefully pointed out to him, this was what he had been paid so handsomely for – even he couldn't argue with that.

Chapter One Hundred and Three

When Jessie opened her eyes again, she knew immediately that there was someone else in the room with her. She tried to steady her breathing which was so loud in the darkness. Then she realised that her hands were free, she wasn't tied up any more. She tried to sit up, but she couldn't manage that immediately. Her legs were still shackled and she was tied to the bed. As she became more aware of her circumstances she felt relief that she had been given at least a modicum of freedom. It took her a few minutes to finally drag herself into a sitting position; she was in a lot of pain – her arms and back felt like they had been broken.

'Who's there? I know you're there.' She could hear the tremor in her voice and she hated herself for her weakness. 'You fucking coward! Talk to me! I can't go anywhere, can I? I can't hurt you, can I?'

She listened intently, trying to penetrate the darkness. 'My dad will kill you for this. You know that, don't you?'

She could hear the person breathing near to her, they were only a few feet away. It was a man, she knew that much, and he clearly wasn't bothered by her words. She could feel that he was totally in control of the situation and of her. She was scared, but she couldn't bow down, she couldn't admit to her fears.

'I know you're there. I know you're near me. I can hear you, for fuck's sake.' Her voice was strong, and that pleased her, even as she braced herself for an attack. But it didn't come. She wasn't sure what she was supposed to do, what she was supposed to say. She lowered her voice, and said huskily, 'I'm starving and I'm thirsty. I had one bottle of water and that's gone.'

She was straining to hear something, but there wasn't anything except the quiet breathing. She lay back down; she was weak, and she was wasting her time trying to get a reaction. She hoped she wasn't going to be starved to death, just left alone to die in the darkness, that was such a terrifying thought. This couldn't be it for her, surely? She huddled into the mattress and, as she curled up, she heard the clinking of the chains around her ankles, felt the weight of them and, for the first time in the whole of her life, she felt completely alone.

'You really are your father's fucking daughter.'

The voice was low, it had a cockney twang to it. It was the voice of an older man. But this person, whoever he was, was a complete stranger to her.

'Why am I here? What did I ever do to you?'

She could hear his footsteps as he walked away from her slowly, heard the heaviness of the door as he pulled it open and, as it shut behind him, she started to cry.

Chapter One Hundred and Four

'I can't believe that no one knows where she is, Michael. It's just not possible. You're wrong. You need to start sorting this out properly.'

Michael looked at his wife, at her perfectly made-up face, and her expensive designer clothes that she wore indoors like other people wore pyjamas. It was the middle of the night and she was fully dressed, acting as if it was the most natural thing in the world to be dressed like a fucking supermodel at three a.m., when it was anything but. And, to top it all, she had the nerve to question him. To challenge him about his missing daughter, as if he wasn't even bothering to try and locate her. This from the mother who didn't care enough to leave her home and help him with his search. He was tired, worried, and now he was also fucking annoyed. How dare she question him, when she hadn't done anything at all to help?

'Do you know what, Josephine? You've got a brass neck on you. I have been searching high and low for Jessie, I've mobilised the whole of the London police force, every fucker on my payroll, and I have made sure that every person our Jessie ever knew has been routed. What have you done? Other than repair your make-up, and reset your fucking hair? Oh, and let little Jake have a few minutes of your *precious* time with you? Playing the devoted nana, and keeping everything he touches as if it means anything to anyone else in the real world! Come on then – tell me, Josephine. I'm so fucking *interested.* You haven't left this house for years. You hide in here like a fucking Nazi war criminal. We pretend it's normal, you living in two rooms in a home that's big enough to house a fucking army, but it's *not*, Josephine, it's not *normal* at all. Then you have the nerve to tell me that I'm not doing enough to find Jessie. Where the *fuck* do you get off?'

Josephine was white-faced at this attack on her, and she wasn't able to answer her husband. His anger was so painful and raw. She had never seen him like this before. Somewhere in her head, she recognised he was telling her the truth, but it didn't make it any easier to hear.

Pulling herself upright in her chair and, squaring her shoulders, she gathered her pride. Looking at the man she had married, and who she still loved with all her heart, she said coldly, 'I don't need you or anyone else to tell me about my life, Michael. *I* am the one who has to live it, and I live it to the best of my ability.'

For the first time ever her words didn't have any effect on him; he didn't care about her problems or her needs. 'Oh, blow it out your arse, Josephine. It's not about you for once, is it? It's about Jessie, and where the fuck she might be. Because I don't think this is her usual old fanny. I think this time she might really be in serious trouble.'

Chapter One Hundred and Five

Jessie woke up to find a stone-cold McDonald's and a large bottle of water on the end of her bed. She was relieved there was finally some light, albeit not that bright, but at least she could peruse her surroundings. There wasn't much to see. As she gobbled down the food left for her, she didn't notice anything of use; the walls were concrete, badly rendered, and there was no furniture in the room other than the bed she was tied to. The smell of her urine was disgusting, but there wasn't anything she could do about that. She just hoped *that* would work in her favour – whoever this man was, he wouldn't want to rape her. She stank like a fucking polecat. But he'd already had his chance for that.

She finished her food and drank a deep gulp of the water; she had never been so hungry in her life. She had a feeling the man was sedating her with the water he allowed her, but she had no choice – she had to drink it. It was better to be asleep, if truth be told. She wasn't going anywhere anytime soon. Her arms were aching from being bound for days and, as she tried to flex her legs to get some feeling back into them, she saw a bundle of clothing on the floor beside her bed.

Grabbing the clothes eagerly, she noticed that he had left her a cheap wraparound skirt that was suitable for the beach and a tracksuit top; it was an ugly grey colour, but at least it looked warm. As she stripped off her clothes, she was ashamed to see just how soiled and dilapidated she had become.

She slipped off the end of the bed, and stood up unsteadily. In the dim light she could make out two thick metal plates fixed into the floor, and these were what held her captive. The chains themselves were tight, and they were very heavy. She couldn't remove them without a weapon of some kind, or the keys to her ankle chains, of course. It was a terrible feeling, being held captive like this, left to lie in her own stench, her own urine, like a fucking animal. But she wasn't going to let this man know how much that affected her. He'd not harmed her since that first night, when he had knocked her unconscious, but she could still feel the pain from where he had hit her. If he had hit her like that once, he wouldn't care about having to do it again.

She dressed herself quickly in the fresh clothes, pulling the skirt she'd been wearing over her head. Her underwear was filthy but she couldn't remove it with the chains. At least the clean clothes gave her a feeling of power and reminded her of how strong she could be if necessary. She could not allow herself to think otherwise; if she gave in to her fears, this man would beat her, and she was determined that she would never give up without a fucking fight. She had fought her father, the big dangerous villain, tooth and nail, so she was fucked if she was going to let anyone else get the better of her now. She forced herself to concentrate on the predicament that she was in, reminding herself that, no matter what might have passed between her and her father, he was the only chance she had to survive; if anyone was capable of finding her, and rescuing her, it was her dad.

She saw how stained the mattress was with her own bodily functions and, using all her strength, she finally managed to turn it over. It was difficult and exhausting, but it was something she needed to do. This was about her refusing to let the man who was holding her captive demoralise her completely. She climbed back on to the bed, pleased at what she had achieved for herself.

She still felt filthy, though. She could smell her own urine and body odour. Her breath was rank, her skin felt greasy, oily and grubby. She could feel the large scab on her scalp – from where the man had beaten her unconscious – which had bled quite badly. She still felt pain whenever she moved her head around.

She pulled the blankets from the floor and, even though they were dirty, she used them to cover herself. She felt the sting of tears again and for all her certainty that her father would come for her, she began to wonder if he was even looking for her yet. Why hadn't he found her already? He was the hardest man in fucking Europe! Why had she been taken? This couldn't be a kidnapping – if it was, surely she would have been forced to make a tape of the kidnapper's demands? Or talk to her father to prove she was still alive? Her father would insist on that. He wouldn't pay a penny until he was assured she was still in one piece. So what the fuck was this about? She still had her very expensive Rolex, and it gave her the time and the date. It was five days since she had been abducted, and the man who was keeping her chained up didn't seem to be bothered about anything. There was no urgency about him, or his movements – in fact, he was a bit *too* laid back. The food, the light and the clean clothes, though, made her think that maybe he wasn't going to leave her to starve to death. Maybe he did have a hidden agenda. But what that might be, she couldn't even hazard a guess.

Chapter One Hundred and Six

Dana O'Carroll was in her late thirties and she knew she wasn't a beauty. She was a heavyset woman with a flat face, heavy lips, and deep brown eyes. She had worked for the Flynns since three months before Jake had been born, employed to look after the child and also Josephine. She was a state-registered nurse, and she had taken this place knowing that she would stay for the duration – the lure of a newborn baby had been too much for her to resist. Jake Flynn was the child she would never have. She absolutely adored him.

Although Dana had ostensibly been brought in to look after Jake, she had known within the first five minutes that Josephine Flynn was seriously in need of psychiatric help. Dana thought the world of Josephine, but there was no getting away from the fact that she was becoming odder by the day, and that was why she was paid so much. She had to watch her like a hawk.

Dana gave Jake everything he needed, and he loved her with all his little heart. As he was getting older, he was starting to question his world and the people in it. His mother Jessie was an anomaly to him; she drifted in and out of his life and didn't know how to treat him when they *were* together. But what would she know about love and caring? It wasn't as though she had learnt it at home. Dana saw that Josephine would always put her husband Michael above anyone, even Jake, if it came to it. How was Jessie supposed to live with that knowledge? Now that Michael had given Josephine a much-needed reality check, forcing her to acknowledge the truth of her life for once, it seemed that Josephine had suddenly forgotten she had a small grandson who needed her. Josephine had locked herself away in her room, broken-hearted and full of self-pity. She had refused to see her little grandson, saying she was too upset. It was shocking and cruel to ignore the little boy like that, but what could she do about it?

Michael Flynn came into the kitchen and, sitting down beside his grandson, he kissed him on his cheek heartily, grabbing the boy out of his chair. Jake laughed loudly with happiness; he loved to be noticed.

'I hear a certain young man is going to Mass this morning with his school. He's learning about his Holy Communion.'

Jake grinned at his granddad. 'I am. That's me! How did you know?'

Michael shrugged theatrically. 'I heard about it, and I wanted to give him a hug before he went! It's a sacrament you know, Jake, Holy Communion, like a deal you make with God. It's very important. It's a big thing for anyone. Remember that. You'll make your First Confession, and then, when you've been absolved of all your sins, you can finally make your First Holy Communion. It's a big event in your life, mate.'

Jake was hanging on his granddad's every word.

'Never forget that you are a very special person, who is going to do a very special thing, and that being a Catholic is very important, OK?'

Jake nodded solemnly. 'Will my mummy be there?'

Michael hugged his grandson tightly. ''Course she will be there, Jake, she wouldn't miss something as important as this!'

As he said the words, he hoped he wouldn't be proved a liar. For all he knew, his daughter was already dead.

Chapter One Hundred and Seven

Declan Costello had spoken to all his workmen, and they said the same thing: Jessie Flynn was on the missing list. It was a fucking joke. Declan had honestly thought that Jessie, true to form, would be discovered tucked up in bed with some piece of shit, and everyone could then sigh with well-deserved relief. Now, he was starting to think that Michael might have a point – that there was something much more serious going on. But what the fuck could it be? And what was the reason behind it? He couldn't think of one person who would even dream of hurting Michael Flynn through his family. There was no logic to it – the fact they had even tried to involve his family would be tantamount to a death warrant. Michael would never swallow anything like that.

He waited patiently for Michael to arrive for the meeting as arranged. This time, though, he would be agreeing with his friend. There was something very off about this whole thing, he could see that now.

Chapter One Hundred and Eight

Josephine was heartbroken that her Michael could have spoken to her like that, lost his temper and insulted her with such viciousness. Especially now, knowing how worried she was, how scared she was for their daughter. He had shouted at her like *she* was the one in the wrong. He knew exactly the willpower it took for her to live even the limited life that she did, yet he had spoken to her with such anger that she had realised what he really thought about her deep down. It had hurt. Every single day was a challenge to her, every moment was so fucking hard, and he had always acted like he understood her pain. That had been a lie. She could feel the ache in her breast, the pain of betrayal. She would never forget what he had said to her. Even when he tried to grovel and apologise – as he would – she would never forget what he had said to her or how he had said it.

She looked at her reflection in the dressing table; she was perfectly made-up, and that was for her husband's benefit. She kept herself looking good for him, so he would appreciate her, remember how much they had meant to each other. She had put her husband before everyone, and she had thought that he had felt the same way about her. As Michael's world got bigger her world got smaller. Now she was trapped, reduced to living in a few rooms, and the outside world was terrifying to her. She had believed that Michael had understood her fears, as irrational as they might be, had accepted them as part of their life as husband and wife. But that wasn't the case.

She had heard him talking to Jake, laughing and joking with him, and she had also heard him leave the house, without even seeing how she was or asking after her. Her Michael had always made a point of saying goodbye to her, of making her feel like she was the centre of his life.

She wouldn't let herself cry; she had no intention of ruining her make-up, not for anyone. She would be here for him, as she had always been. He knew that he was all she had ever really cared about. She had placed him above everyone else and, as far as she was concerned, that alone should guarantee her his loyalty.

Chapter One Hundred and Nine

'How can there be no news, Declan? It's a fucking joke.'

Declan didn't say a word. What could he say? It was the truth. 'I think you might be right, Michael. There's a definite bad smell here.'

Michael laughed, but there was no mirth there. They were in the offices at Canary Wharf.

'At last! You can finally see what I've been fucking saying all along. *Five* days, Declan, and not a fucking dicky-bird. My daughter hates my fucking guts, she flaunts every fucking thing she does in my face, so why not this time? If this was about her, she would make sure I knew about it.'

Declan got up from his seat and poured them both a coffee. The underlying worry in Michael's voice was clear. Giving Michael his mug, Declan said honestly, 'I really don't know, Michael, I can't answer that. All I do know is, I think you're right. I think you sussed this out before anyone else.'

Michael sipped at his coffee, glad to finally have someone agree with him. He had known from the off that this was suspect.

'I want to put the reward up to fifty grand cash. That will guarantee a good fucking shake down, get the word out there. If anyone's information leads me to my daughter – even if it's to her dead body – I will put the money in their pocket myself. I've got to find her, Declan. I need to know what's going down. I know this is trouble, I can feel it.'

Declan nodded. 'I'll do it, Michael, but remember that *you* were the one who said dead or alive. Not me.'

It had crossed Declan's mind that she might be dead somewhere; considering the life she had insisted on living that wouldn't be unlikely.

'I just need to know what's going on, Declan, either way.'

Declan could understand that; he would feel the same if it was him.

Chapter One Hundred and Ten

Josephine heard the knocking on her door, and she guessed it was Dana – no one else bothered to knock. She plastered a smile on her face, and tried to look relaxed, but she knew that Dana had heard everything that had been said between her and Michael. Dana slipped into the room, and Josephine saw that she was holding a letter.

'This was in the post box outside the gates, Josephine. It's handwritten and addressed to you. I thought I should give it to you straight away. You know, just in case . . .'

Josephine took the letter from her warily. 'Thank you.'

Dana waited a few seconds, expecting Josephine to open it, but she didn't. Instead, she placed it carefully on the table beside her chair.

Dana smiled easily. 'Don't you think you should open it, Josephine? It might be important, with what's going on at the moment.'

Josephine smiled right back at her. 'I'll open it later, if it's all the same to you. How did Jake get on today?'

Dana shrugged. 'He had a good day, he's a good kid. He enjoyed the Mass, he hasn't stopped going on about it.'

'Good. Bring him up to me after his tea.'

Dana nodded. 'Of course. I'd best get on, then.'

She left the room as fast as decently possible. She cared about

Josephine very much, but sometimes she could be very creepy.

Dana went back down to the kitchen. Bringing up a tray of tea and biscuits a few hours later, she didn't ask Josephine if she had finally opened the letter. It was still lying on the table, unopened.

Dana had a feeling that it might be important. She rang Michael, telling him everything she knew and, as she had expected, he was back home within the hour.

Chapter One Hundred and Eleven

'I can't fucking believe you sometimes, Josephine! Why haven't you even opened the fucking thing?' Michael snatched the letter off the table.

His annoyance bothered Josephine. He was looking at her as if she had done something wrong. Who the hell did he think he was?

He ripped open the envelope. It had one sheet of paper inside, folded up perfectly. He opened it up slowly, and Josephine realised that, just like her, he was frightened of what it might contain. She watched him as he read the contents.

'Well? Come on then, what does it say, Michael?'

He bent down, until he was level with his wife's face. 'Not fucking too much, Josephine. It just has a number that we were *supposed* to ring at three thirty this afternoon. Bit late for that now, though, don't you think? You silly bitch!'

Josephine was stricken with guilt, Michael could see that, but he didn't care. His wife wouldn't open a letter if you paid her a million pounds – she couldn't. She hadn't opened a letter for years; it was another one of her foibles. He had always accepted her eccentricities, tried his hardest to be supportive, because he loved her so much. Now he wasn't so sure he had done the right thing. All his support seemed to have achieved was to allow his wife to become more and more reclusive. He had enabled her to give in to her fears.

'Why didn't you fucking ring me, Josephine? Or get Dana to? Didn't it occur to you that this letter might be about your daughter? I mean, when was the last time anyone sent you a fucking letter? I can't believe that you didn't care enough about your own child to open it or at least ask someone else to do it for you. Now we've missed the chance to talk to whoever might be holding her. Can't you see how fucking wrong this is? How fucking dangerous you are? Because you still can't bring yourself to do something as normal as opening a fucking letter!' He was bellowing at her now, shouting at her with all his might, venting all the anger and frustration that had been brewing inside him for such a long time.

'For years I have pretended that there is nothing wrong with you. I loved you so fucking much I went along with everything – your fucking hoarding, your fucking refusal to accept reality. I even swallowed you becoming a recluse. I've paid out fortunes for the best doctors available. I've done everything in my power to help you. But do you know what? I wish I'd fucking known then what I know now. I think you *like* being a recluse, you *like* living in these two rooms, surrounded by your boxes of old fucking *crap*. It gives you the excuse you need to justify your life. Even Jake doesn't matter any more, does he? Like me and Jessie, he can't compete with the world you've created for yourself. No one can. How could they? Because it's all about you, isn't it?' Michael opened his arms out wide. 'Look around you, Josephine. This is *it*, darling. This is your crowning achievement. Two rooms and a poxy little bathroom. I hope you think it was worth it.'

Josephine was unable to retaliate. As Michael looked at her he felt guilty. The colour had drained from her face; even with her make-up she looked awful. His words had finally hit home. He had needed to say what he really wanted to, just once. His anger at her utter selfishness was so voracious, he just couldn't stop himself. He had been a good husband to her, no matter what she might think. He had gone along with whatever she wanted, *always.* Anything to make Josephine happy. And what had it got them in the long run? Nothing, that's what. Sweet fuck-all. She had left the real world behind, and he had let her do it, even though he had known it was wrong. Now he would never forgive her.

Chapter One Hundred and Twelve

Jessie felt ill. She had eaten the food left for her so quickly, she now had chronic indigestion. She didn't eat that much normally, but now she felt she should eat whatever she got, to keep her strength up, thereby making sure that, if it ever came to it, she could fight her own end. The man appeared to be immune to her charms and, as she had always used her feminine wiles to get what she wanted, she didn't know how to deal with him. He wouldn't talk to her for a start; in fact, he ignored her with such disdain it was an insult in itself. When he did look at her it was carefully, almost as if he was trying to get inside her head.

He was very nondescript, not very tall, and he looked to be well into his fifties. Although it was hard to tell in the dimness of the basement.

Even though she was still scared, she didn't think the man was capable of harming her without provocation. She had lived around violent men all her life, and this bloke didn't have the same feel to him as her father or her uncle Declan. They both had an air about them that warned you that these were men who would be capable of extreme violence, if the circumstances warranted it. Her nana Hannah, her father's own mother, had happily told her everything she wanted to know about her father and, unlike everyone else in her world, she had not tried to sanitise any of it. She had listened to her nana Hannah's stories.

Even though she spent a lot of time with her, she had never really liked her; her nana Hannah was a vicious old bitch. But Jessie had needed her to tell her everything.

She looked at the man now and shouted angrily, 'Talk to me! Don't just fucking stand there staring at me.'

The man grinned at her for a few moments. Then he walked away, and she heard him leave the room, shutting the door behind him.

Jessie felt the fear building inside her chest again. How the hell had she ended up like this? How the fuck had this happened to her?

Chapter One Hundred and Thirteen

'I tried the number over and over, Declan, but no one answered. I could fucking lamp Josephine one. Why the fuck didn't she open the fucking letter? It's not fucking rocket science, is it? Her daughter's missing, and a letter arrives. Two and two springs to mind! But that's her all over, isn't it? Can't open a fucking letter, can't use the fucking stairs, can't leave the fucking house. The list of things that she can't do any more is fucking endless! I lived with her problems, you know I did. But today her fucking refusal to think about her daughter's welfare tipped me over the edge. I've seen her for the selfish cunt she really is.'

Declan didn't say anything, but Michael didn't expect an answer from him anyway. He already knew Declan's opinion of Josephine and her so-called 'problems'. Declan had never said anything outright, but his silence over the years had spoken volumes. His less-than-complimentary opinion of Josephine had always been there between them.

Michael was so worried about his daughter and what might be happening to her. 'I have more than most people could ever even dream of. I deal in millions of pounds. I single-handedly changed the whole infrastructure of British crime. Yet do you know something, Declan? I've really got fuck-all. My daughter treats me like a fucking leper, and my wife lives on her own fucking planet. Did you know that Josephine won't use the stairs nowadays? She lives in two rooms. The size of that fucking house, and she lives in less space than if she lived in a council flat. How insulting is that?'

Michael was more distressed than Declan had ever seen him. Michael Flynn was always in complete control of his emotions; seeing his friend so vulnerable was a first for Declan Costello. But these were difficult times, and he could understand Michael allowing his hard-man persona to slip.

Declan had poured them a large Scotch each and, as he handed Michael his drink, he wished there was something he could think of to say that might ease the man's plight.

'I love my daughter, Declan. For all our problems, I never stopped loving her. Now she's on the missing list, and I can't help her.'

'You should give the letter to the Old Bill, Michael, they might find a fingerprint or something.'

Michael looked at his old friend as if he had never seen him before. 'Oh, stop it, Declan. This isn't *CSI*, for fuck's sake. Gil Grissom isn't going to miraculously find the cunt's name out before the sixty minutes is up. You and I both know that's a fucking big stretch for anyone's imagination. Most people's fingerprints aren't on any database, unless you've been nicked, and DNA takes weeks to process. Even then they can only match it with a name if they happen to have the fucker's DNA there to start with. Can't see that, can you?'

'I just think you should use whatever you can, Michael.'

Michael shook his head sadly. 'All I can do now is wait until the bastard contacts me again.'

Chapter One Hundred and Fourteen

Michael had rung the number from the letter over and over again. Nothing. It was a waste of his time, but he couldn't stop himself. The phone didn't even fucking ring; it was probably a cheap throwaway. He couldn't understand why the person involved didn't seem bothered about making contact with him. If this had been a shake-down, a call for cash, then he would have heard something long before now. Michael felt sick with apprehension. There wasn't anyone he could think of with the guts to do something like this to him; he was too big, too respected for anyone to think they could dare get away with something like this. But he couldn't find out a fucking thing – even the police were stumped. He just sat in his home, waiting for a call, for another letter to be delivered, anything at all that might lead him to his daughter.

Jake bowled into the room, all smiley-faced. He smelt clean, and his sturdy little body looked bigger than ever. Michael ruffled his hair, pleased to see him, proud of the boy.

'Hello, Granddad! I've been learning my seven times table.'

Michael laughed at his grandson's complete enjoyment of his little life.

'Have you now! Very important, you know, learning your times tables.'

Jake nodded in absolute agreement. 'I know that, Granddad!

Dana reckons it's what sorts the men from the boys!'

Dana laughed at his words. She was already making Jake's breakfast, and Michael laughed with her.

'Well, Dana knows about these things, Jake, so listen to her.'

Jake was pleased to hear his granddad sound happy. Jake hated the tension in the house. His nana was very sad, she didn't seem like her usual self. His nana had fallen out with his granddad, he had heard them shouting at each other. It was very worrying – other than Dana they were all he had in the world. He hadn't seen his mum for a long time and he was feeling very anxious about her too.

Dana placed his porridge on the table before him, and he started to eat it slowly. He liked it with honey and sugar, and Dana always made it perfectly for him.

Dana was leaning against the fridge, drinking a cup of coffee. She looked at Michael and, raising her eyebrows, she asked carefully, 'Any news?'

Michael shook his head sadly. 'No. Nothing. Not a dicky-bird.'

Jake listened to the talk between them, and he knew that they were talking about his mummy. He had heard enough to work out that she was in some kind of trouble. But then his mummy was always having some kind of problem. It wasn't anything unusual for her. Her whole life was one problem after another. His nana always seemed to think that was the case anyway. She always said to Dana, that her Jessie attracted trouble like other people contracted a rash. It was there before you knew it and it itched until it was scratched raw.

'You get yourself off to school, Jake. Have a good day, son.'

Jake liked it when his granddad called him 'son'. He finished his porridge quickly.

'I've got to take my drawing in, Granddad. It's a picture of me, you, Dana and Nana. We had to draw our family. It's going on the wall for our Communion. I drew us all in the garden. Even Nana!' He laughed, and Michael laughed with him, even though he was sad to think that the child knew, as young as he was, that his nana didn't use the garden, and also sad to think he had left his mother out of the equation.

'That sounds lovely. Nana would be pleased to know you've drawn a picture of her.'

Jake shrugged, a childish shrug that was as honest as it was natural. 'I suppose so, Granddad. But she won't see me, you know. Even though I've been a good boy.'

Michael was sorry to the heart for his grandson's predicament. Josephine forgot that her lifestyle affected everyone around her, little Jake especially. Her living in a fucking bubble when her daughter was missing just proved to him how selfish she really was.

'Your nana is not very well, Jake.'

Jake got off his chair slowly, and smiling at his Granddad, he said with false gaiety, 'Dana told me already. I know that she's not well. Nana's never well.'

Chapter One Hundred and Fifteen

Jessie could feel the eyes of her captor on her. He watched her sometimes while she slept, and she hated knowing that he did that. It was creepy. She was feeling so sore, her ankles were bleeding as the cuffs were rubbing away her skin every time she moved. It was agony.

She sat up on the bed and shouted, 'I'm hungry, you know! Fucking starving! I need a real meal. I need a bath. I need to use a proper toilet. *Please* let me use a proper toilet!' She hated the whine in her voice, but she couldn't help herself. 'I'm bleeding, for fuck's sake. My ankles are rubbed raw. At least give me something to ease the pain.'

She was crying now, even as she was determined not to show him any weakness. She didn't want him to know that he had beaten her. But he had. No matter how much she tried to act tough, he had her shackled to a bed in a filthy basement. He had won from the moment she had woken up tied and bound and unable to free herself.

She was crying noisily now. She was hurting, bleeding and so frightened. Her resolve was breaking down by the second. Strong or weak, it made no difference to him. He just sat and watched as she screamed at him. Her fears and her worries had finally overwhelmed her; she was broken. Gut-wrenching sobs broke from her uncontrollably.

Her captor continued to watch her, only now she saw through her tears that he was smiling.

Chapter One Hundred and Sixteen

Detective Inspector Timothy Branch was nervous. He had never been to Michael Flynn's scrapyard before, but he knew that many people *had* gone there and never been seen again. That was the power of a crushing machine – an errant body placed in the boot of a car didn't really stand much chance of being located. Once the car was put into the crusher, it was reduced to a two-foot-by-two-foot cube of metal.

He drove into the yard slowly. The gates were already open for him, and he saw the men who had waved him inside so cheerfully closing the gates behind him.

He regretted taking Flynn's money for so many years. Now he was asking him for a favour and he couldn't deliver, and that wasn't sitting well with him. He had a feeling it wasn't sitting well with Michael Flynn either.

He pulled up outside the Portakabins and, as he stepped out of his car, he noticed that there were a few men scattered around. They were all watching him as he walked up the rickety stairs that led into the offices.

He looked at Michael and, nodding politely towards him, he said quietly and respectfully, 'I'm sorry, Michael. Still nothing. I've had my blokes out there again. They've pulled in everyone who knows Jessie, and they all say the same thing. They haven't seen her, she hadn't fallen out with anyone, and she isn't holed up anywhere. It's a fucking mystery. No one can just disappear overnight.'

Michael Flynn could see that Branch was genuinely disappointed.

'I even pulled the CCTV from the general area around Jessie's flats. Fuck-all again. The cameras that should show the outside of her flats had been disabled. According to the company who should be monitoring them, they only noticed the next morning. Well, I put a fucking rocket up their arses, but there's nothing we can do about it now, is there?'

Declan Costello got up from his chair reluctantly; he was comfortable. He pulled out a typist's chair from behind the desk, and offered it to Timothy Branch.

'Sit there. I'll get us all a drink. Same again, Michael?'

Michael gave him his empty glass. Declan busied himself pouring out the whiskies.

Timothy Branch took his drink gratefully, and he gulped at it, enjoying the taste.

Michael sipped his drink slowly.

'I wish I could tell you different, Michael, I really do. But I hear your blokes are getting the same reaction as mine.'

Michael nodded. 'You're right. No one seems to know sweet fuck-all. But I want to ask you something, Timothy, and I want you to tell me the truth. If this was a real police matter, if a girl went missing like my Jessie, how long before you would assume she was dead?'

Declan Costello had never thought he would feel sorry for DI Timothy Branch; the man was a fucking arsehole. But he did now. The man didn't know what to say for the best.

'The thing is, Michael, every case is different. I mean, there's no way I can answer that.'

Sighing with annoyance, Michael said quietly, 'Don't fucking mug me off, I'm not an idiot. I am asking you: if a girl was abducted, like my Jessie, how long would you give her before you assumed she was fucking *dead*?' He bellowed out the last word.

Timothy Branch shrugged, saying honestly, 'A couple of days. The fact that no one can explain her disappearance is not a good sign, to be honest. But, saying that, you know she is being held by someone. Your wife had that letter, it was hand delivered. So that's a good thing, Michael.'

Michael Flynn shook his handsome head in a gesture of denial. 'But that's just it, though. Anyone could have her, couldn't they?'

Chapter One Hundred and Seventeen

Jessie woke to see the man standing over her. Up close he looked decidedly odd; there was no emotion on his face, nothing to say he even registered her presence. It was unnerving. He had pale grey eyes, and his skin was a dirty yellow. His mouth was partly open, and she could see his teeth – which were rotten – and smell his awful breath. She felt her stomach heaving; he actually made her feel physically sick. The stench was overpowering, a sickly sweetness of old food and long-neglected cavities. It was putrid.

He had not given her any food for over thirty-six hours, all he had given her was a bottle of water, which she still suspected was drugged. She hadn't seen him this close to her before and she was frightened of him. He looked crazy, like people you saw on the streets and knew at a glance were dangerous so you avoided eye contact and passed as fast as possible.

She just wanted to go home, get away from him, from here. She wanted to see her mum, her little boy – for the first time in years, she wanted her family around her.

The man licked his lips slowly, deliberately. Jessie knew he was taking some kind of chemical, because he looked stoned. His eyes didn't focus properly and over the course of the last few days he had seemed to be unravelling more and more. He smiled at her suddenly and as he laughed he started to cough, and the stench from his breath hit her directly in her face, spraying her skin with droplets of his saliva. It took all her willpower not to vomit everywhere.

He looked at her for long moments, before saying flatly, 'You must be starving. Are you starving?'

She nodded, wondering what this was leading to. She didn't shout at him or demand anything from him – she was too weak, too scared of him. He knew that – she had felt the change in him the last few days. It seemed the weaker she became, the stronger he felt. She had expected her father to have rescued her by now, but he hadn't. She was so worried that he wasn't bothered about her, had left her to her own devices. Or, worse still, that her parents had heard nothing from this man, and just assumed she was on the missing list. It wouldn't be the first time she had disappeared without telling anyone her whereabouts.

The man told her nothing. He rarely even spoke to her. He just watched her.

He stepped away from her and, taking out a packet of cigarettes, he lit one for himself. Then, almost as an afterthought, he offered the packet to her.

She took the pack of Lambert & Butler from him, pleased to have a distraction. Taking one out, she pulled herself upright on the mattress, and then he lit her cigarette with his lighter. His actions were very old-fashioned; he even cupped the lighter in his hand to ensure it didn't go out.

She pulled on the cigarette deeply and felt light-headed – it was the first cigarette she'd had in ages.

'Thank you. I appreciate this.'

He bowed, and she knew he was mocking her. She took another few puffs on the cigarette, feeling the nicotine as it hit her brain, enjoying it because it seemed to wake her up, break through the malaise that she was feeling constantly.

'My father, does he know you've got me? He will pay you a

lot of money if you ask him to. Have you asked him for anything? What does he know?'

The man didn't answer; he just stared at her, as if he couldn't hear her. It was a very nerve-racking experience.

He dropped his cigarette on to the floor and put it out, slowly grinding it under his foot into the concrete floor. Then he shook his head, smiling at her as if it was a great joke. 'No, of course I haven't contacted him. Why on earth would I do that?'

His voice was almost conversational as though he expected her to have an answer for him. He was even looking at her quizzically. She felt the cold hand of fear clutching at her heart. None of this made any sense. Why had this man taken her?

'But surely money is what this is about? My father will pay for me, my mum will see to that. I mean, why else would you even bring me here in the first place? It doesn't make any fucking sense.'

He lit another cigarette, drawing on it noisily, but he didn't bother to answer her. Jessie threw her cigarette butt on to the floor at his feet, getting more worked up.

'Do you even know *who* my father is? Don't you *realise* exactly *who* you are dealing with? My father is not a man to try and have over in any way. He is very dangerous if he's crossed. He will be searching everywhere for me. You better understand that, and stop this before it goes too far.' She sounded petulant even to her own ears, but she was still reeling from his words. If he hadn't been in touch with anyone, how was she ever to escape? How could anyone find her? If this wasn't about money, about shaking down her old man, then what the hell did this fucking nutbag want with her?

The man settled himself on the end of the bed and, shrugging gently, he looked at her frightened face, and he said seriously, 'This isn't about *you*, Jessie. It never was. This is about your father. Michael Flynn. This is about payback. This is about reminding him that the past is always there, no matter how much he might have tried to forget about it. I certainly haven't. When I finally decide to deliver you to your parents, young lady, you will be as dead as a fucking doornail. That was always the plan.'

'But why? What have I ever done to you?' Jessie was sobbing now.

He laughed again, as if she was amusing him. 'You? You've never done anything to me, you silly girl. Like I said, this is not about you.' He stood up abruptly. 'By the way, I'm not going to be bringing you food any more. I think it's only fair to tell you that. You deserve that much from me, Jessie. You deserve to be treated decently. It's all in the Bible. John chapter eight, verse thirty-two: then you will know the truth, and the truth will set you free. Never forget that, Jessie Flynn – it's a statement of fact. The truth is important, the *truth* is worth dying for.'

Jessie shouted angrily, 'But I don't want to fucking die! I have a little boy. He needs me.'

The man smiled once again. 'You see? You're lying again. It's the truth you need to hang on to, Jessie. You're just a fucking trollop. Your little boy is being brought up by your mum and dad. *Everyone* knows what a fucking piece of shit you are. I've done my homework, Jessie Flynn.'

Jessie was unable to answer the man; he was without reason. There was nothing she could do to make him listen to her.

The man looked at her sadly. 'I wasn't going to tell you this, but I think you need to know the truth, Jessie. I sent your mother a number to ring me on – that was last week. I was going to torture her, to be honest. I had no intention of ever letting you leave here. But do you know something? She didn't even call me. Three thirty that day, there I was, ready and waiting, and nothing – not a fucking peep. That is a truth you need to acknowledge.

I gave her that one chance, a chance to contact *you*. Your mother didn't even bother herself. Now your dad, on the other hand, from what I can gather, has been looking for you all over. There's even a fifty grand reward for information about your whereabouts. See what I'm saying? The truth will set you free, Jessie.'

She watched him as he walked away from her, and she knew that she was without hope. She was bloodied and bleeding and this man didn't care. She was nothing to him, her suffering meant nothing to him. She heard the door slam, and the scraping noise as he pulled the bolts into place, and she wondered if this was it for her. Was this how she was going to die, alone and frightened, starved to death, and without ever having the chance to tell her little son how much she had really loved him?

Chapter One Hundred and Eighteen

'With respect, Josephine, do you really believe for a fucking moment that I haven't been searching high and low for Jessie? No one knows a fucking thing. Not the Filth, not our workers. It's fucking outrageous.'

Josephine felt awful. 'I didn't mean it how it came out, Michael, but I'm so worried about her. You need to get out there again and retrace her steps, there has to be someone who knows something.'

Michael interrupted his wife. He was still furious with her for losing them the only lead they'd had with the letter. How could she kid herself like this? 'Are you having a fucking laugh? I've been out there looking for her since she first went AWOL. Unlike *you*, of course, Josephine, who still can't bring yourself to leave your fucking bedroom. Who has sat here on your arse the whole time, drinking wine and watching your DVDs to take your mind off it all, and couldn't even open a fucking letter! It's a joke, Josephine. Your whole *life* is a fucking joke. This is your fault. *Your life* is what helped our Jessie to go off the rails. You always pretended everything was all right, but it wasn't, Josephine. How dare you even try to tell me what I should be doing, when you have done fuck-all! You really can't see how hard it's been for me, can you? Watching you waste your life away up here like a fucking character from a storybook. It's a fucking excuse of a life,

Josephine, it has been for years. And it's cost us our daughter.'

The pain Michael had caused his wife with his words was evident. She was white-faced, her eyes so big and wide she looked like a bush baby. He had hurt her badly, but he didn't care. His daughter, for all she might be, was missing and could be dead, and he couldn't play this game with his wife any more. He was sick of pretending that everything was normal. He couldn't protect her from the truth any more – he didn't want to. Josephine needed a reality check, and it had been a long time coming.

As she dropped her eyes from his, and turned away from him – acting like she was the only one of them who was hurting – he felt his anger building up inside his chest once more. She really knew how to play the victim.

'Do you know what, Josephine? I can see what you're doing, acting the innocent, as always. Poor old Josephine, who can't be expected to do anything useful, not with all her problems, eh? Well, do you know what? You can go and fuck yourself because, unlike *you*, I've done everything in my power to locate Jessie. I know that and, more to the fucking point, *you* know that.'

Josephine Flynn was aware that she had finally used up all the goodwill that her husband had always shown to her. She was feeling thoroughly ashamed of herself. She had always known that Michael had given her more love than she had ever deserved from him. He had been losing patience with her for a while now, and she didn't know how to make it better, how to make him understand that she couldn't help herself, that she hated herself for her weakness.

'Please, Michael . . .'

He turned away from her, waving his arms in dismissal. 'I can't listen to you, Josephine. I'm sorry, but I've got to go.'

Chapter One Hundred and Nineteen

Declan wasn't sure if he was doing the right thing, but he couldn't, in all good conscience, ignore the woman's request for a meeting any longer. Nor could Michael either – he was already on his way to the meet.

She had contacted him personally, and she had waited a long time to be heard, refusing to discuss her business with anyone but Michael. She had been ringing his offices for over a week, but hadn't explained why. Declan had finally called her back, and realised from her tone she might have important information.

He smiled at the woman sitting opposite him, sipping her cup of tea, and she smiled back at him, a serene smile, that made him feel better about everything. No matter what the outcome might be, she was at least being genuine. What more could anyone ask for?

Michael arrived at the address he had been given by Declan, and he parked his Range Rover carefully outside the house in question. This was his old stomping ground; he had grown up round the corner from this street, and he was pleased to see the change in it. East London was now a desirable place to reside. The houses that were once barely one step above slums, were now changing hands for exorbitant amounts of money. It was a fucking joke – everyone else dreamt of getting away from the area; now it seemed certain people were determined to buy a property there. Wonders would never cease.

He was already feeling guilty about turning on Josephine, even though he knew she had been asking for it for a long time. But he did love her, and he felt as much to blame for the way she lived as she was, because he had never once challenged her about her lifestyle. Until now.

Michael got out of his Range Rover, and locked it behind him. He walked up the short pathway to the front door of the house, and rang the doorbell. The front door was opened by Declan Costello, and Michael was ushered inside the tiny house.

This was what used to be called a parlour-type house, and Michael knew the layout off by heart. He followed Declan down the narrow passageway into the front room. Mrs Singh, as he had always known her, was waiting for him patiently. She was sitting on a small two-seater sofa in a deep burgundy colour, and the two armchairs that matched it sat either side of the fireplace. There was a light wood cabinet against the party wall, and a matching coffee table in front of the fireplace. The carpet was expensive, a good Axminster, and where the only real money had been spent. The sole ornaments in the room were photographs of her family, and these were plentifully scattered round.

Michael took the woman's hand gently in his. 'It's very good to see you again, Mrs Singh. It's a long time since I've been in here.'

She stood up to greet him. She was as tiny as he remembered, under five feet tall, as thin as a rake, her thick dark hair streaked with grey now, but she still had the power to make him feel like a kid again.

'Sit down, Michael, it's lovely to welcome you here once again.'

Michael and Declan both settled themselves into the armchairs by the fireplace. Mrs Singh poured Michael a cup of tea, and he took it from her carefully.

'I appreciated you coming to my husband's funeral, Michael, it would have pleased him so much. He always thought a lot of you. I'll never forget that, you know, never forget that you remembered the people from your childhood.'

Michael sipped his tea, embarrassed now. 'You and your husband were always very good to me. He was a good man, a decent man.'

She nodded in agreement. 'He was. I was very lucky.' She smiled widely. 'I always knew, Michael, that it was you who stopped the trouble we were experiencing at the shop. The threats and the hate all stopped overnight. Mr Singh always said that it could only be you. We were aware of how you had got on in life, and we were pleased for you.'

Declan Costello sat back in his armchair and relaxed; this was a woman Michael obviously respected, who he was happy to listen to.

'I did nothing really, Mrs Singh, I just put out a few feelers, explained that you were dear friends of mine. But if it helped you both then I am very pleased about that.'

She looked at him kindly with her deep brown eyes; she was a shrewd woman, that much was evident.

She was wearing a deep-green sari, and she looked to Declan as if she had dressed for the occasion. She looked well-to-do, like a woman of substance, her jewellery was gold, very heavy, and well made. She had diamonds in her ears, and in the rings on her fingers.

'I have been trying to contact you for a while now, Michael. I heard about your Jessie going missing, and I heard you were looking for information about her.'

Michael immediately sat forward in his armchair, he knew this woman wouldn't have asked him here without good reason.

'Go on. I'm listening.' Michael's voice was quiet, interested.

'I must explain, Michael, I don't even know if this is anything of relevance. All I can say is, *I* found it odd and, considering what's been going on, I just thought I should let you know about it.'

Declan butted in quickly, 'There's also a fifty-grand reward for any information that leads to Jessie.'

Michael Flynn's head snapped sideways, looking at Declan with complete and utter disgust.

Mrs Singh shook her head slowly in denial. Holding her hand over her heart she said with real meaning, 'I can assure you, *Mr* Costello, that means very little to me.' That she was deeply offended by what Declan had said to her was more than obvious.

Michael Flynn was out of the armchair he was sitting in within nanoseconds and, kneeling down on the carpet in front of his old friend, he grabbed Mrs Singh's hands in his. Squeezing them tightly, he said, 'Ignore him, Mrs Singh, he's fucking ignorant at times. Just tell me what you know.'

She grasped Michael's hands, pulled them to her chest, knowing that he would listen to what she had to say.

'I was in the shop a few weeks ago. I rarely spend that much time there these days, but I still pop round once or twice a week. My eldest son Davinda and his wife took it over after my husband died, as you know. Anyway, I saw a man in there, and I could see he wasn't right, that he was, you know, what the cockneys always called "radio rental"? A bit mental? Remember how Mr Singh always loved the rhyming slang? But I knew this person. You know when you see someone and you can't place them? That is how I felt. He bought forty Lambert and Butlers, and a bottle of cheap vodka. My son Davinda served him and, as the man was leaving, he looked directly at me, and he smiled. It was a strange smile, Michael. I can't explain it. Anyway, it took me a day or two, but then I remembered who he was.'

She pushed Michael gently away from her, and she sat back on the settee. Michael could see the turmoil in her face, knew that she was worried about what she was going to say to him. 'It's so many years ago but I'm sure that it was Steven Golding.'

Declan Costello was quietly watching everything that was happening, and he saw the way that Mrs Singh looked at Michael as she told him who she thought she had seen. He also saw Michael Flynn's face drain of all its colour.

'I hope I was wrong, Michael, but I really don't think I was. Then I heard that your Jessie was missing.' She sighed heavily. 'I really don't know if any of this is related. I just thought that you should know.' She looked at Michael steadily, saying quietly, 'I always wondered about it, Michael.'

Michael was shaking his head slowly. Declan could see he had been thrown by the woman's revelations. It was absolutely amazing to witness this first-hand.

'I never planned it, I *swear*. It should never have happened.'

Mrs Singh opened her arms wide, she was crying now. 'I always knew that, Michael, I never doubted you.'

Michael enveloped the tiny woman in his arms, hugging her to him tightly, and she hugged him back. Declan watched with disbelief. He knew one thing, though – he should have brought these two together at the start, when she first rang them, asking for Michael Flynn, instead of fobbing her off. He had a terrible feeling that this might be too late now.

Chapter One Hundred and Twenty

Declan opened the door to his penthouse, and stood aside to allow Michael to enter before him. Once inside he shut the door and locked it. He followed Michael into the lounge, turning on the lights as he went.

Michael was standing by the patio doors that led out on to a large terrace. He was looking over London, and Declan left him to it for a while, going into his kitchen – a large airy room, twenty feet by sixteen – and pouring them each a large drink. The kitchen was state of the art; the cooker alone wouldn't have looked out of place in an expensive restaurant. Not that he had ever used it, of course, just like the American-style fridge or the two dishwashers. He made instant coffee and a slice of toast at a push. The black granite work surfaces he used as a bar. He didn't care to use the gadgets, but he liked to own them; they gave the place class.

He brought the drinks into the lounge, and he passed one to Michael. 'So, Mrs Singh? Nice lady.'

Michael tossed his drink back in one. 'How long was she trying to get hold of me, Declan?'

Declan tossed his own drink back then; he needed it. 'Since last week, I think. But be fair, Michael, we had no idea who she was or what she wanted. It was only because she was so persistent that I called her myself. And then came to you. I realise the error of my ways now, we should have been on top of it. But it wasn't deliberate, you know that.'

Michael held his empty glass out, and followed Declan out to the kitchen, where he waited for him to pour them both more Scotch.

'She *is* a nice lady, Mrs Singh.'

Declan nodded his agreement. 'I could see that, Michael. I could also see that you really think a lot of her, and her husband as well.'

Michael Flynn took out his cigarettes and lit one. 'She was very good to me, both her and her husband were. I went to school with Davinda, their oldest son, we were good mates. They are Sikhs and, years ago, the Sikhs and the Muslims sent their kids to a faith school – in other words, a Catholic school. So we all grew up together. It was nice. Davinda – Dave, as we called him – was a real fucking brainiac. He went on to university – that was Mr Singh's dream, you know? Education. He saw it as the jewel in the crown of the United Kingdom. He used to say, "Remember, boys, this country has the best education system in the world, and it's *free.*" I didn't appreciate that until it was too late. But I used to spend a lot of time round there when I was a kid. Mrs Singh looked after me when my mum was working.'

Declan listened to his friend without interrupting. He knew he had to let him say what he needed to in his own time.

'When I went to work for your brother, I lost contact with the Singhs and a lot of the people I had gone to school with. That was deliberate on my part. I wanted to pursue my own agenda but, to be absolutely honest, I also didn't want Davinda or anyone to get dragged into any of my shit, if it all went tits up.'

Declan shrugged. 'I can understand that, Michael. There're people we don't bring into our working lives. That's par for the course. But I have to ask you, who the fuck is Steven Golding?'

Michael Flynn looked Declan Costello straight in the eyes, and Declan knew that whatever had happened with this Steven Golding, Michael had buried a long time ago.

Michael lit another cigarette, and he drew on it deeply. He needed to calm himself down, needed to remind himself that he had come a long way since those days. He was at the top of his game, and there was no one with the strength to challenge his position.

'Steven Golding was one of the first jobs that your brother ever gave to me. Well not him, but his father. His father was Daniel Golding. Ringing any bells now, is it?'

Declan nodded; it had all just slipped into place. 'That was you? Fucking hell. I knew Patrick had something to do with it, but you'd only just come onboard. I never thought you'd be involved.'

Michael nodded. 'Patrick told me to go to an address in South London and burn the house down. It was about a debt he was owed. He said that if the house was torched, the insurance would pay out and everything would be hunky-dory. I did what he asked of me. I never knew there was anyone in there – I had been told it was an empty property. But, as I found out afterwards, it wasn't empty. Daniel Golding, his wife, and his two young daughters were in there. Steven survived because he was staying the night at a friend's. I only realised later that Patrick had known all along that the house wasn't empty – he had planned for it to go down that way.'

Declan Costello was looking at Michael as if he was a stranger, as if he was someone who had gate-crashed his way into his home.

'I never knew. I never even dreamt that it might have anything to do with you. Everyone was up in arms about it – those girls were only twelve and fourteen years old. And it was *you*? *You* who poured the petrol through the letter box and burned them to death in their beds?'

Declan was outraged, absolutely disgusted. He was remembering the shock waves the deaths had sent through their community. Daniel Golding had owed money to everyone – like any compulsive gambler he had no real care about borrowing from all and sundry; he believed he could win anything he borrowed back. But no one he owed money to would have taken it out on his family, that just wasn't done. Daniel deserved whatever he might get, but his kids and wife were sacrosanct.

Michael Flynn grabbed hold of Declan's shirt front, dragging him roughly towards him and, looking into his face, Michael said furiously, 'I did what your fucking brother told me to do! I thought the house was fucking empty. Patrick had assured me of that. Afterwards, do you know what he said? He said, "Typical fucking Danny Golding. Always in the wrong place at the wrong time." '

Declan pulled himself away from Michael's grip. 'I'm sorry, Michael, I know that my brother was a fucking looney. Why do you think I stepped back after we took Patrick out? I loved him as my brother, but I knew that he needed to be culled, like a fucking wild animal. Now you've told me, I can see it perfectly. You were a young lad, taking his word at face value, and that would have appealed to him. The knowledge that you were unaware of the truth would have appealed to him.'

Michael laughed nastily. 'I swallowed it, I really believed that it was an accident at first, and I put it out of my mind. I convinced myself that it wasn't my fault. And do you know what, Declan? It *wasn't* my fault. I did what Patrick told me to do. When it went fucking pear-shaped, he stood by me and I appreciated that. But, years later, when I really knew him, I realised he was too shrewd not to have known that the house wouldn't be empty.'

Declan Costello poured them both more whisky. Michael took his drink gratefully.

'That was my brother Patrick all over, Michael. I know what he was capable of. That night, when we took him out, deep down I didn't feel guilty about it. I was relieved – so relieved to know that he was gone at last, and that I didn't have to police him any more. But, that aside, why would this Mrs Singh warn you about Steven Golding?'

Michael Flynn looked at Declan warily. He had just told this man the biggest secret of his life. The biggest shame of his life. But he trusted him.

'Mrs Singh saw me that night. I bumped into her husband outside their shop, and she came out to talk to me. She knew by then that I was working for your brother – she even tried to warn me off! She told me that night to get home and have a bath because I stank of petrol. Of course she didn't know *why* then but, as the Golding family only lived a few streets away, it wasn't long before she did the sums. I knew I could trust her. I never told Patrick about her – I knew that he would have seen her as a threat to him, to his world. It never occurred to him that some people might just be naturally loyal.'

Declan laughed then. 'My brother never trusted the concept of loyalty, Michael, that was his problem.'

Michael sighed heavily. 'I told you all this because you needed to know. But I can only tell myself that I did what I was told to do.'

Declan felt so sorry for Michael; he knew first-hand just how manipulative his brother had been.

'Look, Michael, what we need to do now is forget this shit, and hunt down Steven Golding. Mrs Singh is a fucking shrewd old bird. I'll get on to the Old Bill now, see what they can find out. About time they earned their fucking keep anyway. Then we can work from there.'

Michael Flynn nodded in agreement. 'I just want to know Jessie's all right.'

Declan patted his friend's shoulder gently. 'Of course you do, Michael, she's your daughter!'

Chapter One Hundred and Twenty-One

DI Timothy Branch was relieved to finally be able to give Michael Flynn some useful information. In fact, he'd excelled himself. He drove into the scrapyard and parked his BMW neatly, walking into the Portakabin like a conquering hero.

Michael and Declan were already there as he had expected. He bowled into the room all smiles and smugness until he registered that both Michael Flynn and Declan Costello looked tired and angry. It occurred to him that Michael's daughter was still missing, so he removed his smile, and settled his face into what he saw as serious work mode.

'I got here as soon as I could. I think you will be pleased with the information I've gathered.'

He waited to be offered a seat. Michael obliged, sweeping his arm out towards the old typist's chair, saying tightly, 'Sit and talk. It's about fucking time you earned your keep.'

Timothy sat down as requested, but his earlier euphoria was gone. Michael Flynn was a very scary man, there was no doubt about that. Declan and Michael were both watching him warily, waiting to hear what he had to say to them.

Timothy Branch knew that this was his only chance to redeem himself. He opened up the file he had on Steven Golding which he had brought with him, and cleared his throat noisily, feeling very nervous once again.

'First of all, from what I have found out, Steven Golding has been under psychiatric care for many years. When he was fifteen, his mother, father, and two young sisters were all killed in a fire. It was an arson attack – deliberate. He had stayed overnight at a friend's so he survived. But he has never fully recovered; he has been in and out of psychiatric facilities for the best part of the last thirty-odd years. He was released again, four months ago, having accrued a large amount of money over the years from his benefits, et cetera. It came to over twelve thousand pounds in total. It seems he removed that from the bank in cash, and no one has seen him since. He hasn't turned up for any of his outpatient appointments, and he hasn't been near the flat he was allocated by the housing trust. He is unknown to the police – never been arrested for anything. According to his doctor, he suffers from delusions, and he is often unable to differentiate between fantasy and reality. But they have assured me that he is *not* violent. He is on quite heavy medication, Dolmatil and – ' Timothy Branch stared down at the page, unable to read his own writing – 'I can't read that, I'm afraid. But I assume it's an anti-psychotic drug of some description. Steven Golding has a very high IQ and is an avid reader – he can read a book in a day. He was last seen three weeks ago when he withdrew all his money out of the bank.'

Michael Flynn opened his arms out in a gesture of supplication. 'Is that it, then?'

Timothy Branch nodded. 'That is everything I could find out. I've got my people watching out for him.' He quickly pulled out a picture from his file, and handed it to Michael. 'This is a recent photo of him.'

Michael Flynn looked at it. Steven Golding appeared older than he actually was – he was as grey as a badger and his eyes were the same dull grey; he looked almost lifeless. He was looking directly into the camera, his mouth was hanging open, his teeth were black, rotten, and his skin looked thick, like orange peel. He was not a man anyone would stop to talk to, that much was obvious.

Timothy Branch took a deep breath, and then said seriously, 'From what I can gather, if he doesn't take his medication he can become paranoid and quite aggressive. But I must stress that, according to his doctor, he is not a violent man – when he is taking his meds, of course.'

Michael handed the photograph to Declan. 'So, Timothy, let me see if I've got this right. Basically, he left the nut house three weeks ago, he cleared his bank account, and he is now on the missing list with twelve grand and, to add insult to injury, without his meds, he has a seriously bad fucking attitude?'

Timothy Branch didn't know what he could say to that. He was hoping that someone spied the fucker somewhere, so he could help Michael to track him down.

Declan passed the photograph back to Michael. 'Fuck me, Michael, what a smooth-looking bastard he is! Mouth full of dog ends, and a face like a bag of fucking hammers. At least he won't be hard to pick out in a crowd!'

Michael Flynn smiled; Declan could make him laugh even at a time like this.

'If he's got my Jessie, he has had to rent somewhere for cash. We need to get our blokes out there asking around. Like you say, Declan, it's not like they wouldn't fucking remember him, is it? He isn't exactly the answer to a maiden's prayer.'

Timothy Branch stood up, a bundle of nerves once more. 'I will get all my people out there. I will let you know if I hear anything.'

Michael Flynn didn't even bother to answer. This man was useless in every way.

When Branch had left, Declan said with incredulity, 'How the fuck can these people just be allowed out of the nut farms? No one is monitoring them, looking out for them – they just let them go out into the community without a fucking thought. It's outrageous.'

Michael Flynn agreed with his friend. 'I tell you this much, Declan – if anything bad happens to my Jessie, whoever signed that cunt out of the funny farm had better be a fucking good runner, because I will hunt them into the ground. I will make sure they never have that kind of responsibility again.'

Declan grinned. 'You're preaching to the converted, Michael. I will be right beside you, mate. But, remember, now we know what he looks like.'

Chapter One Hundred and Twenty-Two

The pavement was alight with rumours. Jessie Flynn was missing and there was a fifty-grand reward up for grabs, so it was in everyone's best interests to keep an eye out. Now they were being shown a photograph of a right strange-looking cove. It wasn't as if it would be hard to pick *him* out of a line up. The word was out.

Michael Flynn had everyone on his payroll asking questions, and insisting on answers. His house was like Fort Knox – there were people watching it twenty-four/seven. There was no doubt in anyone's mind that this was the real deal. The fifty grand was an incentive, for everyone concerned. It was not just a big chunk of change, it was also proof of how serious Michael Flynn was about finding his daughter and, more to the point, punishing the person who had caused him so much aggro.

Michael Flynn was a legend in his own lunchtime; no one in their right mind would take him on. After seeing the photo of the man he was looking for, it was obvious that he was a fucking nutbag – he had to be.

A few of the people had heard the name Golding, and put two and two together. He had lost his whole family – of course he was a fucking nutter. But why had he singled out Michael Flynn's only daughter? The gossip was Michael Flynn had refused to pay a ransom for her, and that seemed feasible; after all, Jessie Flynn wasn't the most lovable of people. She hated her dad as well, everyone knew that. She talked about him like he was a piece of dirt – she had always enjoyed the shock and awe she had caused when people heard her cunt her father into the ground.

That was shocking enough, but what was more so was the way that Michael Flynn ignored it. It had to be hard for him, knowing that his only daughter talked about him as if he was nothing. If anyone else had dared to say what his Jessie had said, they would have been dead within twenty-four hours.

So people were willing to believe that he wouldn't pay the ransom asked for his daughter, and a big majority of those people didn't blame him. They thought that the fifty-grand reward was so he could locate the fucker responsible – and if Jessie was there then that was just an added bonus.

The whole underbelly of the British Isles was looking for Steven Golding. His photo was being shown everywhere. He was famous, but for all the wrong reasons.

Chapter One Hundred and Twenty-Three

Josephine was listening to her grandson as he chattered away to her about school. Dana had brought him in to her, along with a tray of drinks and cake, and she tried her hardest to concentrate on what he was telling her.

Michael had been so right – she *didn't* have any true interest in her grandson. She loved him, but she didn't want to be bothered with the day-to-day care that was required. Dana saw to that. Josephine was always nervous that he would somehow interfere with her belongings.

Ever since Michael had let rip at her, she was deeply worried that they were never going to be able to recover. She had not seen him since – he had not even called her. She wondered if this was the end of the line for them. She didn't even encourage sex any more – she didn't want it. If she *did* succumb to him, she didn't take an active part, she just lay there and waited for it to be over. Michael wouldn't force her into something she didn't want – he was too decent, too kind to ever make her do anything she didn't want to. But now she wondered if she had inadvertently shot herself in the foot. He was still a handsome, vibrant man, and he could easily find a young woman to fulfil his needs. She had always believed that his love for her had been enough, but now she wasn't so sure. She always looked perfect, but that wasn't enough.

'Will you answer me, Nana!' Jake was cross, and his strident voice had broken into her reverie.

Josephine smiled at him. 'I'm sorry, my little darling. What were you saying?'

But Jake didn't answer her, he was feeling very cross. It was hard trying to talk to his nana when she was so obviously not listening to him. She *never* listened to him!

'Please, Jake, I'm *so* sorry. I didn't hear you. Nana has a lot on her mind today.'

Jake stood up, he had been sitting at her feet as usual, but he wasn't in the mood for his nana's strangeness today. 'I'm going, Nana. If you won't talk to me then I want to be in the garden.'

Josephine was mortified. Jake looked so cross with her. He really was Michael's double – he even had her husband's expressions, especially now as he stood before her with folded arms, his handsome face dark with anger.

'I'm going to ask Dana to play with me outside and when Granddad comes home, I'm going to ask him when my mummy will be back.'

He stormed out of the room, and Josephine didn't stop him. She sat back in her chair, aware that she should have chased after him, made him feel wanted. But how could she do that when, in all honesty, she didn't really want to?

She leant down and picked up his sweet wrappers; he had eaten a Kit Kat and a miniature Mars Bar. She folded both of the wrappers up neatly and carefully and placed them in the box beside her chair.

She started to tremble all over. She was having trouble breathing, and she closed her eyes and concentrated on taking deep, long breaths. It was an awful feeling. Her doctor said the panic attacks came on when she was feeling stressed. Well, of course she was stressed! Her daughter was missing and her grandson was cross with her. Coupled with her husband's angry shouting, it was inevitable.

She forced back the tears that were threatening and, going to her dressing table, she repaired her make-up carefully. It didn't make her feel better as it usually did. She sat back down in her chair and wondered if her husband was going to ring her, and put her mind at rest. She poured herself out another large glass of red wine and, as she sipped it, she decided that she would put on one of her favourite DVDs.

Chapter One Hundred and Twenty-Four

'Look, Lana, I am doing all I can to locate my daughter. If I was *you*, I'd try and fucking sort out your *own* daughter – my *wife*! In case it's escaped your notice, she hasn't left her fucking bedroom since the old King died! Now fuck off and stop ringing me. If I have any news, you will be one of the first to hear it.'

Michael slammed down the phone. He was so angry. Who did she think she was? Lana was like Josephine and his mother – they expected him to miraculously sort everything out for them. And he did, most of the time, but the only thing he wanted to concentrate on now was finding Jessie, and chasing down that fucker Golding. The last thing he needed was to spend time on the phone with people he would happily avoid if he wasn't related to them!

Declan Costello laughed. 'Well, that fucking told her, anyway!'

Michael looked at Declan; he was such a good friend to him, despite everything that had happened in the past. 'Fucking Lana! She's a pain in the arse. Josephine takes after her. She thinks that everything in the world revolves around her and fuck everybody else. Do you know something, Declan? Josephine hasn't left the house for years. That mad cunt who's got my Jessie sent her a letter with a number to call, and she didn't even fucking ring me to tell me! She now can't even make a phone call apparently! The fucking mad bitch. But she can take a call. You tell me where the logic is in that?'

Declan sighed. 'I know, Michael, you told me this before, mate. We all know your Josephine is a bit eccentric. But don't say anything you'll regret tomorrow, eh?'

Michael had always played down Josephine's oddities. Personally, Declan thought she was fucking barking. But then he wasn't married to her, thank fuck.

Michael snorted with derision. '*Eccentric?* Is that what you really think? She is a fucking card-carrying, bona fide head banger. I just wish I'd admitted it to myself ages ago. My mother, another fucking so-called "strong" woman, warned me about her from the off. She said she was a bit fucking doolally tap. But I had to have her. I loved Josephine so much, like she was a fucking terminal disease I'd contracted. I let her get away with murder. No matter how fucking nutty she got, I just kept pretending that it was perfectly normal. But it's not, Declan. She doesn't give a fuck about Jessie, not really, or little Jake – or even me for that matter. All she cares about is herself, and her fucking problems. I am so fucking sick of it.'

The phone rang and Declan picked it up quickly, glad to shut off Michael's conversation. It was not like him to say anything derogatory about his Josephine.

Michael watched closely as Declan listened to whoever was on the other end of the phone.

'Are you a hundred per cent sure?'

Declan was once again the listener, and Michael was watching his every nuance. 'Good man. Fucking result. Tell them to bring it here. Canary Wharf.'

Declan replaced the receiver and, looking at Michael, he said quickly, 'It appears our Mr Golding has been spotted. That was

Jack. It seems that one of his blokes is visiting his old mum in Essex – she lives in Canewdon, near Rochford – and he thinks he saw him coming out of the local SPAR there. By the time the geezer had got parked – and we all know what Essex is like for parking – he'd lost sight of him. But he's purchased the CCTV from the shop, and it's being brought to us now. So at least this is something, Michael. If it is him, we have a location.'

Michael Flynn felt tearful; the relief he felt was so potent, and overwhelming. Never before, in the whole of his life, had he felt so useless. He was the main man, everyone came to him for their earn, he dealt with the Colombians, he basically held Europe in the palm of his hand and yet, for all that, he still couldn't locate his own daughter. The irony.

Chapter One Hundred and Twenty-Five

The CCTV footage wasn't exactly HD, but it was good enough for what Michael needed. 'That's him, Declan! It's fucking him! At long last.'

Declan could feel Michael's euphoria. It was over two weeks since Jessie had gone missing, and not a soul had seen or heard anything of her since. That is, except her own mother, and she had kept the information to herself. What the fuck was that about? Everyone knew that Josephine was running on fucking fumes. She was a strange fucker at the best of times, but when Michael told him she had been contacted about her daughter and she hadn't bothered to follow it up, it proved how much of a fucking nut she really was. It was the only opportunity they had been given to find out the girl's location and Josephine Flynn had put her own fucking mentalness above her only child's welfare. That was harsh, by anyone's standards.

But now, *finally*, Michael had something to work with, something tangible he could use. He deserved every second of his relief; it had been a long time coming.

Michael was writing everything down in a notebook. 'He bought Lambert and Butler cigarettes, and a bottle of the cheapest vodka, just like he did at Mrs Singh's. We know that he has never passed his driving test, but that doesn't mean he hasn't got a vehicle. It just means it's not insured. But why isn't he buying food?'

Declan shrugged. He had wondered that himself, but he didn't want to say it and worry Michael.

'The Filth are combing everywhere, and so are our lads. If he has rented a place we will know about it. He can't fucking hide out for ever, Michael. It's not feasible. No one can drop off the radar these days.'

Michael grinned. This was the best he had felt since this nightmare had started.

The phone rang and Michael picked it up, hoping it was someone with the man's location, or something else he could use to find his daughter.

Declan was watching Michael with a wide grin on his face, expecting to hear that the man had been found, and they could finally do something constructive – like kill the fucker, torture him at their leisure, and wipe him off the face of the earth.

'You've got to be fucking kidding me!'

Declan could hear the disappointment in Michael's voice; whoever was calling them didn't have good news.

'OK, OK. We will wait for it – just get it here quickly.' Michael put the phone down slowly.

Declan held his breath as he waited for Michael to tell him the latest news.

Michael lit a cigarette and, after drawing on it a few times, he said helplessly, 'You're not going to fucking believe this, Declan. That was John Freed of all people. It seems there is another CCTV on its way here. This time Golding was spied in a Tesco Express in Kent. He bought the same things – forty Lambert and Butler and a bottle of cheap vodka. He was recognised by the woman working the till. She rang John, and he's looked at the CCTV for himself. He reckons it is definitely Golding.'

Declan was silent; this was getting a bit too creepy now. It was as if the man was goading them, deliberately sending them on different trails. It was a good tactic, but it was guaranteed to make Michael Flynn angry and vicious.

'He's fucking laughing at us, Declan! This mentally retarded fucking headcase is laughing at us, for fuck's sake! He is telling me that he has the upper hand. I get that – it's standard procedure to keep the enemy guessing. But what is happening to my Jessie while this is going on? Is he hurting her? Has he already fucking murdered her?'

Declan waved his hands in despair. 'You mustn't think like that, Michael. For fuck's sake, if he hurt Jessie, he wouldn't have a bargaining chip any more, would he? Think about it. Plus, from what we know about him, he isn't a violent person. He's a fucking nutbag granted, but there's no history of violent behaviour.'

Michael jumped up out of his chair. He was feeling so angry and so impotent. How was it possible this fucking Golding could operate under his radar? It was a nightmare. This man couldn't be underestimated, he knew that much – he was far more intelligent than anyone was giving him credit for.

'Declan, have a fucking day off, will you! Read the papers! Every other day some fucking head banger kills somebody for no fucking reason. They stab them or attack them in a shopping centre in full view of everyone around them. And, the worst thing of all is, these people – these nutters – are only roaming the streets because some fucking shrink decides that they are not a danger to anyone. But they are. This cunt is a fucking Grade A looney. I don't care what the doctors in the nut house might have said about him – he had the nous to fucking take my baby.

He has a very high IQ, remember? And he reads a lot. Well, when I finally get my hands on him – Mr Fucking *Intellectual* – I will personally remove his brain from his skull and I will then cheerfully force feed it to the useless cunt who decided he was fit enough to rejoin society. I can't believe this ponce is actually getting the better of *me*. That is the hardest part of all, Declan – this fucking no-mark, this mentally challenged fucker, is actually getting one over on me.'

Declan agreed with Michael wholeheartedly; this ponce was either very clever or very lucky; Declan had a feeling it was a combination of the two. But that wasn't what Michael needed to hear at this precise moment in time.

'That is fucking mental, Michael. Listen to yourself! He is a nut – granted – but that is his weakness, not his strength. He doesn't even want a ransom, for fuck's sake. That alone should tell you something.'

'It does, Declan. It tells me this isn't about money, this is fucking personal, and we both know why that is, don't we?'

Declan didn't answer.

'Patrick knew what he was asking of me. He *knew* the house wasn't empty. He was using me to vent his fucking spleen. It was one of his biggest failings – his narrow-mindedness. He could hold a grudge for the tiniest of reasons, an imagined slight, or a small loan that was overdue – something he should have been big enough to overlook. But he couldn't. When he got that bee in his fucking bonnet . . .' He trailed off. His anger was threatening to take over, and he knew he had to calm himself down, think logically, not let his heart rule his head. 'You know what I am saying as well as I do, Declan.'

Michael Flynn looked out of his window. Today he wasn't enjoying the view he'd always loved. Today he was wondering how a man like Steven Golding could get the better of him. That was something Michael Flynn couldn't live with, something he would never be able to overcome. The man was on a fucking death wish, and Michael was going to make sure he got *exactly* what he was asking for.

Chapter One Hundred and Twenty-Six

Jessie woke up to see the man taking photos of her. She didn't even try to hide herself from him, she was too tired, too sore to move. Her ankles were so painful, the shackles had rubbed most of her skin away, and she could actually see her ankle bones poking through now. It was so disgusting to look at. The metal rings that held her in place were covered with dried blood and hardened lumps of her skin, a constant reminder of her predicament.

The man was laughing to himself, as if he was party to some private joke. Jessie had lost most of her fight – it was pointless trying to convince him of anything. He had already told her the worst – that he was going to let her die. She believed him. He was too fucking unbalanced to lie to her. He was on a mission, that much was evident; he lived on another planet, on another wavelength.

Now she was starving and in such agony she might welcome death at some point in the near future; anything had to be better than living like this. He had even taken the bucket from her, so she couldn't even open her bowels or have a pee with ease. She had been reduced to using the concrete floor. But what else could she do? She was limited by the shackles and, as her dad used to say, even a dog doesn't shit in its own basket. The less food her body got, the more she seemed to need to evacuate her bowels. It was like water, just diarrhoea, but it was very painful for her. And humiliating.

She wasn't sure how long it would be before it would be too difficult for her to move. Then she would have no choice but to lay in her own filth.

She wanted to cry again, but she didn't think she had any tears left. She opened the bottle of water – he still made sure she had that at least – and she drank it straight down, welcoming the oblivion of the drugged liquid. The sores on her ankles were infected, and she could smell her own rotting flesh. It was so disgusting, it even overshadowed her body odour, though the smell of faeces was overpowering.

The man himself didn't seem to notice anything was amiss; he didn't wrinkle his nose, or register the stench surrounding her. Jessie decided that he just wasn't interested enough to care. Like he kept telling her, this wasn't about her. It was as if he didn't even see her most of the time.

The man stepped closer to her, smiling inanely.

'Do you remember that quiz show that was on years ago? When people had to guess the price of things? It was a really good show.'

Jessie shook her head. 'No, I don't remember it. Probably before my time.'

The man grinned. 'Oh, you would have liked it. I did, I loved it. The man who asked the questions was very clever. I remember now, it was called *Sale of the Century*. I like quiz shows. I like questions. I always liked questions.'

Jessie forced herself to smile at him. 'Really? Can I ask you a question, then?'

He smiled at her, positively beaming with pleasure. 'Of course you can, silly! Ask me anything you like, anything at all. I bet I can answer it.'

Jessie pulled herself up on to her elbows and, looking the man straight in the eyes, she asked quietly, 'Why are you doing this to me? What have I ever done to you?'

He turned away from her, but when he turned back to face her, he was laughing again. 'I told you before, Jessie, this isn't about *you*! You are the weapon I need, Jessie, to bring your father to his knees. When I finally deliver you to him, starved, shackled and, of course, *dead*, he will finally understand the meaning of despair. Complete and utter despair. It's a pain that is unique. You see, one thing I have learnt, Jessie, is the worst pain of all is not your *own* suffering, but knowing about the suffering of the people you really care about. That's a far worse pain, worse than any physical harm you might have to endure yourself.'

He was smiling at her again, as if he had just given her the secret of eternal happiness. Then he said matter-of-factly, 'Think about your little boy Jake. Imagine if I starved him to death. That would be a far worse pain to you, than what you're experiencing now, wouldn't it? Do you see what I mean? Understand what I'm getting at?'

Jessie didn't answer him; she felt sick at what he had said to her. This was surreal, unbelievable, and yet it was really happening.

Chapter One Hundred and Twenty-Seven

'There are people searching Kent as well as Essex, Michael. He can't fucking evade us for ever. I have mobilised everyone that we work with throughout the British Isles, and they are all on the hunt as well. The fifty grand is a big incentive but, also, I think this cunt has really put a lot of backs up.'

Michael didn't reply. He was so tired, but he just couldn't sleep. He was still holed up in the offices at Canary Wharf with Declan. It was where everyone knew to contact them.

Michael didn't want to go home; he talked to little Jake on the phone, but there was no way he wanted to go back there and face Josephine. She was the last person he wanted to see. Every time he thought about her keeping that letter to herself, putting her own needs before her daughter's, he felt angry enough to strangle her with his bare hands. If she had told him, this might have been resolved by now. If this bloke was as big a nut as they all reckoned, maybe not phoning had sent him over the edge; after all, no one had heard a fucking word from him since.

'How the fuck can this ponce evade not just the police, but every fucking Face in the country? It's fucking impossible, surely?'

Declan shrugged casually. 'Well, look at that Bin Laden bloke. He'd been on the trot for years when they caught him.'

Michael ran his hands through his hair; sometimes Declan didn't have a clue. He just opened his mouth before he put his brain in gear.

'Oh, by the way, Michael, I spoke to Jack earlier on, while you were in the shower. He has tracked down Golding's medical records. It cost him an arm and a leg, but he has all the addresses where he's ever lived – everything about him. Who knows – he might have a place he goes to regularly. It's worth a chance.'

Michael snorted with derision. 'I suppose so. It's amazing what you can fucking buy, isn't it?'

Declan laughed at Michael's sarcasm. Money could get literally anything usually.

Michael went on: 'If I could only know for certain that she was alive, Declan, I would feel so much better. I can't bear to think that she might be frightened, you know? Scared and alone somewhere, and wondering why I haven't rescued her.'

Declan was very blasé as he said honestly, 'I'm sorry, Michael, but it would take a lot to scare your Jessie. She isn't what anyone would call a shrinking violet, is she? Jessie Flynn is a woman who lives her own life. Fuck me – if *you* can't control her, how the fuck could anyone else?'

Michael didn't laugh with Declan this time; he appreciated his friend was just trying to allay his fears, but no one could do that now.

'I'm not so sure about that, Declan. She isn't as hard-faced as she acts. There is a softness there that few people ever see. She would ring her mum almost every day, because she knew that she worries about her. She also asks about Jake, of course. She loves that little boy, I know that for a fact.'

Declan wasn't so sure Jessie was this sweet young thing her father was describing, but if that was what Michael wanted to believe, he was happy to go along with it. In his opinion, Jessie

Flynn was a selfish little fucker, who never had the sense to see how fucking lucky she was, and who had never appreciated just how loved and adored she was. She was a user, and she had used everyone around her. But Declan was shrewd enough to keep his own counsel; there were some things you couldn't tell people – they just didn't want to hear them.

'Well, Michael, you know her better than anyone, mate.'

Michael's phone vibrated and he picked it up, opening the text message. He was shocked to see a picture of his Jessie. She was shackled to a bed, looking ill and very frightened.

'Oh, my God.'

He passed the phone to Declan, who looked at the picture with abject horror. Jessie looked terrified, and she also looked like she was starving. He could see her ribcage in startling detail. He zoomed in so he could see the picture better, and he could see that her ankles were rubbed raw from the iron shackles. It looked as if the bones were exposed, and there were faeces on the floor around the bed. It was a wicked, vicious picture sent to cause the maximum of hurt.

It was her eyes, though, that really bothered him. They were looking right into the camera, and there was no life in them. They were already dead. He was so shocked, he couldn't speak for a few minutes.

Michael had crossed his arms over his chest and he was hugging himself. As he rocked himself to and fro, Declan was shocked to realise that the man was openly crying. Michael Flynn was sobbing like a baby; it was terrible to see him brought so low.

Declan forced himself into action. He picked up his phone and he rang a man called Arthur Hellmann. He was a technological wizard, and he had worked for everyone who was anyone. He also had a serious gambling habit, and he had owed money all over the Smoke. It had been Michael's idea to pay his debts off and get him into the firm. Now Declan hoped the man could use his expertise to track down the mobile phone Golding was using. It was clutching at straws, but it was all they had. Michael Flynn needed to feel like he was doing something, now more than ever. That image of young Jessie had achieved its goal; it was further proof that they didn't have any control over this situation whatsoever.

When he came off the phone, he looked at Michael sadly. 'I'm going to up the security at your house, Michael. I think this proves we can't take any chances.'

Michael nodded. 'Put them inside the house. I'll ring Dana, make sure that she doesn't even take Jake to school. Until this is over, we daren't chance anything.' Michael looked at the photo of his daughter again. 'She's fucking terrified, you can see it in her eyes. How in *fuck's* name has this happened? How the fuck has this mad cunt managed to get this far?'

Declan shrugged; he was genuinely disturbed himself now. This was well outside their usual remit. Until now, he would have bet his last penny that a situation like this would have been an impossibility. They were too big, too well known. But Declan knew, from bitter experience, that the greatest of threats nearly always came from the people you least expected.

Chapter One Hundred and Twenty-Eight

Hannah Flynn couldn't understand why Michael had not been around to see her for days. It wasn't like him – he always made a point of dropping in to see her. She was particularly worried after what Josephine had told her. If her Michael had lost his temper with his wife then there was something serious going on. Josephine had never been able to do any wrong in Michael's eyes. Now, it seemed, he had finally lost his patience, and she had found herself actually feeling sorry for Josephine. That alone had been a shock. The woman had been completely devastated by her husband's attack on her. But Christ Himself knew – she blessed herself automatically at the use of the Lord's name in vain – Josephine Flynn was one of the most selfish fuckers that had ever been put on this earth. Hannah sat down at her kitchen table. She was a bundle of nerves lately, she couldn't seem to settle. What had happened to Jessie was playing on her mind. The girl always kept in touch with her nana Hannah.

She poured herself out a glass of good Irish whisky, and took a large gulp to steady herself. Then she poured herself another. She heard her doorbell, and sighed with annoyance. Few people sought her company, and that suited her. She had never suffered fools gladly. But, as she walked to her front door, she hoped against hope that it was someone with news about her Jessie.

She opened the front door, expecting to see someone she knew. Instead she saw a skinny, grey-haired man, with sallow skin and a twisted smile. She detected a sour odour coming off him. She went to ask him what the hell he wanted, but before she could say a word, he lunged at her. As she tried to step back from him, she felt a sharp pain in her chest. Looking down, she saw the handle of a knife sticking out of her breast. It occurred to her that its blade was obviously buried deep inside her chest. It had all happened so quickly. The man was still smiling at her and, as she sank to her knees, he stepped away from her casually, and began taking photos of her on his phone. All she could do was watch him. She was trying to call out, get help, but there was nothing she could do. Her mouth was slowly filling up with blood, and it made her want to vomit. It tasted disgusting, it was so thick and it was suddenly dribbling out of her mouth. She could feel its warmth as it ran down her chin. She was lying on her back now, and she knew she would eventually choke on her own blood. She could feel her heartbeat getting slower by the second, and she could hear herself wheezing as she tried to breathe. She could feel the light-headedness as she gradually started to lose consciousness, and she welcomed the oblivion. Anything was better than this battle to take a single breath.

Chapter One Hundred and Twenty-Nine

Arthur Hellmann was a strange-looking man. He was tall, very thin, and he had deep brown eyes and white-blond hair. It was a startling combination. Whereas on some people, it would have given them striking good looks, on Arthur it just seemed to add to his general air of strangeness. He was a man who found it very difficult to socialise with other people, and who much preferred the anonymity of cyberspace.

As he walked into the office, Michael and Declan didn't even bother to greet him, and that suited him. He liked that Michael Flynn didn't feel the need to engage him in conversation unless it was of some relevance. Too many people talked for the sake of it, and they rarely had anything of interest to say.

He sat at the desk, and set up his laptop, before saying to no one in particular, 'I can access most phones. As long as this one's turned on, I can get a location on it. I can also work out where any calls were made – the area, that is.'

Michael Flynn passed his BlackBerry to him, and Arthur glanced at the photograph. It was shocking.

'I got that about three hours ago, Arthur. I need you to try and find the sender.'

Arthur nodded. He was aware that time was obviously of the

essence. 'Well, there is one thing I can tell you straight off, this isn't the usual cheap throwaway phone. This picture has a lot of detail, which tells me the phone used was a fairly decent model.'

Michael Flynn wasn't even listening to the man. 'Just try and track the fucker down.'

The phone vibrated once more. Arthur Hellmann automatically opened the text. After a quick glance at the contents, he passed the phone to Michael Flynn without a word.

Michael looked at the photo of his mother lying in her hallway, a knife poking out of her right breast, and he shook his head slowly in disbelief. For the first time in his life he felt vulnerable, frightened. His mother was dying before his eyes, his daughter was dying somewhere, tied up like a fucking animal and obviously in extreme pain, and he couldn't do a thing. This man was taunting him. The phone in the office started ringing, and Michael Flynn knew exactly what the call would be about.

Chapter One Hundred and Thirty

Josephine sat on her balcony with a glass of red wine, looking out over the gardens and wondering if the man who had her daughter and who had murdered her mother-in-law was coming for her and Jake.

It felt unreal knowing that Hannah was dead. Stabbed in her own home, by some mad fucker who had evaded capture. Now her home was overrun with armed men, sent by Michael to protect them. Little Jake was loving the company, bless him, unaware of the danger they were in.

She had a twelve-gauge shotgun by her side, and a Glock 22 handgun lying on the table in front of her. If anyone was coming here, she was more than ready to fight her end. It was odd, but she had always found handling guns very easy from the time Michael taught her to use one. She liked the feel of them, the knowledge that they were capable of so much destruction. It was the secret of guns: the weakest person in the world could protect themselves from the biggest of enemies, because a gun was relatively lightweight, and had the power over life and death.

Even though Michael had seen fit to *drown* their home with his armed men, she felt much safer knowing that she was armed too. Hannah had been taken out on her doorstep, stabbed like a fucking animal, and whoever had done that also had her daughter in his clutches. If only she had been capable of passing his message on to Michael, this might have been avoided. She had been hoping that he would come to see her and, if he had, then she would have been able to show him the letter.

It was a learning curve, she supposed – she was unable to justify her actions any longer. It didn't mean she was going to be able to change overnight; this wasn't a fucking film, where everything was resolved in an hour and a half, this was her real fucking *life*. But she could at least make a conscious decision this time to get the help that she so desperately needed. Surely that was a start?

Jake came running into her room, hyper with excitement.

'Nana, one of Granddad's friends said he would teach me to play poker! Can I learn it, please?'

Josephine was grateful Jake was distracted. ''Course you can! It's a very tricky game, though, so make sure you listen to what the man tells you carefully.'

Jake Flynn was dressed in his favourite Peppa Pig pyjamas – he was obsessed with Peppa, and would happily wear these until they fell apart. He was holding his favourite book which he had tucked under his arm – he adored *The Gruffalo* and he had read it over and over again. He looked very handsome and so vulnerable, that Josephine felt almost tearful as she looked at him. He deserved much more than she had ever given to him. She had lost out on so much of his little life.

'I like playing cards. I told the man that and he laughed! He said I was Granddad's double, and I think that's a good thing, Nana, don't you? Dana is going to learn with me, so that we can play poker together.'

Josephine hugged him to her tightly. She kissed his thick, dark hair, drinking in the smell of Matey bubble bath and jojoba shampoo.

He hugged her back with one arm, before pulling away from her. Then he noticed the gun on the table in front of her. He said solemnly, 'Nana, you better be very careful with that.'

Josephine could hear the underlying fear in his voice. He was six years old and already he knew that guns were dangerous. One day, of course, he would have to understand that, in the world his granddad lived in, guns were a necessity – a part of their everyday life. The charmed life that they lived came at a price, and that price was often higher than anyone realised. It was a dangerous life, and that was more apparent now than ever before.

'I will, darling. I will be very careful. Now, you go and learn how to play poker. Don't worry about anything. No one will ever let anything bad happen to you, I promise.'

As he ran back down to the kitchen, she wondered if she could keep that promise. She remembered the night that the Cornel brothers had arrived at her door, remembered Jessie's shock and horror at the night's events. She could see herself telling her daughter to lock herself in her bedroom, and not to be frightened of anything. She had found an inner strength that night to protect her home, her sanctuary, from the threat of the outside world. Jessie had seen her with the gun that night, and it had terrified her. Jessie had understood the danger they were in. It had changed her daughter – she had been forced to grow up that night.

Now her only child was being held captive, and that was harder for Josephine to comprehend than anything else in her life so far. That her daughter's dire predicament had still not been enough to make her use a telephone, was something she was finding very hard to forgive herself for. But it was actually her Michael's reaction that she was really worried about. She feared he wouldn't be forgiving her any time soon.

A part of her hoped that this unknown man would come here and give her the chance to take him out. It might be her only opportunity to redeem herself.

Chapter One Hundred and Thirty-One

Timothy Branch was watching Michael Flynn as the man tried to take in the news of his mother's death; the woman had been slaughtered on her doorstep. It was unbelievable – no one could have predicted anything like this. Who would have thought that a man like Michael Flynn could ever have been game-played by a fucking toe rag like Steven Golding? Golding was a fucking no-mark. But, somehow, he had managed to get the better of Michael Flynn. He had not only taken the man's daughter, he had also stabbed the man's mother to death in her own home.

It was Steven Golding's complete disregard for the consequences of his actions that truly bothered Timothy Branch. His was the mindset of a terrorist, someone whose only aim in life was to carry out the duty required of them, regardless of their own safety. It was only about the end game. This man Golding didn't seem to have an agenda that any of them could understand – there wasn't room for bargaining; he honestly didn't seem to want anything of value from any of them. He was only interested in hitting Michael Flynn where it hurt. All he seemed to want was revenge. That was the only thing this could be about – not that Michael Flynn had been very forthcoming about his dealings with the man in the past. But he had read the man's medical reports, knew that his family had been wiped out in a fire – a fire that had been started deliberately. It didn't take an Albert fucking Einstein to work out that Michael Flynn had been involved in that shit somewhere along the line. Branch had been around long enough to suss out what was *really* going on, but it wasn't in his interests to pursue this train of thought – he knew when to leave well alone.

'I've had your mother's body taken to the morgue, and I have hushed it up for the moment, but you have to understand, Michael, I can't sit on this for too long. None of the neighbours saw anything – it was very fast. And, from what I can gather, your mum wasn't a woman who encouraged her neighbours' friendships, if you get my drift.'

Michael laughed wryly. 'You got that right. My mother was the female equivalent of Jack the Giant Killer. She saw most people in her orbit as completely fucking useless ponces. She wasn't known for her sparkling personality.'

Declan Costello could detect the catch in Michael's voice underneath his bravado. He had loved his mother, in spite of everything. She wasn't a woman who encouraged displays of affection, but she had loved her son too.

Timothy Branch was aware of Hannah Flynn's reputation as a woman of limited patience; it was well known she had a tongue in her head and she used it to her advantage. He sighed. 'Look, Michael, the bottom line is, this bloke is either very fucking clever, or very fucking lucky. In all my years on the force I have never seen anything like it. He's obviously watched you for a while and he's aware of your daily routine. How else could he know so much? One thing I do know, though, is he's not that far away. I'd say that he's operating from within an hour's journey of your house. He has to be. It stands to reason.'

Declan and Michael exchanged glances; at last the man was

making sense. It was about time he earned his fucking keep! Branch was like all bent Filth – he wasn't liked or trusted by the people who paid his extra-curricular wages, *or* the people he had to work with in his capacity as an Old Bill. They would all know that he wasn't kosher or to be completely trusted. Word travelled fast, and that was something no one could prevent. It was a double-edged sword. He was paid a good wage to ensure that he was on their side if it ever went pear-shaped, but he was automatically suspect because he was selling out his own. Treachery wasn't looked on lightly in either of the circles Timothy Branch moved in.

Declan poured Michael another drink; he needed it – the man was in absolute shock. 'Come on, Michael, sit down and drink this. You've had a shock to your system.'

Michael allowed himself to be seated and took the drink offered to him. He had never felt so useless in his whole life. He kept seeing Jessie, the fear on her face, and the picture of his mother, dying in front of his eyes. No one seemed to be able to give him any information of use. He had a very large workforce, and not one of them could find out even the simplest thing about Steven Golding.

Timothy Branch cleared his throat noisily. 'I've had my blokes comb through his medical records, and there's nothing of value, Michael. They have been to every address where he's been registered, checked with his doctors, and not a fucking whisper.'

Michael Flynn started to laugh loudly, but it was an unnatural sound, too high pitched and too heartbreaking to be normal.

Declan and Timothy watched Michael laughing, warily.

Arthur Hellmann looked up from his computer in the corner of the room and he said triumphantly, 'I've got him. I think I've found the fucker.'

Declan knelt down in front of Michael and, grabbing the man's shoulders, he shook him roughly. 'Stop it, Michael! Will you just stop laughing. Listen to me! This isn't over yet.'

Eventually Michael began to quieten down, and then he seemed to pull himself together. Pushing Declan away, he picked up the glass of brandy from the table, and swallowed it in one gulp. He looked into Declan's eyes, saw the worry there and the genuine concern for his wellbeing. Michael wiped his hand across his mouth roughly; he had no choice left but to face this.

'It's OK, Declan. I'm fine. I'm OK.'

Declan was still kneeling on the floor, shocked by Michael's reaction. It wasn't like him to lose the plot. The man had every reason to – it just wasn't something he had expected. Michael Flynn was a hard man, harder than anyone Declan had ever known.

'Fucking hell, Michael, you can't lose it now. We're so close. You need to pull yourself together, get a fucking grip.'

Michael took a deep breath and expelled it slowly. He was aware that he needed to keep himself on an even keel. 'I'm all right now, Declan. It's over.'

Arthur Hellmann was embarrassed at such a naked display of emotion, especially from a man like Michael Flynn. It was unseemly, humiliating – the man was almost hysterical.

Declan turned to him and said angrily, 'Well, come on then, Arthur. Where is the fucker?'

Chapter One Hundred and Thirty-Two

Jessie woke up as the man shook her. She felt so drained, so ill. She didn't even know where she was for a few moments; it was a while before she remembered the truth. Then it all came rushing back, and she closed her eyes in distress. She blinked back tears, looking at the man's filthy smile which was as familiar to her now as her mother's beautiful one, and she wondered if it would be the last thing she ever saw in this life. It was such a frightening thought. She hoped not. She hoped she would just go to sleep and slip away, that she could at least take away some of his power and die without him witnessing it. He was looking at her intently, and she couldn't turn away from his gaze. Her legs were swollen, and they felt like they were burning. Her toes were black, and she knew she had a serious infection. She had a temperature and she was burning up, sweating like a pig. Her hair was stuck to her head, and she couldn't concentrate any more. She just wanted it to be over.

The man was smiling at her as he said conversationally, 'You look awful, Jessie. Really bad.'

She didn't answer him; he didn't expect one anyway.

'I must tell you this.' He was giggling like a girl, and she could see the euphoria he was experiencing – it was almost tangible. He was sitting on the bed, with his hands underneath his behind, like a teenage girl who had just found out a juicy piece of gossip about her worst enemy.

'I want to show you a photograph. I know you will understand the importance of it. You're a very intelligent girl. I must be honest with you, it wasn't something I expected.'

He held his phone out to her, and she looked at the picture he showed her, as she knew he wanted her to. She didn't have a choice – her fight was gone. She saw her nana Hannah dead or dying. There was blood everywhere. It was sickening. Her nana had died violently, for no reason other than because this weirdo had decided it was her time. Seeing her nana stripped of her dignity and left to die was so very wrong. Hannah Flynn was a woman who had brought up her child alone, who had worked every hour God sent, to give her son the best that she could. It was an awful way to die, and worse at the hands of someone like this. Jessie felt a spark of hatred threaten to erupt, but made sure that she kept her face neutral.

'That's my nana. I assume she's dead?' She was pleased with how nonchalant her voice sounded, pleased that she had taken away some of his glory. He wanted a reaction from her, and she would give him one – just not the reaction he was expecting.

The man sat upright; he was so stiff it was like he had a board up his jumper.

Jessie sighed. 'No one liked her anyway. You did us all a favour. I bet my dad would shake your hand if he knew.'

The man was sitting on the bed, staring at her, but she knew he wasn't seeing her – he was once more on his own private planet. What kind of person was he to kill an old lady, and show the pictures to her grandchild? Her fear of him was gone. She was dying – it was only a matter of time now. But she would die without giving this fucker another inch – she was not going to give him the satisfaction of knowing she was frightened of him any more. Seeing her nana Hannah like that, so brutally murdered, was the last straw. As tired and as ill as she felt, she wasn't going to let him think that he had broken her completely. Her nana Hannah deserved that much from her, surely?

She made herself laugh then, a low, deep-throated chuckle. 'God, I bet she was surprised to see you, eh? Hannah Flynn, the hardest woman in the East End, murdered on her doorstep. It's so ironic. You're lucky she didn't stab you first.'

She could sense the man was annoyed with her. He didn't like what she was saying, and that suited her – she hoped he would do the kind thing and finish her off as well. It wasn't as if she was ever going to leave this place alive. He had already made that abundantly clear to her.

'Me and my dad have had more fights than Michael Tyson. We *loathe* each other. My mum hasn't left the house for fucking years, she lives in two rooms and she's a hoarder. I bet you didn't know that, did you? She keeps everything, every scrap of paper, every fucking thing that someone she loves has touched. It's mental, I tell you. She still has sweet wrappers from when I was a toddler. And I can tell you now, mister, the minute I went on the missing list my dad would have made sure my mum had more bodyguards than fucking Whitney Houston. He *adores* her – she's his reason for living. When you deliver my body, as you promised, he will hunt you down like a dog, but not because of what you've done to me – he won't give a flying fuck about that. He will come after you, because you took something he owned. It's all about face with my dad, about front.' She laughed again, much harder this time. She could see the bafflement on his face and was enjoying his discomfort, and the knowledge that she had royally pissed all over his fireworks. If nothing else, she was going to make sure he didn't have the last laugh.

The man stood up abruptly, and she looked him right in the eyes. Then he punched her hard in her face. She didn't react, she let him hit her, and even as she felt her eye begin to swell, she still didn't say anything.

Suddenly, he was shouting at her, a deafening roar that was as unexpected at it was potent. 'I will *not* allow you to laugh at me. I will *not* let you do that.'

He hit her again, this time on her jaw. It was an uppercut, and she felt the blow snap her head back with its power. The next punch hit her straight in the mouth; he was so much stronger than she would have believed possible. Her lip split open and it started to bleed profusely. She could taste her own blood, feel it as it dripped down her face. She instinctively braced herself for the next onslaught, but it didn't come. She heard him walking away from her, leaving her all alone once more.

She didn't move. She waited until she heard the door clang shut, and then she opened her eyes, glad to be by herself again. She couldn't help feeling like she had won something. It was a small victory, but it was a victory nonetheless. She spat the blood out of her mouth. She could feel the throb of her eye as it started to close, and the stinging from the cut on her lip. She tried to pull herself up into a sitting position, but she couldn't manage it. She welcomed the pain from her face; the fresh hurt took her mind off her other ills. She lay there, unable to move her body any more, praying to God for sleep to take her. While she was asleep she couldn't feel pain, she wasn't reminded of the state she was in, or the fact she was going to die chained to a bed. She couldn't think about how she had neglected her little son, or how she had wasted her young life, and all because she had seen the dark side of her parents' lives. Jake had been a constant reminder of her mistakes – she had always seen him as a symbol of her stupidity. Now, after this, she would give anything to turn back the clock, and do everything right – do what her father had urged her to do from the very beginning: stand up and face her responsibilities. She had fought him every step of the way and now it seemed so fucking futile. She had lain here and thought it over in depth, and accepted that she had not hurt anyone except herself.

She looked up at the ceiling. Her tears were rolling down her face – she could feel them dripping into her ears, and she didn't even wipe them away.

Chapter One Hundred and Thirty-Three

'Right then, people.' Arthur Hellmann was oblivious to most of what had been going on around him; that was his biggest failing as a human being, and his biggest asset as a computer whiz. 'From what I can work out, the person you're looking for is located within a one-quarter mile radius. He is in Essex, within two miles of Romford. The phone itself is registered to someone called Malcolm Briers, whose address, believe it or not, is within two miles of Romford. The address is White Farm on the Rainham Road. It was a clever fucking scam, I tell you. If I didn't have access to every fucking mobile number on the planet, we would never have located the fucker. He was well hidden. And if he had not left his phone on, I would never have found the bastard.'

Michael was listening to the man with absolute amazement. After all this time, this fucking weirdo had actually managed to track the bastard down, when even the police couldn't manage to do it. Michael was almost beside himself with euphoria – at last he had a fucking lead.

Arthur looked at the men around him warily. 'Look, it doesn't mean he's *there*. It just means that is where it's all registered. But the phone *was* used within that area recently.'

Michael hugged the man to him. 'You fucking *diamond*! Whatever happens, mate, you get your wedge. At least you have given us a place to start. I could fucking kiss you!'

Declan was laughing now. He felt the same euphoria as Michael; this was a real fucking result.

Timothy Branch watched the two men as they bowled out of the room together. He felt he had failed; and of course he had – miserably. Turning to Arthur Hellmann, who was one weird-looking fucker, he said arrogantly, 'What you just did is illegal, you do know that?'

Hellmann laughed in his face. He couldn't give a toss what this man thought of him or his methods. If he worked within the law he would never have found out anything! No one would. Their hands were tied, Freedom of Information Acts, etc., etc. It was laughable. This was why he earned the big bucks – this man had to know that better than anybody.

Poking a finger into Branch's face, he said sarcastically, 'So fucking arrest me then! I *dare* you.' Hellmann hoped that he was fifty grand up on this deal – that was the asking price for locating Michael Flynn's daughter. He had followed the phone, followed the trail, he just hoped that he had done enough.

Chapter One Hundred and Thirty-Four

Michael was buzzing as they drove out of East London – *finally* he was actually doing something constructive. It had been a long time coming; this mad fucker was so elusive, he was beginning to think he would never find him. It was the first time in his life that he had been unable to meet a problem head on. He had been at the top of his game for so long, it was unbelievable to think that anyone could have got the better of him. It galled him, it *unnerved* him, if he was honest.

'I am going to kill this cunt with my bare hands, Declan. How *dare* he bring this to my door? Whatever might have happened in the past, his fucking beef was with *me*, not my family. I'm the one who fucked up.' He laughed sarcastically. 'Or, more to the point, *Patrick* was the one who fucked up. He knew what he was asking me to do. But what I can't get my head round is that, of all the people I have taken out for whatever fucking reason, the only time it's come back to bite me on the arse, is the one time I never intended to hurt a fucking soul. I would never have done that for anyone. Taking out women and children? That's a fucking no-brainer. I would never have agreed to that.'

Declan sighed. He could understand Michael's feelings. He kept his voice neutral as he said calmly, 'It's all relative. That's in the past, Michael. All you can do now is sort out this shit as best you can.'

They were sitting in traffic at the Lodge Avenue roundabout in Barking. It was so frustrating. Michael was grasping the steering wheel with both hands, he was sweating all over, his fury and impatience intense now. He had no other choice – he had to sit there patiently until the traffic moved. There was nothing else he could do.

Declan could feel the man's tension – it was understandable, but it was also threatening to get out of control. He lit them both cigarettes, and he passed one to Michael. Then they were on the move. Michael manoeuvred his Mercedes through the traffic skilfully and, as they edged towards Dagenham, he said with obvious relief, 'Another five minutes in that traffic and I would have run fucking riot through Barking.'

Declan laughed with him; he felt the same way. It was dark now, and the sky was heavily laden with rain clouds. It was close, stormy, and it added to the feeling of urgency. As it started to spit, Michael put on the windscreen wipers. He was already relaxing as they passed the Ford Motor Works along the A13, and slipped into Rainham. After all this time, he finally had a fucking goal to head for.

'Every time I think of that picture of my Jessie I feel like screaming. And my mum's dead, Declan – I know it's true, but I just can't take it in. She was struck down in her own home, on her own fucking doorstep. How the fuck can this have happened to *me*? It's like a fucking living nightmare.' He wanted to cry again. The absolute power of his emotions amazed him. 'My old mum, for all her attitude, was always fucking good to me, Declan. She worked every hour God sent when I was a kid, and I never wanted for anything. She would have given me the food out of her mouth, I know that. I've always known that.'

Michael drove past Rainham Clocktower, and out towards the country lanes. They were nearly there now, and he could feel the adrenaline starting to kick in.

'My mum always said that Josephine was a selfish cunt, and she was right. I wouldn't listen to her. When Josephine first started hoarding food, all those years ago, my mum said I needed to nip it in the bud. But I didn't listen to her – I treated her like she was the fucking enemy. I just pretended that it wasn't happening. But she was proved right. If I had put my foot down from the off, I know that all this shit with Josephine would never have got this far. I stood by as my wife gradually retired from real life. All that money I have shelled out on psychiatrists for her, and they say the same thing – it takes *time*. She is mentally ill! Well, fuck me, Declan, I don't know about them, but I had already fucking worked that one out for myself. Hardly rocket science, is it? If it wasn't for Dana, Jake would never leave the house. That great, big, expensive *fucking* house, situated in its *own* grounds, with its thirty-grand kitchen, and its two full-time gardeners, and my wife lives in two rooms and, it seems, can't bring herself to make a phone call that might save her only daughter's life. All that money I have weighed out to get her help, and she is still unable to open a letter or dial a fucking telephone. How fucking messed up is that? This new bloke she's got on her case now – a right fucking arrogant cunt he is and all – is giving *me* lists of books I should be reading to acquaint myself with my wife's condition. Well, I pointed out to him, in the nicest possible way, that I was paying him good money to do all of that *for* me, and there was an old saying: why have a fucking dog and bark your fucking self. I was very angry at the time, and I think he noticed that. Suffice to say, Declan, he soon got with the fucking project.'

He slowed the car down. They were on the Rainham road,

and he parked in a layby. 'We're here. The farm entrance is down the end of this lane.'

Michael got out of the car. It was raining hard now. Opening up the boot, he took out a large handgun, and passed it to Declan. He took out a Glock 22 for himself. It was his weapon of choice – lightweight, and easy to use; it was also easy to dispose of. It could be stripped down to nothing.

'I am so looking forward to meeting Mr Steven Golding, and blowing his fucking head right off.'

He shut the car boot carefully. He turned towards his old friend, and said gravely, 'I will never forget how good you've been to me, Declan, through all of this. I really have appreciated how you've stood by me through everything. I know that you have talked me down on more than one occasion, and stopped me from screwing this up completely. I appreciate just how good a friend you are, Declan.'

Declan was moved by Michael's words; he knew how hard it was for him to even say them. 'Look, Michael, you know that I will always have your back.'

Michael grinned sadly. 'Do you know the worst thing about this for me? The one thing that I've learnt from this shit is that it all means *nothing*. Everything that we've worked for, everything that we've achieved, all the fucking stunts we've pulled to get what we wanted from life, all that planning, and forward thinking, all those fucking years we put into it and it turned out that it was for sweet F A, sweet fuck-all. We chased the fucking dollar day and night, living the so-called dream! The leaders of everyone around us, responsible for every fucking earn, as well as the people who we allow to gather up said earn for us. And it was a fucking waste of time. We have squandered so much of our lives accumulating money, power, *things* and, in reality, neither of us has a single thing of use to show for any of it. How fucking sad is that?'

Declan shrugged theatrically, and he said with a laugh, 'Well, when you put it like that, Michael . . .'

Michael was amazed to hear himself laughing, but he was. If anyone had said that he could have found any amusement in this situation he would have thought them mad. But Declan Costello had made him laugh, and that was something good. It felt so good to laugh, to really laugh, to find some humour at last.

They looked at each other for a few moments and then they walked side by side towards White Farm.

Chapter One Hundred and Thirty-Five

White Farm was a smallholding, and it had been a rental property for over two years. There were no animals there any more, but the barns and the outbuildings were still in a very good state of repair. The old couple who had lived there since before the War had died within a few days of each other. Their only son, a grammar-school boy they had both doted on, had emigrated to Canada in the early sixties. His education had eventually alienated him from the people who had happily bankrolled him through university, and who had eventually paid his fare out to Toronto. They had never seen him again – or met his wife, or his children, or their great-grandchildren – but they had been very proud of him, and they had cherished the Christmas cards and photos he had sent to them sporadically. When they died he had arranged his parents' burials, and he had then arranged for the farm he had grown up on to be rented out until property prices started to rise in the UK once again. It had all been done over the phone, and, like all absentee landlords, he had no idea of who might be occupying his old homestead. The rental agents had even less interest and, for someone like Steven Golding, that was a situation he could exploit without fear of anyone ever bothering to chase him up, or even having to meet with anyone face to face. As long as the rent was paid promptly and, in his case, three months in advance, no one could give the proverbial flying fuck.

He had found all the old couple's belongings stored in the attic; their whole lives were packed into a few boxes. A life of occasional letters and greetings cards, the haphazard affection of a son who had left them both behind as soon as he could. He had hated the son who had walked away from parents who had loved him dearly.

Steven Golding sat at the kitchen table, a big scrubbed-pine monstrosity, that was very old and very scarred. It had seen a lot of use over its lifetime, that was evident. There were people who would pay a lot of money for it, he knew that. People who had to buy other people's lives, other people's possessions, because they didn't have anything of such value in their own families. It was a sad fact, but it was true.

The rain had stopped, but the wind was gathering momentum. It was early October, and autumn was already settling in. Steven Golding stood up quickly, and glanced around him, pleased that the kitchen looked so clean and tidy. He looked at his watch – it was after eight, and he made his way down into the cellar, locking the heavy door behind him carefully. No one was ever getting past that door, it was like Fort Knox. The smell assailed his nostrils, and he smiled at the discomfort he knew it must be causing Jessie Flynn. He stepped carefully down the stairs, and walked to where she was still lying on her bed.

She looked terrible. Her legs were swollen and they looked so painful. Her face was porcelain white, the skin tight on her skull, and her eyes had sunk back into their sockets. She was dying, and she knew that as well as he did. Her breathing was laboured – every breath she took was a long and drawn out wheeze, loud in the quiet of the basement.

'Jessie, Jessie, wake up, lovely.' He was shaking her roughly and, as she opened her eyes, he bent over her. 'I need to talk to you, Jessie. You're dying, but I think you've worked that out for yourself, haven't you? Your dad should have been here by now. I really thought he would have found you a lot quicker than this.'

She didn't say anything; she was still trying to focus on him, trying to pull herself into the real world.

Steven Golding could see that Jessie Flynn was too far gone for him to have any kind of meaningful conversation with her; she had deteriorated rapidly in the last twelve hours. Her condition shocked him – he had thought she was a much stronger person, and thought she would have fought much harder than she had done. In the beginning she had been so cocky, so arrogant, threatening him with her dad. She had been convinced that he would help her. She had assumed this was about money – money was all people like the Flynns understood. When she had finally realised that it wasn't about him getting a ransom, that she was *never* going to be rescued, never going to leave this basement, she seemed to have succumbed to the inevitable. It was not what he had expected – he was not pleased about this turn of events.

He walked over to the tap by the stairs, and filled a bucket with cold water. Walking back over to her, he threw the contents into her face, drenching her. But, other than trying to catch her breath, which was a natural reaction, the shock of the cold water did nothing to revive her. He could see her trying to focus on him, on her surroundings, and he felt a sudden, fleeting moment of sorrow for her. He had quite liked her, and that wasn't something he had been prepared for – had certainly never expected.

He looked down at her; she was clearly unable to understand what was happening around her. It occurred to him that the infection from her ankles had probably entered her bloodstream, and she was likely suffering from blood poisoning. Even with the stench of faeces in the room, he could still detect the underlying odour of her rotting flesh. It was a sour smell, a heavy, cloying stench that seemed to rise up from her skin, and envelop the very air around her body. It was sharp in the nostrils, made your eyes water, and it smelt like imminent death.

He grabbed her hand, and held it gently between his palms. She was in a sorry state all right. But what could he do? This was what he had intended to happen. He had been left with nobody, all because Patrick Costello had held a grudge against his father. Costello had a perfect alibi for that night, and Steven had finally worked out that Michael Flynn, Costello's up-and-coming young wannabe, had done the dirty deed in his name. He had poured the petrol through the letterbox, and he had wiped out a whole family to better *himself*. All that so he could become Patrick Costello's blue-eyed boy. Well, as the Bible said, be sure your sins will find you out.

Chapter One Hundred and Thirty-Six

Michael and Declan had made their way around the property, carefully and quietly creeping towards the back of the house. It wasn't a large property – a pre-war, two-storey, red-brick house, with no aesthetic value. It was still in possession of its old-style Crittall windows – there was nothing of any beauty to give the house its own identity. It was very well built, but it needed a lot of work on it if anyone was going to live there for any length of time. It had been neglected, and that showed.

Michael looked through the kitchen window; other than this room, the house was in utter darkness. There were no outside lights either, and that was something both Michael and Declan were glad about. It made their life much easier. The kitchen was fairly large, and it looked like something from the Discovery Channel. It had faded yellow linoleum and hand-made wooden cupboards, the cooker was an old gas model, with an eye-level grill pan, and only three burners. The oven didn't look large enough to cook anything bigger than a family-sized chicken. Other than a modern electric kettle, the place could have been a museum.

Michael Flynn looked inside, and whispered to his friend, 'Fucking hell, Declan, this place is like something from fucking *Z Cars*!'

He moved quickly to the back door and, turning the handle slowly, he was relieved to find that it wasn't even locked. This fucker obviously didn't think anyone was going to find him. Stepping into the room, he held his breath, and listened carefully. The place smelt of neglect and poverty.

Declan followed him in, and he shut the door carefully behind him. The place felt totally empty, as if it hadn't been occupied for a long time.

Michael whispered huskily, 'Listen, Declan, can you hear that?'

Declan Costello listened to the house, straining his ears for any sound whatsoever. He shook his head slowly. 'No.'

Michael rolled his eyes in annoyance. He walked slowly across the kitchen. There was a door that was open which led into the hallway and, to the side of it, there was another door. Michael guessed that it led to a cellar. These old places were built to last, and they were also built with farmers in mind – a cellar was essential, an important storage facility, especially in the winter months.

Suddenly the two men heard music. It was very loud, and out of place in the grand scheme of things. It threw them both for a few seconds. Michael recognised the melody – it was 'Almaz' by Randy Crawford. The whole thing was getting more bizarre by the second and, when they heard the basement door being unbolted, they both slipped into the darkness of the hallway.

Michael could feel the thrumming of his heart as he waited for the man to emerge from the basement. He was holding his breath, frightened to even breathe in case he gave himself away. All he wanted was to find his Jessie, his baby, and to finally prove to her that he loved her no matter what. Then he wanted to destroy this cunt, this man who had somehow snuck past him, had somehow got the better of him, had threatened his family, his life.

The door opened slowly. It was obviously a very heavy door, and it wasn't easy to negotiate. Declan and Michael waited with bated breath for Steven Golding to come into the kitchen, and to finally enter their orbit.

He did so slowly and, as he turned to face the men he knew would be waiting for him, he grinned amiably, saying cheerfully, 'I've been waiting for you, and so has Jessie.'

Chapter One Hundred and Thirty-Seven

Steven Golding looked so much smaller than Michael had expected. He was almost puny. It was hard to believe that this was the man who had caused him so much grief, who had been so fucking elusive. It was a joke, surely?

Golding laughed. 'You're too late, Mr Flynn. We waited for you, but you never came. Now your little Jessie is dying, I'm afraid.'

Michael stepped towards the man, intent on murder, and Declan grabbed him. 'Stop it, Michael. That's what he wants. Let's find Jessie first. I wouldn't believe a word this slippery fucker says.'

Michael knew that Declan was right, he couldn't do anything until he had found his daughter.

Steven Golding shrugged. 'Be my guest, she's down there.' He gestured towards the basement door. 'She's been down there since day one.'

Declan grabbed the man by his throat, and dragged him unceremoniously down the basement stairs behind Michael. The music was much louder inside the room, and it added to the surreal feeling that was enveloping them.

Declan was unsure for a few moments if he was actually seeing what was before his eyes. The stench alone was bad enough, but Jessie, if that really *was* Jessie, was like something from a horror film.

She was so bloated, and her feet, her lovely little feet, were almost devoid of skin. He looked at Michael; he could see the man's disbelief at what he was witnessing. He too was wondering if this was some kind of joke, even though they both knew that wasn't possible.

The photo Michael had been sent had been bad enough but, in the hours since then, it was obvious that Jessie had deteriorated. She looked dead already.

Declan went to the CD player and, kicking it with all his might, he watched as it rose up into the air, and then hit the wall. The ensuing silence was almost deafening.

Michael looked at his daughter, at the condition she was in. It was like a fucking nightmare, beyond anything he could ever have imagined. This was his baby girl – no matter what had happened in the past, she was his only child, and he loved her with a passion.

'Oh my fucking God. Oh dear God. Please don't do this to me . . .' Michael was trying to pick his daughter up in his arms, trying to comfort her. But she was unresponsive, her eyes were closed. Michael was openly crying, sobbing in despair.

Declan punched Golding in the side of his head, and he watched as the man skidded through the shit that was everywhere, and sprawled on the floor. Then grabbing him back up, he bellowed into his face, 'Where's the fucking keys, you fucking piece of shit!'

He was already pulling the man's jacket off him, and searching his trouser pockets. He finally found a set of keys in the man's jacket and, calling out Michael's name, he threw them to him.

As he did so, Jessie let out a long slow breath and opened her

She tried to follow the sound of her father's voice, as he shouted loudly, 'Jessie darling, Jessie, it's me, your dad. Stay with me, love. Please . . .'

Declan screamed at his friend with annoyance, 'Will you unlock her, Michael? For fuck's sake! We need to phone a fucking ambulance! Get her some help! Pull yourself together, man. She needs you!'

Michael seemed suddenly to understand what was needed from him. He was visibly shaking as he picked up the keys from the floor and, taking out his mobile phone, he called for an ambulance. He was as coherent as possible, and he gave the address of White Farm, quickly and succinctly. He also explained the seriousness of his daughter's condition. Then he turned to Declan. 'It's not a key we need. He's fucking screwed these fuckers into place. We need a spanner.'

He turned on Steven Golding then, and, after kicking and punching him to the floor, he grabbed him by his prematurely grey hair and, pulling him back on to his feet, he pushed his face into his and demanded, 'You shackled her, so you can fucking get her loose.'

Both Michael and Declan watched as Golding dropped to the floor. He then crawled through the filth and, pulling himself up with difficulty, he took a spanner from the windowsill, and he held it out to the men like an offering.

'It's too tight, I can't undo it. Her blood has dried all over it. Now it's like fucking glue.'

He was still taunting them. Declan moved quickly to stop Michael from attacking him once more. 'This is like suicide by cop, Michael, but the ambulance will be here soon, remember? Get her free, get her help, and I will keep this cunt on ice, OK? I'll take him to the scrapyard. You've got Branch to smooth your path with the hospital et cetera. He will make sure this doesn't bite anyone's arse. All you need to do is get her help, OK?'

Declan watched as Michael did as he was told and, leaving him to it, he dragged Steven Golding out of basement, walked him down the lane, and forced him into the boot of Michael's Mercedes.

He sat in the car and waited until the ambulance had arrived before he drove sedately though the London traffic to the scrapyard. Declan guessed that the nut case wanted Michael to kill him. He had done what he had set out to do, and now he wanted to die. It was all so fucking mental. His punishment could be arranged, only at a later date. He wasn't getting away with this that easily, not by a long chalk.

Chapter One Hundred and Thirty-Eight

Timothy Branch arrived at the hospital, aware that he would be expected to smooth everything over for Michael Flynn, and to make sure that Michael could get on with the business at hand with the minimum of fuss.

When he saw young Jessie Flynn he was, for the first time in his life, speechless. The girl was lying on a bed in intensive care, and Michael Flynn was standing beside her bed, holding her hand. *He* looked seriously ill too – his face was devoid of colour, even his lips were white.

But Jessie, young Jessie, was a terrifying sight.

'Fucking hell, Michael, I'm so sorry. I'm so very sorry.'

And he meant it. Michael could hear it in the man's voice.

'He fucking planned this, Timothy. He shackled her to a bed, and he left her there to rot. Her heart gave out. The infection in her blood weakened it. Twenty-two years old and she had a massive fucking coronary. I got there too late. I was too late to help her.'

Michael started to cry again.

Timothy Branch automatically put his arm around the man's shoulders; he couldn't even imagine the pain that he must be feeling. To lose a child was hard enough for anyone, but to know she had been murdered – had died a slow and painful death – had to be unendurable.

'Listen, Michael, I will sort this, don't worry. I swear to you.'

Michael nodded. He appreciated the man's promise – for the first time he actually felt that the man was trustworthy. But it was the way Jessie had died. Even a fucking no-mark like Branch couldn't help but be affected. Just looking at her broken body was hard enough.

'That bastard soaked her with cold water, he starved her, he fucking held her there with home-made manacles. You should see her poor legs. The fetters were so fucking tight they rubbed away every piece of her skin – they even scraped against her bones. She must have been in absolute agony, Timothy. My baby lived her last few weeks on this earth in excruciating pain, waiting for me to find her, to help her. But I was too late.'

Detective Inspector Timothy Branch would never have believed that he would feel any kind of pity for Michael Flynn, but he did. He felt the man's pain as if it was his own. No one should ever have to see a child like this. It was outrageous – it took a certain kind of hate to be capable of harming another person so wickedly. Child murderers, rapists, were capable of such viciousness, of such cowardice, because *they* were cowards. They bullied the weakest people in society, little children and anyone who was smaller or weaker than them. Now Jessie Flynn, whose father was the hardest man in Europe, let alone London or the UK, who was responsible for every earn available, was dead. Murdered.

If this could happen to Michael Flynn's child, what chance did anyone else have? This just proved that no one was immune to hatred. As a police officer, Timothy had always known that – he had seen so much mindless violence, so many pointless murders. But when something like this happened to a man like Michael Flynn, a man who was by all accounts at the pinnacle of his power, it was food for thought. Here he was, crushed and weeping as he looked at his daughter's bruised and broken body. It was an eye-opening situation.

Michael Flynn looked at Timothy Branch, and he smiled eerily. 'I've got him though, Timothy, I've got the fucker, and I will make him pay. Don't you worry about that.'

Timothy Branch didn't answer him. He just stood there, silently thanking the Good Lord that it wasn't *his* child lying there dead.

Chapter One Hundred and Thirty-Nine

As Josephine heard her husband running up the stairs, she checked her make-up in her dressing table mirror, pleased to see that she looked perfect.

She sat up straighter in her chair, and turned off her DVD player. She knew that Michael hated her films, especially that she watched the same ones over and over again.

As he came into her bedroom, she was ready for him, she had a half smile on her face, and she looked towards him quizzically. It was a look she had practised and perfected over the years. There was no way she would lower herself to ask him why he had not bothered to get in touch with her. She still had her pride.

He stood before her, like an avenging angel, and she could see that he wasn't his usual self. In fact, he looked terrible. His clothes were crumpled as if he had slept in them, and he was badly in need of a shave. She looked him up and down, very slowly, taking in his dishevelled appearance, and letting him know she had noticed it.

'I thought I heard you, Michael, but it's been a while so I wasn't holding out too much hope of seeing you.'

He didn't say anything to her, and she looked at him straight in the eyes.

'Is that all you've got to say to me, Josephine? My mother is dead. I assumed that even *you* might have worried about how I was coping with that! She was murdered, remember?'

Josephine could hear the antagonism in his voice, the sarcasm that was dripping from every word he spoke. She wasn't going to say anything that would give him reason to attack her again, as he had the last time she had seen him. She had not been willing to accept his conduct then, and she wasn't prepared to accept it now. Even if he did have a right to call her out about her behaviour, that didn't mean that he should do it. They were married and, no matter what had happened to them in the past, they had always loved each other.

'I'm sorry about your mum, Michael. Of course I am. How can you even say something like that to me?'

She sounded so offended, so insulted by him. It was crystal clear to him now just how devious she actually was – had always been. He gave a low, mocking laugh. He was seeing her with fresh eyes. She looked wonderful – why wouldn't she? Her whole life was taken up with her appearance, with repairing her make-up, making sure her eyebrows were plucked and shaped, that her lipstick was faultless. Her hair looked salon-perfect twenty-four/seven, and her nails were coloured, shaped and buffed with a diligence that had to be seen to be believed.

'You're a piece of work, Josephine, do you know that? In case you were wondering, your only daughter's dead. Jessie had a massive heart attack today. Twenty-two years old, and her heart gave out. The man who had taken her, who had contacted *you*, if you remember, that man who you ignored, basically *tortured* our Jessie to death. She died in fucking agony waiting for someone to find her. Now she is gone from us, Josephine, like my old mum.'

Josephine knew that Michael was telling her the truth, but it was hard to take it all in.

'I am waiting for some kind of reaction from you, Josephine. I just told you that your only child is dead, and nothing. Not a fucking word.'

He stood there, looming over her, and waited for her to say something – anything – to acknowledge her only child's demise. But she didn't say a word.

'Do you know what, Josephine? Patrick Costello said something to me many years ago, and I never understood the real meaning of it until recently. You were just at your hoarding stage, and I was really worried about you, about your mental health. He knew that, and we were out one night, and he said to me, "Always remember this, Michael – people only do to you what you let them." I didn't understand what he meant until recently. He was a wise fucking man in some ways – mad as a fucking Russian road map – but he had you sussed out right, lady.'

Josephine could not believe that her Jessie was dead. It wasn't something she had ever contemplated, but now a part of her was relieved. It meant that Jake would now be wholly hers – hers and Michael's. He was the son they had never had.

'I can't believe what you're telling me, Michael. My baby girl, my Jessie is dead. Poor Jake. He's an orphan. We are all he's got left.'

Michael shook his head angrily. 'Oh, save it for someone who cares! Jake will survive, I will see to that. But I'm warning you now, Josephine, you are going to the nut farm, and this time I'm not going to stop it. If you don't go, then I will turn my back on you completely. Do you hear me? I'm deadly serious this time. I will *never* forgive you, Josephine, for what happened to our Jessie – for not even *trying* to let me know immediately when you heard from that cunt who was holding her hostage. You put yourself first as always, and I know now that you always will. You're going to end up a lonely old woman because I'm finished with you. Any love I had for you – and I loved you with all my heart – has died. It's gone.'

Josephine jumped from her chair, and she tried to grab her husband's hands. She couldn't live without him, without her Michael. He was the only thing that she really cared about.

But he pushed her away from him, unwilling to even touch her. 'I'm arranging with your shrink that if you don't go into hospital voluntarily in the next five days, I will have you sectioned. I can do that, Josephine, and I fucking will if I have to. Don't bank on your latest shrink to get you out of it. I pay him, and he will do whatever I ask him to.'

She sat back in her chair, panic overwhelming her. He meant every word he was saying, and she didn't know how she could stop him. He turned away from her in disgust.

At the door, he turned back to look at her, and said sadly, 'Jessie is dead, and you don't even seem able to fucking take that onboard. She died a death I wouldn't wish on my worst enemy and you've not even asked me anything about her at all. I know that you won't even bother to go to your daughter's fucking funeral, but you *will* go to the nut house this time, Josephine.'

She looked at her husband, her handsome husband, who had always stood by her no matter what, and suddenly she felt so very lonely and frightened. She had pushed him away for years. She had known that he would never have done the dirty on her – he was too decent, too nice a person. She had relied on that, she had relied on his love for her.

He was still standing there, in the doorway, watching her intently. 'By the way, I'm burying Jessie with my mum. They were close and I want them to be together. I can't stand the thought of our Jessie down there in the ground all alone.' He swallowed back the tears once more. 'There was a lot of my mum in Jessie. I realise that now.'

He walked out of the room, and she heard him walking away from her, his tread heavy as he went down the stairs. She could hear Jake's shrieks of excitement as he was picked up and thrown in the air by his granddad. But it meant nothing to her – all she cared about was that her husband was going to walk away from her. She was finally without his protection, and it terrified her. Every time one of her doctors had recommended that she needed serious treatment, needed to be hospitalised, she had made sure that Michael replaced them. He had always tried to do whatever she wanted him to do. He had always done everything in his power to make her happy.

She put her head in her hands. She had never felt such a feeling of despair before in her whole entire life. She wouldn't cry, though, even though she wanted to. She *couldn't*, she could *not* let *anything* interfere with her make-up. She stood up quickly and, pulling out the small padded stool from underneath the dressing table, she sank down on to it. She stared at her face for long moments in the mirror, automatically checking her make-up, and she sighed with relief as she saw that it was all still in place. It was her mask. It was the façade that she showed to the world. But, deep down inside, she knew that she had not faced the real world for years. She registered suddenly that her daughter was really gone. That her Jessie would never again ring her, or come to visit her son. Her Jessie, her baby girl, was dead.

She closed her eyes in distress. Michael was right. She honestly didn't care enough about anyone; all she was really bothered about was Michael's threat of putting her into a mental institution. She wasn't a fucking fool. If she went into one, she knew that it would be a long time before she would ever get out again.

Chapter One Hundred and Forty

Michael drove through the gates of the scrapyard slowly. The old boy who worked the night shift was a stickler for fucking social etiquette. Michael waved at him in a suitably friendly fashion, and he saw his gratified smile. He sighed in annoyance. He was a nice old geezer, a Face in his younger days, but that didn't warrant all this fucking babysitting and smiles every time he drove into the yard. Declan had always said, it takes two minutes of your life to recognise a good worker, and that recognition would guarantee their loyalty for twenty years. He was absolutely right, of course. But tonight Michael wasn't in the mood.

He parked his Range Rover next to his Mercedes and, as he got out and stood on the tarmac stretching, he was gratified to hear that whoever was in the boot of his Merc was making one hell of a racket.

Declan came out of the Portakabin doorway. He looked huge against the lights. Declan had gradually got bigger and bigger over the years, and it was only now that Michael was really noticing that.

'Drink first?' Declan was miming drinking a cup of tea with his little finger raised up like an old biddy.

Michael laughed despite himself. You couldn't not like Declan Costello – the man was a genuine diamond. Even at a time like this he could bring a smile to Michael's face.

'Pour me a large brandy, but first up, open this fucking boot.'

Declan took the Mercedes keys from his trouser pocket, and opened the boot quickly.

Steven Golding was lying there, and he blinked as his eyes adjusted to the sudden light. He trained his gaze on Michael warily.

Michael looked around him. He was aware that there was no way this man could escape from the scrapyard's premises. There was a very high brick wall surrounding the place for a start, and the barbed wire that had been placed on the top of it years before had always been a very good deterrent. The gates were electric, and they too were very high. The nightwatchman had a large German Shepherd who wasn't that enamoured of new people. There were also three other large dogs – two Dobermans and a Rottweiler bitch, which roamed the grounds during the daytime. The people who owned them worked there. It suited everyone to let the animals run free. There were people who came in ostensibly to look for a specific part for a specific car, who were quite capable of going on the rob. The hounds made sure they didn't feel the urge to come back later, when it was dark.

He looked once more at Steven Golding; it was patently obvious that the man wasn't going to climb out of the boot by himself. Michael laughed again, this was a fucking joke.

'Do you know something, Steven? I never knew there was anyone in your house that night. I really believed it was empty. I wasn't happy about burning people's possessions, you know? But it was for Patrick Costello, and I wanted to prove myself to him. I wanted to make something of myself. I wanted to be able to give my mum a few quid, make her life that bit easier. She had brought me up all on her own since I was a baby. I never would have dreamt of harming anyone. It was Patrick Costello who wanted that. He could be a very petty man, a very vicious man.'

Steven Golding was still lying in the boot of Michael's Mercedes. It was a fucking big boot, and Steven Golding was more than comfortable it seemed.

'If you had just come to me, if you had fucking had the sense to call me out, confront me, I would have done anything to make amends – I swear that to you. I've never really got over it. Even now I still wake up sweating. But I did learn how to put it aside. If I hadn't managed to do that, I would have ended up as big a fucking headcase as you are.'

Steven Golding looked feral. The man had no saving graces at all, from his rotten teeth to his pock-marked and scarred skin. He was obviously a loner. Michael knew that the man was mentally ill, and that he had been in and out of different institutions for the best part of his life. That was sad. But Michael couldn't change anything that had happened, even if he had wanted to. Steven Golding looked exactly what he was – a broken-down, disillusioned fantasist, who had been deprived of his whole family as a teenage boy. He was quite obviously madder than a fucking bull with a red-hot poker up its arse, and had managed to infiltrate every aspect of Michael's life, eventually destroying not just his only daughter but his mother as well.

'Do you know what, Steven? Stay where you are.'

Michael shut the boot noisily. Then he walked leisurely to one of the outbuildings. It was a shed that had been constructed over twenty years before from a job-lot of corrugated iron, and it was where they kept most of the flammable liquids.

Michael went inside and he felt around for one of the petrol cans that he knew would be there. He felt the weight of it in his hand, and then he shook it gently, relishing the noise of the liquid as it moved around.

He walked back to his Mercedes, calling out to Declan, who he knew had been watching everything from the Portakabin window. When Declan appeared, he gestured to him to open the boot once more. Declan Costello, as always, was more than happy to oblige.

Steven Golding was still curled up. As Michael opened the petrol can and started to pour it all over him, Golding attempted to get up and tried to get out of the boot. Michael Flynn punched him back down. The stench of petrol fumes was heavy in the air.

Steven Golding was terrified, and Michael could see that. His eyes were bulging out of his head with the fear of being burned alive.

'Answer me one last thing – would you have harmed my grandson?'

Steven Golding shook his head. 'Of course not. I would have left him alone.'

Michael snorted with derision. 'Why didn't you just come after me? *I* was the culprit, for fuck's sake!'

Golding looked him in the eye as he said, 'Too easy. I know you will suffer much more over your Jessie and your mum's death. Guilt is a very destructive force.'

Michael didn't answer him. After all, who could argue with the truth? He took a book of matches out of his pocket and, smiling slightly, he said steadily, 'The truth is, Steven, I'm actually going to enjoy this.'

Steven Golding tried to get out of the boot, and Michael Flynn hammered him over and over again until the man couldn't move. Michael felt the man's face collapse beneath his fists and he still didn't stop battering him. He carried on hitting the man until he was completely spent.

He picked the book of matches up from the ground and tore off a match. Lighting it, he used it to ignite the whole pack, which he threw casually on to the man's chest.

As the whole car went up in flames, Declan shouted, 'What

the fuck are you doing, Michael? Your car! What about your fucking car?'

Michael Flynn stood watching the man responsible for the vicious murders of his mother and daughter squirming and screaming in pain without blinking. Then he looked at Declan Costello and, laughing loudly, he said, 'Relax, Declan, for Christ's sake! I reported this car stolen hours ago.'

Declan went back into the Portakabin and came back with two large drinks. He handed one to Michael, and he stood beside him as Steven Golding was burned beyond recognition.

When the car finally blew they were both sitting side by side on the steps of the offices.

'It's over, Michael.'

Michael sipped his brandy, savouring the taste. 'Do you know the worst of it for me now, Declan? I wish that cunt had been in the house that night. I wish I had burned him to death with his sisters and his mum and dad. So what does that make me?'

Declan put his arm around his friend's shoulders and, sighing heavily, he said, '*Human*, Michael. Unfortunately, that's what it makes you – *human*.'

Epilogue

The house of the righteous contains great treasure,
but the income of the wicked brings them trouble

Proverbs 15:6

Chapter One Hundred and Forty-One

'Nana looks different.'

Michael laughed at his grandson's seriousness. 'I know she does. She's not well. But she's getting better, that's the main thing.'

Jake nodded, but he wasn't so sure about anything any more. He knew his real mum was dead. He had seen her grave and she was buried with his great-nana Hannah. His granddad went to visit them a lot, and he sometimes went with him. It was funny thinking his mum was dead, up in heaven, but one of the nuns at school had told him that sometimes Jesus missed people so much that he called them back up to heaven early. He liked to think that was true, but he wasn't sure if it was. His mum had been a bit of a cow – at least that is what his nana Josephine had used to say about her. Now his nana Josephine was in a hospital, and she acted very strangely. He could see her walking towards them, and Jake felt his heart sink inside his chest.

'Here she comes, Jake.'

Jake could hear the false gaiety in his granddad's voice.

Josephine walked across the grass towards her husband and her grandson slowly. The drugs were responsible for that; she couldn't bring herself to break into a sprint these days. She sat down at the picnic table opposite her husband. He still looked so good, so very handsome. He got better looking as he got older; it was unfair.

Michael smiled at her. 'You're looking well, Josephine.'

But she wasn't. She looked awful these days. She didn't bother with her appearance any more. It was a good thing, according to her doctor. He wasn't so sure himself.

She didn't answer him. Instead she looked at Jake and, holding her arms out, she said sadly, 'I could do with a hug, young man.'

Jake looked at his granddad and, when Michael nodded slightly, he went around the table, and allowed his nana to squeeze him to her tightly. When Jake finally managed to pull himself away from her, he went straight back to sit beside his granddad.

Josephine knew that she had been well and truly rejected by her grandson, but there was nothing she could do about it.

'Really, Josephine, you do look much better. The doctor told me that you were finding it much easier to go outside. It's wonderful to see you out here with us now.'

Josephine looked at her husband for long moments. He visited her twice, sometimes three times, a week and he seemed genuinely interested in her progress. But it was bullshit. She wasn't stupid. She knew him better than he knew himself. He was just doing his duty. That was his trouble, he didn't have a treacherous bone in his body. He was determined to divorce her, though, she knew that.

'How are you, Michael? Good?'

He smiled gently. 'Yeah, I'm fine. You know me, same old, same old.'

Josephine nodded in agreement. 'I hear you're having a right old time of it. Katherine Rourk, Danny's *daughter*. I bet she could be *your* daughter, eh? She's young enough.'

Michael didn't answer her; it wasn't any of her business.

She laughed nastily. 'I still hear everything, Michael. I'm not fucking dead yet.'

He smiled back at her but his voice was steely as he said, 'If you don't watch your fucking mouth, that could be arranged sooner than you think, Josephine.'

'Are you threatening me?'

He saw how she narrowed her eyes, and he wondered how he had let her rule him for so long. 'Why would I do that, Josephine? If I was threatening you, believe me, you'd know it. I come here to see how you are and to bring your little grandson in to visit you. There's no hidden agenda.'

Then she said angrily, 'It's been nearly six months, Michael. I want to go home.'

Michael turned to Jake. 'You can go inside now, and spend the pound I gave you in the sweet shop. Wait in the reception and I'll be there in a minute, OK?'

Jake nodded.

'Say goodbye to Nana.'

Jake waved at her quickly and, running off, he called out 'Goodbye' over his shoulder.

Michael knew that the lad found Josephine a trial – as *he* did if he was honest. She was stranger than ever now, but it was all to the good, according to the doctors. Personally, he thought she was getting madder by the day.

'Look, Josephine, I can't control everything any more. This is a proper hospital – you can't just buy the doctors here, and choose your own fucking meds. Look how far that got you. You need to do whatever the doctors tell you to do. For once in your life, Josephine, you can't rely on me to bail you out. You were *sectioned*, for fuck's sake! You can't just fucking *choose* what you want to do any more. It's out of our hands. The doctors decide when you can go home and, when that day comes, I have purchased a lovely little cottage for you. You will love it.'

'I've already got a home.'

He sighed heavily; he was sick and tired of this. 'Not any more you haven't. Once we get the divorce, I will see you all right. But you will never come back to that house again. It's in Jake's name now anyway.'

Josephine grinned nastily. 'You're loving this, aren't you? You dumped me, and then you put me away. Katie Rourk must be a blinding fuck, Michael. Got you right where she fucking wants you!'

Michael stood up slowly. 'I'm not doing this, Josephine. I've told you before. It's over between us. I will *never* forgive you for what happened to our Jessie. I will take care of you up to a point – I owe you that much. But don't treat me like a fucking earhole, OK? I come here so you can see Jake, so I can see how you're getting on. After all, I *am* the one footing the *fucking* bill for this, aren't I? If I pull out, lady, you will end up in a local NHS nut ward somewhere, so don't bite the hand that feeds you.'

Josephine couldn't believe that her Michael couldn't find it in his heart to forgive her; he had *always* forgiven her in the past, no matter what she had done. She grabbed his hands in hers, and she tried to pull him back into his seat, to make him sit down and talk with her.

'Please, Michael, I promise you I will do anything . . . But don't do this to me . . .'

He pulled away from her and, stepping back, he said gently, 'I've got to go, Josephine. But if you don't stop this I can't visit you any more. I've told you over and over again I will bankroll your treatment, and I will always look out for you. But our marriage is over.'

He walked away from her purposefully, aware that he didn't

have even a small sliver of doubt abo
had ceased to exist for him when he had hat he was doing. She
like he had woken from a coma, and seen his that letter. It was
really was. It had been a revelation. He had sudd for what she
much she had manipulated him over the years and, en how
thing was, he knew that he had gone along with it al st
agoraphobia, her fear of telephones, her fear of fucking everything that didn't suit her. But she didn't have a fear of wine – she could neck that all day and night. He had swallowed it until he had seen that letter which resulted in his daughter dying in such pain and with such injuries. Knowing that if Josephine had just *once* put someone else first it might have all have been avoided wasn't something he could excuse.

He walked into the reception room. Jake was waiting for him – he looked so worried, bless him.

'Is Nana OK?'

Michael grinned. ''Course she is. Come on, let's get home, shall we? Dana is cooking us a shepherd's pie! With real shepherds in!'

Jake smiled a real smile at last. 'That's my favourite dinner!'

'And mine too! What's the chances of that, eh?' He grasped his grandson's hand and walked him out to the car park. Jake stopped in front of the Mercedes, and Michael looked at him quizzically.

'What's wrong, Jake?'

The little boy suddenly looked vulnerable and frightened. Michael smiled at him gently. 'You can tell me anything, Jake, you know that.'

Jake started to cry, and Michael rushed over to him, and he swept him up into his arms, hugging the boy to his chest tightly.

'Nana scares me. I don't like coming here, Granddad.'

Michael knew then, without a shadow of a doubt, that he

would never come back h again. ‘Then we won’t come here any more, Jake.’

Jake pulled hi away from his granddad’s chest and looked into his fac said seriously, ‘Promise?’

Mic miled at the little lad; he loved him so very much.

‘P

Chapter One Hundred and Forty-Two

Declan was well on the way to getting drunk. He was on the borderline at the moment, but he was feeling good. He watched the doorway, expecting Michael. Declan thought it was good for Michael to get out more, he had spent so much of his life pussy-footing around Josephine, it was good for the man to finally just do whatever he wanted to. It had been a hard year for him, he had buried his mother and his daughter, and he had seen his wife, the love of his life, sectioned, and dragged out of his home kicking and screaming. He deserved a bit of R and R. He had been getting that with young Katie Rourk, by all accounts, and good luck to him. Michael had never been the unfaithful type. He was a one-woman man. If anyone else had married Josephine they would have been out on the nest in no time, but not Michael.

Declan looked around the bar. There was no doubt that, for a private drinking club, it had a very good feel to it. No one got in unless they were members, and Michael and he agreed the memberships! How fucking neat was that? He could come here knowing that he wouldn't have to deal with anyone that he didn't want to.

He gestured to the barmaid for another drink, and she did as he requested immediately. It was early evening and the place was nearly empty. It didn't really liven up till later, so he was enjoying the quiet. He picked up his Jack Daniel's and Coke and, raising his glass towards the barmaid, he took a long drink.

Michael came down the stairs a few seconds later, all smiles, which pleased Declan. The man was finally looking relaxed again.

The barmaid was tiny – under five feet tall, and she had the smallest hands and feet Declan had ever seen on a grown woman. Her hair, on the other hand was *huge*. It was beautiful, her crowning glory, and she was always smiling. She had that kind of nature – she was a glass-half-full girl, as she had told Declan on more than one occasion. She automatically mixed Michael Flynn a large vodka and tonic.

He took it from her with a smile and, turning to Declan, he said happily, 'I needed this, Declan. It's been a fucking mad day.' He took a large gulp of his drink; it was strong, even for him.

'So? How was Josephine?'

Michael shrugged. 'Same old, same old!'

Declan laughed then. 'Hark at you! Who'd have thought it, eh?'

Michael lit a cigarette, and he pulled on it quickly. As he blew out the smoke, he said honestly, 'I never thought we would ever have broken up. But we have, and I'm glad.' Michael grinned suddenly. Then, leaning forward, he said quietly, 'I have some news for you, Declan – you're the first person to know.'

Declan laughed at his mate's cloak-and-dagger voice. 'Oh yeah? So what is it, then?'

Michael Flynn grinned happily. 'Katie's pregnant. It wasn't planned, but I've got to tell you, Declan, I'm over the fucking moon.'

Declan Costello was taken aback, but he recovered quickly. 'Congratulations, mate. How old is Katie anyway?'

Michael gestured to the barmaid to refill their glasses.

'She's twenty-six. Not as young as she looks. But still a lot younger than me! Josephine has already pointed that out today. But I don't give a toss, Declan. I really care about her, and I think she does me. And I want a child, I want a child of my own. I will marry her, Declan, and I will give her and my babies the world.'

Declan Costello was speechless.

Michael Flynn looked into his friend's stunned countenance and he said gaily, 'I'm the wrong side of fifty, and I have nothing left, other than Jake, of course. I want what I never had, Declan – a couple of kids, *nice* kids, and a woman who isn't a fucking walking headcase. Josephine's doctor told me that nothing I could have done would have changed her life. She has a personality disorder. I always thought it was my fault that she wasn't the full five quid. But it would have happened anyway, no matter what. Katie is fun, she makes me laugh. So much of my life was spent holding Josephine's hand, or living down my only daughter's antics, pretending that I didn't care, when I did care. I cared more than I could ever let on. But not any more. That's all over now. She's gone – my Jessie is dead and gone. Josephine and all her fucking problems are gone. This time around I want what everyone else takes for granted. I just want a normal fucking life.'

Declan Costello smiled. He raised his glass in a toast, and he said sincerely, 'To you, Michael, and the next generation of Flynns.'